The Rosie Effect

Graeme Simsion is a full-time writer. Previously an IT consultant with an international reputation, he wrote his first book in 1994 – the standard reference on data modelling, now entering its fourth edition – and taught at four Australian universities. He is married to Anne, a professor of psychiatry who writes erotic fiction. They have two children.

His first novel, *The Rosie Project*, was a bestseller all over the world.

The Rosie Effect

GRAEME SIMSION

MICHAEL JOSEPH
an imprint of
PENGUIN BOOKS

MICHAEL JOSEPH

Published by the Penguin Group
Penguin Books Ltd, 80 Strand, London WC2R ORL, England
Penguin Group (USA) Inc., 375 Hudson Street, New York, New York 10014, USA
Penguin Group (Canada), 90 Eglinton Avenue East, Suite 700, Toronto, Ontario, Canada M4P 2Y3
(a division of Pearson Penguin Canada Inc.)
Penguin Ireland, 25 St Stephen's Green, Dublin 2, Ireland (a division of Penguin Books Ltd)
Penguin Group (Australia), 707 Collins Street, Melbourne, Victoria 3008, Australia
(a division of Pearson Australia Group Pty Ltd)
Penguin Books India Pvt Ltd, 11 Community Centre, Panchsheel Park, New Delhi – 110 017, India
Penguin Group (NZ), 67 Apollo Drive, Rosedale, Auckland 0632, New Zealand
(a division of Pearson New Zealand Ltd)
Penguin Books (South Africa) (Pty) Ltd, Block D, Rosebank Office Park,
181 Jan Smuts Avenue, Parktown North, Gauteng, Johannesburg 2193, South Africa

Penguin Books Ltd, Registered Offices: 80 Strand, London WC2R ORL, England

www.penguin.com

First published in Australia by The Text Publishing Company 2014
First published in Great Britain by Michael Joseph 2014
001

Set in 13.5/16 pt Garamond MT Std
Typeset by Jouve (UK), Milton Keynes
Printed in Great Britain by Clays Ltd, St Ives plc

A CIP catalogue record for this book is available from the British Library

HARDBACK ISBN: 978–0–718–17947–2
TRADE PAPERBACK ISBN: 978–0–718–17948–9

www.greenpenguin.co.uk

Penguin Books is committed to a sustainable
future for our business, our readers and our planet.
This book is made from Forest Stewardship
Council™ certified paper.

To Anne

I

Orange juice was not scheduled for Fridays. Although Rosie and I had abandoned the Standardised Meal System, resulting in an improvement in 'spontaneity' at the expense of shopping time, food inventory and wastage, we had agreed that each week should include three alcohol-free days. Without formal scheduling, this target proved difficult to achieve, as I had predicted. Rosie eventually saw the logic of my solution.

Fridays and Saturdays were obvious days on which to consume alcohol. Neither of us had classes on the weekend. We could sleep late and possibly have sex.

Sex was absolutely *not* allowed to be scheduled, at least not by explicit discussion, but I had become familiar with the sequence of events likely to precipitate it: a blueberry muffin from Blue Sky Bakery, a triple shot of espresso from Otha's, removal of my shirt, and my impersonation of Gregory Peck in the role of Atticus Finch in *To Kill a Mockingbird*. I had learned not to do all four in the same sequence on every occasion, as my intention would then be obvious. To provide an element of unpredictability, I settled on tossing a coin twice to select a component of the routine to delete.

I had placed a bottle of Elk Cove pinot gris in the refrigerator to accompany the divers' scallops purchased that morning at Chelsea Market, but when I returned after retrieving our laundry from the basement, there were two glasses of orange juice on the table. Orange juice was not compatible with the wine. Drinking it first would desensitise our tastebuds to the slight residual sugar that was a feature of the pinot gris, thus creating an impression of sourness. Waiting until after we had finished the wine would also be unacceptable. Orange juice deteriorates rapidly – hence the emphasis placed by breakfast establishments on 'freshly squeezed'.

Rosie was in the bedroom, so not immediately available for discussion. In our apartment, there were nine possible combinations of locations for two people, of which six involved us being in different rooms. In our ideal apartment, as jointly specified prior to our arrival in New York, there would have been thirty-six possible combinations, arising from the bedroom, two studies, two bathrooms and a living-room-kitchen. This reference apartment would have been located in Manhattan, close to the 1 or A-Train for access to Columbia University medical school, with water views and a balcony or rooftop barbecue area.

As our income consisted of one academic's salary, supplemented by two part-time cocktail-making jobs but reduced by Rosie's tuition fees, some compromise was required, and our apartment offered none of the specified features. We had given excessive weight to the Williamsburg location because our friends Isaac and Judy Esler lived there and had recommended it. There was no logical reason why a (then) forty-year-old professor of genetics and a thirty-year-old postgraduate medical student would be suited to the same neighbourhood as a fifty-four-year-old psychiatrist and a fifty-two-year-old potter who had acquired their dwelling before prices escalated. The rent was high and the apartment had a number of faults that the management was reluctant to rectify. Currently the air-conditioning was failing to compensate for the exterior temperature of thirty-four degrees Celsius, which was within the expected range for Brooklyn in late June.

The reduction in room numbers, combined with marriage, meant I had been thrown into closer sustained proximity with another human being than ever before. Rosie's physical presence was a hugely positive outcome of the Wife Project, but after ten months and ten days of marriage I was still adapting to being a component of a couple. I sometimes spent longer in the bathroom than was strictly necessary.

I checked the date on my phone – definitely Friday, 21 June. This was a better outcome than the scenario in which my brain had developed a fault that caused it to identify days incorrectly. But it confirmed a violation of the alcohol protocol.

My reflections were interrupted by Rosie emerging from the bedroom wearing only a towel. This was my favourite costume, assuming 'no costume' did not qualify as a costume. Once again, I was struck by her extraordinary beauty and inexplicable decision to select me as her partner. And, as always, that thought was followed by an unwanted emotion: an intense moment of fear that she would one day realise her error.

3

'What's cooking?' she asked.

'Nothing. Cooking has not commenced. I'm in the ingredient-assembly phase.'

She laughed, in the tone that indicated I had misinterpreted her question. Of course, the question would not have been required at all had the Standardised Meal System been in place. I provided information that I guessed Rosie was seeking.

'Sustainable scallops with a mirepoix of carrots, celeriac, shallots and bell peppers and a sesame oil dressing. The recommended accompanying beverage is pinot gris.'

'Do you need me to do anything?'

'We all need to get some sleep tonight. Tomorrow we go to Navarone.'

The content of the Gregory Peck line was irrelevant. The effect came entirely from the delivery and the impression it conveyed of leadership and confidence in the preparation of sautéed scallops.

'And what if I can't sleep, Captain?' said Rosie. She smiled and disappeared into the bathroom. I did not raise the towel-location issue: I had long ago accepted that hers would be stored randomly in the bathroom or bedroom, effectively occupying two spaces.

Our preferences for order are at different ends of the scale. When we moved from Australia to New York, Rosie packed three maximum-size suitcases. The quantity of clothes alone was incredible. My own personal items fitted into two carry-on bags. I took advantage of the move to upgrade my living equipment and gave my stereo and desktop computer to my brother Trevor, returned the bed, linen and kitchen utensils to the family home in Shepparton, and sold my bike.

In contrast, Rosie added to her vast collection of possessions by purchasing decorative objects within weeks of our arrival. The result was evident in the chaotic condition of our apartment: pot plants, surplus chairs and an impractical wine rack.

It was not merely the quantity of items: there was also a problem of organisation. The refrigerator was crowded with half-empty containers of bread toppings, dips and decaying dairy products. Rosie had even suggested sourcing a second refrigerator from my friend Dave. One fridge each! Never had the advantages of the Standardised Meal System, with its fully specified meal for each day of the week, standard shopping list and optimised inventory, been so obvious.

There was exactly one exception to Rosie's disorganised approach. That exception was a variable. By default it was her medical studies, but currently it was her PhD thesis on environmental risks for the early onset of bipolar disorder. She had been granted advanced status in the Columbia MD program on the proviso that her thesis would be completed during the summer vacation. The deadline was now only two months and five days away.

'How can you be so organised at one thing and so disorganised at everything else?' I'd asked Rosie, following her installation of the incorrect driver for her printer.

'It's *because* I'm concentrating on my thesis, I don't

worry about other stuff. Nobody asks if Freud checked the use-by date on the milk.'

'They didn't have use-by dates in the early twentieth century.'

It was incredible that two such dissimilar people had become a successful couple.

2

The Orange Juice Problem occurred at the end of an already-disrupted week. Another occupant of our apartment complex had destroyed both of my 'respectable' shirts by piggybacking on our washing load in the shared laundry facilities. I understood his desire for efficiency, but an item of his clothing had dyed our light-coloured washing a permanent and uneven shade of purple.

From my perspective there was no problem: I was established as a visiting professor in the Columbia medical school and no longer needed to worry about 'creating a good first impression'. Nor could I imagine being refused service in a restaurant because of the *colour* of my shirt. Rosie's outer clothing, which was largely black, had not been affected. The problem was restricted to her underwear.

I argued that I had no objection to the new shade and that no one else should be seeing her undressed, except perhaps a doctor, whose professionalism should prevent him or her from being concerned with aesthetics. But Rosie had already tried to discuss the problem with Jerome, the neighbour whom she had identified as the offender, to prevent a recurrence. This seemed a reasonable course of action, but Jerome had told Rosie to go screw herself.

I was not surprised that she had encountered resistance. Rosie habitually took a direct approach to communication. In speaking to me, it was effective, indeed necessary, but others frequently interpreted her directness as confrontational. Jerome did not convey an impression of wanting to explore win-win solutions.

Now Rosie wanted me to 'stand up to him' and demonstrate that we 'wouldn't be pushed around'. This was exactly the sort of behaviour that I instruct my martial arts students to avoid. If both parties have the goal of establishing dominance and hence apply the algorithm of 'respond with greater force', the ultimate result will be the disablement or death of one party. Over laundry.

But the laundry situation was minor in the context of the week as a whole. Because there had been a *disaster*.

I am often accused of overusing that word, but any reasonable person would accept that it was an appropriate term to describe the failure of my closest friends' marriage, involving two dependent children. Gene and Claudia were in Australia, but the situation was about to cause further disruption to my schedule.

Gene and I had conversed over a Skype link, and the communication quality had been poor. Gene may also have been drunk. He seemed reluctant to divulge the details, probably because:

1. People are generally unwilling to talk openly about sexual activity involving themselves.
2. He had behaved extremely stupidly.

After promising Claudia that he would abandon his project to have sex with a woman from each country of the world, he had failed to honour his commitment. The violation had occurred at a conference in Göteborg, Sweden.

'Don, show a bit of compassion,' he said. 'What were the odds of her living in Melbourne? She was *Icelandic*.'

I pointed out that I was Australian and living in the United States. Simple disproof by counter-example of Gene's ludicrous proposition that people remain in their own countries.

'Okay, but *Melbourne*. And knowing Claudia. What are the odds of that?'

'Difficult to calculate.' I pointed out that Gene should have asked this question *before* adding to his tally of nationalities. If he wanted a reasonable estimate of the probability, I would need information about migration patterns and the size of Claudia's social and professional network.

There was another factor. 'In calculating the risk, I need to know how many women you've seduced since you agreed not to. Obviously the risk increases proportionately.'

'Does it matter?'

'If you want an estimate. I'm presuming the answer is not zero,' I said.

'Don, conferences – overseas conferences – don't count. That's why people go to conferences. Everyone understands that.'

'If Claudia understands, why is there a problem?'

'You're not supposed to get caught. What happens in Göteborg stays in Göteborg.'

'Presumably Icelandic Woman was unaware of this rule.'

'She's in Claudia's book club.'

'Is there some exception for book clubs?'

'Forget it. Anyway, it's over. Claudia's thrown me out.'

'You're homeless?'

'More or less.'

'Incredible. Have you told the Dean?' The Dean of Science in Melbourne was extremely concerned with the public image of the university. It seemed to me that having a homeless person in charge of the Department of Psychology would be, to use her habitual expression, 'not a good look'.

'I'm taking a sabbatical,' said Gene. 'Who knows, maybe I'll turn up in New York and buy you a beer.'

This was an amazing thought – not the beer, which I could purchase myself, but the possibility of having my longest-standing friend in New York.

Excluding Rosie and family members, I had a total of six friends. They were, in descending order of total contact time:

1. Gene, whose advice had often proved unsound, but who had a fascinating theoretical knowledge of human sexual attraction, possibly prompted by his own libido, which was excessive for a man of fifty-seven.

2. Gene's wife, Claudia, a clinical psychologist and the world's most sensible person. She had

shown extraordinary tolerance of Gene's infidelity prior to his promise to reform. I wondered what would happen to their daughter Eugenie and Gene's son Carl from his first marriage. Eugenie was now nine and Carl seventeen.

3. Dave Bechler, a refrigeration engineer whom I had met at a baseball game on my first visit to New York with Rosie. We now convened weekly on the scheduled 'boys' night out' to discuss baseball, refrigeration and marriage.

4. Sonia, Dave's wife. Despite being slightly over-weight (estimated BMI twenty seven), she was extremely beautiful and had a well-paid job as the financial controller for an in-vitro fertilisation facility. These attributes were a source of stress for Dave, who believed that she might leave him for someone more attractive or rich. Dave and Sonia had been attempting to reproduce for five years, using IVF technology (oddly, not at Sonia's place of employment, where I presumed she would receive a discount and access to high-quality genes if required). They had recently succeeded and the baby was scheduled to be born on Christmas Day.

5. (equal) Isaac Esler, an Australian-born psychiatrist whom at one time I had considered the most likely person to be Rosie's biological father.

5. (equal) Judy Esler, Isaac's American wife. Judy was a pottery artist who also raised funds for charity and research. She was responsible for some of the decorative objects cluttering our apartment.

Six friends, assuming the Eslers were still my friends. There had been zero contact since an incident involving bluefin tuna six weeks and five days earlier. But even four friends were more than I had ever had before. Now there was a possibility that all but one of them – Claudia – could be in New York with me.

I acted quickly and asked the Dean of Medicine at Columbia, Professor David Borenstein, if Gene could take his sabbatical there. Gene, as his name coincidentally indicates, is a geneticist, but specialises in evolutionary psychology. He could be located in psychology, genetics or medicine, but I recommended against psychology. Most psychologists disagree with Gene's theories, and I forecast that Gene would not need any more conflict in his life. It was an insight which required a level of empathy that would not have been available to me prior to living with Rosie.

I advised the Dean that, as a full professor, Gene would not want to do any proper work. David Borenstein was familiar with sabbatical protocol, which dictated that Gene would be paid by his university in Australia. He was also aware of Gene's reputation.

'If he can co-author a few papers and keep his hands off the PhD students, I can find an office for him.'

'Of course, of course.' Gene was an expert at getting published with minimal effort. We would have vast amounts of free time to talk about interesting topics.

'I'm serious about the PhD students. If he gets into trouble, I'll hold you accountable.'

This seemed an unreasonable threat, typical of university administrators, but it would provide me with an excuse to reform Gene's behaviour. And, after surveying the PhD students, I concluded it was unlikely that any would be of interest to Gene. I checked when I called to announce my success at finding him employment.

'You've got Mexico? Correct?'

'I have passed time with a lady of that nationality, if that's what you're asking.'

'You had sex with her?'

'Something like that.'

There were several international PhD students, but Gene had already covered the most populous developed countries.

'So, are you accepting the job?' I asked.

'I need to check my options.'

'Ridiculous. Columbia has the world's best medical school. And they're prepared to take someone who has a reputation for laziness and inappropriate behaviour.'

'Look who's talking about inappropriate behaviour.'

'Correct. They accept me. They're extremely tolerant. You can start Monday.'

'Monday? Don, I don't have anywhere to live.'

I explained that I would find a solution to this minor

practical problem. Gene was coming to New York. He would again be at the same university as me. And Rosie.

As I stared at the two orange juices on the table, I realised that I had been looking forward to the alcohol to counteract my anxiety about conveying the Gene news to Rosie. I told myself that I was being unnecessarily concerned. Rosie claimed to welcome spontaneity. This simple analysis, however, ignored three factors.

1. Rosie disliked Gene. He had been her PhD supervisor in Melbourne and technically still was. She had numerous complaints about his academic conduct and regarded his infidelity to Claudia as unacceptable. My argument that he had reformed had now been undermined.
2. Rosie considered it important that we had 'time to ourselves'. Now I would inevitably be devoting time to Gene. He was insistent that his relationship with Claudia was over. But if there was any chance that we could help to save it, it seemed reasonable to give temporarily lower priority to our own healthy marriage. I was certain that Rosie would disagree.
3. Factor Three was the most serious, and possibly a result of misjudgement on my part. I put it out of my mind to focus on the immediate problem.

The two highball glasses filled with orange fluid reminded me of the night that Rosie and I first 'bonded' – the Great Cocktail Night where we secured a sample of DNA from every male in attendance at the reunion of her mother's medical year and eliminated all of them as candidates for Rosie's biological father. Once again, my cocktail-making skills would provide a solution.

Rosie and I worked three nights per week at The Alchemist, a cocktail bar on West 19th Street in the Flatiron neighbourhood, so drink-making equipment and ingredients were tools of trade (although I had not been able to convince our accountant of this). I located vodka, Galliano and ice cubes, added these to the orange juices and stirred. Rather than commence my drink before Rosie, I poured myself a shot of vodka on ice, added a squeeze of lime, and drank it rapidly. Almost instantly, I felt my stress level returning to its default state.

Finally Rosie emerged from the bathroom. Other than the change in direction of travel, the only difference in her appearance was that her red hair was now wet. But her mood appeared to have elevated: she was almost dancing towards the bedroom. Obviously the scallops had been a good choice.

It was possible that her emotional state would make her more receptive to the Gene Sabbatical, but it seemed advisable to defer the news until the next morning, after we had had sex. Of course, if she realised that I had withheld data for that purpose, I would be criticised. Marriage was complex.

As Rosie reached the bedroom door, she spun around: 'I'll be five minutes getting dressed and then I'm expecting the world's best scallops.' Her use of the words 'world's best' was an appropriation of one of my own expressions – a definite indication of a positive mood.

'Five minutes?' An underestimate would have a disastrous impact on scallop preparation.

'Give me fifteen. No hurry to eat. We can have a drink and a chat, Captain Mallory.'

The Gregory Peck character's name was a further good sign. The only problem was the chat. 'Anything happen in your day?' she would say, and I would be obliged to mention the Gene Sabbatical. I decided to make myself unavailable by undertaking cooking tasks. In the meantime, I put the Harvey Wallbangers in the freezer, as they were in danger of warming above optimum temperature when the ice melted. Cooling would also reduce the rate of deterioration of the orange juice.

I returned to dinner preparation. I had not used this recipe before and it was only after commencing that I discovered that the vegetables needed to be chopped into quarter-inch cubes. The list of ingredients made no mention of a ruler. I was able to download a measuring application to my phone, but had barely finished production of the reference cube when Rosie re-emerged. She was now wearing a dress – highly unusual for dinner at home. It was white and contrasted dramatically with her red hair. The effect was stunning. I decided to delay the Gene news only slightly, until later in the evening. Rosie could hardly complain about that. I would reschedule aikido practice for the next morning. That would leave time for sex after dinner. Or before. I was prepared to be flexible.

Rosie sat in one of the two armchairs that occupied a significant percentage of the living room.

'Come and talk to me,' she said.

'I'm chopping vegetables. I can talk from here.'

'What happened to the orange juices?'

I retrieved the modified orange juices from the freezer, gave one to Rosie, and sat opposite. The vodka and Rosie's friendliness had relaxed me, although I suspected the effect was superficial. The Gene, Jerome and juice problems were still running as background processes.

Rosie raised her glass as if proposing a toast. This turned out to be exactly what she was doing.

'We've got something to celebrate, Captain,' she said. She looked at me for a few seconds. She knows that I am not fond of surprises. I assumed that she had achieved some important milestone with her thesis. Or perhaps she had been offered a place in the psychiatry-training program on completion of the medical course. This would be extremely good news, and I estimated the probability of sex at greater than ninety per cent.

She smiled – then, presumably to increase the suspense, drank from her glass. Disaster! It was as if it contained poison. She spat it out, over her white dress, and ran to the bathroom. I followed her as she removed the dress and ran water over it.

Standing in her half-purple underwear, pumping water in and out of the dress, she turned back to me. Her expression was far too complex to analyse.

'We're pregnant,' she said.

3

I struggled to process Rosie's statement. Reviewing my response later, I realised that my brain had been assaulted with information that appeared to defy logic on three counts.

First, the formulation *'we're* pregnant' contradicted basic biology. It implied that *my* state had somehow changed as well as Rosie's. Rosie would surely not have said, 'Dave's pregnant'. Yet, according to the definition implicit in her statement, he was.

Second, pregnancy was not scheduled. Rosie had mentioned it as a factor in her decision to cease smoking, but I assumed that she had simply used the eventual possibility of pregnancy as motivation. Furthermore, we had discussed the matter explicitly. We were having dinner at Jimmy Watson's Restaurant in Lygon Street, Carlton, Victoria, Australia, on 2 August of the previous year, nine days before our wedding, and a couple had placed a baby container on the floor between our tables. Rosie mentioned the possibility of us reproducing.

We had by then decided to move to New York, and I argued that we should wait until she had finished her medical course and specialisation. Rosie disagreed – she thought that would be leaving it too late. She would be thirty-seven by the time she qualified as a psychiatrist.

I suggested that, at a minimum, we wait until the completion of the MD program. The psychiatric qualification was not essential to her planned role as a clinical researcher in mental illness, so if the baby permanently derailed her studies, the impact would not be disastrous. My recollection is that she did not disagree. In any case, a major life decision requires:

1. Articulation of the options, e.g. have zero children; have a specific number of children; sponsor one or more children via a charity.
2. Enumeration of the advantages and disadvantages of each option, e.g. freedom to travel; ability to devote time to work; risk of disruption or grief due to actions of child. Each factor needs to be assigned an agreed weight. 1051, 872/AFP
3. Objective comparison of the options using the above.
4. An implementation plan, which may reveal new factors, requiring revision of (1), (2) and (3).

A spreadsheet is the obvious tool for (1) through to (3), and if (4) is complex, as it would be in preparing for the existence of a new human being and providing for its needs over many years, project-planning software is appropriate. I was unaware of any spreadsheet and Gantt chart for a baby project.

The third apparent violation of logic was that Rosie was using the combined oral contraceptive pill, which has a failure rate of less than 0.5 per cent per annum

when used 'perfectly'. In this context, 'perfectly' means 'correct pill taken daily'. I could not see how even Rosie could be so disorganised as to make an error with such a simple routine.

I am aware that not everyone shares my view of the value of planning rather than allowing our lives to be tossed in unpredictable directions by random events. In Rosie's world, *which I had chosen to share*, it was possible to use the language of popular psychology rather than biology, to welcome the unexpected, and to forget to take vital medication. All three of these events had occurred, culminating in a change of circumstances that made the Orange Juice Problem and even the Gene Sabbatical appear minor.

This analysis, of course, did not happen until much later. The situation as I stood in the bathroom could not have been worse in terms of mental stress. I had been taken to the edge of an unstable equilibrium, and then struck with the maximum conceivable force. The result was inevitable.

Meltdown.

It was the first occurrence since Rosie and I had met – in fact the first time since my sister Michelle's death from an undiagnosed ectopic pregnancy.

Perhaps because I was now older and more stable, or because my unconscious mind wanted to protect my relationship with Rosie, I had a few seconds to respond rationally.

'Are you okay, Don?' said Rosie.

The answer was a definite no, but I did not attempt to

voice it. All mental resources were diverted to implementing my emergency plan.

I made the timeout sign with my hands and ran. The elevator was at our floor, but the doors seemed to take forever to open and then to close again after I stepped inside. Finally I could release my emotions in a space that had no object to break or people to injure.

I doubtless appeared crazy, banging my fists against the elevator walls and shouting. I say doubtless, because I had forgotten to push the button for street level, and the elevator went all the way to the basement. Jerome was waiting with a washing basket when the doors opened. He was wearing a purple t-shirt.

Although my anger was not directed towards him, he did not appear to discern this subtlety. He pushed his hand against my chest, probably in an attempt at pre-emptive self-defence. I reacted automatically, grabbing his arm and spinning him around. He crashed against the elevator wall, then came at me again, this time throwing a punch. I was now responding according to my martial-arts training rather than my emotions. I avoided his punch, and opened him up so he was undefended. It was obvious he understood his situation and was expecting me to strike him. There was no reason to do so, and I released him. He ran up the stairs, leaving his washing basket behind. I needed to escape the confined space, and followed him. We both ran out onto the street.

I initially had no direction in mind, and locked in to following Jerome, who kept looking back. Eventually he ducked down a side street and my thoughts began to clear. I turned north towards Queens.

I had not travelled to Dave and Sonia's apartment on foot before. Fortunately, navigation was straightforward as a result of the logical street numbering system, which should be mandatory in all cities. I ran hard for approximately twenty-five minutes and by the time I arrived at the building and pushed the buzzer I was hot and panting.

My anger had evaporated during the altercation with Jerome; I was relieved that it had not driven me to punch him. My emotions had felt out of control, but my martial-arts discipline had trumped them. This was reassuring, but now I was filled with a general feeling of hopelessness. How would I explain my behaviour to Rosie? I had never mentioned the meltdown problem, for two reasons:

1. After such a long time, and with my increased base level of happiness, I believed that it might not recur.
2. Rosie might have rejected me.

Rejection was now a rational choice for Rosie. She had reason to consider me violent and dangerous. And she was pregnant. To a violent and dangerous man. This would be terrible for her.

'Hello?' It was Sonia on the intercom.

'It's Don.'

'Don? Are you okay?' Sonia was apparently able to

detect from my voice – and possibly the omission of my customary 'greetings' salutation – that there was a problem.

'No. There's been a disaster. Multiple disasters.'

Sonia buzzed me up.

Dave and Sonia's apartment was larger than ours, but already cluttered with baby paraphernalia. It struck me that the term 'ours' might no longer be applicable.

I was conscious of extreme agitation. Dave went to fetch beer, and Sonia insisted that I sit down, even though I was more comfortable walking around.

'What happened?' said Sonia. It was an obvious thing to ask but I was unable to formulate an answer. 'Is Rosie all right?'

Afterwards, I reflected on the brilliance of the question. It was not only the most logical place to begin, but it helped me gain some perspective. Rosie was all right, physically at least. I was feeling calmer. Rationality was returning to deal with the mess that emotions had created.

'There is no problem with Rosie. The problem is with me.'

'What happened?' Sonia asked again.

'I had a meltdown. I failed to control my emotions.'

'You lost it?'

'Lost what?'

'You don't say that in Australia? Did you lose your temper?'

'Correct. I have some sort of psychiatric problem. I've never told Rosie.'

I had never told anyone. I had never conceded that I suffered from a mental illness, other than depression in my early twenties, which was a straightforward consequence of social isolation. I accepted that I was wired differently from most people, or, more precisely, that my wiring was towards one end of a spectrum of different human configurations. My innate logical skills were significantly greater than my interpersonal skills. Without people like me, we would not have penicillin or computers. But psychiatrists had been prepared to diagnose mental illness twenty years earlier. I had always considered them wrong, and no definitive diagnosis other than depression was ever recorded, but the meltdown problem was the weak point in my argument. It was a reaction to irrationality, but the reaction itself was irrational.

Dave returned and handed me a beer. He had also poured one for himself, and drank half of it rapidly. Dave is banned from drinking beer except on our joint nights out, due to a significant weight problem. Perhaps these were extenuating circumstances. I was still sweating despite the air-conditioning, and the drink cooled me down. Sonia and Dave were excellent friends.

Dave had been listening and had heard my admission of the psychiatric problem. 'You never told me either,' he said. 'What sort of –?'

Sonia interrupted. 'Excuse us a minute, Don. I want to speak to Dave alone.' She and Dave walked to the kitchen. I was aware that conventionally they would have needed to employ some form of subterfuge to disguise

24

the fact that they wanted to talk about me without me hearing. Fortunately, I am not easily offended. Dave and Sonia know this.

Dave returned alone. His beer glass had been refilled.

'How often has this happened? The meltdown?'

'This is the first time with Rosie.'

'Did you hit her?'

'No.' I wanted the answer to be 'of course not', but nothing is certain when logical reasoning is swamped by out-of-control emotions. I had prepared an emergency plan and it had worked. That was all I could claim credit for.

'Did you shove her – anything?'

'No, there was no violence. Zero physical contact.'

'Don, I'm supposed to say something like, "Don't fuck with me, buddy," but you know I can't talk like that. You're my friend – just tell me the truth.'

'You're also my friend and therefore aware that I am incompetent at deception.'

Dave laughed. 'True. But you should look me in the eye if you want to convince me.'

I stared into Dave's eyes. They were blue. A surprisingly light blue. I had not noticed before, doubtless as a result of failure to look him in the eye. 'There was no violence. I may have frightened a neighbour.'

'Shit, it was better without the psycho impression.'

I was distressed that Dave and Sonia believed I might have assaulted Rosie, but there was some comfort in realising that things could have been worse, and that their primary concern was for her.

Sonia waved from the entrance to Dave's office where she was talking on her phone. She gave Dave a thumbs-up signal, then jumped up and down with excitement like a child, waving her free hand in the air. Nothing was making sense.

'Oh my God,' she called out, 'Rosie's pregnant.'

It was as though there were twenty people in the room. Dave clinked his glass against mine, spilling beer, and even put his arm around my shoulder. He must have felt me stiffen, so he removed it, but Sonia then repeated the action and Dave slapped me on the back. It was like the subway at rush hour. They were treating my problem as a cause for celebration.

'Rosie's still on the phone,' said Sonia, and handed it to me.

'Don, are you all right?' she said. She was concerned about *me*.

'Of course. The state was temporary.'

'Don, I'm so sorry. I shouldn't have just sprung it on you like that. Are you coming home? I really want to talk to you. But, Don, I don't want this to be temporary.'

Rosie must have thought that I was referring to *her* state – her pregnancy – but her answer gave me vital information. Riding home in Dave's van, I concluded that Rosie had already decided that it was a feature rather than a fault. The orange juice provided further evidence. She did not want to harm the fertilised egg. There was an extraordinary amount to process, and my brain was now functioning normally, or at least in the manner that I was accustomed to. The meltdown was perhaps the psychological equivalent of a reboot following an overload.

Despite my growing expertise in identifying social cues, I nearly missed one from Dave.

'Don, I was going to ask you a favour, but I guess with Rosie and everything . . .'

Excellent was my first thought. Then I realised that the second part of Dave's sentence, and the tone in which it was delivered, indicated that he wanted me to overrule him, to enable him to avoid feeling guilty for asking for my assistance at a time when I was occupied with other problems.

'No problem.'

Dave smiled. I was aware of a surge of pleasure. When I was ten, I had learned to catch a ball after an amount of practice far in excess of that required by my schoolmates. The satisfaction every time I completed what for others would have been a routine catch was similar to the feeling I now experienced as a result of my improved social skills.

'It's no big deal,' Dave said. 'I've finished the beer cellar for the British guy in Chelsea.'

'Beer cellar?'

'Like a wine cellar, except it's for beer.'

'It sounds like a conventional project. The contents should be irrelevant from a refrigeration perspective.'

'Wait till you see it. It turned out pretty expensive.'

'You think he may argue about the price?'

'It's a weird job and he's a weird guy. I figure British and Australian – you guys might connect. I just want a bit of moral support. So he doesn't walk over me.'

Dave was silent and I took the opportunity to reflect. I had been given a reprieve. Rosie had presumably thought that my timeout request had been to consider the consequences of her announcement. The actual meltdown had been invisible to her. She seemed extremely happy with the pregnancy.

There need be no immediate impact on me. I would jog to the Chelsea Market tomorrow, teach an aikido class at the martial-arts centre and listen to the previous week's *Scientific American* podcasts. We would revisit the special exhibition of frogs at the Museum of Natural History, and I would make sushi, pumpkin gyoza, miso soup and tempura of whatever whitefish was recommended by the employees of the Lobster Place for dinner. I would use the 'free time' that Rosie insisted we schedule on the weekend – and which she was currently using for her thesis – to attend Dave's client meeting. At the homewares shop, I would purchase a specialised stopper and vacuum pump to preserve the wine that Rosie would normally have consumed, and substitute juice for her share.

Other than the amendment to beverage management, life would be unchanged. Except for Gene, of course. I still needed to deal with that problem. Given the circumstances, it seemed wise to postpone the announcement.

It was 9.27 p.m. when I arrived home from Dave's. Rosie flung her arms around me and began crying. I had learned that it was better not to attempt to interpret such behaviour at the time, or to seek clarification as to the specific emotion being expressed, even though such information would have been useful in formulating a response. Instead, I adopted the tactic recommended by Claudia and assumed the persona of Gregory Peck's character in *The Big Country*. Strong and silent. It was not difficult for me.

Rosie recovered quickly.

'I put the scallops and stuff in the oven after I got off the phone,' she said. 'They should be okay.' This was an uninformed statement, but I concluded that the damage would probably not be increased significantly by leaving them for another hour.

I hugged Rosie again. I was feeling euphorically happy, a characteristic human reaction to the removal of a terrible threat.

We ate the scallops an hour and seven minutes later, in our pyjamas. All scheduled tasks had been completed. Except for the Gene announcement.

4

It was fortunate that sex had been brought forward to Friday evening. When I returned from my market jog the following morning, Rosie was feeling nauseated. I knew that this was a common symptom in the first trimester of pregnancy, and, thanks to my father, I knew the correct word for it. 'If you describe yourself as nauseous, Don, you're saying you make people sick.' My father is meticulous about correct use of language.

There is a good evolutionary explanation for morning sickness in early pregnancy. In this critical stage of foetal development, with the mother's immune system depressed, it is essential that she does not ingest any harmful substances. Hence the stomach is more highly tuned to reject unsuitable food. I recommended that Rosie not take any drugs to interfere with the natural process.

'I hear you,' said Rosie. She was in the bathroom, steadying herself with both hands on the vanity unit. 'I'll leave the thalidomide in the cupboard.'

'You've got thalidomide?'

'Kidding, Don, kidding.'

I explained to Rosie that many drugs could cross the placental wall, and cited a number of examples, along with descriptions of the deformities they could cause.

I did not think Rosie was likely to take any of them, and was really only sharing some interesting information that I had read many years earlier, but she closed the door. At that point, I realised that there was one drug that she had definitely taken. I opened the door.

'What about alcohol? How long have you been pregnant?'

'About three weeks, I guess. I'm going to stop now, okay?'

Her tone suggested that answering in the negative would not be a good idea. But here was a stunning example of the consequences of failing to plan. Those consequences were important enough to have their own special pejorative term, even in a world that does not value planning as much as it should. We were dealing with an *unplanned pregnancy*. If the pregnancy had been planned, Rosie could have stopped drinking in advance. She could also have arranged for a medical assessment to identify any risks, and we could have acted on research indicating that the DNA quality of sperm can be improved by daily sex.

'Have you smoked any cigarettes? Or marijuana?' Rosie had given up smoking less than a year ago, and had occasionally relapsed, typically in conjunction with alcohol consumption.

'Hey, stop freaking me out. No. You know what you should be worried about? Steroids.'

'You've been taking steroids?'

'No, I haven't been taking steroids. But you're making me stressed. Stress creates cortisol, which is a steroid hormone; cortisol crosses the placental wall; high levels of cortisol in babies are associated with depression in later life.'

'Have you researched this?'

'Only for the last five years. What do you think my PhD's about?' Rosie emerged from the bathroom and stuck her tongue out, a gesture that seemed inconsistent with scientific authority. 'So your job for the next nine months is to make sure I don't get stressed. Say it: *Rosie must not get stressed*. Go on.'

I repeated the instruction. 'Rosie must not get stressed.'

'Actually, I'm a bit stressed now. I can feel the cortisol. I think I might need a massage to relax me.'

There was another critical question. I tried to ask it in a non-stress-inducing tone as I warmed the massage oil.

'Are you sure you're pregnant? Have you consulted a doctor?'

'I'm a medical student, remember? I did the test twice. Yesterday morning and just before I told you. Two false positives are highly unlikely, Professor.'

'Correct. But you were taking contraceptive pills.'

'I must've forgotten. Maybe you're just super potent.'

'Did you forget once or multiple times?'

'How can I remember what I forgot?'

I had seen the pill packet. It was one of the numerous female things that had appeared in my world when Rosie moved in. It had little bubbles labelled according to the day of the week. The system seemed good, although a mapping to actual dates would have been useful. I envisaged some sort of digital dispenser with an alarm. Even in its current form, it was obviously designed to prevent errors by women who were far less intelligent than Rosie. It should have been easy for her to notice an oversight. But she changed the subject.

'I thought you were happy about having a baby.'

I was happy in the way that I would be happy if the captain of an aircraft in which I was travelling announced that he had succeeded in restarting one engine after both had failed. Pleased that I would now probably survive, but shocked that the situation had arisen in the first place, and expecting a thorough investigation into the circumstances.

Apparently, I waited too long to respond. Rosie repeated her statement.

'You said you were happy last night.'

Since the day Rosie and I participated in a wedding ceremony in a *church* in memory of Rosie's atheist mother's Irish ancestry – with her father, Phil, performing a 'giving away' ritual that surely violated Rosie's feminist philosophy, Rosie wearing an extraordinary white dress and veil that she planned never to use again, and escaping having chopped-up coloured paper thrown over us only because of a (sensible) regulation – I had learned that, in marriage, reason frequently had to take second place to harmony. I would have agreed to the confetti if it had been permitted.

'Of course, of course,' I said, trying to maintain a rational and non-confrontational conversation while processing memories and rubbing oil into Rosie's naked body. 'I was just wondering how it happened. As a scientist.'

'It was the Saturday morning after you went out and got breakfast and did your Gregory Peck in *Roman Holiday*.' Rosie attempted her own impression. 'You should always wear my clothes.'

'Was I wearing my shirt when I did it?'

'You do remember. You're right. I had to tell you to take it off.'

First of June. The day my life changed. Again.

'I didn't think it would happen straight away,' she said. 'I thought it might take months, maybe years, like Sonia.'

In retrospect, this was the perfect moment to tell Rosie about Gene. But I did not realise until later that she was admitting that the contraception failure was deliberate and thus giving me an opportunity to make my own revelation. I was focused on the massage process.

'Are you feeling less stressed?' I asked.

She laughed. 'Our baby is out of danger. Temporarily.'

'Would you like a coffee? I put your blueberry muffin in the refrigerator.'

'Just keep doing what you're doing.'

The net result of continuing to do what I was doing was that the time window between breakfast and my aikido class disappeared, and there was no chance to discuss the Gene Problem. When I returned, Rosie suggested we cancel the museum visit to enable further work on her thesis. I used the freed-up time to research beer.

Dave drove us to a new apartment building between the High Line and the Hudson River. I was amazed to discover that the 'cellar' was actually a small bedroom in an apartment on the thirty-ninth floor, immediately below the top-floor apartment that it was to serve. The lower apartment was otherwise vacant. Dave had insulated the room with refrigeration panels and installed a complex cooling system.

'Should've done more to insulate the ceiling,' said Dave. I agreed. Any costs would have been rapidly recouped in electricity savings. I had learned a great deal about refrigeration since meeting Dave.

'Why didn't you?'

'Building management. I think they would have caved, but the client isn't too worried about running costs.'

'The client is presumably extremely wealthy. Or extremely fond of beer.'

Dave pointed upwards.

'Both. He bought two four-bedroom apartments: he's using this one just for the beer.'

He moved his finger to his lips in the conventional signal for silence and secrecy. A short, thin man with a craggy face and long grey hair tied in a ponytail had appeared in the doorway. I estimated his BMI as twenty and his age as sixty-five. If I had to guess his profession, I would have said plumber. If he was a former plumber who had won a lottery, he might be a very exacting client.

He spoke with a strong English accent. "Ullo, David. Brought your mate?' The plumber extended his hand. 'George.'

I shook it according to protocol, matching George's pressure, which was medium. 'Don.'

Formalities completed, George inspected the room.

'What temperature you setting it at?'

Dave gave an answer that I deduced as likely to be wrong. 'For beer, we generally set it at forty-five degrees. Fahrenheit.'

George was unimpressed. 'Bloody hell, you want to freeze it? If I want to drink lager, I'll use the fridge upstairs. Tell me what you know about real beer. Ale.'

Dave is extremely competent, but learns from practice and experience. In contrast, I learn more effectively by reading, which is why it took me so long to achieve competence in aikido, karate and the performance aspects of cocktail-making. Dave probably had zero experience with English beer.

I responded on his behalf. 'For English bitter, the recommended temperature is between ten and thirteen degrees Celsius. Thirteen to fifteen for porters, stout and other dark ales. Equivalent to fifty to fifty-five point four degrees Fahrenheit for the bitter and fifty-five point four to fifty-nine Fahrenheit for the dark ales.'

George smiled. 'Australian?'

'Correct.'

'I'll forgive you that. Go on.'

I proceeded to describe the rules for proper storage of ale. George seemed satisfied with my knowledge.

'Smart fellow,' said George. He turned to Dave. 'I like a man who knows his limitations and gets help when he needs it. So it'll be Don looking after my beer, will it?'

'Well, no,' said Dave. 'Don's more of a . . . consultant.'

'I hear you loud and clear,' said George. 'How much?'

Dave has strong ethics about business practice. 'I'll have to work it out,' he said. 'Are you happy with the fit-out?' Dave indicated the refrigeration equipment, insulation and plumbing that rose through the ceiling.

'What do you reckon, Don?' asked George.

'Insufficient insulation,' I said. 'The electricity consumption will be excessive.'

'Not worth the trouble. Had enough strife with the building manager already. Doesn't like me putting holes in the ceiling. I'll save it up till I put the spiral staircase in.' He laughed. 'All right otherwise?'

'Correct.' I trusted Dave.

George took us upstairs. It was incredible as an apartment, but totally conventional as an English pub. Walls had been removed to incorporate three of the bedrooms into the living room, which was furnished with multiple wooden tables and chairs. A bar was equipped with six taps connected by lines to the beer cellar below, and a large TV screen was angled high on the wall. There was even a platform for a band with piano, drums and amplifiers in place. George was very friendly, and got us micro-brewery beers from one of the bar fridges.

'Rubbish,' he said as we drank them on the balcony, looking out over the Hudson to New Jersey. 'The good stuff should be here on Monday. It came over on the same boat as us.'

George went back inside and returned with a small leather bag.

'So, tell me the bad news,' he said to Dave, who interpreted this as a request for an invoice and passed over a folded piece of paper. George looked at it briefly, then pulled out two large wads of hundred-dollar bills from his bag. He gave one to Dave and counted a further thirty-four bills from the second.

'Thirteen thousand, four hundred. Close enough. No need to trouble the fiscal fiend.' He gave me his card. 'Call me any time you've got a worry, Don.'

George had made it clear that he wanted me to check the cellar morning and night, at least for the first few weeks. Dave needed the contract. He had left a secure job to start his own business before Sonia became pregnant, and was not making much money. Recently he had lacked funds for baseball tickets. Sonia planned to stop working when she had the baby, which would incur costs in its own right.

Dave was my friend, so I had no choice. I would have to change my schedule to accommodate a twice-daily detour via Chelsea.

Outside my apartment building I was intercepted by the superintendent, whom I generally avoided due to the probability of some sort of complaint.

'Mr Tillman, we've had a serious complaint from one of your neighbours. Apparently you assaulted him.'

'Incorrect. He assaulted me, and I used the minimum level of aikido necessary to prevent injury to both of us. Also, he turned my wife's underwear purple and insulted her with profanities.'

'So you assaulted him.'

'Incorrect.'

'Don't sound incorrect to me. You just told me you used karate on him.'

I was about to argue, but before I could say anything he made a speech.

'Mr Tillman, we have a waiting list so long for apartments in this building.' He spaced his hands in a way that was presumably meant to provide evidence for his assertion. 'We throw you out, your apartment will be taken by someone, someone *normal*, the next day. And this isn't no warning – I'll be talking to the owners. We don't need weirdos, Mr Tillman.'

5

My mother's Saturday night Skype call from Shepparton came through on schedule at 7.00 p.m. Eastern Daylight Time; 9.00 a.m. Australian Eastern Standard Time.

The family hardware store was surviving; my brother Trevor needed to get out more and find himself someone like Rosie; my uncle appeared to be in remission, thank God.

I was able to reassure my mother that Rosie and I were fine, work was also fine and any thanks for my uncle's improved prognosis should be directed to medical science rather than a deity who had presumably allowed my uncle to develop cancer. My mother clarified that she was just using an expression, and not submitting scientific evidence of an interventionist god, God forbid, which was also just an expression, Donald. Our conversations had not changed much in thirty years.

Dinner preparation was time-consuming, as the mixed sushi platter had a substantial number of components, and by the time Rosie and I sat down to eat I had still not conveyed the Gene information.

But Rosie wanted to talk about the pregnancy.

'I looked it up on the web. You know, the baby isn't even a centimetre long.'

'The term *baby* is misleading. It's not much advanced from a blastocyst.'

'I'm not calling it a blastocyst.'

'Embryo. It's not a foetus yet.'

'Attention, Don. I'm going to say this once. I don't want forty weeks of technical commentary.'

'Thirty-five. Gestation is conventionally measured from two weeks prior to conception and our best guess is that the event occurred three weeks ago, following the *Roman Holiday* impression. Which needs to be confirmed by a medical professional. Have you made an appointment?'

'I only found out I was pregnant yesterday. Anyway, as far as I'm concerned, it's a baby. A potential baby, okay?'

'A baby under development.'

'Right.'

'Perfect. We can refer to it as the Baby Under Development. BUD.'

'Bud? It makes him sound like a seventy-year-old man. If it's a "he".'

'Ignoring gender, it's statistically likely Bud will reach the age of seventy, assuming successful development and birth and no major change to the environment on which the statistics are based, such as nuclear holocaust, meteorite of the kind that caused the dinosaur extinction –'

'– being talked to death by his father. It's still a male name.'

'Also the name of a plant component. A precursor to a flower. Flowers are considered feminine. Your name

41

has a flower connection. *Bud* is perfect. Reproductive mechanism for a flower. Rosebud, *Rosie*-bud –'

'Okay, okay. I was thinking that the *baby*, speaking in the future tense, could sleep in the living room. Until we can find a bigger place.'

'Of course. We should buy Bud a fold-up bed.'

'What? Don, babies sleep in cribs.'

'I was thinking of later. When it's big enough for a bed. We could buy one now. So we're prepared. We can go to the bed shop tomorrow.'

'We don't need a bed yet. We don't even need to buy the crib for a while. Let's wait till we know that everything's okay.'

I poured the last of the previous evening's pinot gris and wished there was more in the bottle. Subtlety was not getting me anywhere.

'We need the bed for Gene. He and Claudia have split up. He has a job at Columbia and he's staying with us until he can find somewhere else to live.'

This was the component of the Gene Sabbatical that may not have been well considered. I should probably have consulted with Rosie before offering Gene accommodation. But it seemed reasonable for Gene to live with us while he looked for his own apartment. We would be providing for a homeless person.

I am well aware of my incompetence in predicting human reactions. But I would have been prepared to bet on the first word that Rosie would say when she received the information. I was correct by a factor of six.

'Fuck. Fuck, fuck, fuck, fuck, fuck.'

Unfortunately, my prediction that she would ultimately accept the proposition was incorrect. My series of arguments, rather than progressively breaking down her resistance, seemed to have the opposite effect. Even my strongest point – that Gene was the best-qualified person *on the entire planet* to assist her in completing her thesis – was rejected on essentially emotional grounds.

'No way. Absolutely no way is that narcissistic, cheating, misogynist, bigoted, unscientific . . . *pig* sleeping in our apartment.'

I felt that accusing Gene of being unscientific was unfair, but when I started to list Gene's credentials Rosie went to the bedroom and shut the door.

I retrieved George's card to enter it into my address book. It included the name of a band: Dead Kings. To my amazement, I recognised it. Due to my musical tastes being formed primarily by my father's record collection, I was familiar with this British rock group whose music had been popular in the late 1960s.

According to Wikipedia, the band had become active again in 1999 to provide entertainment on Atlantic cruises. Two of the original Dead Kings were actually dead, but had been replaced. George was the drummer. He had accumulated four marriages, four divorces and seven children, but he appeared, relatively, to be the psychologically stable member. The profile did not mention his love of beer.

When I went to bed, Rosie was already asleep. I had

made a list of further advantages of Gene living with us, but decided it would be unwise to wake her.

Rosie was, unusually, awake before me, presumably as a result of commencing her sleep cycle early. She had made coffee in the plunger.

'I figured I shouldn't be drinking espresso,' she said.

'Why?'

'Too much caffeine.'

'Actually, plunged coffee has approximately 2.5 times the caffeine content of espresso.'

'Shit. I try to do the right thing –'

'Those figures are approximate. The espressos I get from Otha's contain three shots. Whereas this coffee is unusually weak, probably due to your lack of experience.'

'Well, you know who's making it next time.'

Rosie was smiling. It seemed like a good time to introduce the additional arguments in favour of Gene. But Rosie spoke first.

'Don, about Gene. I know he's your friend. I get that you're just being loyal and kind. And maybe if I hadn't just discovered I was pregnant . . . But I'm only going to say this once and we can get on with our lives: we do not have space for Gene. End of story.'

I mentally filed the 'end of story' formula as a useful technique for terminating a conversation, but Rosie contradicted it within seconds as I swung my feet out of the bed.

'Hey, you. I've got writing to do today, but I'm going to kick your arse tonight. Give me a hug.'

44

She pulled me back to the bed and kissed me. It defies belief that a person's emotional state could be deduced from such an inconsistent set of messages.

In reviewing my interaction with Rosie, I concluded that her reference to kicking my arse was metaphorical, and should be interpreted positively. We had established a practice of attempting to outperform each other at The Alchemist. In general, I consider the artificial addition of competition to professional activities to be counter-productive, but our efficiency had shown a steady improvement. Time at the cocktail bar appeared to pass quickly, a reliable indication that we were enjoying ourselves. Unfortunately there had been a change of ownership. Any alteration to an optimum situation can only be negative, and the new manager, whose name was Hector but whom we referred to privately as Wineman, was demonstrating this.

Wineman was approximately twenty-eight years old, estimated BMI twenty-two, with a black goatee and heavy-framed glasses in the style that had once marked me as a nerd but was now fashionable.

He had replaced the small tables with longer benches, increased the intensity of the lighting and shifted the drinks focus from cocktails to Spanish wine to complement the revised menu, which consisted of paella.

Wineman had recently completed a Master of Business Administration, and I assumed his changes were in line with best practice in the hospitality industry. However, the net effect had been a fall in patronage, and the consequent firing of two of our colleagues, which he attributed to difficult economic conditions.

'They brought me in just in time,' he said. Frequently.

Rosie and I held hands on the walking component of the journey to the Flatiron neighbourhood. She seemed in an excellent mood, despite her ritual objection to the black-and-white uniform that I, personally, found highly attractive. We arrived two minutes ahead of schedule at 7.28 p.m. Only three tables were occupied; there was no one sitting at the bar.

'You're cutting it fine,' said Wineman. 'Punctuality is one of your performance measures.'

Rosie looked around the sparsely populated room. 'Doesn't look like you're under any pressure.'

'That's about to change,' said Wineman. 'We've got a booking for sixteen. At eight.'

'I thought we didn't take bookings,' I said. 'I thought that was the new rule.'

'The new rule is that we take money. And they're VIPs. VVIPs. Friends of mine.'

It was a further twenty-two minutes before anyone ordered cocktails, due to absence of clientele. A party of four (estimated ages mid-forties, estimated BMIs between twenty and twenty-eight) arrived and sat at the bar, despite Wineman attempting to direct them to a table.

'What can I get you?' asked Rosie.

The two men and two women exchanged glances. It was extraordinary that people needed the advice of their friends and colleagues to make such a routine decision.

46

If they insisted on external counsel, however, it was best that it came from a professional.

'I recommend cocktails,' I said. 'As this is a cocktail bar. We can accommodate all known taste and alcohol requirements.'

Wineman had taken up a position to my left, on the client side of the bar.

'Don can also show you our new wine list,' he said.

Rosie put a closed copy of the leather-bound document on the bar top. The group ignored it. One of the men smiled.

'Cocktails sound good to me. I'll have a whiskey sour.'

'With or without egg white?' I asked, in line with my responsibility for order negotiation.

'With.'

'Straight or over ice?'

'On the rocks.'

'Excellent.' I called to Rosie, 'One Boston sour over ice,' slapped my hand on the bar and started the timer on my watch. Rosie was already standing at the liquor shelves behind me, and I knew that she would be sourcing the whiskey. I put a shaker on the bar, added a scoop of ice and halved a lemon as I solicited and clarified the remaining three orders. I was conscious of Wineman watching. I hoped that, as a business-administration graduate, he would be impressed.

The process I had designed and refined makes best use of our respective capabilities. I have the superior database of recipes, but Rosie's dexterity level is higher than mine. There are economies of scale in one person squeezing the total lemon juice requirement or performing all of the pours of a particular liquor. Of course, such opportunities need to be identified in real-time, which necessitates an agile mind and some practice. I considered it highly unlikely that two bartenders working on individual cocktails could perform as well.

As I poured the third cocktail, a cosmopolitan, Rosie was tapping her fingers, having already garnished the mojito. She had kicked my arse, at least in the first round. As we served the cocktails with the simultaneous movement of our four arms, our clients laughed, then applauded. We were accustomed to this response.

Wineman was also smiling. 'Take a table,' he said to our customers.

'We're fine here,' said Boston Sour Man. He sipped his drink. 'Enjoying the show. Best whiskey sour I've ever had.'

'Please, sit down and I'll organise some tapas – on the house.'

Wineman took four wineglasses from the rack. 'Did you see *Indiana Jones and the Temple of Doom*?' he said.

I shook my head.

'Well, Don, you and Rosie just reminded me of the scene where Mr Jones's assailant shows off his skills with a sword.' Wineman pointed to our clients drinking their cocktails and made some moves that were presumably meant to simulate swordsmanship.

'*Whoosh, whoosh, whoosh, whoosh*, very impressive, four cocktails, seventy-two dollars.'

Wineman picked up an opened bottle of red wine.

'Flor de Pingus.' He poured four glasses and made a sign with his hand, holding his index finger and thumb at ninety degrees with his remaining fingers folded. 'Bang, bang, bang, bang. One hundred and ninety-two bucks.'

'Jerk,' said Rosie as Wineman delivered the drinks to a group of four who had arrived during our cocktail-making. This time her tone was not affectionate. 'Check out their faces.'

'They look happy. Wineman's argument is valid.'

'Of course they're happy. They hadn't ordered anything yet. Everybody's happy when the drinks are on the house.' Rosie put a highball glass in the rack with unnecessary force. I detected anger.

'I recommend going home,' I said.

'What? I'm okay. Just pissed off. Not with you.'

'Correct. Stressed. Creating cortisol, which is unhealthy for Bud. Based on experience, there is a high probability that you will initiate an unpleasant interaction with Wineman and be stressed for the remainder of the shift. Restraining yourself will also be stressful.'

'You know me too well. Can you cope without me?'

'Of course. Numbers are low.'

'That's not what I meant.' She laughed and kissed me. 'I'll tell Wineman I'm feeling sick.'

At 9.34 p.m. a group of eighteen arrived, and the table that had remained reserved and unused for the entire evening was extended to accommodate them. Several were noticeably intoxicated. One woman, aged in her mid-twenties, was the focus of attention. I automatically estimated her BMI: twenty-six. Based on the volume and tone of her speech, I calculated her blood alcohol level as 0.1 grams per litre.

'She's shorter in real life. And a bit porkier.' Jamie-Paul, our bartending colleague, was looking at the group.

'Who?'

'Who do you think?' He pointed to Loud Woman.

'Who is she?'

'You're kidding me, right?'

I was not kidding, but Jamie-Paul offered no further explanation.

A few minutes later, with the party seated, Wineman approached me. 'They want the cocktail geek. I'm guessing that's you.'

I walked to the table where I was greeted by a male with red hair, though not as dramatically red as Rosie's. The group appeared to be made up entirely of people in their mid- to late-twenties.

'You're the cocktail guy?'

'Correct. I am employed to make cocktails. What would you like?'

'You're the guy with – like – a cocktail for every occasion, right? And you keep all the orders in your head? You're that guy?'

'There may be others with the same skills.'

He addressed the rest of the table, loudly, as the ambient noise was now significant.

'Okay, this guy – what's your name?'

'Don Tillman.'

'Hello Dan,' said Loud Woman. 'What do you do when you're not making cocktails?'

'Numerous activities. I'm employed as a professor of genetics.'

Loud Woman laughed again, even more loudly.

Red Hair continued. 'Okay, Don is the king of cocktails. He's memorised every cocktail on the planet and all you need to say is bourbon and vermouth and he'll say martini.'

'Manhattan. Or an American in Paris, boulevardier, Oppenheim, American sweetheart or man o' war.'

Loud Woman laughed. Loudly. 'He's Rain Man! You know. Dustin Hoffman when he remembers all the cards. Dan's the cocktail Rain Man.'

Rain Man! I had seen the film. I did not identify in any way with Rain Man, who was inarticulate, dependent and unemployable. A society of Rain Men would be dysfunctional. A society of Don Tillmans would be efficient, safe and pleasant for all of us.

A few members of the group laughed, but I decided to ignore the comment, as I had ignored the error with my name. Loud Woman was intoxicated and would likely be embarrassed if she saw a video of herself later.

Red Hair continued. 'Don's going to pick a cocktail to fit whatever you want, then he's going to memorise everybody's orders and come back and give them to the right people. Right, Don?'

'As long as people don't change seats.' My memory

does not handle faces as well as numbers. I looked at Red Hair. 'Do you wish to commence the process?'

'Got anything with tequila and bourbon?'

'I recommend a highland margarita. The name implies Scotch whisky but the use of bourbon is a documented option.'

'Oh Kaaaay!' said Red Hair, as though I had hit a home run to win the game in the bottom of the ninth inning. I was one eighteenth of the way to completing my task. I refocused on the drinks orders rather than on constructing a more detailed baseball analogy around this interesting number. It could wait until my next meeting with Dave.

Red Hair's neighbour wanted something like a margarita but more like a long drink but not just a margarita on the rocks or a margarita with soda but something – you know – different, like to make it more unique. I recommended a paloma made with pink grapefruit juice and rimmed with smoked salt.

Now it was Loud Woman's turn. I looked carefully but did not recognise her. This was not inconsistent with her being famous. I largely ignore popular culture. Even if she had been a leading geneticist, I would not have expected to know her face.

'Okay, Rain Man Dan. Make me a cocktail that expresses my personality.'

This suggestion was met with loud sounds of approval. Unfortunately I was in no position to meet the requirement.

'I'm sorry, I don't know anything about you.'

'You're kidding me. Right?'

'Wrong.' I tried to think of some way of asking politely about her personality. 'What is your occupation?'

There was laughter from everyone except Loud Woman, who seemed to be considering her answer.

'I can do that. I'm an actor and a singer. And I'll tell you something else. Everybody thinks they know me but nobody truly does. Now what's my cocktail, Rain Man Dan? The mysterious chanteuse, maybe?'

I was unfamiliar with any cocktail of that name, which probably meant she had invented it to impress her friends. My brain is highly efficient at cocktail searching based on ingredients, but is also good at finding unusual patterns. The two occupations and the personal description combined to produce a match without conscious effort.

A two-faced cheater.

I was about to announce my solution when I realised that there might be a problem – one that placed me in danger of violating my legal and moral duty as the holder of a New York State Liquor Authority Alcohol Training Awareness Program Certificate. I took remedial action.

'I recommend a virgin colada.'

'What's that supposed to mean? That I'm a virgin?'

'Definitely not.' Everybody laughed. I elaborated. 'It's like a pina colada but non-alcoholic.'

'Non-alcoholic. What's *that* supposed to mean?'

The conversation was becoming unnecessarily complicated. It was easiest to get to the point. 'Are you pregnant?'

'What?'

'Pregnant women should not drink alcohol. If you're only overweight, I can serve you an alcoholic cocktail, but I require clarification.'

As I rode the subway home at 9.52 p.m., I reflected on whether my judgement had been affected by the Rosie situation. I had never suspected a client of being pregnant before. Perhaps she *was* merely overweight. Should I have interfered with a stranger's decision to drink alcohol in a country that valued individual autonomy and responsibility so highly?

I made a mental list of the problems that had accumulated in the past fifty-two hours and which now required urgent resolution:

1. Modification of my schedule to accommodate twice-daily beer inspections.
2. The Gene Accommodation Problem.
3. The Jerome Laundry Problem, which had now escalated.
4. The threat of eviction due to (3).
5. Accommodating a baby in our small apartment.
6. Paying our rent and other bills now that Rosie and I had both lost our part-time jobs as a result of my actions.
7. How to reveal (6) to Rosie without causing stress and associated toxic effects of cortisol.
8. Risk of recurrence of the meltdown and fatal damage to my relationship with Rosie as a result of all of the above.

Problem-solving requires time. But time was limited. The beer was due to arrive within twenty-four hours, the super-intendent would probably accost me by tomorrow evening and Jerome could attempt an act of revenge at any time. Gene was about to arrive and Bud was only thirty-five weeks away. What I required was a means of cutting the Gordian knot: a single action that would solve most or all of the problems at once.

I arrived home to find Rosie asleep, and decided to consume some alcohol to encourage creative thinking. As I reshuffled the contents of the fridge to access the beer, the answer came to me. The fridge! We would get a bigger fridge, and all other problems would be solved.

I phoned George.

6

It is generally accepted that people enjoy surprises: hence the traditions associated with Christmas, birthdays and anniversaries. In my experience, most of the pleasure accrues to the giver. The victim is frequently under pressure to feign, at short notice, a positive response to an unwanted object or unscheduled event.

Rosie insisted on observing the gift-giving traditions, but she had been remarkably perceptive in her choices. Colleagues had already commented positively on the shoes that Rosie had given me for my forty-first birthday ten days earlier and which I now wore to work in place of expired running shoes.

Rosie claimed to enjoy surprises, to the extent of saying 'surprise me' when I sought her advice on which play or concert or restaurant to book. Now I was planning a surprise that would exceed all previous instances, with the exception of the revelation of her biological father's identity and the offer of an engagement ring.

It is considered acceptable to engage in temporary deception in support of a surprise.

'You coming, Don?' said Rosie as she departed the following morning. Although Rosie was technically on vacation, she was continuing to work on her thesis at

Columbia on weekdays, as the apartment gave her 'cabin fever'.

She was wearing a short dress with blue spots that I suspected was a recent purchase. The belt, also blue, was wider than necessary to perform its presumed function of emphasising her body shape. The overall effect was positive, but largely due to the exposure of Rosie's legs rather than the aesthetic properties of the costume.

I had switched from riding my new bike to accompanying her on the subway to increase contact time. I reminded myself: the deception is temporary and in support of a surprise; surprises are positive; Rosie had not revealed my birthday weekend excursion to the Smithsonian. I stepped into the bathroom to prevent Rosie interpreting my body language.

'I'm running a bit late. I'll get the next train,' I said.

'You're *what*?'

'Running late. It's not a problem. I don't have any lectures today.' All three statements were technically true, but the first was deceptive. I planned to take the whole day off.

'Are you okay, Don? This pregnancy thing has thrown you, hasn't it?'

'Only by a few minutes.'

Rosie had joined me in the bathroom and was examining some component of her face in the mirror. 'I'll wait for you.'

'Not necessary. In fact, I'm considering riding my bike. To make up time.'

'Hey. I want to talk to you. We hardly talked all weekend.'

It was true that the weekend had been disrupted and that communication had thus been reduced. I began to formulate a response but, now that I was in deception mode, it was difficult to conduct a normal conversation.

Fortunately, Rosie conceded without further input from me. 'All right. But call me for lunch or something.'

Rosie kissed me on the cheek, then turned and left our apartment for the last time.

Dave arrived in his van eight minutes later. We needed to move swiftly as he was required at the Cellar in the Sky to take delivery of the English ale.

It took fifty-eight minutes to pack the furniture and plants. Then I tackled the bathroom. I was astonished by the number of cosmetic and aromatic chemicals that Rosie owned. It would presumably have been insulting for me to tell her that, beyond the occasional dramatic use of lipstick or perfume (which faded rapidly after application due to absorption, evaporation or my becoming accustomed to it), they made no observable difference. I was satisfied with Rosie without any modifications.

Despite the quantity, the chemicals fitted in a single garbage bag. As Dave and I packed the remaining contents of the apartment into Rosie's suitcases, cardboard boxes and additional polythene bags, I was amazed by the sheer quantity of *stuff* we had accumulated since arriving. I remembered a statement Rosie had made prior to leaving Melbourne.

'I'm leaving all the crap behind. I'm hardly bringing

anything.' It was true that she had contradicted this statement by bringing *three suitcases*, but her intent was clear: moving was an opportunity to review possessions. I decided to discard anything not essential to our lives. I recalled some advice I had read in a magazine, waiting for the dentist, on 5 May 1996: 'If you haven't worn it or used it for six months, you don't need it.' The principle seemed sensible and I began applying it.

Dave accompanied me to the doorman's office to surrender my key. Rosie's would need to be returned later. We were greeted by the superintendent. He was, as usual, unfriendly.

'I hope you're not here to complain about anything, Mr Tillman. I haven't forgotten about talking to the owners,' he said.

'Unnecessary. We're leaving.' I gave him the key.

'What, no notice? You got to give thirty days' notice.'

'You indicated that I was an undesirable tenant who could be replaced tomorrow with a desirable one. It seems like a good outcome for everyone.'

'If you don't care about a month's rent.' He laughed.

'That seems unreasonable. If you have a new tenant in the apartment, you would be receiving double rent for a month.'

'I don't make the rules, Mr Tillman. Take it up with the owner if you want.'

I was conscious of becoming annoyed. Today was inevitably going to involve a high level of stress, beginning with the abandonment of scheduled Monday activities. It was time to practise my empathy skills. Why was the supervisor consistently so unpleasant? The answer did not require much reflection. He was required to deal with tenants who complained about problems that he was powerless to rectify, due to his low status and the recalcitrance of the company that owned the building. He was constantly dealing with people in conflict. His low status alone put him at increased risk of coronary heart disease due to elevated cortisol. World's worst job. I suddenly felt sorry for him.

'I apologise for causing you trouble. Can you connect me with the owner, please?'

'You want to speak with the owner?'

'Correct.'

'Good luck.' Incredible. My simple exercise in empathy now had the superintendent on my side, offering his good wishes. He made a call.

'I've got the tenant in 204 with me. He's leaving – right now, today – you got it, no notice – and thinks he should get his deposit back.' He laughed and handed me the phone.

Dave took it from me. 'Let me do this.'

Dave's voice changed. The tone was difficult to describe, but it was as if Woody Allen had been cast instead of Marlon Brando in *The Godfather*.

'My friend here's got a problem with the legality of the air-conditioning system. Might be a safety risk.'

There was a pause.

'A licensed air-conditioning inspector,' said Dave. 'You got self-contained units all over the building like warts on a toad. We don't act unless we get a

60

complaint, but then we'd be obliged to look at the whole damn building. I guess if my friend's paying the rent for another month, he might just want to do that: make a complaint. Which could be very expensive for you. Or maybe you'd like to let him go now. With his security deposit.'

There was a longer pause. Dave's face registered disappointment. Perhaps the 'warts on a toad' metaphor had confused the owner. Toads are presumed to *cause* warts, not to *have* warts. He handed me the phone.

'You done?' said a male voice down the line.

'Greetings.'

'Oh shit, it's you. You're leaving?'

I recognised the voice now. It was not the owner. It was the employee I frequently spoke to about problems that the owner was contractually responsible for but the superintendent considered outside his domain: the stability of temperature, the speed of the internet service, regularity of fire drills. *Et cetera.*

'Correct. Actually, until now, I was unaware of the air-conditioning compliance problem. It sounds extremely serious. I recommend –'

'Forget it. Just drop by and I'll have a cheque waiting for you.'

'What about the air-conditioning?'

'Forget about the air-conditioning and we'll write you a lovely reference for your next landlord. We're going to miss you, Professor.'

In the van, Dave's hands were shaking.

'Is there a problem?'

'I need something to eat. I hate doing that stuff. Confrontation. I'm no good at it.'

'You didn't need to –'

'Yes, I did. Not just for your rent. I need the practice. People think they can take me down.'

George was waiting for us and the beer when we arrived at the Cellar in the Sky.

'I'm impressed,' he said to Dave. 'Don tells me he cares so much about the beer that he's going to sleep with it.'

'Not because I care so much about the beer. Because it's high-quality accommodation that would otherwise be unused.'

'In the best location in New York City. And you're getting it for free.'

'No rent, no complaints,' said Dave. He was practising his tough-guy voice.

'You know we practise upstairs?' said George. 'Loud. There's bugger-all sound insulation.'

'So it's unrentable,' said Dave.

Incredible. A three-bedroom apartment plus coolroom considered unrentable because of an occasional noise problem, easily counteracted with earplugs. Or George could have advertised for deaf tenants.

George shrugged. 'I'm not allowed to rent it. I bought it so the kids could visit. You know, any time they're in New York and want to see their father. I don't think that's going to be a risk for you.'

'How often do you practise?' I asked.

George laughed. 'About once a year. But maybe the beer will inspire me.'

We were interrupted by the arrival of the beer: six large barrels with stands. There was a minor accident carrying the last of these through the living room, resulting in a spillage which I estimated at twenty litres. By the time Dave obtained cloths and mops, it had soaked into the carpet.

'Sorry,' said George. 'But no complaints, remember. I've got a hairdryer, if you want.'

While Dave dried the carpet with Rosie's hairdryer, I unpacked the garbage bags. The Cellar in the Sky had three bathrooms, which was patently excessive. The non-ensuite bathroom was large enough to serve as an office, so I installed my computer and work table there. There was no room for a chair, but the toilet seat was at the correct height. I covered it with a towel for hygiene and comfort. Now I would be able to work all day without ever needing to come out, except for nourishment.

I pulled my mind away from the fantasy of permanent isolation. I had practical tasks to complete in a limited timeframe.

I designated the largest bedroom as Rosie's office and with Dave's help moved in the plants and surplus chairs. I selected the smallest and least well-lit bedroom as our sleeping quarters. Sleeping, I explained over Dave's objections, requires minimal space, and light is an impediment. There were still a few square metres of unused floor after we installed the bed.

We finished at 6.27 p.m. Rosie seldom left Columbia before 6.30 p.m., to avoid subway crowds in the heat. To maximise the surprise, I delayed communicating our change of accommodation until the last possible moment. A few seconds after I sent the text message, I heard a sound from her handbag – the one she took to work at The Alchemist rather than the larger one she used for university. She had left her phone at home. It was not the first time and was the predictable result of owning more than one handbag.

Dave came back from returning George's hairdryer and offered to intercept her at our former apartment.

'While I'm gone, you better get rid of the stink,' he said. I had become accustomed to it, but the beer smell was now mingled with the acrid fumes that the motor in Rosie's hairdryer had produced when it burned out. George's was obviously of a higher quality and had lasted almost three times as long. I decided that a strong-smelling fish would be appropriate to mask the smell and also solve the dinner problem.

At the delicatessen, my phone rang with an unfamiliar number. It was Rosie.

'Don, what's happened? They won't let me in.'

'You left your phone at home.'

'I know. This is Jerome's phone.'

'Jerome? Are you in danger?'

'No, no, he apologised about the washing. He's right

here. What did you say to him?' She did not allow adequate time to answer. 'What's going on?'

'We've moved. I'll text you the address. I need to ring Dave.'

I hung up and texted our new location to Jerome's phone. Dave, Rosie, Jerome, Gene, the fish. I was at my limit of multitasking.

The smoked mackerel was already in the oven and generating aromas of similar intensity to the stale beer and burned wiring when the doorbell rang. It was Rosie. I released the building entrance lock, and approximately thirty seconds later she knocked.

'You don't have to knock,' I said. 'This is our apartment.'

I opened the door dramatically to display the large living room.

Rosie looked around, then walked straight to the windows and looked out over the balcony. The view! Of course, Rosie was interested in views. I hoped she did not have a problem with looking at New Jersey.

'Oh my God,' she said. 'You're kidding me. What's it costing?'

'Zero.'

I retrieved our list of desirable apartment attributes from my pocket and showed her. It was like the Wife Project questionnaire, which, despite Rosie's criticisms, had indirectly brought us together, except now every box was ticked. The perfect apartment. It was apparent that Rosie agreed. She opened the doors to the balcony and spent approximately six minutes looking across the Hudson before stepping back inside.

'What are you cooking?' she asked. 'Is that fish? I've been craving something smoked all day. I thought being pregnant was making me want to smoke again. Which is totally weird. But smoked fish is brilliant. You've blackened it and cooked it in beer, right? You read my mind.' She dropped her phone-free handbag on the floor and hugged me.

I had not read Rosie's mind, nor created the culinary disaster which it contained. But there was no point in undermining her happiness. She wandered around without any obvious purpose for a while, then started exploring in a more systematic manner, starting with her bathroom, which seemed an odd choice.

'Don, my cosmetics! All my stuff. How could you do this?'

'I've made some sort of error?'

'The opposite. It's like – everything is exactly where it was. In the same position.'

'I took photos. Your system was impossible to understand. I did the same with your clothes.'

'You moved everything today?'

'Of course. I had planned to do some culling, but I couldn't remember everything you'd worn in the last six months. I generally don't notice what you wear. So I had to retain everything.'

'This is where you're planning to work?' she said, a few seconds after opening the door to my bathroom-office.

'Correct.'

'Well, I won't be invading your personal space. Given I won't know what you're using it for.'

When she discovered the beer room, I explained the arrangement with George.

'It's like house-sitting. Instead of a dog, he has beer. Which, unlike a dog, does not require feeding.'

'I gather it still managed to do the equivalent of pee on the floor.'

I had forgotten the smell. Humans rapidly become accustomed to their environments. I doubted that Rosie's long-term happiness would be significantly decreased if the beer smell remained. Nor, for that matter, would it be increased by the change of apartments. After the most basic physical requirements are satisfied, human happiness is almost independent of wealth. A meaningful job is far more important. One day in the life of Ivan Denisovich laying bricks in Siberia probably generated a higher level of happiness than one day in the life of a retired rock star in a Manhattan penthouse with all the beer he could drink. Work was crucial to sanity. Which was probably why George continued to perform on the cruise ship.

Rosie was still talking. 'You're serious about not paying rent?'

'Correct.'

'How would you feel if I gave up the cocktail bar job? It's not the same any more. It's probably only a matter of time before Wineman fires me anyway.'

Incredible. It appeared that our being fired by

Wineman was a positive, or at least had zero impact. An item of bad news that would have detracted from my day's success had been rendered irrelevant.

'We can both give it up,' I said. 'It would be vastly less enjoyable without you.'

Rosie hugged me again. I was hugely relieved. I had undertaken a major, risk-prone project, solving multiple problems simultaneously, with complete success. I had cut the Gordian knot.

Rosie's only negative reaction was to the use of the smallest room as our bedroom, as predicted by Dave. But then she said, 'You gave me the biggest room for my office. And, of course, we'll need an extra bedroom.'

It was good that she had accepted my solution to the Gene problem without further discussion. I texted him the good news along with our new address.

I served the fish with a Robert Mondavi Reserve chardonnay (me) and celery juice (Rosie). I had not bothered to buy the vacuum pump for the wine. Any surplus could be kept cool in the beer storage room. For the next eight months, I would be drinking for two.

Rosie raised her juice glass, clinked it with my wine, and then, with just a few words, reminded me of the problem, the terrible problem that had been hiding behind all the others.

'So, Professor Tillman, how do you feel about being a father?'

7

My thoughts about being a father had progressed in the following sequence:

1. Prior to my late teens, I assumed that fatherhood would occur as my life proceeded according to the most common pattern. I did not contemplate it in any more detail.
2. At university I discovered my incompatibility with women, and gradually abandoned the idea, due to the improbability of finding a partner.
3. I met Rosie and fatherhood was back on the agenda. I was initially concerned that my general oddness would be an embarrassment to any children, but Rosie was encouraging and clearly expected us to reproduce at some point. As the actual creation of children had not been scheduled, I forgot about it.
4. Then everything changed as a result of a critical event. I had planned to discuss it with Rosie, but had not given it any priority, again because nothing had been scheduled and also because it reflected badly on me. Now, due to lack of planning, a child was almost inevitable and I had not disclosed important information.

The critical event was the Bluefin Tuna Incident. It had occurred only seven weeks earlier, and the memory of it returned as soon as Rosie raised the topic of fatherhood.

We had been invited to Sunday lunch with Isaac and Judy Esler, but Rosie had forgotten that she had scheduled a study-group meeting. It made sense for me to proceed alone. Isaac had asked for my recommendation as to venue. My automatic response was to select a restaurant I had visited several times before, but Rosie had persuaded me to do otherwise.

'You're way better at restaurants than you used to be. And you're a foodie. Pick somewhere interesting and surprise them.'

Following substantial research, I selected a new Japanese fusion restaurant in Tribeca and advised Isaac.

On arrival, I discovered that Isaac had booked a table for five, which was slightly annoying. A three-person conversation involves three pairs of human interactions, three times as many as a two-person conversation. With familiar people, the complexity is manageable.

But with five people, there would be ten pairs, four involving me directly and six as an observer. Seven of these would involve unfamiliar people, assuming that Isaac and Judy had not coincidentally invited Dave and Sonia or the Dean of Medicine at Columbia, statistically unlikely in a city the size of New York. Keeping track of the dynamics would be virtually impossible and the probability of a faux pas would be increased. The scene was set: unfamiliar people, a restaurant I had not visited before, no Rosie to monitor the situation and provide an early warning. In retrospect, disaster was inevitable.

The additional people were a man and a woman who arrived in advance of Isaac and Judy. They joined me at the table where I was drinking a glass of sake, and introduced themselves as Seymour, a colleague of Isaac (hence presumably a psychiatrist), and Lydia, who did not specify her profession.

Seymour was aged approximately fifty and Lydia approximately forty-two. I had been trying (with minimal success) to eliminate a habit acquired during the Wife Project of calculating body mass index, based on estimates of height and weight, but in this case it was impossible not to notice. I estimated Seymour's BMI at thirty and Lydia's at twenty, primarily due to their difference in height. Seymour was approximately 165 centimetres tall (or, more descriptively, short), about the same height as Isaac, who is thin, while Lydia's height was approximately 175 centimetres, only seven centimetres less than mine. They formed a striking counter-example to Gene's assertion that people tend to select partners who resemble them physically.

Commenting on the contrast seemed to be a good way to get the conversation started and to introduce an interesting topic on which I was knowledgeable. I was careful to attribute the research to Gene to avoid appearing egotistical.

Despite my not using any pejorative words for height and weight, Lydia responded in a manner that appeared cold.

'To begin with, Don, we're not a couple. We just met outside the restaurant.'

Seymour was more helpful. 'Isaac and Judy invited us separately. Judy's always talking about Lydia, so it's great to meet her at last.'

'I'm in Judy's book club,' said Lydia, addressing Seymour rather than me. 'Judy's always telling us stories about *you*.'

'Good ones, I hope,' said Seymour.

'She says you've improved since your divorce.'

'People should be forgiven everything they do three months either side of a divorce.'

'On the contrary,' said Lydia. 'That's exactly what they should be judged on.'

Lydia's information that they were merely two people who had coincidentally been invited to the same lunch was in line with Gene's theory. It gave me an opportunity to re-enter the conversation.

'A victory for evolutionary psychology. The theory predicts that you would not be attracted to each other; I observe evidence that is counter to the theory; more detailed examination of the data supports the theory.'

I was not seriously offering a scientific analysis, but using scientific language for the purpose of amusement. I have considerable experience with the technique, and it usually results in some level of laughter. In this case it did not. If anything, Lydia's expression became less happy.

Seymour at least smiled. 'I think your hypothesis rests on some invalid assumptions,' he said. 'I've got a bit of a thing for tall women.'

This seemed like very personal information. If I had shared what I found physically attractive about Rosie, or women in general, I am sure it would have been judged as inappropriate. But people with better social skills have more leeway to take risks.

'Luckily,' Seymour continued. 'Or I'd be limiting my options in a big way.'

'You're searching for a partner?' I asked. 'I recommend the internet.' My extraordinary success in finding the perfect partner as a result of random events did not invalidate the use of more structured approaches. At this point, Isaac and Judy arrived, increasing the conversational complexity by a factor of 3.33 but improving my comfort level. If I had been left alone with Seymour and Lydia for longer, I would probably have made some sort of social error.

We exchanged formulaic greetings. Everyone else ordered tea, but I concluded that if I had made a mistake in drinking sake, it was too late to recover, and ordered a second flask.

Then our waiter brought the menu. There was an array of fascinating food, consistent with the research I had undertaken on the restaurant, and Judy suggested we order one plate each and share. Excellent idea.

'Any preferences?' she asked. 'Isaac and I don't eat pork, but if someone else wants to order the gyoza, that's fine.' She was obviously being polite, and ordering the gyoza would have made their meals less interesting than the others due to reduced variety. I did not make that mistake. When my turn came, I took advantage of

73

Rosie's absence to try something that would normally have provoked an argument.

'The bluefin tuna sashimi, please.'

'Oh,' said Lydia. 'I didn't see that. Don, you might not be aware that bluefin is an endangered species.'

I was aware of this fact. Rosie ate only 'sustainable seafood'. In 2010, Greenpeace had added the southern bluefin tuna to its seafood Red List, indicating a very high risk of it being sourced from unsustainable fisheries.

'I know. However, this one is already dead and we will only be sharing a single portion among five people. The incremental effect on the world tuna population is likely to be small. In exchange we have an opportunity to experience a new taste.' I had never eaten bluefin tuna and it had a reputation for being superior to the more common yellowfin, which is my favourite food component.

'I'm up for it, as long as it's definitely dead,' said Seymour. 'I'll skip my rhino horn pills tonight to make up.'

My mouth was open to comment on Seymour's extraordinary statement but Lydia spoke first, giving me time to consider the possibility that Seymour was making a joke.

'Well, I'm *not* up for it,' she said. 'I don't accept the argument that individuals can't make a difference. That's the attitude that's stopping us doing anything about global warming.'

Isaac offered a useful if obvious contribution. 'Plus the Indians and Chinese and Indonesians wanting to have our standard of living.'

Lydia may or may not have agreed. But she was talking to me.

'I suppose you don't think about what sort of car you drive or where you shop.'

Her supposition was incorrect, as was the implication that I was environmentally irresponsible. I do not own a car. I ride a bike, use public transport or run. I have relatively few clothes. Under the Standardised Meal System, only recently abandoned, I had virtually zero waste in food and I now treated the efficient use of leftovers as a creative challenge. But I consider my contribution to reducing global warming negligible. My position on rectifying the problem seems to be unattractive to many environmentalists. I had no desire to spoil our lunch with unproductive arguments, but Lydia seemed to be already in irrational greenie mode, so, as with the sake, there was no point in holding back.

'We should be investing more in nuclear power,' I said. 'And finding technological solutions.'

'Such as?' said Lydia.

'Removing carbon from the atmosphere. Geoengineering. I've been reading about it. Incredibly interesting. Humans are poor at restraint but good at technology.'

'Do you know how abhorrent I find that type of thinking?' said Lydia. 'Do whatever you like and hope that someone will come along and fix it. And get rich doing it. Are you going to save the tuna that way too?'

'Of course! It's highly possible we could genetically engineer the yellowfin tuna to taste like bluefin. Classic example of a technological solution to a problem created by humans. I would volunteer for the tasting panel.'

'You do whatever you want. But I don't want us, as a group, to order the tuna.'

It is incredible what complex ideas can be conveyed by a human facial expression. Although no guide was likely to include it, I believe I was correct in interpreting Isaac's as *For fuck's sake, Don, don't order the tuna.* When our server arrived, I ordered the scallops with *foie gras de canard.*

Lydia began to stand up, then sat down again.

'You're actually not trying to upset me, are you?' she said. 'You're really not. You're just so insensitive you don't know what you're doing.'

'Correct.' It was easiest to tell the truth and I was relieved that Lydia did not consider me malicious. I saw no logical reason why a concern about sustainability should be a predictor of what I assumed was an objection to the treatment of farmed poultry. I consider it wrong to stereotype people, but it might have been useful in this situation.

'I've met people like you,' she said. 'Professionally.'

'You're a geneticist?'

'I'm a social worker.'

'Lydia,' said Judy, 'this is getting too much like work. I'm going to order for the whole table, and we should all start again. I've been dying to hear about Seymour's book. Seymour's writing a book. Tell us about your book, Seymour.'

76

Seymour smiled. 'It's about growing meat in laboratories. So vegetarians can have a guilt-free burger.'

I began to respond to this unexpectedly interesting topic but Isaac interrupted.

'I don't think this is the right time for a joke, Seymour. Seymour's book is about guilt, but not about burgers.'

'Actually I do mention lab burgers. As an example of how complex these issues are and the way deeply rooted prejudices come into play. We need to be more open to thinking outside the box. That's all Don's been saying.'

This was essentially correct, but it started Lydia off again.

'That's not what I'm complaining about. He's entitled to an opinion. I let the evolutionary psychology stuff go before, even though it's crap. I'm talking about his insensitivity.'

'We need truth-tellers,' said Seymour. 'We need technical people. If my plane's going down, I want someone like Don at the controls.'

I would have assumed he would want an expert pilot rather than a geneticist flying the plane, but I guessed he was attempting to make a point about emotions interfering with rational behaviour. I noted it for future use as perhaps less confronting than the story about the crying baby and the gun.

'You want some guy with Asperger's flying your plane?' said Lydia.

'Better than someone who uses words they don't understand,' said Seymour.

Judy tried to interrupt, but Lydia and Seymour's argument had acquired a momentum that excluded the rest of us, even though the topic of conversation was me. I had some familiarity with Asperger's syndrome from preparing a lecture sixteen months earlier when Gene had been unable to meet the commitment due to a sexual opportunity. Consequently, I had helped to initiate a research project looking for genetic markers for the syndrome in high-achieving individuals. I had noted some of my own personality traits in the descriptions, but humans consistently over-recognise patterns and draw erroneous conclusions based on them. I had also, at various times, been labelled schizophrenic, bipolar, an OCD sufferer and a typical Gemini. Although I did not consider Asperger's syndrome a negative, I did not need another label. But it was more interesting to listen than to argue.

'Look who's talking,' said Lydia. 'If anyone doesn't understand Asperger's, it's psychiatrists. Autism, then. You want Rain Man flying your plane?'

The comparison made no more sense than it did later when Loud Woman drew it. I certainly would not have wanted Rain Man flying my plane, if I owned one, or a plane in which I was a passenger.

Lydia must have assumed that she was causing me distress. 'Sorry, Don, this isn't personal. *I'm* not calling you autistic. He is.' She pointed to Seymour. 'Because he and his buddies don't know the difference between autism and Asperger's. Rain Man and Einstein – it's all the same to them.'

Seymour had not called me autistic. He had not used any labels, but had described me as honest and technical, essential attributes for a pilot and positive in general. Lydia was attempting to make Seymour look bad for some reason – and the complexities of the three-way interaction between us had now exceeded my ability to interpret them.

Seymour addressed me. 'Judy tells me you're married. I've got that right?'

'Correct.'

'Stop, enough,' said Judy. Four people. Six interactions.

Isaac raised his hand and nodded. Seymour apparently interpreted the combination of signals as approval to continue. All five of us were now involved in a conversation with invisible agendas.

'You're happy? Happily married?' I wasn't sure what Seymour's questioning was about, but I concluded that he was a fundamentally nice person who was trying to support me by demonstrating that at least one person liked me enough to live with me.

'Extremely.'

'In touch with your family?'

'Seymour!' said Judy.

I answered Seymour's question, which was benign. 'My mother phones me every Saturday; Sunday, Australian Eastern Standard Time. I don't have any children of my own.'

'Gainfully employed?'

'I'm an associate professor of genetics at Columbia. I

consider that my work has social value in addition to providing an adequate income. I also work in a bar.'

'Mixing comfortably with people in a generally relaxed but sometimes challenging social environment with an eye on the commercial imperatives. Enjoying life?'

'Yes' seemed to be the most useful answer.

'So you're not autistic. That's a professional opinion. The diagnostic criteria require dysfunction and you're enjoying a good life. Go on enjoying it and stay away from people who think you've got a problem.'

'Good,' said Judy. 'Can we pull some food now and have a pleasant lunch?'

'Screw you,' said Lydia. She was talking to Seymour, not Judy. 'You need to pull your head out of your diagnostic manual and go into the street. Go visit some real people's homes and see what your airline pilots do.'

She stood and picked up her bag. 'Order whatever you want.' She turned to me. 'I'm sorry. It's not your fault. You're not going to undo whatever trauma happened in your childhood. But don't let some fat little shrink tell you it doesn't matter. And do me and the world one favour.'

I assumed she was going to mention the bluefin tuna again. I was wrong.

'Don't ever have children.'

8

'Earth to Don. Are you still reading me? I asked how you were feeling about becoming a father.'

I did not need Rosie's reminder. My reflections on the Bluefin Tuna Incident had been replaced by a struggle to answer her question and I was not making much progress. I suspected that Claudia's recommended response to difficult personal enquiries – *Why are you asking?* – would not work here. It was obvious why Rosie was asking. She wanted to ensure that I was psychologically ready for the most challenging and important task of my life. And the truth was that I had already been judged, *professionally* judged, by a social worker accustomed to dealing with family disasters, as unfit.

In describing the lunch to Rosie seven weeks earlier, I had focused on matters that would be of immediate interest to her: the restaurant, the food and Seymour's book about guilt. I did not mention Lydia's assessment of my suitability as a father, since it was only a single – albeit expert – opinion, and of no immediate relevance.

My mother had given me a useful rule when I was young: before sharing interesting information that has not been solicited, think carefully about whether it has the potential to cause distress. She had repeated it on a number of occasions, usually after I had shared some interesting information. I was still thinking carefully when the doorbell rang.

'Shit. Who's that?' said Rosie.

I could predict who it was, with a high degree of certainty, taking into account the scheduled arrival time of the Qantas flight from Melbourne via Los Angeles and travel time from JFK. I released the security lock and Rosie jumped up to open the door. When Gene emerged from the elevator, he was carrying two suitcases and a bunch of flowers, which he immediately gave to Rosie. Even I could see that his arrival had caused a change in the human dynamics. A few moments earlier, I was struggling to find the correct words to say. Now, the problem had been transferred to Rosie.

Fortunately, Gene is an expert in social interaction. He moved towards me as if to hug me, then, detecting my body language or remembering our past protocols, shook my hand instead. After releasing it, he hugged Rosie.

Gene is my best friend, yet I find hugging him uncomfortable. In fact, I only enjoy close contact with people with whom I have sex, a category containing one person only. Rosie dislikes Gene, yet she managed to hug him for approximately four seconds without a break.

'I can't tell you how much I appreciate this,' said Gene. 'I know you're not my biggest fan.' He was speaking to Rosie, of course. I have always liked Gene, although this has required forgiveness for some immoral behaviour.

'You've gained weight,' I said. 'We need to schedule some running.' I estimated Gene's BMI as twenty-eight, three points higher than when I had last seen him ten months earlier.

'How long are you staying?' said Rosie. 'Has Don told you I'm pregnant?'

'He has not,' said Gene. 'That's wonderful news. Congratulations.' He used the wonderful news as an excuse to repeat the hug and avoid answering the question about the duration of his visit.

Gene looked around. 'I really do appreciate this. What a great place. Columbia must pay better than I thought. But I'm interrupting dinner.'

'No, no,' said Rosie. 'We shouldn't have started before you. Have you eaten?'

'I'm a bit jet-lagged. Not sure what time my body thinks it is.'

Here, I could help.

'You should drink alcohol. Remind your body that it's evening.' I went to the coolroom to collect a bottle of pinot noir while Gene began unpacking in what, until now, had been the spare room. Rosie followed me.

Rosie stared at the barrels of beer, then looked suddenly ill and dashed out. It was true that the smell was much stronger inside the coolroom. I heard the bathroom door slam. Then there was a loud noise, a crash, but not from the bathroom. It was followed by a booming sound at similar volume. It was drumming from upstairs. An electric guitar joined in. When Rosie returned from the bathroom, I had the earplugs ready, but I suspected that her level of satisfaction had dropped.

She went to her new study while I fitted my own

earplugs and finished my meal. Fifty-two minutes later the music stopped and I was able to talk with Gene. He was certain that his marriage was over, but it seemed to me that he merely needed to rectify his behaviour. Permanently.

'That was the plan,' he said.

'It was the only reasonable plan. Draw up a spreadsheet. Two columns. On one side you have Claudia, Carl, Eugenie, stability, accommodation, domestic efficiency, moral integrity, respectability, no more inappropriate-conduct complaints, vast advantages. On the other, you have occasional sex with random women. Is it significantly better than sex with Claudia?'

'Of course not. Not that I've had a chance to compare recently. Can we talk about this later? It's been a long flight. Two flights.'

'We can talk tomorrow. Every day until we get it resolved.'

'Don, it's over. I've accepted it. Now, tell me how it feels to be an expectant father.'

'I don't have any feelings about it yet. It's too early.'

'I think I might ask you every day until we get it resolved. You're a bit nervous, aren't you?'

'How can you tell?'

'All men are. Worried they'll lose their wives to the baby. Worried they'll never have sex again. Worried they won't cut it.'

'I'm not average. I expect I will have unique problems.'

'And you'll solve them in your own unique way.'

This was an extremely helpful contribution. Problem-solving is one of my strengths. But it failed to address the immediate dilemma.

'What do I tell Rosie? She wants to know how I feel.'

'You tell her that you're excited about being a father. Don't burden her with your insecurities. Got any port?'

The music started again. I didn't have any port, so substituted Cointreau and we sat without talking until Rosie came out to get me. Gene had fallen asleep in the chair. It was probably more comfortable than sleeping on the floor. It was certainly better than being homeless in New York.

In the bedroom, Rosie smiled and kissed me.

'So the Gene situation is acceptable?' I said.

'No. It's not. Nor is the beer smell, which we're going to have to do something about if you don't want me throwing up in the evenings as well as the mornings. And obviously you need to talk to the people upstairs about the noise. I mean, you can't give earplugs to a baby. But the apartment is just stunningly, wonderfully brilliant.'

'Sufficient to compensate for the problems?'

'Almost.' She smiled.

I looked at the world's most beautiful woman, dressed only in a too-large t-shirt, sitting up in my bed – our bed. Waiting for me to say the words that would allow this extraordinary situation to continue.

I took a deep breath, expelled the air, then took another breath to allow speech. 'I'm incredibly excited about becoming a father.' I was using the word *excited* in the sense that I would use it to say an electron was excited: activated rather than in a particular emotional state. Hence I was speaking sincerely, which was a good thing, as Rosie would have detected a lie.

Rosie flung her arms around me and hugged me for longer than she had hugged Gene. I was feeling much better. I could allow my intellect to rest and enjoy the experience of being close to Rosie. Gene's advice had been excellent and had, at least for me, justified his presence. I would solve the noise problem and the beer problem and the fatherhood problem in my own way.

I woke with a headache, which I attributed to the stress associated with recalling the Bluefin Tuna Incident. My life was becoming more complex. In addition to my duties as professor and spouse, I was now responsible for monitoring beer, Gene and, potentially, Rosie, whom I suspected would continue to be neglectful of her health, even during this critical period. And, of course, I needed to do some research to prepare myself for fatherhood.

There were two possible responses to the increased load. The first was to put in place a more formal schedule to ensure that time was allocated efficiently, taking into account the relative priority of each task and its contribution to critical goals. The second was to embrace chaos. The correct choice was obvious. It was time to initiate the Baby Project.

I suspected Rosie would have a negative reaction to the installation of a whiteboard in the living room. I discovered a brilliant solution. The white tiles on the walls of my new bathroom-office were tall and narrow: approximately thirty centimetres high and ten centimetres wide. They provided a ready-made grid with a surface suitable for a whiteboard marker. On one wall were nineteen columns of seven tiles, interrupted only by the toilet-roll holder which occupied one tile and obscured another – an almost perfect template for a rolling eighteen-week calendar. Each tile could be divided into seventeen horizontal slots to cover waking hours, with the possibility of further vertical subdivision. Rosie was unlikely to see the schedule, given her statement about respecting my personal space.

Of course I could have used a computer spreadsheet or calendar application. But the wall was much bigger than my screen and filling in my scheduled research meetings, martial-arts training and market jogs for the first four weeks induced an unexpected sense of wellbeing.

The morning after Gene's arrival, we travelled together on the subway to Columbia. The journey from our new apartment was much shorter and I had rescheduled my departure time accordingly. Rosie had not yet adjusted her daily routine and took an earlier train.

I used the time to talk to Gene about his family problem. 'She rejected you because you cheated on her. Multiple times. After you lied to her about stopping. Therefore she needs to be convinced that you are no longer a cheat and a liar.'

'Not so loud, Don.'

I had raised my voice to emphasise these critical points and people were looking at us – and Gene particularly – with disapproval. A woman stepping off at Penn Station said, 'Shame on you.' The woman behind her added, 'Pig.' It was useful to have my argument reinforced but Gene attempted to change the subject.

'Thought any more about fatherhood?'

I had not yet included any baby-related activities in my new white-tile schedule, although they had been the original motivation for creating it. It was possible my mind was responding to an unexpected event by activating primitive defence mechanisms and pretending it did not exist. I needed to do two things: acknowledge the upcoming birth by stating it out loud to others and undertake some actual research.

After installing Gene in his office at Columbia, we had coffee with Professor David Borenstein. Rosie joined us, in her role as my partner, rather than as a medical student. David had been extremely helpful in supporting our visas and relocation. 'So what's news with you, Don?' he asked.

I was about to give David an update on my investigation of genetic predisposition to cirrhosis of the liver in mice, which was nearing completion, when I remembered my earlier decision to acknowledge my impending fatherhood.

'Rosie's pregnant,' I said.

Everyone was silent. I knew immediately that I had made an error, as Rosie kicked me under the table. It was obviously ineffective; the statement could not be retracted.

'Well,' said David. 'Congratulations.'

Rosie smiled. 'Thanks. It's not really public yet, so –'

'Of course. And with my faculty hat on, I can assure you that you're not the first student to have some disruption to their studies.'

'I'm not planning to let it disrupt my studies.' I recognised Rosie's 'Don't fuck with me' voice. It seemed inadvisable to use it on the Dean.

But David did not detect the tone, or chose to ignore it. 'I'm not the person to talk to,' he said. 'When you're ready, have a chat to Mandy Rau. You know Mandy? She's the counsellor. Make sure you tell her you're covered by Don's medical plan.'

Rosie was about to speak again, but David raised both hands in a double 'Stop' signal and the subject changed to Gene's program.

David declined a second coffee. 'Sorry, I have to go, but I need to speak to Don about the cirrhosis research. Walk back with me? You're welcome to join us, Gene.'

Gene, despite having no interest in my research, joined us.

'I gather you've finished the component of the study that needs a visiting professor,' said the Dean.

'There's still a vast quantity of data to be analysed,' I said.

'That's what I meant – it's mainly legwork. I thought you might like some assistance.'

'Not if it means applying for a grant.' It is generally less time-consuming to do work myself than to get involved in the paperwork required to get help.

'No, you don't need to apply for a grant. *In this specific instance.*' He laughed and Gene joined in. 'But I've got a post-doc researcher, strong on statistics, on loan to us – it's a bit of a personal favour to a colleague, but there's got to be meaningful work. Not least in case they audit the visa.'

'Take him,' said Gene.

Gene's publication list was populated by work performed by such people under his notional supervision. I did not want my name on papers I had not written. But I owed it to David Borenstein to not waste my time on tasks that could be performed by a more junior person who would benefit from the experience.

'Her name's Inge,' said David. 'She's Lithuanian.'

Gene left us, and the Dean and I walked for a while without speaking. I presumed he was thinking – a pleasant change from most people who regard a gap in the conversation as a space that requires filling. We were almost at his office when he spoke again.

'Don, the counsellor is going to suggest Rosie takes time off. That's sensible. But we don't want to lose her. We like to keep our students and she's a good one. The timing's not great. She'll probably need to defer the first six months of her major clinical year, then have the baby and come back second semester, or the following year. I'd say take the whole year. It'll give you time to work out the care arrangements, which will probably involve you.'

I had not thought about this practical issue, and David's advice seemed sound. 'Some women take a month or two off and come right back, and arrange to pick up what they've missed in the vacation. I think that's a mistake. Especially for you two.'

'Why specifically us?'

'You don't have local support. If you both had parents or siblings living here – maybe. There's only so much child care you can contract out. I'd say, defer the whole year. Or the baby will suffer, the study will suffer, she'll suffer. And let me tell you from bitter experience, you'll suffer too.'

'Seems like excellent advice. I'll tell Rosie.'

'Don't tell her it came from me.'

The Dean of Medicine, our sponsor, an experienced parent. Could there be anyone with greater authority to offer advice on balancing medical studies and parenthood? Yet I suspected he was right in recommending I not mention his name. Rosie would instinctively reject the advice of an older male in authority.

My prediction was correct.

'I'm not taking a year out of the program,' Rosie said when I presented David's advice that evening without citing its source. We were having dinner with Gene, our new family member, who was making use of one of the surplus chairs.

'A year out is nothing in the long term,' said Gene.

'Did you take time off when Eugenie was born?' said Rosie.

'Claudia did.'

'Then just equate me to you rather than Claudia. Or is that too big a leap?'

'So Don's going to look after the baby?'

Rosie laughed. 'I don't think so. I mean, Don has to work. And . . .'

I was interested to hear what other reasons Rosie might cite for my not being able to look after Bud, but Gene interrupted.

'So who's going to look after it?'

Rosie thought for a few moments.

'I'll take her – or him – with me.'

I was stunned. 'You'll take Bud to Columbia – to the hospitals?' By the time Bud was born, Rosie would be working with actual patients – people riddled with infectious diseases – in situations where a baby underfoot could cause life-threatening disasters. Her approach seemed impractical and irresponsible.

'I'm still thinking about it, okay? But it's time they considered the needs of women with children. Instead of telling us to go away and come back when the baby's grown up.' Rosie pushed her plate aside. She had not finished her risotto. 'I need to do some work.'

Once again, Gene and I were left to talk. I made a mental note to replenish the liquor stocks.

Gene selected the conversation topic before I could mention his marriage.

'Feeling any better about being a dad?'

The word 'dad' sounded odd, applied to me. I thought of my own father. I suspected his role in my life when I was a baby had been minimal. My mother had resigned from her teaching job to manage three children while my father worked at the family hardware store. It was a practical, if stereotypical, allocation of the workload. Given that my father shares some of the personality traits that give me the most trouble, it was probably advantageous to maximise the amount of input from my mother.

'I've considered it. I suspect the most useful contribution is to stay out of the way to avoid causing problems.' This was consistent with the assessment of me given by Lydia during the Bluefin Tuna Incident and in keeping with the medical maxim: *First do no harm*.

'You know, you may get away with it. Rosie's a rusted-on feminist, so philosophically she wants you to wear a skirt, but she also thinks she's Superwoman. Independence is an Australian female trait. She'll want to do it all.' Gene drained his Midori and refilled both glasses. 'Whatever women say, they're biologically bonded to the baby in a way we're not. It won't even recognise you for the first few months. So don't worry about that. Look ahead to when it's a toddler and you can interact.'

This was helpful. I was fortunate to be able to source advice from an experienced father and head of a psychology department. He had more.

'Forget everything you hear from psychologists. They fetishise parenthood. Make you paranoid you're doing something wrong. If you hear the word *attachment*, run a mile.'

This was *extremely* helpful. Lydia doubtless belonged to the group Gene was describing.

Gene continued. 'You don't have any nieces or nephews, right?'

'Correct.'

'So you've got no real experience with kids.'

'Only Eugenie and Carl.' Gene's children were almost familiar enough to be included in my list of friends, but too old for toddler orientation.

Rosie emerged from her office and walked towards the bedroom, making hand motions which I interpreted as *You've had enough to drink, both of you, and it's time to come to bed instead of sharing more interesting information.*

Gene started to get up and collapsed back in the chair. 'Here's my last bit of advice before I fall over. Watch some kids, watch them play. You'll see they're just little adults, only they don't know all the rules and tricks yet. Nothing to worry about.'

9

Rosie was sitting up in bed when I joined her.

'Don, before you get undressed – could I ask you a favour?'

'Of course. As long as it doesn't require mental or physical coordination.' Gene's topping-up of my glass had resulted in an accidental overdose of alcohol.

'What time does the deli close? The one where you got the smoked mackerel?'

'I don't know.' Why did I need to remain dressed to answer the question?

'I'd really love some more.'

'I'll buy some later today.' It was 12.04 a.m. 'We can have it cold as an appetiser.'

'I meant now. Tonight. With dill pickles. The ones with chilli if you can find them.'

'It's too late to eat. Your digestive system –'

'I don't care. I'm pregnant. You get cravings. It's normal.'

Normal had clearly been redefined.

I predicted that finding smoked mackerel and pickles after midnight would involve significant effort, especially as my intoxication precluded the use of my bicycle, but this was the first opportunity I had been offered to do something directly related to the pregnancy.

Random jogging in an unfamiliar neighbourhood failed to uncover any smoked mackerel. The streets were still busy and my directional choices were being influenced by the need to dodge pedestrians. I decided to proceed to Brooklyn where I knew there was a well-stocked all-night delicatessen on Graham Avenue. Statistically, my expected time to find mackerel was probably lower if I continued to search Manhattan, but I was prepared to pay a price for certainty.

As I jogged over the Williamsburg Bridge, I analysed the problem. It seemed likely that Rosie's body was reacting to some deficiency, the intensity of the desire magnified by the importance of proper nutrition during pregnancy. She had rejected the mushroom and artichoke risotto but wanted mackerel. I made a provisional conclusion that her body required protein and fish oil.

As with the management of my increasingly complex life, I saw two possible approaches. An on-demand sourcing of nutrition, driven by cravings which probably occurred only after the deficiency was recognised by her body, was going to be disruptive and inefficient, as my search for mackerel was demonstrating. A planned approach, recognising the specialised diet required for pregnancy and ensuring all ingredients were on hand in a timely manner, was obviously superior.

When I arrived home at 2.32 a.m. in the City That Never Sleeps, I had run approximately twenty kilometres and acquired mackerel, pickles and chocolate (Rosie always craved chocolate). Rosie was asleep.

Waving the mackerel under her nose did not stimulate any response.

When I woke, Rosie and Gene were already preparing to leave for Columbia and I had a headache again, this time doubtless due to lack of sleep. The correct amount of relatively undisturbed sleep is critical to optimum physical and mental functioning. Rosie's pregnancy was taking a severe toll on my body. Purchase of pregnancy-compatible food in advance would at least obviate the need for midnight excursions. As a short-term solution, I took a day's leave to concentrate on the Baby Project.

I was able to use the freed-up day productively, first to catch up on sleep, then to source further information on Rosie's statement about the link between cortisol and depression. The evidence was convincing, as it was for the link with heart disease. It was definitely important to minimise Rosie's stress levels in the interests of both Bud's health and her own.

I allocated the remainder of the morning, after completion of scheduled body-maintenance tasks, to researching nutrition in pregnancy. The time I allowed turned out to be manifestly insufficient. There was so much conflicting advice! Even after rejection of articles that helpfully advertised their lack of a scientific basis by the use of words such as *organic, holistic* and *natural,* I was left with a mass of data, recommendations and recipes. Some focused on foods to include, others on foods to avoid. There was substantial overlap. A commercial but impressive baby-oriented website offered a Standardised

Meal System for each trimester, but its meals included meat, which would be unacceptable to Rosie. I needed more time, or a meta-study. Surely others had faced the same problem and codified their findings.

The pregnancy websites also contained vast amounts of information about foetal development. Rosie had been clear that she did not want a technical commentary, but it was so *interesting*, especially with a case study progressing in my apartment. I selected one of the wall tiles above the bath and labelled it '5' to represent the estimated number of weeks of gestation up to the preceding Saturday. I made a dot the size of an orange seed to represent Bud's current size, then added a sketch. Even after forty minutes' work, it was crude compared with some of the diagrams available online. But, as with the schedule on the tiles opposite, its production gave me a distinct sense of satisfaction.

To solve the immediate nutrition problem, I selected a vegetarian recipe at random from one of the websites. A jog via Trader Joe's sufficed to source all the necessary ingredients for a tofu and squash flan.

I was left with an afternoon of unscheduled time – an ideal opportunity to do some research in line with Gene's advice. It seemed wise to delay the shower and change until after my excursion, especially as the weather forecast indicated a thirty per cent probability of rain. I put my light raincoat on over my jogging costume and added a cycling hat for hair protection.

There was a small playground on 10th Avenue, only a

few blocks away. It was perfect. I was able to sit on a bench, alone, and watch children with their guardians. Binoculars would have been helpful, but I could observe gross motor actions and even hear some conversation, especially as much of it was shouted. I was not disturbed – in fact on the sole occasion that a child approached me it was immediately summoned back.

I made several observations in my notebook.

The children explored for short distances but routinely checked and returned to their guardians. I recalled seeing a documentary in which this behaviour was made more obvious by fast-motion replay, but could not recall what type of animal was involved. My phone had substantial available memory, so I began shooting my own video. Gene would definitely be interested.

My recording was interrupted by some kind of communal activity: the guardians and children gathered together for approximately twenty seconds and then moved to the other end of the playground, where my view of them was obscured by a central island of foliage. I followed and sat where I could observe them again, but they did not resume their play. I decided to wait and used the time to change the video resolution on my phone in case there was an opportunity to film a longer segment. Due to my focus on the camera-operating task, I did not notice the approach of two uniformed male police officers.

In retrospect, I may not have handled the situation well, but it was an unfamiliar social protocol in unexpected circumstances driven by rules which I did not know. I was also struggling with the video application which I had downloaded because of its superior compression algorithm, without due attention to its user-friendliness.

'What do you think you're doing?' This was the (marginally) older policeman. I guessed they were both in their thirties, and in good physical shape – BMIs approximately twenty-three.

'I *think* I'm configuring the resolution, but it's possible I'm doing something different. It's unlikely you will be able to assist unless you're familiar with the application.'

'Well, I guess we should get out of your way and leave you with the kids.'

'Excellent. Good luck fighting crime.'

'Get up.' This was an unexpected change of attitude on the part of the younger colleague. Perhaps I was seeing a demonstration of the 'good cop, bad cop' protocol. I looked to Good Cop to see if I would receive contrary instructions.

'Do you also require me to stand up?'

Good Cop assisted me to stand. Forcefully. My dislike of being touched is visceral, and my response was similarly automatic. I did not pin or throw my assailant, but I did use a simple aikido move to disengage and distance him from me. He staggered back and Bad Cop pulled his gun. Good Cop produced handcuffs.

At the police station, the officers sought a statement in which I conceded that I had been in the park observing children and that I had resisted arrest. I was finally given an answer to the obvious question: what had I done wrong? It is illegal in New York to enter a designated children's playground without the company of a child under the age of twelve. Apparently there was a sign posted on the fence to that effect.

Incredible. If I had actually been, as presumably suspected by the police and anticipated by the lawmakers, someone who gained sexual satisfaction from observing children, I would have had to kidnap a child in order to gain entry to the playground. Good Cop and Bad Cop were not interested in this argument, and I eventually provided an account of events that seemed to satisfy them.

I was then left alone in a small room for fifty four minutes. My phone had been confiscated.

At that point an older man, also in uniform, joined me, carrying what I guessed was the printed version of my statement.

'Professor Tillman?'

'Greetings. I need to call a lawyer.' The time spent alone had been useful in allowing me to collect my thoughts. I remembered a 1–800 phone number for criminal lawyers from a subway advertisement.

'You don't want to call your wife first?'

'My priority is professional advice.' I was also conscious that news of my arrest would cause Rosie stress, particularly as the problem was still unresolved and she could do little to help.

'You can call a lawyer if you want. Maybe you won't need one. You want something to drink?'

My answer was automatic. 'Yes, please. Tequila – straight

up.' My interrogator looked at me for approximately five seconds. He made no signs of getting the drink.

'Sure you wouldn't like a margarita? Maybe a strawberry daiquiri?'

'No, a cocktail is complex to prepare. A tequila is fine.' I suspected that they would not have fresh juice available. Better a neat tequila than a margarita made with lemon syrup or sweet-and-sour mix.

'You're from Melbourne, Australia, right?'

'Correct.'

'And now you're a professor at Columbia?'

'An associate professor.'

'You got someone we can call to verify that?'

'Of course. You can contact the Dean of Medicine.'

'So you're a pretty smart guy, right?' It was an awkward question to answer without appearing arrogant. I just nodded.

'Okay, Professor, answer me this. With all your intelligence, when I offered you a margarita, did you really think I was going to go to the tearoom and squeeze a few limes?'

'Lemons are fine. But I only asked for a tequila. Squeezing citrus fruit for cocktails seems an inappropriate use of time for a law-enforcement professional.'

He leaned back. 'You're not kidding, are you?'

I was under extreme pressure, but conscious that I must have made an error. I did my best to clarify.

'I've been arrested and am at risk of incarceration. I was unaware of the law. I am not intentionally making a joke.' I thought for a moment, then added, only because it might reduce the chances of jail and consequent low-quality food, dull conversation and unwanted sexual advances, 'I'm somewhat socially incompetent.'

'I sorta figured that out. Did you really say "Good luck fighting crime" to Officer Cooke?'

I nodded.

He laughed. 'I've got a nephew a lot like you.'

'He's a professor of genetics?'

'No, but if you want to know about World War II Spitfires, he's your boy. Knows everything about planes, nothing about how to stay out of trouble. You must've done all right at school. To make professor.'

'I got excellent marks. I didn't enjoy the social aspects.'

'Problems with authority?'

My instinctive answer was 'no': I am observant of rules and have no desire to cause trouble. But unbidden memories of the religious education teacher, the head-master and the Dean of Science in Melbourne entered my mind, followed by Wineman, the superintendent at the Brooklyn apartment and the two cops.

'Correct. Due to honesty – lack of tact – rather than malice.'

'Ever been arrested before?'

'This is the first time.'

'And you were in the playground to' – he checked his document – 'observe children's behaviour in preparation for fatherhood.'

'Correct. My wife is pregnant. I need to acquire familiarity with children.'

'Jesus.' He looked at the paper again, but his eyes did

not indicate that he was reading. 'All right. I don't think you're a danger to kids, but I can't just let you walk away. If next week you go and shoot up a school, and I've done nothing –'

'It seems statistically unlikely –'

'Don't say anything. You'll talk yourself into trouble.' It seemed like good advice. 'I'm going to send you to Bellevue. This guy will see you and, if he thinks you're safe, you're off the hook. We're all off the hook.'

He gave me back my phone and waved the handcuffs. 'Brendan's a good guy. Just make sure you show up. Or we do it the hard way.'

IO

It was 6.32 p.m. when I left the police station. I immediately phoned Bellevue to make an appointment. The receptionist asked me to call back the next day unless it was an emergency. Approximately four minutes into my description of the situation, she made an apparently irreversible decision that it was not.

On the subway, I debated whether I needed to inform Rosie of the Playground Incident. It was embarrassing, and suggested a lack of familiarity with rules. Knowing the rules is one of my strengths. Rosie would be upset that something unpleasant had happened to me and angry with the police – in short, *stressed*. My earlier decision to insulate Rosie until the matter was resolved remained valid. I had avoided the worst-case scenario at the police station. The assessment at Bellevue was the only remaining obstacle.

I told myself that there was *no reason* for anxiety about meeting with the psychologist. In my early twenties I was interviewed by numerous psychologists and psychiatrists. My circle of friends included Claudia, a clinical psychologist; Gene, head of a psychology department; Isaac Esler, a psychiatrist; as well as Rosie, a psychology graduate and PhD candidate. I was experienced and comfortable in the company of these professionals. Nor was there any reason for the psychologist to consider me dangerous. There was thus *no reason* for anxiety about the assessment. In the absence of a reason, it was irrational to be anxious.

Rosie was already home, working in her new study, when I arrived. I had missed my stop, and then walked in the wrong direction. I blamed the change of location. I began dinner preparation. It would provide a less-dangerous topic of conversation than the day's activities.

'Where have you been?' Rosie called out. 'I thought we were having lunch together.'

'Tofu. Nutritious and easy to digest and a great source of iron and calcium.'

'Hello?' She emerged from the study, and came up behind me as I focused on the food. 'Do I get a kiss?'

'Of course.'

Unfortunately the kiss, despite my best efforts to make it interesting, was insufficient to distract Rosie from her inquisition.

'So, what have you been doing? What happened to lunch?'

'I hadn't realised lunch was confirmed. I took the day off. I went for a walk. I was feeling unwell.' All true statements.

'No wonder. You were up all night drinking with Gene.'

'And purchasing smoked mackerel.'

'Oh shit. I'd forgotten. I'm sorry. I had some eggs and vinegar and went to sleep.'

She pointed to the tofu, which I was in the process of preparing.

'I thought you were going out with Dave.'

'This is for you.'

'Hey, that's nice of you, but I'll get a pizza.'

'This is healthier. Rich in betacarotene, essential for a healthy immune system.'

'Maybe, but I feel like pizza.'

Should I rely on the instincts that indicated pizza or the website that specified tofu? As a geneticist I trusted instincts, but as a scientist I had some confidence in research. As a husband, I knew that it was easier not to argue. I put the tofu back in the refrigerator.

'Oh, and take Gene with you.'

Boys' night out was defined as being Dave, me and sometimes Dave's former workmates. However, it was also defined as Rosie 'having time to herself'. The only way of maintaining both components of the definition was to require Gene to eat alone, which would have broken another rule of ethical behaviour. Change seemed unstoppable.

As Gene and I exited the elevator and stepped into the street, George was leaving a limousine carrying a bag. I intercepted him.

'Greetings. I thought you were returning to England.' An online search had revealed the name of George's cruise ship, which had departed a few hours earlier.

'Bit quiet for you, eh? No, we've got a few months off, courtesy Herman's Hermits. Agent's looking for gigs in New York. How's the beer?'

'The temperature is correct and stable. There's a minor leak that produces occasional odours, but we've become accustomed to them. Are you planning to practise tonight?'

'Funny you should ask. Can't say I feel like it, but Jimmy – the bass player – said he might fetch up. Three days in New York City and he's run out of things to do so why not get together and drink beer and play some music.'

'Do you want to watch baseball instead?' The idea popped into my head as a solution to the noise problem that George might create for Rosie. It may have been the first occasion in my life that I had spontaneously asked someone other than a close friend to join me for social purposes.

'You going out, then?' he said.

'Correct. To eat food, drink alcohol and watch baseball. We also talk.'

I had selected Dorian Gray, a bar in the East Village, as our regular meeting place. It offered the best combination of television screens, noise level (critical), food quality, beer, price and travel time for Dave and me. I introduced George as my vertical neighbour, and explained that Gene was living with me. George did not appear concerned about having an extra non-paying tenant.

Dave is adaptable to changes in plans and was happy to have George and Gene join us. We ordered burgers with all available extras. Dave's diet is suspended on boys' nights out. Gene ordered a bottle of wine, which was more expensive than the beer that we usually drank. I knew this would worry Dave.

'So,' said Gene, 'what happened to you today? I had to show your new assistant the ropes.'

'You make it sound like it wasn't too much of a burden,' said George. 'This'd be a young lady, would it?'

'That'd be exactly what it were,' said Gene, possibly mimicking George's accent. 'Name's Inge. Very charming.'

In keeping with the primary purpose of the boys' night out, which was to provide mutual assistance with personal problems, I was wondering whether I should seek advice on the Playground Incident. I wanted a second opinion on my decision to withhold information from Rosie, but it seemed unwise to tell George, who was effectively my landlord, that I had been arrested.

'I have a minor problem,' I said. 'I committed a social error which may have consequences.' I did not add that the error was a direct result of following Gene's advice to observe children.

'Well, that's all clear enough,' said Gene. 'You want to tell us a bit more?'

'No. I just want to know whether I should tell Rosie. And if so, how.'

'Absolutely,' said Gene. 'Marriage needs to be based on trust and openness. No secrets.' Then he laughed, presumably to indicate that he was making a joke. This was consistent with his behaviour as a liar and cheat.

I turned to Dave. 'What do you think?'

Dave looked at his empty plate. 'Who am I to talk? We're going broke and I haven't told Sonia.'

'Your refrigeration business is in trouble?' said George.

'The refrigeration part is okay,' said Dave. 'It's the business part.'

'Paperwork,' said George. 'I'd tell you to get someone to do it, but one day you wake up and find you've been working for them instead of the other way around.'

I found it hard to see how such information would become available at the point of waking, but agreed with George's broad thesis: administration was a major inconvenience to me also. Conversely, Gene was an expert at using it to his own advantage.

The conversation had lost focus. I brought it back to the critical question: should I tell Rosie?

'Seriously, does she need to know?' said Gene. 'Is it going to affect her?'

'Not yet,' I said. 'It depends on the consequences.'

'Then wait. People spend their lives worrying about things that never happen.'

Dave nodded. 'I guess she doesn't need any more stress.' That word again.

'Agreed,' said Gene. He turned to George. 'What do you think?'

'I think this wine is surprisingly palatable,' said George. 'Chianti, is it?' He waved to our server. 'Another bottle of your finest Chianti, squire.'

'We've only got one kind of Chianti. The one you were drinking.'

'Then bring us your finest red wine.'

Dave's expression indicated horror. I was less worried. Dorian Gray's finest red wine was unlikely to be expensive.

George waited for the wine to arrive. 'How long have you been married?' he said.

'Ten months and fifteen days.'

'And already you're doing things you can't tell her about?'

'It seems so.'

'No kids, I presume.'

'Interesting question.' It depended on the definition of 'kid'. If George was a religious fundamentalist, he might consider that a kid had been created at some time between an hour and five days after the removal of my shirt on the life-changing Saturday, depending on the speed of travel of the successful sperm.

While I was thinking, Gene answered the question. 'Don and Rosie are expecting their first child . . . when, Don?'

The mean human gestation period is forty weeks; thirty-eight weeks from conception. If Rosie's reporting was correct, and conception had occurred on the same day, the baby was due to be born on 21 February.

'Well,' said George, 'that answers your question about whether to put her in the picture. You don't want to say anything that's going to upset her.'

'Good principle,' said Gene.

Even without the scientific evidence linking stress to Bud's future mental health, my companions had reached essentially the same conclusion as I had. The news needed to be withheld until the problem was resolved. Which needed to happen as quickly as possible if I was to avoid becoming a victim of cortisol poisoning myself.

Gene tasted the wine on behalf of the group and continued. 'It's natural for people to deceive their partners. You don't want to go against nature.'

George laughed. 'I'd like to hear you argue that one.'

Gene proceeded to give his standard lecture on women seeking the best genes, even from outside their primary relationship, and men seeking to impregnate as many women as possible without being caught. It was fortunate that he had given the talk many times, as I detected significant intoxication. George laughed a lot.

Dave did not laugh at all. 'Sounds like baloney. I've never seriously thought of cheating on Sonia.'

'How can I put this?' said Gene. 'There's a hierarchy. The further up the pecking order you go, the more women are available to you. A colleague of ours is head of the Medical Research Institute in Melbourne and he just got caught with his pants down – almost literally. Couldn't have happened to a nicer guy.' Gene was referring to my co-researcher in Melbourne, Simon Lefebvre, and it was good to know that he now regarded him as a 'nice guy'. In the past there had been some unhealthy competitiveness.

Gene poured the last of the wine. 'So, no offence, but Don is an associate professor and I'm a department head. I'm at about the same level as Lefebvre, but up the ladder from Don. I probably don't get as many opportunities as Lefebvre, whose dedication to the task is an example to all of us, but I get more than Don.'

'And I'm a refrigeration engineer, which is lower than both of you,' said Dave.

'In terms of the social hierarchy, that's probably true. It doesn't make you any less worthwhile as a person. If I need my fridge fixed, I'm not going to call Lefebvre, but on average someone in your profession is going to get fewer opportunities for sex with women who are unconsciously – or consciously for that matter – focused on status. You're probably a better man than I am in lots of ways, but in this group I'm the alpha male.'

Gene turned to George. 'Sorry, *squire*, I'm being presumptuous. I'm assuming you're not the vice chancellor of Cambridge or an international soccer player.'

'Too dumb for the first,' he said. 'Would've liked to be the second. Got a try-out with Norwich, not good enough.' The waiter brought the bill and George grabbed it, put a pile of notes on it, and stood up.

George, Gene and I took a taxi back to the apartment building. When the elevator doors had closed in front of George, Gene said, 'A free meal. Shows what a guy will do to challenge the alpha male. Do you know what he does for a living?'

'Rock star,' I said.

*

Rosie was in her sleeping costume, but still awake, when I entered the bedroom.

'How was your night?' she asked, and I had a moment of panic before realising that no deception was required.

'Excellent. We drank wine and ate hamburgers.'

'And talked about baseball and women.'

'Incorrect. We never talk about women in general – only you and Sonia. Tonight we talked about genetics.'

'I'm glad I stayed home. I'm guessing talking genetics meant Gene giving Dave the "men are programmed to deceive" lecture. Am I right?'

'Correct. I consider it unlikely that Dave will modify his behaviour as a result.'

'I hope nobody modifies their behaviour because of anything Gene says to them,' she said and looked at me strangely. 'Is there something you're not telling me?'

'Of course. There are vast numbers of things I don't tell you. You'd have information overload.' This was an excellent argument, but it was time to introduce a change of topic, shifting the focus to Rosie. I had prepared a suitable question during the taxi ride home.

'How was your pizza?'

'I ended up cooking the tofu. It wasn't that bad.'

A few minutes after I joined Rosie in bed, George began drumming. Rosie proposed that I go upstairs to ask him to stop.

'I'll go up myself, if you won't,' she said.

I was faced with three choices: a confrontation with

my landlord, a confrontation with my wife or a confrontation between my landlord and my wife.

Judging from his appearance when he opened the door, George must have been playing in his pyjamas. I have a theory that everyone is as odd as I am when they are alone. I was also in pyjamas, of course.

'Making too much noise for you and the missus? And Don Juan?'

'Just the missus.' I was trying to reduce the magnitude of my complaint by sixty-seven per cent. My voice sounded uncannily like my grandfather's.

George smiled. 'Best night out in living memory. Used me brain, didn't talk about football.'

'You were fortunate. Normally we talk about baseball.'

'Bloody interesting, that stuff about genetics.'

'Gene is not always technically accurate.'

'I'll bet he's not.' He laughed. 'Don't know what the connection is, but this is the first time I've felt like practising for donkey's years. Reckon your mate's brought out the alpha male in me.'

'You're drumming to annoy Gene?'

'People pay money for this. You're getting it for free.'

I could not think of a good counter-argument, but George smiled again.

'I'll play a chaser for him and call it a night.'

Deceiving Rosie the next morning was not straight-forward.

'What's going on, Don?'

'I'm feeling a bit unwell again.'

'You too?'

'I might go to the doctor.'

'I've got a better idea. Why don't you join me on the orange juice wagon? You smelled like a brewery when you came in last night.'

'It was probably the beer leaking again.'

'Don, I think we need to talk. I'm not sure you're coping.'

'Everything is fine. I'll be back at work this afternoon. Everything will be back on schedule.'

'Okay. But I'm just a little bit stressed too. My thesis is a mess.'

'You need to avoid stress. You still have eight weeks. I recommend talking to Gene. You're supposed to talk to your supervisor about your thesis.'

'Right now I need to get the stats sorted, which is not exactly Gene's thing. It was bad enough having to report to him once a month without him living in the house and knowing I'm in trouble. And getting my husband drunk.'

'I'm an expert in statistics. What are you using?'

'You want to help me cheat in front of my supervisor? Anyway, I need to do this myself. I'm just having trouble concentrating. I get something in my head and suddenly my brain's somewhere else and I have to start again.'

'You're sure you're not getting early-onset Alzheimer's or some other form of dementia?'

'I'm *pregnant*. And I've got a lot of stuff going on. I walked past the counsellor today and she said, just casually, "I heard the news; any time you want to have a chat." Shit, I can barely keep my head straight with what I'm doing and she's talking about something that's months away.'

'Presumably the counsellor is an expert –'

'Don't. Just leave it for the moment. What did Gene say about moving out? You spoke to him last night, right?'

'Of course. I'll speak to him again today.' Both statements were technically correct. Elaborating would have added to Rosie's stress.

My second attempt to book an assessment at Bellevue was a *disaster*. Brendan, the person the senior police officer had referred me to, was on stress leave, joining Rosie and me and presumably much of New York in needing to lower his cortisol to safe levels. There were no other appointments available for eight days. I decided it would be more useful to appear in person, in the expectation that there would be cancellations or no-shows.

The clinic was at approximately the same latitude as our apartment, but on 1st Avenue on the East Side of Manhattan. I used the cross-town bicycle ride to plan my approach and had my speech ready when I arrived at the psychiatric-assessment unit. The sign above the receptionist's barred window said *Check-in.*

'Greetings. My name is Don Tillman and I am a suspected paedophile. I wish to put myself on standby for an assessment.'

She looked up from her paperwork for only a few seconds.

'We don't have a waiting list. You need to make an appointment.'

I had prepared for this tactic.

'Can I speak to your manager?'

'I'm sorry, she's not available.'

'When will she be available?'

'I'm sorry, Mr –' She waited as if expecting me to say something, then continued. 'You really have to make an appointment. Those are the rules. And you need to take your bike outside.'

I restated my case for immediate assessment, this time in detail. It took some time, and she made multiple attempts to interrupt. She finally succeeded. 'Sir, there are people waiting.'

She was right. I had a growing audience who seemed impressed by my arguments. I addressed my summary to them.

'Statistically, at some time this morning, there will be a psychologist, supported by taxpayers, drinking coffee and surfing the internet due to failure of a client to keep his or her appointment, while a potential psychopathic paedophile is free to roam the streets of New York City, unassessed –'

'You're a paedophile?' A woman of about thirty, wearing a tracksuit, BMI approximately forty, was asking the question.

'An *accused* paedophile. I was arrested in a children's playground.'

She spoke to the receptionist. 'Someone oughta see this guy.' It was clear that she had the support of the other people in the waiting area.

The receptionist scanned a list and picked up the phone. Approximately a minute later she said, 'Ms Aranda will see you in an hour if you're prepared to wait.' She gave me a form to complete. A victory for rationality.

'I gather you were anxious to talk to someone,' said Ms Aranda (estimated age forty-five, BMI twenty-two), who introduced herself as Rani. She listened for the forty-one minutes required to explain the events of the previous day. I observed a progressive improvement in her facial expression from frown to smile.

'This is not the first time you have gotten yourself into a sticky situation?' she said when I had finished.

'Correct.'

'But there has been no problem with children before?'

'Only when I was at school. When children were my contemporaries.'

She laughed. 'You have survived so far. If you had not been a bit awkward with the police they would have probably just told you the rules and sent you off. It's not against the law to be awkward.'

'Fortunately. Or I would have already been sentenced to the electric chair.' It was only a small joke, but Rani laughed again.

'I'll write something for the police, and you will be free to get back to your research about children. I suggest visiting your relatives, which is a good thing to do in any case. Wish your wife good luck with the birth.'

A huge burden was lifted from my shoulders. I had solved the problem without stressing Rosie. Tonight I would tell her the story and she would say, 'Don, I said when I agreed to marry you that I was expecting constant craziness. You're incredible.'

Then I realised that someone was looking at us through the glass. It was not until she signalled to Rani, who left the interview room to join her, that I recognised her. It had been fifty-three days since our encounter but the tall stature, low BMI and associated deficit of fat deposits on her face were unmistakable. Lydia from the Bluefin Tuna Incident.

Rani talked to Lydia for a few minutes, then walked away. Lydia joined me in the office.

'Greetings, Lydia.'

'My name is Mercer. Lydia Mercer. I'm the senior social worker and I'm taking responsibility for your case.'

'I thought everything was resolved. I assumed you had recognised me –'

She interrupted. 'Mr Tillman, I'm prepared to believe we may have crossed paths in the past, but I think it would be helpful if you put it out of your mind. You've been arrested for a crime, and a . . . conservative . . . assessment from us could put the police in a position of having to follow through. Am I being clear enough for you?'

I nodded.

'Your wife's pregnant?'

'Correct.'

Don't ever have children, she had said. I had violated her instruction, though not through any deliberate action of my own. I added, in my defence, 'It wasn't planned.'

'And you think you're equipped to be a father?'

I recalled Gene's advice. 'I'm expecting that instinct will ensure essentially correct behaviour.'

'As it did when you assaulted the police officer. How's your wife coping?'

'Coping? There's no baby yet.'

'She works?'

'She's a medical student.'

'You don't think she might require some additional support at this time?'

'Additional to what? Rosie is self-sufficient.' This was one of Rosie's defining characteristics. She would have been insulted if I suggested she required support.

'Have you talked about child care?'

'Minimally. Rosie is currently focused on her PhD thesis.'

'I thought you said she was a medical student.'

'She's completing a PhD concurrently.'

'As you do.'

'No, it's extremely uncommon,' I said.

'Who does the housework, the cooking?'

I could have answered that housework was shared and that the cooking was my responsibility, but it would have undermined my statement about Rosie's self-sufficiency. I found a neat way around it. 'It varies. Last night she cooked her own meal and I purchased a hamburger independently at a sports bar.'

'With your buddies – your *mates* – no doubt.'

'Correct. No need to translate. I am familiar with American vernacular.'

She looked again at the file.

'Does she have any family here?'

'No. Her mother is dead, she's *passed*, hence being here is not possible. Her father is unable to be here as he owns a gym – *a fitness centre* – which requires his presence.'

Lydia made a note. 'How old was she when her mother died?'

'Ten.'

'How old is she now?'

'Thirty-one.'

'Professor Tillman. I don't know if this makes any sense to your mind, but what we have is a first-time mother, an independent professional high achiever, an *over-achiever*, loss of mother before the age of eleven, no role model, no supports, and a husband who hasn't a clue about any of this. As a professor, as an intellectual, can you see the point I'm making?'

'No.'

'Your wife is a sitting duck for postnatal depression. For not coping. For ending up in hospital. Or worse. You're not doing anything to prevent it and won't see it if it happens.'

Much as I disliked what Lydia was saying, I had to respect her professional expertise.

'You're not the only unsupportive partner out there, not by a long way. But you're one I can do something about.' She waved the file. 'You're going to do some work. You assaulted a police officer. I don't know how that lack of control translates into a domestic situation, but I'm referring you to a group. Attendance is compulsory until the convenor says you're safe. And I want to see you in a month for an assessment. With your wife.'

'What if I fail?'

'I'm a social worker. You've been referred to me because of inappropriate and illegal behaviour around children. At the end of the day, people will listen to me. Police: I only have to write a report to put this back in their hands. Immigration: I'm guessing you're not a citizen. And there are protocols for fathers we consider dangerous.'

'What should I do to improve my suitability?'

'Start paying attention to your wife – and how she's coping with becoming a mother.'

Lydia was not scheduled to work on 27 July, and I wondered briefly if that would solve the problem of bringing Rosie in for assessment in 'a month's time'. The receptionist was adamant that it was not a valid reason for non-attendance, and made an appointment for 1 August, five weeks away. I had previously been stressed by the idea of waiting eight days for an appointment; now I would have thirty-five days of higher-level anxiety with no option but to involve Rosie.

There was a more critical issue. Lydia had raised the problem of Rosie's mental state. I was fortuitously equipped to take immediate action. When my sister died three years earlier, I had been concerned that I might have become clinically depressed as a result. With some reluctance, Claudia had administered the only depression questionnaire she had at home: the Edinburgh Postnatal Depression Scale.

I had continued to use the EPDS to assess my emotional state, putting consistency ahead of the fact that I was not a new mother. Now it was the perfect instrument: despite the name, the accompanying guide specified that it was designed for use antenatally as well as postnatally. If the instrument indicated that Rosie was not at risk, I could present the results at the next appointment and Lydia would have to withdraw her intuitive diagnosis in the face of scientific evidence. Perhaps, with the data in hand, I would not even need to bring Rosie.

I knew Rosie well enough to predict that she would be unwilling to complete the questionnaire, and even if she did she might falsify the answers to reassure me of her happiness level. I would need to slip the questions unobtrusively into conversation. The EPDS has only ten short questions with four possible answers each, so it was trivial to memorise.

In the meantime, I needed to spend some time at Columbia after a day and a half absent. I planned to see Gene to raise the issue of moving out, then meet with my new research assistant.

My sequencing of the tasks turned out to be irrelevant. Inge was in Gene's office, where he was explaining his research on human sexual attraction. Gene's methods and findings are not intrinsically humorous, but he is experienced in supporting them with anecdotes and comedic observations, and Inge was laughing. I estimated both her age and BMI as twenty-three. Gene considers that no woman under the age of thirty is unattractive and Inge provided support for this proposition.

I took Inge to the lab, without Gene, and introduced her to the alcoholic mice – collectively rather than individually. It is unwise to form attachments to individual mice. Given her attractiveness and nationality, I thought it important to offer a subtle warning. The mice provided an opportunity.

'Basically, they get drunk, have sex and die. Gene's life is similar except for his duties as a professor. He may also have some incurable sexually transmissible disease.'

'Excuse me?'

'Gene is extremely dangerous and should be avoided socially.'

'He didn't seem dangerous to me. He seemed very nice.' Inge was smiling.

'That's why he's dangerous. If he seemed dangerous, he would be less dangerous.'

'I think he's lonely here in New York. He told me he's just arrived. We are in similar situations. There is no rule against me having a drink with him this evening, is there?'

Rosie arrived home before Gene, which gave me the opportunity to screen her for depression. She kissed me on the cheek then took her bag into her study. I followed.

'How was your week?' I asked.

'My *week*? It's only Thursday. My *day* has been okay. Stefan emailed me a tutorial about multiple-regression analysis. Made heaps more sense than the textbook.'

Stefan had been one of Rosie's fellow PhD students in Melbourne. He had a careless attitude to shaving and had accompanied her to the faculty ball before Rosie and I became a couple. I found him irritating. But the immediate problem was to situate our discussion in the timeframe specified by the EPDS.

'A single day is a poor indication of your overall happiness. Days vary. A week is a more useful indicator. It's conventional to say "How was your day?" but more useful to say "How was your week?" We should adopt a new convention.'

Rosie smiled. 'You could ask me how my day was every day, and then average it out.'

'Excellent idea. But I need a starting point. So, just for today, how have things been since this time last Thursday? Have things been getting on top of you?'

'Since you ask — a bit. I'm feeling like crap in the morning. I'm behind with the thesis; there's Gene; I've got the counsellor on my case — I think she's being wound up by David Borenstein; I've got to organise an OBGYN; and the other night I felt that you were sort of putting pressure on me to think about stuff that's months away. It's pretty overwhelming.'

I ignored the elaboration that followed the basic quantification: *a bit*. Not very much.

'Would you say you're not coping as well as usual?'

'I'm okay.'

Zero points.

'Are the problems causing you to lose sleep?'

'Did I wake you up again? You know I'm a lousy sleeper.'

From *lousy sleeper* to *lousy sleeper* was no change.

It seemed a good point to throw in a random question, unrelated to the EPDS, to disguise my intent.

'Are you confident of my ability to perform as a father?'

'Of course, Don. Are you?'

Improvisation was getting me into trouble. I ignored Rosie's question and moved on.

'Have you been crying?'

'I didn't think you'd noticed. Just last night when it all got on top of me and you were out with Dave. It's got nothing to do with you not being a good father.'

One occasion only.

'You're sad and miserable?'

'No, I'm coping okay. Just under pressure.'

No. Zero.

'Anxious and worried for no good reason?'

'Maybe a little. I think I get it out of perspective sometimes.' Oddly, given that this was the first answer that indicated some depressive risk, she smiled. The simplest means of quantifying *maybe* and *sometimes* was to reduce the score for the question by fifty per cent. One point.

'Scared and a bit panicky?'

'Like I said, a little. I'm really pretty okay.'

One point.

'Possibly you're blaming yourself unnecessarily for things.'

'Wow. You're being remarkably perceptive tonight.'

I decoded her response. She was saying I had got it right – hence yes. Full points.

She stood up and hugged me.

'Thank you. You're being really sweet. When we were talking about me taking time off, I thought we weren't connecting . . .'

She started crying! A second occasion. But it was a few minutes outside the one-week survey period.

'Are you looking forward to dinner?' I asked.

She laughed, an extraordinarily rapid mood swing. 'As long as it's not tofu again.'

'And to the future in general?'

'More than I was a few minutes ago.' Another hug, but there was an implication that Rosie had been looking forward to things *rather less than she used to* over the week, taken as a whole.

The last question was tricky, but I had laid a foundation for enquiry.

'Have you thought about harming yourself?' I asked.

'What?' She laughed. 'I'm not going to top myself over multiple regression and some jerk in admin being stuck in the 1950s. Don, you're hilarious. Go and make dinner.'

I counted this as *able to laugh and see the funny side of things*, but, considering the full week, there had been some diminution.

Nine points. A score of ten or greater indicated a risk of depression. Lydia was probably right to have been concerned, but the application of science had provided a definitive answer.

As I walked to the kitchen, Rosie called out, 'Hey, Don. Thanks. I'm feeling a lot better. You surprise me sometimes.'

The following evening, Gene arrived home at 7.38 p.m.

'You're late,' I said.

He checked his watch. 'Eight minutes.'

'Correct.' There would be no impact on the quality of dinner, but my own schedule had now been thrown out. It was frustrating to be the only person in the house affected: Rosie and Gene would barely notice the shift. Having Gene as part of our family significantly increased the chances of such disruption.

Rosie was still in her study. It was a good time to confront Gene.

'Were you drinking with Inge?'

'I was. She's quite charming.'

'You're planning to seduce her?'

'Now, now, Don. We're just two adults free to enjoy each other's company.'

This was technically true, but there were two reasons I needed to prevent Gene from adding another nationality to his list.

The first was the directive from David Borenstein, which I had been blackmailed into accepting in order to secure Gene's sabbatical. The Dean's requirement was that Gene keep his hands off PhD students, but I suspected he would extend it to a twenty-three-year-old researcher, though there is no law against professors having sex with junior researchers or even students, assuming the person is of legal age and the professor is not involved in their assessment.

The second reason was that, if Gene demonstrated celibacy, Claudia might forgive him, and his unfulfilled desire for sex might drive him back to her. I had expected that Gene would be unhappy at the breakup of his marriage and that Rosie and I would be required to console him. To date, I had seen no evidence of unhappiness on Gene's part. I was faced with another human problem that would not be resolved without action by me.

Over the following week, I attempted to leave the Lydia situation for my subconscious to work on. Creative thinking benefits from an incubation period. On the Saturday evening, after my regular VoIP call to my mother, I initiated another interaction.

Greetings, Claudia.

I typed the message rather than attempting to establish a voice link. It was possible she was with a patient. I

131

was operating at maximum personal empathy level, facilitated by isolation in my bathroom-office, a recent jog and a pink grapefruit margarita that I was still consuming. My schedule was up to date, and the previous night I had drawn the outline of Bud on the tile for Week 7.

Hi, Don. How are you? Claudia typed back.

I had changed my view on social formulas. I now realised that they were actually an advantage for people who found human interaction difficult.

Very well, thank you. How are you?

Fine. Eugenie's keeping me on my toes, but otherwise good.

We should use audio – more efficient.

This is fine, Claudia typed.

Talking is superior. I can speak faster than I can type.

Let's stay with text.

How is the weather in Melbourne?

I'm in Sydney. With a friend. A new friend.

You already have vast numbers of friends. Surely you don't need any more.

This one is special.

Formalities had taken us off track. It was time to get to the point.

You and Gene should get back together.

I appreciate your concern, Don, but it's a bit late.

Incorrect. You've only been apart a short time. You have a vast investment in the relationship. Eugenie and Carl. Gene's infidelity is irrational; trivial to correct compared with the cost of divorce, marital disruption, potentially finding new partners.

I continued in this vein. One of the advantages of

text is that the other person cannot interrupt, and my argument quickly filled several windows. In the meantime a message arrived from Claudia, thanks to the asynchronous capabilities of Skype.

Thanks, Don. I really do appreciate your concern. But I have to go. How are you and Rosie?

Fine. Do you want to talk to Gene? I think you should.

Don, I don't want to be harsh, but I'm a clinical psychologist and you're not an expert on interpersonal relations. Maybe leave this one to me.

Not harsh. I have a successful marriage and yours has failed. Hence my approach is prima facie more effective.

It was approximately twenty seconds before Claudia's response came through – the connection was obviously slow.

Maybe. I appreciate you trying. But I have to go. And don't take your successful marriage for granted.

Claudia's icon turned orange before I could text a standard goodbye message.

I was not taking my marriage for granted. After a further week of incubating the Lydia Problem, I decided that I could present it to Rosie as an opportunity to receive advice on our parenting. I attempted to introduce the idea over dinner, which of course included Gene, but as I was unable to disclose information about the Playground Incident, my intentions were misinterpreted. Rosie thought my mention of parenting responsibilities was a reference to her taking leave from the medical program.

133

'If I was a male student having a baby, we wouldn't even be having this discussion.'

'The situation is biologically different,' I said. 'For the male, the birth process has minimal impact; he could be working or watching baseball concurrently.'

'He better not be. Technically, I only need a few days off. *You* take a week off if you have a sniffle.'

'To prevent the spread of disease.'

'Yeah, yeah, I know, but it doesn't change the argument. I just need to find out how much time I can take without having to defer the whole year.'

Gene offered a more compelling, if disturbing, analysis. 'Rightly or wrongly, if a male student didn't take time off, the assumption would be that his partner was doing the child care. Are you thinking of Don taking time off?'

'No, of course I'm not expecting Don to stay home with the baby . . .'

I had not envisaged baby care, but I had not envisaged much at all about life after Bud's birth. It seemed that Rosie's assessment of my abilities as a father was consistent with Lydia's.

She must have seen my expression. 'Sorry, Don. I'm just being realistic. I don't think either of us are thinking of you being the main carer. I told you – I'll take the baby with me.'

'It seems unlikely that it would be permitted. Have you spoken to the counsellor?'

'Not yet.'

I had raised Rosie's idea of taking Bud to work with the Dean, and he had stated unambiguously that it would not be possible. But again, he recommended not citing the authoritative source of advice.

Rosie addressed Gene. 'Don can't take time off anyway. We need an income. Which is why I want to finish this program. So I can have a job and not be dependent on someone else.'

'Don's not someone else. He's your partner. That's how marriage works.'

'You would know.' Rosie, having complimented Gene on his knowledge, then inexplicably apologised. 'Sorry, I didn't mean that. I just don't have time to think about it right now.'

It was a good opportunity to raise the Lydia issue.

'Maybe you need some expert advice.'

'Stefan's been helping me,' Rosie said.

'With parenthood information?'

'No, not with parenthood advice. Don, I've got about fifty problems in my life at the moment, and none of them is how to look after a baby that's eight months away.'

'Thirty-two weeks. Which is closer to seven months. We should prepare in advance. Have an assessment of our suitability as parents. An external audit.'

Rosie laughed. 'Bit late now.'

Gene also laughed. 'I think Don is being characteristically methodical. We can't expect him to take on a new project without research, right, Don?'

'Correct. It would probably require only a short interview. I'll schedule a date.'

'I've got no problems with you having a talk to someone,' said Rosie. 'It's great that you're thinking about it. But I can look after myself.'

13

Our three-person household was settling into a regular schedule. After dinner, Rosie went to her office while Gene and I consumed cocktail ingredients.

'What's the deal?' said Gene. 'You've signed up for some sort of assessment?'

'You were able to deduce that from my conversation?'

'Only because of my professional knowledge of the subtleties of human discourse. I'm amazed Rosie didn't grill you harder.'

'I think her mind is occupied with other matters,' I said.

'I think you're right. So?'

I was in a quandary. My EPDS questioning had absolved Rosie of postnatal depression risk, but her answers had revealed the presence of stress. Should I add to it by telling her the full story, or fail to meet Lydia's requirement, which in turn would result in an adverse report to the police, possible arrest and incarceration, and hence even greater stress to Rosie?

Gene seemed to offer my only hope. His social skills and manipulative abilities are more sophisticated than mine will ever be. Perhaps he could propose a solution that did not involve telling Rosie or going to jail.

I told him the story of the Playground Incident, reminding him that the sequence of events was initiated by his suggestion. His overall reaction appeared to be one of amusement. I took no consolation from this: in my experience, amusement is often correlated with embarrassment or pain on the part of the person causing it.

Gene poured himself the last of the blue Curaçao. 'Shit, Don. I'm sorry if I've somehow contributed to this, but I can tell you that just turning up with a completed questionnaire isn't going to work. I can't see any way out that doesn't involve telling Rosie or going to jail.' I could see that he was unhappy with his conclusion: as a scientist he regarded an unsolved problem as a personal insult. He emptied his glass. 'Got anything else?'

While I visited the coolroom, Gene must have continued to work on the problem.

'All right,' he said. 'I think we've got to take this woman – Lydia – at her word. What's the difference between a social worker and a Rottweiler?'

I was unable to see the relevance of the question, but he answered it himself.

'The Rottweiler gives you your baby back.' It was a joke, probably in bad taste, but I understood that we were two buddies who had been drinking and this was the context in which such jokes were told. 'God, Don, what is this stuff?'

'Grenadine. It's non-alcoholic. You require a clear head. And you're getting distracted. Continue.'

'So the essence is this: you have to front the social worker and you have to bring Rosie. You can make an excuse –'

'I could say she was ill due to pregnancy. Highly plausible.'

'You're only buying time. You might provoke her into submitting the report anyway. You don't want to provoke a Rottweiler.'

'I thought your point was that social workers and Rottweilers are different.'

'My point was that they are only *slightly* different.'

Slightly different. The concept prompted an idea.

'I could hire an actress. To impersonate Rosie.'

'Sophia Loren.'

'Isn't she older?'

'Joking. Seriously, the problem would be that she wouldn't know you well enough. I figure that's what the social worker's going to be focused on – can this woman handle Don Tillman? Because you're not –'

I finished his sentence for him '– exactly average. Correct. How long do you think it would take to know me adequately?'

'I'd say six months. Minimum. Sorry, Don, but I think telling Rosie is the lesser of two evils.'

I delegated the problem to my subconscious for a further week: Week 9 of Bud's gestation. The mark on the tile representing his size was now 2.5 centimetres long, and my drawing of his slightly changed shape was more accomplished, due to practice.

The actor idea was attractive, and I found it difficult to abandon. In problem-solving parlance I had become *anchored* – unable to see alternatives. But Gene was right:

there was no time to brief a stranger on my personality to the extent that she could answer probing questions from a professional. In the end, there was only one person who could help me.

I told her the story of the Playground Incident, and the requirement for an assessment. I tried to make it clear that my priority was to avoid causing stress and that the EPDS questionnaire had indicated that Lydia's fears were unfounded. Nevertheless, I needed to emphasise the risk of not cooperating.

'We have to show up and be assessed as parents and take her advice or I'm going to be prosecuted, deported and banned from contact with Bud.' I may have exaggerated slightly, but Gene's image of a Rottweiler was still in my mind. Martial-arts training did not cover attack dogs.

'Bitch. She's got to be way out of line doing this.'

'She's a professional who has detected risk factors. Her requirement seems reasonable.'

'I think you're being kind. Which is so like you. Anyway, I'm happy to do whatever I can to help.'

This was an incredibly generous response. I had been agonising over whether to proceed with my strategy, but the offer was clear.

'I need you to impersonate Rosie.'

I interpreted Sonia's expression as shock. I had not discussed the plan with Gene, but I was aware of his opinion that accountants were skilled at deception. I was relying on it being accurate.

'Oh my God, Don.' She laughed, but I detected

nervousness. 'You're kidding me. I'm just saying that – I know you're not. Oh my *God*. I don't think I could be Rosie.'

'Morally or in terms of competence?'

'Oh, you know me. Totally immoral.' This was not my impression of Sonia, but was consistent with Gene's view of her profession. 'Rosie and I are so different.'

'Correct. But Lydia hasn't met Rosie. She doesn't even know she's Australian. Just that she's a medical student with no friends.'

'No friends? What about Dave and me?'

'She only sees you because of me. Most of her interaction is with her study group. Occasionally she sees Judy Esler. She's primarily interested in intellectual conversation.'

'I'll have to catch up on my reading. You want a coffee?'

We were at Dave and Sonia's apartment. It was a Sunday, but Rosie had gone into university in violation of the 'weekend free time' rule and Dave was also working. Sonia claimed that her Italian heritage required regular espresso coffee, and had a high-quality machine. Coffee was an excellent idea, but not the first priority.

'After we resolve the impersonation question.'

'After I have my coffee.'

When Sonia returned with my double espresso and her pregnancy-compatible decaffeinated cappuccino, she appeared to have prepared a speech.

'All right, Don, it's just one session, no more?'

I nodded.

'And no forms to fill in or anything, nothing to sign?'

'I don't think so.' Nothing was certain, but as Lydia was officially assessing me as a paedophile, it seemed unlikely that she would report anything about Rosie or the parenthood aspect. Sonia was probably right in characterising her behaviour as 'way out of line'.

'All right. I'm going to do this for you, for two reasons. The main one is because you've been so great to Dave. I know he'd be insolvent without the cash he gets from George the Drummer. I know that.'

Dave definitely did not know that Sonia knew that. Dave was extremely concerned to ensure that Sonia was unaware of his business problems. Which was a ridiculous expectation, considering Sonia's profession.

Sonia finished her coffee. 'But I don't want you to tell Dave,' she said.

'Why not?'

'He's got enough on his mind. You know Dave, he's a worrier.'

This was true. The motivation for the deception was to avoid causing stress to Rosie. It would be a terrible outcome if the solution caused stress to Dave, leading to a heart attack or stroke, which he was already susceptible to because of his weight. But secrets were accumulating. I am extremely poor at deception. I promised Sonia that I would do my best, but that my best was likely to be significantly below the average human ability to lie. I was in need of Gene's skills, but his skills were a result of his personality which I was not in need of.

'What's the second reason?' I asked.

142

'To put that bitch back in her box,' said Sonia. She was laughing.

Rosie was putting flowers into our two vases and the wine decanter when I arrived home. She was wearing shorts and a sleeveless t-shirt. Her shape was not visibly different from its normal state of perfect.

'I need a break from study,' she said. 'You were right about things getting out of perspective.'

'Excellent idea,' I said. 'You need to minimise stress.'

'How is Sonia doing?' said Rosie.

'Sonia is doing extremely well. Dave is nervous about becoming a father. As is normal for men.'

Rosie laughed. 'Hey, I've been thinking. About what you said last week about us getting some counselling. I was probably a bit defensive. Maybe it would be a good idea. If you feel you need it.'

'No, no, I was only thinking of you. I'm feeling highly confident. Excited.'

'Okay. Well, I'm okay too. Let me know if you change your mind.'

Eight days earlier, I would have accepted Rosie's offer. But now the Sonia approach seemed a better solution. There would be less stress for Rosie, less risk of the process being derailed by her becoming confrontational and less danger that she might be exposed to a negative assessment of my readiness for fatherhood.

I arranged to meet Sonia at her place of work on the Upper East Side in the hope that I might be able to

143

combine the pre-interview briefing with learning about advances in reproductive technology. But 'place of work' translated into 'nearby coffee shop'.

'I don't work anywhere near the labs. I only met Dave because I thought his company had overcharged us.'

'Had they?'

'No, Dave screwed up the paperwork. But he was so honest about it, I bought him a coffee. Here.'

'Leading to sex after only two dates.'

'Dave told you that?'

'It's incorrect?'

'Completely untrue. We didn't sleep together until we were married.'

'Dave lied?' Incredible. Dave was scrupulously honest.

Sonia laughed. 'No, *I* lied. You couldn't tell?'

I shook my head. 'I'm extremely gullible.' Fooling Lydia, who was probably accustomed to dealing with welfare cheats, alimony avoiders and accountants within her own organisation, would be more difficult.

'You definitely didn't tell her that Rosie was Australian?'

'I said that she didn't have any family here. She – you – can be from any location except New York.'

'All right. Take me through this depression test.'

'She may use some other. I've researched several. The common factor appears to be that risk of depression is detected via the respondent feeling unhappy and anxious.'

'Isn't psychology amazing? I wonder what these people get paid for sometimes.'

'Do you think we'll be able to deceive her?'

'Don't worry, Don. The trick is only to lie about the things you have to lie about. You be you, I'll be me, except for the name. I'm happy. And completely normal.'

I almost failed to recognise Sonia in the enormous foyer of the Bellevue Hospital. I had only ever seen her in her work costume and, on social occasions, in jeans. She was wearing a large patterned skirt and a white frilled shirt, creating an overall impression of a folk dancer. She greeted me effusively.

'*Ciao*, Don. It's a beautiful day, no?'

'You're sounding strange. Like a comedian pretending to be Italian.'

'I *am* Italian. I'm only living here one year. I've got no family here, like you say to the lady. But I'm very happy! Because of the *bambino*!' She rotated on the spot, and the centrifugal force caused her skirt to extend. She laughed.

Sonia's grandparents on her father's side were Italian, but she did not speak Italian. If Lydia brought in an interpreter, we would be in trouble. I recommended Sonia keep the use of the accent subtle. But it was a brilliant idea to create a foreign Rosie without imitating an Australian accent, which would appear inauthentic next to mine.

'I'm sorry to take you away from your studies,' said Lydia after indicating that we should sit down. 'You must be very busy.'

'I'm very busy all the time,' said Sonia. She looked at her watch. I was impressed by the acting.

'How long have you been in the States?'

'Since the start of the medical course. I come here for study.'

'And before that, what were you doing?'

'Working in an IVF facility in Milano. It is from this that I become interested in medicine.'

'How did you and Don meet?'

Disaster! Sonia looked at me. I looked at Sonia. If one of us had to invent a story, it was best that it be Sonia.

'At Columbia. Don is my teacher. Everything is happening *rapido*.'

'When are you due?'

'December.' This was the correct answer for Sonia.

'Did you plan to get pregnant so quickly?'

'When you work in IVF, you learn how precious it is to have a baby. I think I'm so lucky.' Sonia had forgotten the accent. But she sounded highly credible.

'And you're planning to defer your studies when you have the baby?'

This was a tricky question. Sonia – the real Sonia – planned to take a year off work, which was causing Dave stress, due to the impact on income. If Sonia answered as herself rather than as Rosie, I would be forced to act as Dave for consistency and would doubtless fail to be convincing. It was better that Sonia gave the answer that Rosie would give. Except that she did not know it. I answered for her.

'Rosie intends to continue her studies uninterrupted.'

'No break?'

'A minimum of a week. Possibly more.'

Lydia looked at Sonia. 'A week? You're only taking a week off to have a baby?'

Lydia's obvious surprise and disapproval was consistent with David Borenstein's advice. Sonia's surprise was consistent with her not being Rosie and her own plans to take indefinite leave. We were all in agreement – except Rosie who was not in the room. I tried to present her position.

'The birth of a baby is no more disruptive than a minor upper respiratory tract infection.'

'You think having a baby is like having a cold?'

'Without the disease aspect.' Rosie's analogy had been faulty in that respect. 'More equivalent to taking a week's leave to attend the baseball play-offs.' Sonia gave me a strange look; my baseball reference had doubtless been prompted by subconscious thoughts of Dave.

Lydia changed the topic. 'So, with Rosie studying full-time, you're the sole breadwinner.'

Rosie would hate me answering 'yes' to this question. My answer was true until recently. 'Incorrect. She works in a bar in the evenings.'

'I guess she'll be giving that up at some point.'

'Absolutely not. She considers it critical to contribute to the finances.' As Sonia had said, most of the time it was possible to tell the truth.

'And what do you see as your role?'

'In what respect?'

'I'm thinking, with Rosie studying full-time and working part-time, you might need to help with the baby.'

'We've discussed it. Rosie requires zero assistance.'

Lydia turned to Sonia. 'Are you comfortable with all that? Is that what *you* think?'

I had temporarily forgotten that Sonia was a virtual Rosie, and had been speaking of Rosie as a person external to our conversation. I hoped Lydia had not noticed. But the answer was a simple 'Yes'. Lydia would have a consistent story, consistent with mine, consistent with Rosie having exactly what she required for happiness, consistent with *reality*.

'Well –'

'Before you answer,' said Lydia, 'tell me a bit about your family. Was your mother allowed to speak for herself?'

'Not really. My father decided what she said and did.'

'So they were very traditional?'

'If you mean, did my father go to work and come home and never cook and expect dinner on the table while my mom who had diabetes had to manage five kids, yes, we were traditional. Tradition was the excuse.' The Italian accent had gone. Sonia was sounding angry.

'Seems like you might be about to follow in her footsteps.'

'Seems like it, doesn't it? It was all about my father's job. Oh, he had to work so hard. So *hard*. Well, you know what, I didn't marry my father. I'm expecting just a little bit more from Dave.'

'Dave?'

'Don.'

There was a pause. Lydia was probably working backwards from Sonia's error to arrive at the inevitable conclusion that she was an imposter. I needed an explanation for the name error. My mind was racing and the solution was so elegant that it overrode my natural aversion to lying.

'My middle name is David. My father's name is also Donald, so sometimes I'm called Dave. To avoid confusion.' The idea was prompted by my cousin Barry and his father who is also named Barry, leading to my cousin being known within the family by his middle name, which is Victor.

'Well, Don-Dave, what do you think of what Rosie just said?'

'Rosie?' Now I was seriously confused. Sonia, Rosie, Don, Dave, Barry, Victor, which was also my grandfather's name. My father's father. I was about to be a father, too. Of a child with a temporary name.

'Yes, Donald-David, Rosie. Your wife.'

With time I could have untangled it. But with Lydia staring at me, I gave the only practicable answer.

'I need to process the new information.'

'When you've processed it, book another appointment.' Lydia waved the police file. We were dismissed. And the problem was not solved.

Sonia had to return to work, so we debriefed on the subway.

'I have to tell Rosie,' I said.

'What are you going to say to Lydia? "Hello, this is the

149

real Rosie? I'm a con man as well as a paedophile and an insensitive slob?"'

'There was no mention of insensitivity and slobbishness.'

'If you were a bit more sensitive, you might have picked it up.' It was Sonia's stop, but I got off too. The conversation was obviously critical, in two senses of the word.

'Sorry, I'm angry with myself,' said Sonia. 'I messed it up. I don't like to mess up.'

'The accidental use of Dave's name was totally understandable. I had to concentrate hard to avoid calling you Sonia.'

'It's a bigger deal than that. Things aren't going the way I'd hoped with Dave and me. We tried for so long and now he's not interested.'

I knew why. Dave was stressed by work and the possibility of business failure, leading to the prospect of Sonia having to work in violation of her plans, leading to rejection of Dave as a suitable partner, leading to divorce, estrangement from his child and all meaning disappearing from his life. We had reviewed this sequence many times.

Unfortunately, I could not share the state of the business with Sonia, as this might accelerate the process. Now Sonia was identifying another path that might lead to the same conclusion.

Sonia continued. 'I've been reading up on everything, trying to do everything right, and he seems to think the pregnancy has nothing to do with him. Do you know what he did last night?'

'Ate dinner and went to bed?' It seemed the most likely scenario.

'You couldn't have put it better. I'd made a meal right out of the pregnancy book, covering seven of the ten power foods. I had it waiting for him when he came in, and you know what he'd done? He'd bought a hamburger. A double cheeseburger with bacon and guacamole. He's supposed to be on a diet.'

'Did it have tomato and leafy greens?'

'What?'

'I'm counting the pregnancy power foods.'

'He sat and ate it in front of me. And then went to bed. Just so inconsiderate.'

I thought it best not to reply. Dave trying to save his marriage, leading to working harder, leading to stress, leading to hamburger consumption and exhaustion, leading to health and marriage problems. More material to process.

Neither of us spoke as we walked from the subway to the IVF facility. Sonia inexplicably went to hug me, but remembered in time. 'Don't say anything to Dave. We'll get through it.'

'Can I tell him that part? About getting through it? He may also be worried about marriage failure.'

'He said that?'

'Correct.'

'Oh God. It's all so hard.'

'Agreed. Human behaviour is highly confusing. I'll tell Rosie about Lydia tonight.'

'No, you won't. It's my fault, and I don't want to be responsible for upsetting Rosie. Sounds like she's already carrying the weight of the world. We'll get it right next time.'

'I'm not sure what we have to do.'

'Lydia and I are saying the same thing. You need to think more about supporting Rosie. No matter what she's saying about being independent, she needs your help.'

'Why would she lie?'

'She's not lying, not deliberately. She's got this idea of herself as Wonder Woman. Or maybe she thinks you don't want to help. Or can't help.'

'So I need to demonstrate a contribution to the pregnancy process?'

'Support. Taking an interest. Being there. That's all Lydia and I are looking for. And Don?'

'You have a question?'

'How many power foods in the hamburger? There was lettuce and tomato. On both of them.'

'Eight. But –'

'No buts.'

This time she did hug me. I kept still and it was over quite quickly.

14

Lydia was right. Six weeks had passed since Rosie's announcement of the pregnancy. Yet despite setting up the tile schedule to support the Baby Project, I had actually done almost zero to prepare for baby production and maintenance, other than the purchase of ingredients for one pregnancy-compatible meal and the research excursion that led to the Playground Incident.

Gene was wrong. Instincts that worked in the ancestral environment were not sufficient in a world that regulated playground visits and allowed choices between tofu and pizza. He was right, however, in recommending that I address the problem in my own way, working from my strengths. But I needed to begin now, not wait until after the baby was born.

My search for appropriate texts on the practical issues of pregnancy produced a substantial list. I decided to begin with a well-regarded book as a broad guide to the field and then refer to the specific papers that it referenced for more detailed information. The sales assistant at the medical school bookshop recommended the fourth edition of *What to Expect When You're Expecting* by Murkoff and Mazel, with the warning that some readers found it too technical. Perfect. It was reassuringly thick.

A quick examination of *What to Expect* identified

some positive and negative attributes. The coverage of topics was impressive, although much was irrelevant to Rosie and me: we did not own a cat that might cause infection via its faeces; we were not habitual users of cocaine; Rosie did not have any fears about her competence as a mother. The referencing was poor, a fault doubtless caused by it being intended for a non-academic audience. I was constantly looking for the *evidence*.

The first chapter I read was 'Nine Months of Eating Well'. It provided the meta study I was looking for, drawing together the best research on diet in pregnancy and using it as the basis for practical recommendations. At least that appeared to be the intent.

The chapter title was yet another reminder that Rosie and the developing foetus – exposed and vulnerable to toxins crossing the placental wall – had experienced nine weeks of *not* eating well, including three weeks of not drinking well, due to the lack of planning. But alcohol already ingested could not be un-ingested. I needed to focus on the things that I could change and accept the things I could not.

The advocacy for organic and local produce was predictable. This was a subject that I had previously researched for obvious economic and health reasons. Any advice on pregnancy based on the premise that 'natural is better' should be accompanied by statistics on birth outcomes in the 'natural' environment, devoid of nutritional diversity, antibiotics and sterile operating theatres. And, of course, a rigorous definition of 'natural'.

The disparity between my well-researched conclusions about organics and the summary in the book was a useful warning not to accept recommendations without checking primary sources. Meanwhile, I had no choice but to rely on *What to Expect* as the best information available. I skimmed the rest of the book, learning some interesting facts, before devoting the remainder of the afternoon to developing a Standardised Meal System (Pregnancy Version) in line with its recommendations. Rosie's rejection of meat and unsustainable seafood made the job simpler by reducing the number of options. I was confident that the resulting menu would provide an adequate nutritional base.

As so often occurs in science, implementation proved more difficult than planning. Rosie's initially negative reaction to the tofu meal should have been a warning. I had to remind myself that my acquisition of more comprehensive knowledge had not of itself changed Rosie's view. Logical, but non-intuitive. Rosie raised the subject without prompting from me.

'Where did you get the smoked mackerel from?' she asked.

'Irrelevant,' I said. 'It was cold-smoked.'

'So?'

'Cold-smoked fish is banned.'

'Why?'

'It could make you sick.' I was conscious of the vagueness of my answer. I had not had time to research the evidence behind the unreferenced claim, but at this point I had to accept it as the best advice available.

'Lots of things can make you sick. I'm sick every morning at the moment and I feel like some more of that smoked mackerel. It's probably my body sending me a signal that I need smoked mackerel. Cold-smoked mackerel.'

'I recommend a tinned salmon and soybean-based mini-meal. The good news is that you can eat it immediately to satisfy your craving.' I walked to the refrigerator and fetched Part One of Rosie's dinner.

'Mini-meal? What's a mini-meal?'

It was fortunate that I was studying pregnancy. Rosie had clearly done minimal research.

'A partial solution to the nausea problem. You should eat six mini-meals per day. I've organised a second meal for you at 9.00 p.m.'

'What about you? Are you eating at nine o'clock?'

'Of course not. I'm not pregnant.'

'What about my other four meals?'

'Pre-packaged. Breakfast and three daytime meals for tomorrow are already in the refrigerator.'

'Shit. I mean, that's really nice, but . . . I don't want you going to so much trouble. I can just grab something from the café at uni. Some of their stuff is okay.'

This was in direct contradiction to previous complaints about the café.

'You should resist the temptation. In the interests of maternal and Bud health, we need to plan, plan and plan some more.' I was quoting The Book. In this instance, the advice offered by *What to Expect* was in line with my own thinking. 'Also, you need to control your coffee consumption. Café measures are inconsistent – hence I recommend drinking one standardised coffee in the morning at home and drinking only decaffeinated at university.'

'You've been reading up, haven't you?'

'Correct. I recommend *What to Expect When You're Expecting*. It's intended for pregnant women.'

Our conversation was interrupted by the arrival of Gene, who now had his own key. He seemed in a good mood.

'Evening all, what's for dinner?' He waved a bottle of red wine.

'Appetiser is New England oysters, entrée is deli meats, main course is rare New York steaks with a spice crust and alfalfa salad, followed by a selection of raw milk and blue cheeses, then affogato with Strega.' As part of the change to the meal system, I had also designed meals suitable for Gene and myself, taking into account that we were neither pregnant nor sustainable pescatarians.

As Rosie was looking a little confused, I added, 'Rosie will be eating a legume-based curry, minus the spices.'

The Book warned of irrational behaviour due to hormonal changes. Rosie refused to eat her mini-meal and instead consumed a sample of every component of Gene's and my dinner, including a small quantity of steak (in violation of her commitment to sustainable-seafood pescatarianism), and even a sip of wine.

The predictable consequence was illness the next morning. She was sitting on the bed, head in her hands, when I alerted her to the time.

'You go by yourself,' she said. 'I'm going to take the morning off.'

'Feeling unwell is normal in pregnancy. It's almost certainly a good sign. Lack of morning sickness is correlated with a higher risk of miscarriages and abnormalities. Your body is probably assembling some critical component, such as an arm, and is minimising the possibility of toxins disrupting the process.'

'You're talking shit.'

'Flaxman and Sherman, *Quarterly Review of Biology*, Summer 2000. "An evolved mechanism to reduce toxin-induced deformities."'

'Don, I appreciate all this, but it's got to stop. I just want to eat normal food. I want to eat what I feel like. I'm feeling crap and tinned salmon and soybeans is going to make me feel more crap. It's my body and I get to choose what I do with it.'

'Incorrect. Two bodies, one of which has fifty per cent of my genes.'

'So I get one and a half votes and you get half a vote. I win. I get to eat smoked mackerel and raw oysters.'

She must have noticed my expression.

'I'm kidding, Don. But I don't want you telling me what to eat. I can do this myself. I'm not going to get drunk or eat salami.'

'You ate pastrami last night.'

'Hardly any. I was making a point. Anyway, I'm not planning to eat meat again.'

'What about shellfish?' I was testing.

'I'm guessing no go?'

'You guess wrong. Cooked shellfish is acceptable.'

'Seriously, how important is all this stuff? I mean, this is so *you* – getting obsessed with every little thing. Judy Esler says she never worried about what she ate twenty-five years ago. I'm guessing I'm more likely to be run over walking to Columbia than poisoned by oysters.'

'I predict you're incorrect.'

'Predict? You're not sure, are you?'

Rosie knew me too well. The Book was short on hard data. Rosie stood up and retrieved her towel from the floor. 'Make me a list of what I can't eat. No more than ten things. And no big generic categories like "sweet stuff" or "salty stuff". You cook dinner, I'll eat what I like during the day. Except for your list. And no mini-meals.'

I remembered an item of extraordinarily unscientific advice from The Book, encouraging the most serious failing of the medical profession. It was in reference to caffeine: 'Different practitioners have different recommendations, so check in with yours ...' Incredible – placing individual judgement ahead of the consensus from research. But it provided me with an opportunity to ask another question.

'What advice has your medical practitioner provided on diet?'

'I haven't had a chance to make an appointment. I've been frantic with the thesis. I'll do it soon.'

I was stunned. I did not need The Book to tell me that a pregnant woman should schedule regular visits to an obstetrician. Despite my reservations about the competence of some members of the medical profession, there was no doubt that, statistically, involvement of a professional led to better outcomes. My sister had died due to medical misdiagnosis, but she would certainly have died if she had not seen a doctor at all.

'You're overdue for the eight-week ultrasound. I'll ask David Borenstein for a recommendation and make an appointment for you.'

'Leave it. I'll sort it out on Monday. I'm meeting Judy for lunch.'

'David is far more knowledgeable.'

'Judy knows everyone. Please. Just leave it to me.'

'You guarantee you'll make an appointment on Monday?'

'Or Tuesday. It might be Tuesday I'm seeing Judy. She changed but we might have changed back. I can't remember.'

'You're too disorganised to have a baby.'

'And you're too obsessional. Lucky I'm the one who's having it.'

What had happened to *We're pregnant*?

15

'I'll let you guys have a romantic dinner alone,' said Gene when I went to his office after completing my scheduled work the following Tuesday. 'I've got a date.'

I had been expecting him to travel home with me on the subway to provide intellectual stimulation. Now I would have to download a paper to read. More seriously, Inge had left early to prepare for dinner at an upscale restaurant. I detected a pattern.

'You're having dinner with Inge?'

'Very perceptive. She's delightful company.'

'I've scheduled dinner for you at our apartment.'

'I'm sure Rosie won't miss me.'

'Inge is extremely young. Inappropriately young.'

'She's over twenty-one. She can drink and vote and associate with unattached men. You're in danger of being ageist, Don.'

'You should be thinking about Claudia. Fixing the problem of your promiscuity.'

'I'm not promiscuous. I'm only seeing one woman.' Gene smiled. 'Worry about your own problems.'

Gene was right. Rosie was pleased with his absence. When we got married, I had assumed I would have to spend uncomfortable amounts of time in the presence of another person. In fact, much of our time was spent apart, due to work and study, and our time together (excluding periods in bed when at least one of us – usually me – was asleep) was now frequently shared with Gene. Dedicated contact with Rosie had now fallen well below the optimum level.

There was one encouraging item in The Book, which I had chosen not to raise in the presence of Gene.

'Have you noticed an increase in libido?' I asked.

'Have you?'

'An increase in sexual appetite is not uncommon in the first trimester. I was wondering whether you were affected.'

'You're hilarious. I guess if I wasn't throwing up or feeling like shit . . .'

It struck me that our practice of having sex in the mornings rather than the evenings was contributing to the problem.

After dinner, Rosie headed for her study to work on her thesis. On average, she was devoting ninety-five minutes to this pre-bed session, although the variance was high. After eighty minutes, I made her a cup of fruit infusion, which I accompanied with some fresh blueberries.

'How are you feeling?' I asked.

'Not so bad. Except for the stats.'

'There's a lot of ugly things in this world. I wish I could keep them all away from you,' I said. Gregory Peck as Atticus Finch in supportive mode. It was probably my most effective line. Opportunities to impersonate

Gregory Peck had been significantly reduced by Gene's presence.

Rosie stood up. 'Good timing. I think I've had enough of ugly things for tonight.' She put her arms around me and kissed me in passionate mode rather than greetings mode.

We were interrupted by a familiar noise from an unfamiliar location: someone was calling Gene on Skype. I was not sure of the rules for answering another person's VoIP communication, but perhaps it was Claudia with an emergency. Or a proposal for reconciliation.

I entered Gene's bedroom and saw Eugenie's face on the screen. Gene and Claudia's daughter is nine years old. I had not spoken to her since we moved to New York. I clicked on *Answer with video*.

'Dad?' Eugenie's voice was clear and loud.

'Greetings! It's Don.'

Eugenie laughed. 'I can tell from your face. I could have told from you saying *greetings*.'

'Your father is out.'

'What are you doing at his house?'

'It's my apartment. We're sharing. Like students.'

'That's so cool. Were you and my dad friends at school?'

'No.' Gene is sixteen years older than I am and would not have belonged to my social group if we had been contemporaries. Gene would have been dating girls, playing sport and soliciting votes for school captain.

'Hey, Don.'

'Hey, Eugenie.'

'When do you think Dad will come home?'

'His sabbatical is six months. Hence, technically December 24, but the semester ends on December 20.'

'It's a long time.'

'Four months and fourteen days.'

'Hey, move your head, Don.'

I looked at the small image of my face in the corner of the monitor and realised that Rosie had walked into the room behind me. I moved to one side and expanded the image. Rosie was wearing her one item of impractical nightwear. It was her equivalent of a blueberry muffin, although it was black rather than white with blue spots. She did a little dance and Eugenie called out to her.

'Hey Rosie, hi.'

'Can she see me?' said Rosie.

'Yep,' said Eugenie. 'You're wearing a –'

'I believe you,' said Rosie, laughing, and left the room, waving to me from the doorway. Eugenie resumed our conversation but I was now distracted.

'Does Dad want to come home?'

'Of course! He misses everyone.'

'Even Mum? Does he say that?'

'Of course. I should go to bed. It's late here.'

'Mum says he needs to sort some things out. Is he?'

'He's making excellent progress. We have a men's group as recommended in my book on pregnancy, consisting of a refrigeration engineer, your father, a rock star and me. I'll give you a progress report in a few days.'

'You're so funny. You haven't really got a rock star . . . Hey, why are you reading a book on pregnancy?'

'To assist Rosie with production of our baby.'

'You're having a baby? Mum didn't tell me.'

'Probably because she doesn't know.'

'It's a secret?'

'No, but I saw no use in giving her the information. She's not required to take any action.'

'Mum! Mum! Don and Rosie are having a baby!'

Claudia pushed Eugenie out of the way, which seemed rude, and it was now obvious that the conversation would continue. I wanted to talk to Claudia, but not now and not with Eugenie present.

'Don, that's wonderful news. How do you feel?'

'Excited, end of story,' I said, combining Gene's recommended answer with the conversation terminator I had learned from Rosie.

Claudia ignored my signal. 'That's wonderful,' she repeated. 'Where's Rosie?'

'In bed. Possibly not sleeping due to my absence. It's extremely late.'

'Oh, sorry. Well, please pass on my congratulations. When is she due?'

After conducting an interrogation on pregnancy-related topics, Claudia said, 'So Gene's out, is he? He'd promised to talk to Eugenie. Where is he?'

'I don't know.' I clicked the video off.

'I've lost your face, Don.'

'Some technical issue.'

'I see. Or I don't see. Well, doing whatever he's doing isn't going to solve Eugenie's science problem.'

'I'm an expert at science problems.'

'And also a decent person. Are you sure you've got time?'

'When does it need to be completed?'

'She was very anxious to get it done tonight. But if you have other things . . .'

It would take less time to answer a primary-school science question than to negotiate an alternative arrangement with Claudia.

'Proceed.'

Eugenie returned and I restored the video. Eugenie turned it off again.

'What's the science problem?' I asked.

'There's no science problem. I just told Mum that. Like I'd have a science problem. Face-palm.'

'Face-palm?'

'Like *der*. I'm top of the class in science. And maths.'

'Can you do calculus?'

'Not yet.'

'So you're probably not a genius. Excellent.'

'Why excellent? I thought it was good to be smart.'

'I recommend being smart but not a genius. Unless the only thing you care about is numbers. Professional mathematicians are usually socially inept.'

'Maybe that's why everyone is saying mean things about me on Facebook.'

'Everyone?'

She laughed. 'No, just lots of kids.'

'Can you construct some sort of filter?'

'I can block them. I kind of don't want to. I want to see what they say. They're still kind of my friends. I'm sounding stupid, right?'

'No. It's normal to want information. It's normal to want to be liked. Is there any threat of violence?'

'Nah. They just say stupid things.'

'Probably a result of being stupid. Highly intelligent people are often bullied. As a result of being different. That difference being high intelligence.' I was conscious of not sounding highly intelligent.

'Did you get bullied? I bet you did.'

'You would win the bet. Initially violently, until I learned martial arts. Then more subtly. Fortunately I am not a subtle person, so once the violence stopped, things were much better.'

We talked for fifty-eight minutes, including the initial conversation and the Claudia interaction, exchanging information about bullying experiences. I could not see any obvious solution to her problem, but if her distress was at the level I had experienced as a child, I was obliged to offer any knowledge that might assist.

In the end, she said, 'I have to go to horseriding. You're the smartest person I know.' In terms of intelligence quotient, she was probably right. In terms of knowledge of practical psychology, she was wrong.

'I would not rely on my advice.'

'You didn't give me any. I just liked talking to you. Can we do this again?'

'Of course.' I had also enjoyed the conversation.

Except for thinking about the alternative activity in the adjacent room.

I terminated the connection. As I was leaving Gene's room, the computer beeped with a text message: *Good night. I <3 you, Don.*

Rosie was barely awake when I joined her in bed.

'Sounds like you had a nice chat,' she said.

'To begin with, this case should never have come to trial,' I said, Atticus Finch defending the innocent Tom Robinson, scapegoated because of a minor genetic difference.

Rosie smiled. 'Sorry, Mr Peck, I'm stuffed. Good night.'

Although I had described the group of males with whom I had recently watched baseball and eaten hamburgers as a men's group, my suggestion that we formalise it was not well received by George.

'I'm already in one,' he said. 'It's ruined my life.'

'Obviously, you should leave it. Join a more suitable one.'

'Ah, but it made my life, too. I owe it.' I realised he was talking about the Dead Kings.

'You don't want to watch the ballgame with us? And converse on non-baseball topics between innings?'

'That's fine by me. Just no beating drums. I get enough of that at work. Are Casanova and the big guy coming?'

I mentally mapped the two descriptions to Gene and Dave and answered after only a brief pause. 'Correct.'

'I'll get my drinking shoes on.'

16

Calculon wants to connect with you on Skype.

I didn't know anyone called Calculon. One of the advantages of having a small number of friends is that communications are easily filtered. I ignored the request. The next evening I had an actual message from Calculon: *It's me, Eugenie.*

I accepted the invitation and within seconds my computer was ringing.

'Greetings, Eugenie.' Her image came into view.

'Oh gross!'

I recognised the problem from previous conversations with Simon Lefebvre, my Melbourne research colleague.

'This is my office. It has its own toilet. I'm not currently using it except as a seat.'

'Weird. I'm definitely going to tell Mum. Except I'm not supposed to be talking to you.'

'Why not?'

'I did what you said. I made it into a joke.'

'What did you make into a joke?'

'This girl was saying my dad had like a hundred girlfriends, so I said that's because he's so cool. And your dad is so not cool he could only score your mother, who's a troll.'

'Like someone who guards a bridge?'

Eugenie laughed. 'No, it's someone who's annoying on social media. Dad said she was one. Anyhow, everyone started laughing at this girl instead of me, and then another girl dobbed us all in and we've all got a week's detention and Mum got a note. So now we're all picking on her.'

'On your mother?'

'No, the girl who reported us.'

'Maybe you should have a schedule, a roster, of whose turn it is to be bullied. It would avoid unfairness.'

'I don't think so.'

'But the problem is solved?'

'We have another problem.' She looked very serious. 'Carl.'

'He's also being bullied?'

'No. He says if Dad ever comes back he's going to kill him. Because of the girlfriends.' Eugenie's voice indicated emotion. I detected a risk of crying. 'And I really want Dad to come back.' Prediction correct. Eugenie was now crying.

'It won't be possible to solve the problem while you're emotionally incapacitated,' I said.

'Can you talk to Carl? He won't talk to Dad.'

Carl's stepmother is a clinical psychologist. His father is head of the Department of Psychology at a major university. Now I – a physical scientist hardwired to understand logic and ideas ahead of interpersonal dynamics – had been selected to counsel their son.

I needed help. Fortunately, it was readily available in the person of Rosie.

'Gene's son wants to kill him,' I said.

'He'll have to wait in line. I can't believe it – he's out with Inge again, isn't he?'

'Correct. I've attempted to warn her. What do I say to Carl?'

'Nothing. You can't take responsibility for everyone's life. The person who needs to talk to Carl is Gene. He's Carl's father. And your housemate. For the last six weeks. Which we need to talk about.'

'There's a vast list of things we need to talk about.'

'I know, but not now, okay? I'll lose my train of thought.'

Two hours later, I knocked on her door and entered. There was screwed-up printer paper on the floor. Screwing it up made it impossible to re-use and more bulky for disposal. I diagnosed frustration on Rosie's part as well.

'Do you require assistance?'

'No, I can do it. It's just so fucking annoying. I talked to Stefan on Skype and it all made sense, and now it doesn't. I don't know how I'm going to get it done in the next three weeks.'

'Does that have serious implications?'

'You know I'm supposed to get it finished over the vacation. Which I might have been able to do if I didn't have baby brain or have to worry about Gene's problems. And my medical appointments. Which I made, by the way. The ultrasound is next Tuesday at 2.00 p.m. Is that okay with you?'

'It's almost two weeks overdue.'

'My doctor said twelve weeks was fine.'

'Twelve weeks and three days. The Book specifies eight to eleven weeks. A published consensus is more reliable than the opinion of one practitioner.'

'Whatever. I've got an OBGYN now. I saw her today and she's really good. We'll do all the rest by the rules.'

'According to best practice? The second ultrasound is due at eighteen to twenty-two weeks. I recommend twenty-two, since the first one was late.'

'I'll book it in at twenty-two weeks, no days, and zero hours. It's called a sonogram here, by the way. But right now I just want to get this analysis done before I go to bed. And I want a glass of wine. Just one.'

'Alcohol is banned. You're still in the first trimester.'

'If you don't pour me a glass of wine, I'm going to have a cigarette.'

Short of physical restraint or violence, there was nothing I could do to stop Rosie drinking. I brought a glass of white wine to her study and sat in one of the spare chairs.

'Not having one yourself?' she said.

'No.'

Rosie took a sip. 'Don, have you watered this down?'

'It's a low-alcohol wine.'

'It certainly is now.'

I watched as she took a second sip, imagining the alcohol crossing the placental wall, damaging brain cells, reducing our unborn child from a future Einstein to a physicist who would fall just short of taking science to a new level. A child who would never have the experience described by Richard Feynman of knowing something about the universe that no one ever had before. Or, given the medical heritage on Rosie's side, perhaps he or she would stand on the brink of a cure for cancer. But a few brain cells, destroyed by a mother driven to irrationality by pregnancy-induced hormones . . .

Rosie was looking at me.

'You've made your point. Go and squeeze me an orange before I change my mind. And then you can show me how to do this fucking analysis.'

Gene was in my office at the university when Inge brought in a small FedEx package.

'This was at reception for Don. From Australia,' she said.

While Gene and Inge made lunch plans, I deciphered the sender's details, written in untidy script: Phil Jarman, retired Australian Rules footballer, current proprietor of a gymnasium, and Rosie's father. Why had he sent a package to Columbia?

'I presume it's for Rosie,' I said to Gene when Inge had gone.

'Is it addressed to Rosie?' said Gene.

'No, it's addressed to me.'

'Then open it.'

It was a tiny box, containing a diamond ring. The diamond was quite small, smaller than the one on the engagement ring I had given Rosie.

'You expecting this?' said Gene.

'No.'

'Then there'll be a letter.'

Gene was correct. There was a folded piece of paper in the package:

Dear Don

I've enclosed a ring. It was Rosie's mother's and she would have wanted her to have it.

It's traditional to give an eternity ring on your first wedding anniversary, and I'd be honoured if you'd accept it as a gift from me and Rosie's mother to give to her.

Rosie's not the easiest person in the world, and I've always been concerned that the man she married might not be up to the job. You seem to be doing all right so far from what she tells me. Tell her I miss her and don't ever take what you have for granted.

Phil (your father-in-law)

PS I've got that aikido move of yours worked out. If you screw up, I will personally come to New York and beat the living shit out of you.

I gave the letter to Gene. He read it, then folded it up again.

'Just give me a minute,' he said. I detected emotion.

'It seems Phil is unimpressed with me,' I said.

Gene stood up and paced around the room. It is a habit we share when thinking about difficult problems. My father would quote Thoreau – '*Henry David* Thoreau, American philosopher, Don,' he would say as I walked around our living room working on a mathematics or chess problem – 'Never trust any thought arrived at sitting down.'

Gene closed the door.

'Don, I want you to do an exercise for me. I want you to imagine that your baby is born, and it's a girl, and she grows up to be ten years old. And one day Rosie crashes your car and you're in the passenger seat because you've been drinking. And – you know how the story goes, and I know because you told me – but the evolutionary imperative cuts in and you save your daughter instead of Rosie. And you're left with just the two of you.'

Gene had to stop due to emotion. I helped him out.

'I'm familiar with the story, obviously.' It was the story of Phil, Rosie's mother and Rosie, with a substitution of names.

'No, you're not. You've only heard it as something that happened to someone else. The same as if you read it in the paper about a family in Kansas. I want you to imagine yourself in it. Be Phil. And then imagine your daughter marrying some guy who broke your nose and isn't exactly average and going away to New York and getting pregnant. Then imagine yourself writing that letter.'

'Too much imagining. Too many overlaps. Rosie is in both stories in different roles.'

Gene looked at me with an expression I had never seen him use. This was possibly because he had never been angry with me before.

'Too much imagining? How long did it take you to get

a black belt? How long to learn to bone a fucking quail? I am telling you, Don, that you will sit down and work this through no matter how long it takes until you *are* Phil fucking Jarman, walking around that car with a smashed pelvis to get his kid out, and then you will write that letter yourself, and then try to come to me and say, "Phil is unimpressed with me".'

I waited a few moments for Gene to calm down.

'Why?'

'Because you're about to be a father. And every father is Phil Jarman.' Gene sat down. 'Go and get us both a coffee. And then I want to talk to you about the anniversary. Which you've planned nothing for, right?'

17

Rosie's exercise habits were random in the extreme, in violation of The Book. Medical classes were due to resume in two weeks, and now seemed like the ideal time to address the problem. My plan was to insert a workout an hour before she would otherwise have departed for university. She could then travel directly from the exercise venue. As a result of our recently improved proximity to Columbia, the net impact on waking time would be only forty-six minutes.

It all seemed straightforward, but new initiatives require piloting.

I woke Rosie forty-six minutes before her usual time. Her reaction was predictable.

'What time is it? It's dark. What's wrong?'

'6.44 a.m. It's only dark because the curtains are closed. The sun rose approximately forty minutes ago and there would have been pre-dawn light prior to that. Nothing is wrong. We're going to the pool.'

'What pool?'

'The indoor swimming pool at the Chelsea Recreation Center on West 25th. You'll require your bathing costume.'

'I don't have a bathing costume. I hate swimming.'

'You're Australian. All Australians swim. Almost all.'

'I'm one of the exceptions. Go by yourself and bring me back a muffin. Or the legal equivalent. I'm feeling a bit better. For this time of the morning.'

I pointed out that Rosie had limited experience of this time of the morning, that she was the person requiring the exercise and that swimming was a recommended form of exercise for pregnant women.

'Swimming is the recommended form of exercise for everything.'

'Correct.'

'So why don't you do it?' she said.

'I don't like the crowds in the pool. I strongly dislike getting water in my eyes. And putting my head under.'

'So there you go,' said Rosie. 'You can empathise. I won't make you swim if you don't make me. In fact, maybe there's a general rule there.'

I began the Phil Empathy Exercise as I jogged to Columbia, imagining myself in his shoes, a practice also recommended by Atticus Finch in *To Kill a Mockingbird*. It was a terrible scenario, but I could not achieve what Gene wanted. I was reaching the conclusion that the exercise would require months, and possibly the intervention of a hypnotist or bartender, when my subconscious took over.

I woke that night from the World's Worst Nightmare. I was in command of a spaceship, typing instructions at the console. Rosie was in the scout capsule, drifting away from the mother ship, and I couldn't bring her back. The keyboard was touch-sensitive and my fingers kept making mistakes. My frustration turned to anger and I was unable to function.

I woke up breathing rapidly and reached out. Rosie was still there. I wondered if Phil had similar nightmares and woke to find that the world was exactly as he had dreamed it.

Our first wedding anniversary was on 11 August. This year it was a Sunday. Gene's instructions were to make a booking at a high-quality restaurant, purchase flowers and acquire a gift made from a material determined by the ordinal year of the anniversary.

'You're suggesting I purchase some object every year? For the duration of the marriage?'

'The two may be related,' said Gene.

'Did you do this for Claudia?'

'You have the opportunity to learn from my mistakes.'

'Rosie agrees that we don't require vast quantities of junk.'

'Claudia said the same thing. I suggest you ignore it and buy something made from paper.'

'Can it be a consumable? Disposable?'

'As long as it's paper. And demonstrates thoughtfulness. You may want to run it past me first. You *will* run it past me first.'

I began to make plans in accordance with Gene's instructions, but they were derailed by an envelope that I found on my bathroom-office floor on the Saturday morning, the day before the anniversary. I had the door closed as I was working on the Bud sketch for Week 12;

Gene or Rosie must have slipped it under the door rather than risk interrupting some bodily function. There were advantages in combining bathroom and office.

It was an invitation – identifiable by the word *Invitation* on the front. Inside was a small, thin notebook with a red cover. On the first page, Rosie had written:

Don: I want to give you the maximum surprise without exceeding your tolerance. Turn the pages until you're happy. The fewer the better. Love, Rosie.

It seemed that the Jarman family had decided to communicate with me via handwritten letters. I turned the page.

Our wedding anniversary is tomorrow. I'm in charge.

I had booked a restaurant, which I would now need to cancel. Already I was being surprised and disrupted by an initiative that was intended to buffer me from these effects.

I was about to turn to the next page when Gene knocked on the door.

'Are you okay, Don?'

I opened the door and explained the situation.

'As a man of integrity, you can't read the whole thing then pretend you haven't,' said Gene.

'My intention is to minimise stress, and then to tell Rosie.'

'Wrong. Accept the challenge. She's not going to do

anything to hurt you. She just wants to surprise you. Which she will enjoy doing. You'll enjoy it too if you loosen up a bit.' Gene snatched the book from me. 'No choice now.'

I cancelled the restaurant and began to prepare my mind for the unexpected.

The unexpected began at 3.32 p.m. on Sunday. The doorbell rang. It was Isaac and Judy Esler, neither of whom I had seen since the Bluefin Tuna Incident. They were on their way to view the *Search for the Unicorn* exhibition at the Metropolitan Museum of Art and wondered if I would like to join them.

'Go,' said Rosie. 'I see Judy every week. I can use the time to work on my thesis.'

We took the subway to the exhibition, which was moderately interesting, but it became clear that the primary purpose of the excursion was to verify that our friendship was still operational following the Bluefin Tuna Incident. Judy did almost all of the talking.

'I couldn't believe Lydia. She hasn't shown up at book club since, and we've had three meetings. I'm so sorry, Don.'

'No apologies required,' I said. 'You did nothing wrong and I was guilty of insensitivity regarding food preferences. Rosie would also object if I ordered bluefin tuna.'

It seemed sensible not to reveal that I had been seeing Lydia for professional assessment. In any case, another matter was more critical.

'Did you inform Rosie of Lydia's assessment of me?' I asked.

'I told her what Lydia said. And that Isaac put her in her place.'

'It was Seymour,' said Isaac.

'I'm sure it was you. It doesn't matter. Lydia has her own issues. I thought she and Seymour would be a good pair. He's not happy unless he's got someone who needs him and she'd have her own private therapist. I'm not telling you both anything when I say she could use one.'

Judy had not answered my question, or at least not provided the information I wanted.

'Did you mention anything to Rosie about what Lydia said concerning my capabilities as a parent?' I said.

'I don't remember Lydia saying anything about that. What did she say?'

I stopped myself just in time. 'These paintings are so interesting.'

Judy obviously did not notice the change in topic. I was getting better at it.

I returned home at 6.43 p.m. having purchased a single high-quality red rose (indicating one year of marriage) on the way. As I opened the door, it occurred to me that Rosie might have organised the Eslers to remove me from the house while she prepared some sort of surprise. I was right, and my worst fears were realised. *Rosie was in the kitchen.*

She was cooking, or at least preparing food. Or attempting to prepare food. On our first date, Rosie had confessed that she 'could not cook to save her life' and I had seen no evidence to contradict this. The scallops on the night of the Orange Juice Incident, when I was unavailable due to meltdown and then sex, were the most recent culinary disaster.

As I headed to the kitchen to deliver advice and render assistance, Gene emerged from his room and pushed me back out the door, which he closed behind us.

'You were about to help Rosie out in the kitchen, am I right?'

'Correct.'

'And you would have started by saying, "Do you need any help, darling?"'

I reflected for a few moments. In reality I would have assessed the situation, and determined what needed to be done. As would be appropriate for a qualified person arriving at the scene of an accident.

Gene spoke before I had formulated a response. 'Before you do anything, think about which is more important: the quality of one meal or the quality of your relationship. If the answer is the second, you are about to have one of the great meals of your life, prepared without any assistance from you.'

Naturally my focus had been on the meal. But I could see the logic of Gene's argument.

'Nice work with the rose,' said Gene.

We walked back inside.

'Are you guys okay?' said Rosie.

'Of course,' I said and gave her the rose without comment.

'Don had dog crap on his shoe. I saved the carpet,' said Gene.

Rosie instructed me to dress formally, which meant wearing my collared shirt and my non-bushwalking jacket. The leather shoes would also be required.

'I assumed we were eating at home,' I said from the bedroom.

Gene came in again.

'I'm going out now. Dress as if you were going somewhere with a dress code. Do whatever you're told. Express unalloyed joy at everything. Reap the rewards for decades.'

I located my formal clothes.

'Go out on the balcony,' called Rosie. I had retreated to my office, where the opportunities to cause relationship damage were minimised. Rationally, the worst that could happen was poisoning, resulting in a slow and agonising death for both of us. I started again. Statistically, the most likely outcome was an unpalatable meal. I had eaten plenty of those – some, admittedly, as the result of errors on my part. I had even served such failures to Rosie. But I was still irrationally tense.

It was 7.50 p.m. Rosie had put out a small table – one of the surplus items of furniture that lived in her study – and set it in restaurant style for two people. I estimated the temperature as twenty-two degrees Celsius. There was plenty of light. I sat.

Then Rosie appeared. I was stunned. She was wearing

the amazing white dress that she had used only once before: on the occasion of our marriage. Unlike the stereotypical wedding dress, it was – to use a technical term – *elegant*, like a computer algorithm that achieved an impressive outcome with just a few lines of code. The impression of simplicity was enhanced by the deletion of the veil that she had worn twelve months earlier.

'You said you could never wear that dress again,' I said.

'I can wear what I like at home,' she said, in direct contradiction to the instructions she had given regarding my own costume. 'It's a bit tight.'

She was correct about the tightness, which was primarily in the upper region. The effect was spectacular. It took me a while to realise that she was holding two glasses. In fact I did not notice until she handed one to me.

'Yes, mine's got champagne in it too,' she said. 'I'm just going to have a little, but I could have a whole glass with virtually zero risk to the baby. Henderson, Gray and Brocklehurst, 2007.' She smiled widely and raised her glass. 'Happy anniversary, Don. This is how it started, remember?'

I had to think hard. Our relationship had developed significantly on our earlier visit to New York, but we had not had dinner on a balcony . . . Of course! She was referring to the Balcony Dinner at my Melbourne apartment on our first date. It was a brilliant idea to reproduce it. I hoped she had not attempted the lobster salad. It was critical not to over-fry the leeks or they would become bitter . . . I stopped myself. Instead I raised my own glass and said the first words that came into my mind.

'To the world's most perfect woman.' It was lucky my father was not present. *Perfect* is an absolute that cannot be modified, like *unique* or *pregnant*. My love for Rosie was so powerful that it had caused my brain to make a grammatical error.

We drank champagne and watched the sun go down over the Hudson River. Rosie brought out tomato slices with buffalo mozzarella, olive oil and basil leaves. They tasted exactly as they should. Possibly better. I was conscious of smiling.

'Pretty hard to screw up stacking cheese slices and tomato,' said Rosie. 'Don't worry, I haven't tried anything too tricky. I want to sit out here with you and watch the lights and talk.'

'Are there any particular subjects you plan to discuss?' I asked.

'There's one, but I'll get to it. It'll be nice to just talk. But let me get the next course. Prepare not to freak out.'

Rosie returned with a plate covered in thin slices of something with a sprinkling of herbs. I looked more closely. Tuna! Sashimi tuna. *Raw* tuna. Raw fish was of course on the banned substances list. I did not 'freak out'. A few seconds of reflection revealed that Rosie, in an act of selflessness, had prepared my favourite food even though she could not share it with me.

I was about to express my thanks when I saw that she

had brought *two* pairs of chopsticks. I could feel a freak-out building.

'I told you not to freak,' she said. 'You know what's wrong with raw fish? It might make me sick, like you said. Like it can any time, pregnant or not, and never has. But it won't directly harm the foetus in the way that toxoplasmosis or listeria would. Mercury is a risk, but not in this quantity. Tuna is a good source of Omega-3 fatty acids which are correlated with higher IQ. Hibbeln et al, "Maternal Seafood Consumption in Pregnancy and Neurodevelopmental Outcomes in Childhood", *The Lancet*, 2007. And it's bluefin. A few grams once in a lifetime can't hurt the planet too much.'

She smiled, lifted a slice of tuna with her chopsticks and dipped it in the soy sauce. I was right. I had married the world's most perfect woman.

Rosie's prediction that it would be nice just to talk was correct. We talked about Gene and Claudia and Carl and Eugenie and Inge, about Dave and Sonia and what we would do when our pseudo-lease expired. George had promised me three months' notice. No conclusions were reached, but I was conscious that Rosie and I had not scheduled sufficient time for talking since we had arrived in New York and become busy with work. Neither of us raised the topic of pregnancy, in my case since it had been the source of recent conflict. Rosie's reason may have been the same.

At intervals, Rosie went to the kitchen and returned with food, in every instance competently executed. We had fried crab cakes and then the main course, which Rosie retrieved from the oven.

'Striped bass *en papillote*,' she said. 'Which is to say *in paper*, since this is our paper anniversary.'

'Incredible. You solved the problem and the result is disposable.'

'I know you hate clutter. So we'll just have the memory.' Rosie waited while I tasted it.

'Okay?' she said.

'Delicious.' It was true.

'So,' she said, 'that brings me to the one thing I wanted to say. It's nothing dramatic. I *can* cook. I'm not going to cook every night, and you're a better cook than I am, but I can follow a recipe if I need to. If I screw up occasionally, no big deal. I love everything you do for me, but I also want you to know that I'm not helpless and incompetent. That's really important to me.'

Rosie took a sip from my wineglass and continued her speech. 'I know I do it to you too. Remember the night I left you at the cocktail bar and was worried you wouldn't cope without me? And you were fine, right?'

I must have been too slow to hide my expression.

'What happened?' she said.

There was no reason now, seven weeks later, to hide the story of Loud Woman and the consequent loss of our jobs. I related the story, and we both laughed. It was a huge relief.

'I knew something had happened,' said Rosie. 'I knew you'd been hiding something. You shouldn't ever worry about telling me stuff.'

188

It was a critical moment. Should I tell Rosie about the Playground Incident and Lydia? Tonight she was relaxed and accepting. But perhaps tomorrow morning she would begin worrying and stress would replace her happy mood. The threat of prosecution was still present.

Instead I took the opportunity to explore a lie by a third party. 'When Gene said I had dog faeces on my shoe, did you believe him?'

'Of course not. He dragged you outside to tell you not to get in my face in the kitchen. Or to give you the flower to give to me. Right?'

'The first one. I purchased the flower independently.' I would of course have been fooled had I been in Rosie's position, but I was not surprised that she had detected Gene's lie.

'Do you think Gene knew that he had failed to deceive you?' I asked.

'I'd think so. It's not like I don't know the two of you.'

'So why did he bother inventing a lie that no one would believe and that made no difference to anyone's feelings?'

'Just trying to be nice,' she said. 'I guess I appreciated the effort.'

Social protocols. Unfathomable.

It was my turn to deliver a surprise. I walked inside. Gene was back and he had helped himself to some of the surplus champagne in the refrigerator.

I returned to the balcony and pulled Rosie's mother's ring from my pocket. I took Rosie's hand and put it on her finger, as I had done with another ring on this date a year earlier. In keeping with tradition, I put it on the same finger: the theory is that the eternity ring symbolically prevents the removal of the wedding ring. This seemed to be consistent with Phil's intent.

It took Rosie a few seconds to recognise the ring and begin crying, and in that time Gene had thrown the full box of confetti over us with one hand and taken multiple photographs with the other.

18

A communal meal was scheduled for Tuesday evening. I reminded Rosie in the morning as I suspected her unreliability at keeping appointments had been exacerbated by pregnancy.

'Don't *you* forget,' she said. 'I've got the sonogram booked today.'

Problems had accumulated. I had made a list of eight critical items.

1. The Gene Relocation Problem. Obviously Gene needed to participate in this discussion.
2. The Banned Substances List. I had left it on Rosie's desk, but she had not indicated her formal approval.
3. Rosie's problem with leave from the medical program. This needed to be resolved as quickly as possible in the interests of certainty.
4. An exercise regimen for Rosie, outstanding after the failure of the swimming program.
5. Rosie's thesis, behind schedule and in danger of interfering with other activities.
6. The Gene and Claudia Marriage Problem. I had made no progress and needed Rosie's help.

7. The Carl and Gene Issue. Gene needed to talk to Carl.
8. Direct action on Rosie's stress. Yoga and meditation are widely recognised as promoting relaxation.

Just making the list gave me a feeling of significant progress. I gave printed copies to Gene and Rosie as they sat down to dinner – wild-caught prawns followed by low-mercury grilled fish with a salad featuring the absence of alfalfa shoots.

Rosie's reaction was not positive.

'Fuck, Don. I've got two weeks to finish my thesis. I don't need all this.'

There was silence for approximately twenty seconds.

'Looking at this list,' Gene said, 'it seems like I've been contributing to Item 8. I've been so occupied with young Carl's difficulties that I've been inconsiderate of you. I didn't realise you were under so much pressure with the thesis.'

'What do you think I've been doing in my study all the time? Why do you think I have no life? Don didn't tell you I was behind?' The words were aggressive, but I recognised a conciliatory tone.

'Not really, no. It seems you and Don have got a lot to talk about, with leave and exercise and banned substances. I'll grab a burger and start looking for somewhere to live tomorrow.'

Rosie had what she wanted, but inexplicably refused it.

'No, no, sorry. Have dinner with us. We'll talk about the food and exercise stuff some other time.'

'We need to discuss it now,' I said.

'It can wait,' said Rosie. 'Tell us about Carl, Gene.'

'He blames me for the split.'

'If you could have your time again?' said Rosie.

'I wouldn't change it for Claudia. But if I'd known how it would affect Carl . . .'

'Unfortunately, the past is not changeable,' I said, wanting to bring the conversation back to practical solutions.

'Acknowledging your regret may help,' said Rosie.

'I doubt it'll be enough for Carl,' said Gene.

At least we had addressed, if not resolved, one item on the agenda. I made a point of checking it off on both of their copies.

We made no further progress with the list. Rosie produced a large envelope from her bag and gave it to Gene. 'This is what I did this afternoon.'

Gene pulled a sheet from the envelope and passed it immediately to me. It was a sonogram picture, presumably of Bud. To a non-expert, it was indistinguishable from the pictures in The Book, which I was very familiar with. It was less clear than the sketch I had added to the Week 12 tile five days earlier. I passed it back to Rosie.

'I guess you've seen it already,' said Gene.

'No, he hasn't,' said Rosie. She turned to me. 'Where were you at 2.00 p.m. today?'

'In my office, reviewing a research protocol for Simon Lefebvre. Is there a problem?'

'Did you forget about the sonogram?'

'Of course not.'

'So why weren't you there?'

'I was expected to attend?' It would have been interesting, but I could see no role for myself. I had never attended a medical appointment with Rosie before, nor she with me. In fact she had had her first medical appointment with the OBGYN the previous week, where she presumably received an initial briefing on the conduct of the pregnancy. If I was to attend any appointment, this was surely the most relevant in ensuring that we had the same information. Yet I had not been invited. The sonogram was a *procedure* involving technicians and technology, and I was conscious from experience that professionals liked to work without the presence of onlookers who asked distracting questions.

Rosie nodded slowly. 'I tried to call but your phone was off. I thought you might have had an accident or something, but then I remembered that I'd only told you the time and the place twice and hadn't actually said, "Use that information to get yourself there." '

It was generous of Rosie to take the blame for the misunderstanding.

'Were there any faults?' I asked. At almost thirteen weeks, the sonogram would be able to pick up neural-tube deficits. I had assumed that, in keeping with normal protocols, Rosie would have informed me if there had been a problem, just as she would have informed me if she had lost her phone on the subway. The Book had implied that abnormalities were statistically unlikely. In any case, there was zero I could do until an issue was identified.

'No, there are no faults. What if there were?'

'It would depend on the nature of the fault, obviously.'

'Obviously.'

'Good news, then,' said Gene. 'Some of us imagine every possible scenario, and some of us cross the bridge when we come to it. Like Don.'

'I've got another item,' said Rosie. 'I forgot to tell you. I've got a study group tomorrow night. Here.'

'The semester hasn't started,' I said. 'You need to focus on your thesis.'

'The thesis is screwed. I'm not going to get it done in ten days.'

'It'll be all right,' said Gene. 'I'll organise an extension.'

Rosie shook her head. 'This is Columbia. They have rules.'

'For ordinary mortals. Relax.'

Rosie did not look relaxed. 'I talked to someone in admin. She wasn't exactly helpful.'

Gene smiled. 'I've already spoken to Borenstein. As long as it's in by the start of your clinical year, you'll be fine.'

The study-group meeting would be a major disruption to my schedule, but Rosie was overloaded. I needed to be supportive during this challenging time of change for both of us, as recommended by The Book. 'I'll scale up the dinner. How many people?'

'Don't worry. We'll get pizza. One night won't hurt.'

'I'm not worried. I can easily cook a vastly superior meal.'

'Maybe you guys could have your night out tomorrow.'

'That's a more serious disruption to the schedule than multiplying the dinner.'

'It's just . . . you're faculty, and it's the first time they've been here. They've never met you.'

'Obviously there has to be a first meeting. I can meet them all together.'

'They're strangers. You don't like meeting strangers.'

'Medical students. Almost scientists. Pseudo-scientists. I can have fascinating arguments with them.'

'Which is why I'd rather you went out. Please.'

'You think I'll be annoying?'

'I guess I just want my own space.'

'It's fine,' said Gene. 'I'll look after Don.'

Rosie smiled. 'Sorry to spring it on you. Thanks for understanding.' She was looking at Gene.

George called as Gene and I were leaving for the bar the following evening. 'Don, do you want to come up here instead? We can send out for pizza. I've got a few things I want to throw at the Gene Genie.'

I called Dave. If George was paying and we could watch the baseball, location was of minor importance.

During the seventh-inning stretch George turned to Gene. 'I've been thinking about what you said about genetics. Quite a bit, actually. It still doesn't explain why one of my sons is a drug addict and two aren't.'

'Two words. *Different genes.* I can't know for sure, but I'd guess he got an overdose of genes that tell his body to keep doing what feels good. Fine in an environment without pharmaceuticals.'

George sat back and Gene continued. 'All of us are programmed – genetically programmed – to keep doing what's worked for us, and to avoid things that didn't work.'

'Ayahuasca,' said George. 'Tried once, never again.'

'Most of the time, what we do works well enough. So here's a principle that most psychologists would agree with but that comes straight out of genetics: *people repeat themselves.*'

I asked the obvious question. 'How do they know what to do the first time?'

'They copy their parents. In the ancestral environment, they were, by definition, successful people. They'd succeeded in breeding. If you want to understand individual human behaviour, the magic words are *repeating patterns.*'

'Tell me about it,' said George. 'I'm a drummer. Repeating patterns. Same songs, same boat, same journey.'

'Why do you continue?' I asked.

'Now there's a good question,' said George. 'When I got this apartment, I had an idea I'd move here, find somewhere that'd give me a solo gig once a week. I play a bit of guitar. Get back to writing my own stuff. Every year I promise myself I'll do it, and every year I get back on the bloody boat.'

He put his beer glass down. 'You gents want to switch to wine? I bought a case of Chianti.'

George fetched a bottle of Sassicaia 2000, which is not technically Chianti, but from the same region.

'Jesus,' said Gene. 'A bit good for pizza.'

'World's best pizza,' I said, to clarify, and everyone laughed. It was a minor but notably good moment, and I was sorry Rosie was not sharing it with me.

George was looking for a corkscrew without success. There was a simple solution.

'I'll get mine.' My cork extractor, selected after a significant research project, would be equal or superior to any George might own.

I went downstairs and opened the door to the apartment, expecting to find it full of medical students. The living room was empty. Rosie was in the bedroom, asleep. The light was on and a novel was open on the bed. On the floor was a single, small pizza box. The receipt was stuck to the top: *$14.50. Meatlovers' Special.*

19

'Is there some problem?' I asked Rosie the next morning.

'I was going to ask you the same thing,' she said. 'You were in the bathroom for over an hour.'

Copying the sonogram picture of Bud onto Tile 13 had been more difficult than reproducing a line diagram from the internet. But it seemed sensible to use the actual picture. Rosie was right: it would have been interesting to watch the moving scan.

'No problem,' I said. 'Maintaining the wall tiles.'

I had also been analysing the Meat Pizza Incident. I saw five possibilities:

1. Rosie's study group had eaten the pizza. That did not explain the box being in the bedroom.
2. Rosie was having an affair with a carnivore. That would explain the location of the box, but surely they would have hidden the evidence.
3. The box was mislabelled and actually contained a vegetarian pizza.
4. A meat pizza had been delivered in error. Rosie had discarded the meat and eaten the remaining pizza. The theory was plausible, but there was no sign of meat in the bin.

5. Rosie had violated her practice of sustainable pescatarianism. This seemed highly unlikely, although there was a recent precedent in her eating a small quantity of Gene's and my steak meal.

Incredibly, the highly unlikely option was the correct one. There had been no study group meeting. Rosie had 'just needed a bit of space'. She had lied to me rather than make a straightforward request. And she had ordered a meat pizza.

I could not blame her for dishonesty. I was guilty of a far greater ongoing deception about the Lydia situation for much the same reasons: to protect Rosie from distress and both Bud and her from the harmful effects of excess cortisol. Rosie had not wanted to hurt me by saying she didn't want me in the apartment with her. There were numerous alternative solutions I could have presented – and would have. Perhaps she had chosen to lie rather than listen to them.

It seemed that Gene was right. Dishonesty was part of the price of being a social animal, and of marriage in particular. I wondered if Rosie was withholding any other information.

The vegetarian violation was more interesting.

'I just felt like meat. I got them to hold the salami,' she said.

'I suspect a protein or iron deficiency.'

'It wasn't a craving. I just decided to do it. I'm so over being told what to do. You know why I'm a pescatarian?'

Sustainable pescatarianism had been one of the initial conditions of the Rosie Package, known to me from the day we met. I had accepted that package in its entirety, in direct contrast to the philosophy of the Wife Project, which had focused on aggregating individual components.

'I assume health reasons.'

'If I was that worried about my health, I wouldn't have been a smoker. I'd go to the swimming pool. And sustainability wouldn't matter.'

'You don't eat meat for ethical reasons?'

'I try to do the right thing by the planet. I don't impose my views on other people. I watch you and Gene scoff down half a cow and I don't say anything. I've at least got the excuse of eating for a second person.'

'Perfectly reasonable. Protein –'

'Fuck protein. Fuck people telling me what to eat and when to exercise and how to study and to go to yoga, which I'm doing with Judy anyway. And no, it's not Bikram yoga, it's the right sort of yoga for pregnancy. I can work that out for myself.'

I suspected that 'people' was an incorrect use of the plural form. But it was better than Rosie saying, 'Fuck you,' which was obviously what she meant.

I offered an explanation. 'I'm attempting to assist with the baby production process. You didn't appear to have time to do the necessary research, due to your thesis and the unplanned nature of the pregnancy.' I could have added that I had been *told* to do this by Lydia and Sonia, a professional and a fellow pregnant woman, and would not have done it without such direction, but that would have involved disclosing my deception. Deception had got me into trouble. It was hardly a surprise.

I could have added that I had made no major recommendations about food or exercise or study since the Anniversary Meal, which represented a high point in our relationship. Why was Rosie becoming upset now?

'I get that you were trying to help,' she said. 'I really do. But let's get this straight: my body, my work, my problems. I'm not going to get smashed, I won't eat salami and I'll get there my own way.'

She walked towards her study and indicated that I should follow. From her bag, she retrieved The Book.

'This the book you've been reading?' she asked.

'Obviously.' I hadn't noticed it missing.

'You could have saved yourself a few bucks and taken my copy. It's a bit basic for me. I'm onto it, Don.'

'You require zero assistance?'

'Keep doing what you were doing. Go to work, eat cow, get drunk with Gene. Stop worrying. We're doing okay.'

I should have been pleased with the outcome. I was relieved of responsibility at a time when I had plenty of other things to worry about. But I had been working hard at building empathy for Rosie and now I had a vague sense that despite her words she was not happy with me.

Her solution to the diet issue – in fact all pregnancy issues that I had seen as joint projects – was to proceed alone. At least I had clear direction for the follow-up meeting with Lydia.

'You're over-functioning,' said Gene. 'You know what my doctor said about that book you've been reading? "Give it to someone you hate." All that obsessing, and the difference you make to the outcome is negligible compared to the big game.'

It was our second boys' night out in five days, encouraged by the proximity of George's baseball-watching and drinking facility. Rosie had not objected.

'And the big game is?' said George.

'You've heard me before,' said Gene. 'Genes are destiny. You guys made your biggest contribution when you supplied a bit of your DNA.'

It was obvious Dave disagreed. 'All the books say that genes are just a start; parenting makes a big difference,' he said.

Gene smiled. 'They would say that. Otherwise no one would buy books on parenting.'

'You said so yourself. Kids pick up behaviour from their parents.'

'Only what's left over after the genes have done their work,' said Gene. 'Let me give you an example from a field in which I have some expertise. Your wife is of Italian extraction?'

'Grandparents. She was born here.'

'Perfect. Italian genes, American upbringing. Now, I'm going to predict that she has a histrionic personality.

A bit loud, a bit flamboyant, a bit of an actress. Panics under pressure, hysterical in an emergency.'

Dave didn't say anything.

'Ask a psychologist about cultural stereotypes and they'll tell you it's all nurture,' said Gene. 'Culture.'

'Correct,' I said. 'Evolution of behavioural traits is far slower than the formation of geographic groups.'

'Except for selective breeding. A certain trait becomes sexually attractive for genetic or cultural reasons, doesn't matter which, and people with that trait breed more. Italian men love histrionic women. *Ergo*, the histrionic gene takes over. Your wife's personality was programmed before she was born.'

Dave shook his head. 'You couldn't be more wrong. Sonia's an accountant. Completely level-headed.'

'I don't think I can do this. It isn't making sense. It's the opposite of what I told her before.' Sonia was becoming increasingly agitated as our appointment with Lydia approached. She seemed to be having difficulty discarding her own personality.

'It's simple. You need to say you made an error; that you don't want any help.'

'You think she's going to believe that?' said Sonia.

'It's the truth. Assuming you're Rosie.'

'If you knew how desperate I am for Dave to just take an interest. Five years we tried and now it's like he doesn't want it.'

'Possibly he's too busy working. Providing financial support.'

'You know something? On their deathbed, nobody ever wishes they'd spent more time at the office.'

It was difficult to see how Sonia's statement contributed to the discussion. Dave was not dying, nor did he work in an office. I brought the conversation back on track.

'As you caused the problem last time, and since I am more familiar with Rosie's position, I propose that I provide the necessary information to Lydia and you merely confirm its accuracy.'

'I don't want to be too passive or she'll think you're oppressing me. She's already got it in her head that I'm some sort of peasant girl.'

It seemed a reasonable conclusion on Lydia's part, given the dress and the accent. Today Sonia was wearing a conventional suit, as she had come from work. It struck me as equally uncharacteristic of medical students.

'Excellent point. Probably you should be like Rosie – angry that I tried to control her.'

'Rosie was angry?'

Now that I had said the word, I realised it was true. I did not need to be an expert at interpreting body language to realise that 'Fuck people telling me what to eat' was an aggressive statement.

'Correct.'

'Are you two okay?'

'Of course.' The answer was accurate, assuming that I was employing the word 'okay' in the way it would be used to describe a meal or a performance: *The play was okay, not great*. I assessed Rosie's current level of satisfaction with me as 'not great'.

'I'll do my best, Don. But if you're talking to Dave, can you let him know that I'm not like Rosie? Maybe give him your book if you don't need it any more. I'd love for him to come home early and make me vegetable curry.'

The session with Lydia did not go as planned. I was only five items into my detailed list of events, enumerating instances of Rosie refusing help, when she interrupted and addressed Sonia.

'Why did you not want Don's advice?'

'No man is telling me what to do with my body.' Sonia said this calmly, but then paused and contorted her face in what I assumed was an impression of anger and hit the table with her fist. '*Bastardos!*'

Lydia seemed surprised. I hoped the surprise was at Sonia's actions and not her use of a Spanish word. 'It sounds like you've had some bad experiences.'

'In my village, there is much oppression by the patriarchy.'

'You came from a village in Italy?'

'*Si*. A small village. *Poco*.' Sonia indicated the size of the village by holding her thumb and forefinger approximately two centimetres apart.

'And has working in an IVF lab and studying at Columbia altered your view of men?'

'I don't want Don to tell me what to eat and how much to exercise and when to go to bed.'

'And that's what you feel he's been doing?'

'*Si*. That is not what I want.'

'I can quite understand.' Lydia turned to me. 'Can you understand that, Don?'

'Totally. Rosie does not require my help.' I did not point out that this had been my original position until Lydia had demanded I interfere.

'So, Rosie, last time we met, you seemed quite passionate about wanting some support from Don.'

'Now that I've experienced it, I've decided it's not such a good idea.'

'I can see why. Don, support isn't about telling Rosie what to do. If you want me to be blunt, the problem's with you. Instead of telling her how to be a mother, maybe you should be doing some preparation for being a supportive father.'

Of course! The baby would have two parents, and I had been focusing all my energies on optimising the performance of one. I was amazed that I had not seen the problem earlier, but as a scientist I recognised that paradigm shifts appear obvious only in retrospect. Also, I had been focused on doing whatever seemed necessary to prevent Lydia giving me an adverse report, under the assumption that there was no actual problem with me as a prospective parent. But recent criticisms from Rosie were evidence that Lydia's original judgement was correct. My respect for her had increased dramatically.

I jumped to my feet. 'Brilliant! Problem solved. I need to gain fatherhood skills.'

Lydia maintained a professional level of calmness. She turned to Sonia.

'How do you feel about that? Do you think Don understands what's required?'

Sonia nodded. 'I'm very happy. I'm happy for all the things he taught me about pregnancy because I am too busy with the study, but now I'll make sure he is thinking only about being a *papa*.'

Lydia picked up the police file that had been sitting on the desk and smiled.

'Well,' she said, 'our time is up. Assisting with your parenting was never the official purpose of these sessions, and in that respect you're going to be picked up by the Good Fathers program. I'll be getting a report from them.'

This was the men's group that she had referred me to at our first meeting to assess my propensity for violence. The program I had booked was still seven weeks in the future.

She waved the police file. 'But as far as parenthood is concerned, if the two of you can keep reminding each other what you've said today –'

'Excellent,' I said. 'A highly productive session. I'll book the next available slot.'

'She was going to let you off,' said Sonia.

'I suspected that. But what she said was so useful.'

'She's still got that police file. Couldn't we – you – find another therapist?'

'A significant percentage of professionals are incompetent. And she is familiar with us now.'

'Us. You and Rosie, the Italian peasant.'

'It doesn't matter. Her insight was incredible. She solved the problem.'

20

In retrospect, I had been on the correct path when I observed the children at the playground. Had I not been interrupted – and sidetracked – by a legal technicality, I would have gained the required background on father-hood, which I now realised was where my attention should be focused.

Recent experience had suggested that I could not ignore the pre-birth stage. Sonia was herself an example of a woman who was unsatisfied with her partner's level of involvement in the pregnancy phase. After some reflection, I decided that there were at least four areas for action and skill development that did not involve interfering with Rosie's autonomy:

1. Acquisition of expertise in dealing with very young children. The Book was clear that men should develop skills in baby management to provide respite for their partner. Although Rosie had been dismissive of my role as carer, The Book (and Sonia and Lydia) presented a strongly opposing view.
2. Equipment acquisition, including environment preparation. The baby would require protection

from sharp objects, poisonous substances, alcohol fumes and band practice.

3. Acquisition of expertise in obstetric observations and procedures. The Book was insistent on the importance of regular medical appointments. Rosie was disorganised in this area and over-reliant on her own medical expertise. Also, there was the possibility of some sort of emergency.

4. A non-intrusive approach to the nutrition problem. I did not trust Rosie to maintain a diet within the guidelines. Her ordering of the meatlovers' pizza suggested that factors other than rational analysis were influencing her choices.

The final item was the easiest. Rosie had implicitly agreed to the list of banned substances. I would make the conservative assumption that food purchased by Rosie outside the apartment had zero nutritional value and design our meals to include all the prescribed nutrients in appropriate proportions.

I would vary the detail of the Standardised Meal System (Pregnancy Version) by choosing different fish varieties and green vegetables, thus hiding its underlying structure from Rosie. It would be simpler now that she was a meat eater. She had also entered the second trimester of the pregnancy, where the risk of damage to Bud by toxins that she might ingest from her unsupervised meals had lessened. The hard work had been done, at some cost to our relationship, but I could now relax a little.

Things were looking much more positive.

Rosie was back at university for the fall semester. She had a tutorial on the Saturday morning and told me that, having made the journey to Columbia, she would spend the remainder of the day there.

I began my solo day by drawing a one-to-one scale, apple-sized Bud on Tile 15. The Book noted that Bud's ears had migrated from his neck to his head, and his eyes to the middle. It would have been fascinating to discuss with Rosie, but she was not present. And I had not forgotten her admonition about providing technical commentary.

The obvious starting point for the equipment-acquisition project was a pram: all babies require prams, and I considered myself better qualified than Rosie to select mechanical items. My bicycle represented the result of a three-month evaluation process, culminating in the selection of the appropriate base model plus a list of modifications. I expected the experience to be largely transferable.

At the end of a fulfilling day, interrupted only by food purchasing, lunch and essential bodily functions, my internet-based investigation had produced a set of requirements for the ideal pram and a shortlist of available models, none perfect, but all potentially viable after some modification. I had a satisfying sense of making progress, but decided not to share this with Rosie. It could be another surprise.

There was a second item of equipment which was more critical, at least in terms of the lead time required for thinking and implementation. Rosie had identified the problem of noise from upstairs. However, I had not informed her of the exact agreement with George, which allowed for unlimited music practice at all hours.

The Skype call came through on schedule at 7.00 p.m. Eastern Daylight Time; 9.00 a.m. Sunday, Australian Eastern Standard Time.

'How's the weather there, Donald?' said my mother.

'Minimal change from last week. Still summer. The weather is normal for late August.'

'What's that in the background? Are you in the toilet? You can call back when you're finished.'

'This is my office. It's very private.' Rosie was home and I did not want her listening while I worked on the second surprise.

'I should hope so. How was your week?'

'Fine.'

'You're well?'

'Fine.'

'And Rosie?'

'Fine.'

If we were using only text messages, I could have replaced myself with a simple computer application. The Fine application. Possibly it would be better than I was at interspersing the occasional 'good' and 'very well'. But this evening/morning, a variation was required.

'I need to speak to Dad.'

'You want to speak to your father?' The speech

quality was excellent – *fine* – but my mother no doubt wanted to confirm the unusual request. 'Is everything all right?'

'Of course. I have a technical problem.'

'I'll get him.' Rather than getting him, my mother shouted, 'Jim! It's Donald. He has a problem.'

My father does not waste time with formalities.

'What's the problem, Don?'

'I require a soundproof crib.' Although earplugs provided a simple solution, it had occurred to me that insulating a baby from sound might affect its development in a negative way.

'Interesting. I suppose breathing is the problem.'

'Correct. Communication is solvable electronically –'

'No need to tell me things we both know. But I'm struggling to imagine a soundproof material that air can pass through.'

'I've done some research. There is a project in Korea –'

'You mean *South* Korea.'

'Correct. They've developed a material impermeable to sound but permeable to air.'

'I presume it's on the internet. Send your mother a link. You've given me enough to work on for now. I'll get your mother back. Adele!'

My mother's face appeared in front of my father's. 'What was that about?'

'Don wants some help designing a crib.'

'A crib? A *baby* crib?' *Baby crib* seemed to be a tautology. My father pointed this out to my mother.

'I don't care,' she said. 'Donald, is this for a friend?'

'No, no, it's for Rosie's baby. Our baby. It requires protection from noise but needs to breathe.'

My mother immediately became hysterical. I should have told her earlier, of course it was relevant, for God's sake we speak every Sunday, when is it due, your aunt would be excited, is Rosie all right, I hope it's a girl, I don't mean that, it just came out, I was thinking of Rosie, girls are easier, do you know what it's going to be, isn't it amazing what they can do these days? Vast numbers of questions and observations that eventually occupied an additional eight minutes beyond the time I had scheduled for the discussion with my father. I have learned that tears do not necessarily equate to sadness and, despite my mother being understandably disappointed that we were in New York rather than Melbourne or Shepparton, she seemed pleased with the situation.

I spent almost two weeks with *Dewhurst's Textbook of Obstetrics and Gynaecology* (Eighth Edition) and looking at videos available on the internet before deciding that these materials needed to be supplemented with practical experience. It was like reading a book on karate – useful to a point, but not sufficient for combat preparation. Fortunately, as a member of the medical faculty, I was in a position to gain access to hospitals and clinics.

I booked a meeting with David Borenstein in his office.

'I'd like to deliver a baby.'

The Dean's expression was difficult to interpret, but 'enthusiastic' was not one of the options.

'Don, when I hired you, I expected some strange requests. So instead of me telling you all the practical and legal reasons why you can't deliver a baby, how about you tell me why you want to do it?'

I began to explain the need to be ready for any emergency, but the Dean interrupted, laughing.

'Let me put it like this. The odds of you having to deliver this baby in Manhattan without assistance are quite a bit lower than the odds of you having to do a competent job of raising it once it's born. Which are 100 per cent. You agree?'

'Of course. I have a separate sub-project –'

'I'm sure you do. And you've just planted a seed in my mind. How's Inge doing? How long has she been with you now?'

'Eleven weeks and two days.' She had started on the day of the Playground Incident, the day that led to my second meeting with Lydia, the recruitment of Sonia as an actress and my obligation to attend a group for violent men. The day the secrets began.

'How is she doing?'

'She's highly competent. She's made a significant change to my default position on research assistants.'

'So maybe it's time to give you something different to do.'

'You have another genetics project?'

'Not exactly. I didn't bring you here because you're a mouse-liver expert, or even a genetics expert. I brought you here because you're a scientist I can trust to care only about the science.'

'Of course.'

'Not "of course". Ninety per cent of scientists have some sort of agenda – whether it's proving something they believe already or getting funding or a promotion or their name on a paper. These guys are no exception.'

'Which guys?'

'The guys I want you to work with. They're looking at attachment-related hormones and different modes of synchrony with mothers and fathers.'

'I know zero about this. I don't even understand the title.' I did recognise the word 'attachment' and remembered Gene's advice to 'run a mile', but I let David continue.

'That's fine. The underlying question is: does a baby benefit from having a parent of each gender, as opposed to one parent only, or two women, or two men? What do you think, Don?'

'I still know zero about the topic. How can I have an opinion?'

'And that's why I want you to take the medical school seat on the project. To make sure that the research design and whatever comes out of it are as free of prejudice as you are.' He smiled. 'And you'll get to play with some babies.'

The Dean did not even make an appointment. We walked immediately to the New York Institute of Attachment and Childhood Development, located four blocks from the Dean's office, where we were greeted by three women.

'Briony, Brigitte and Belinda: I'd like you to meet Professor Don Tillman.'

'The B Team,' I said, making a small joke. Nobody laughed. It was an encouraging sign that they were not inclined to over-recognise patterns, but I mentally registered them as B1, B2 and B3. I had been assigned to the project to provide objectivity and it was important to avoid forming personal relationships with the other researchers.

'Don's one of my people,' the Dean continued. 'He's a committed Catholic and a passionate Tea Party supporter.'

'I hope you're kidding me,' said B1. 'This project has had enough –'

'I am kidding,' said David. 'But it shouldn't matter. I said Don is one of my people. His personal philosophy won't affect his judgement.'

'They're inseparable. But we won't have that argument now. If that's what you want, you could have sent us a computer.' B1 again. She appeared to be the team leader.

'Don's not so easy to shut down. As I think you'll discover.'

'You know this is an all-women project? With substantial finance from the Women Working for Women Foundation?'

'*Was* an all-women project,' said the Dean. 'Don, as you can see, changes the picture. I believe the funding is contingent on the College of Medicine and Surgery approving the research design and the analysis. I can't imagine there were any gender restrictions placed on our nominee. I'm sure that would have been considered most inappropriate. I want Don to do whatever he needs to do to ensure the work is scientifically bulletproof. Which is in everybody's interest.'

'Is he approved for working with children?' said B1.

'Aren't their mothers with them all the time?'

'I'm assuming the answer is no. He'll need a clearance. Which I imagine will take some time.'

B1 looked at me for approximately seven seconds.

'What do you think of two women raising a child?'

In a scientific setting, I considered her question equivalent to asking, 'What do you think of potassium?'

'I don't have any relevant knowledge. It's outside my field.'

She turned to the Dean. 'You didn't think some appreciation of family models was relevant?'

'I'd have thought your team had that well covered. I chose Don because he'll offer something you might have a need for.'

'And that would be?' The question was addressed to me.

'Scientific rigour,' I said.

'Oh,' she said. 'Well, we can certainly use that, just being psychologists and all.' She examined me again. Another seven seconds. 'Do you have any gay friends?'

I was about to tell her that I didn't, as a result of having only seven friends, including George, rather than because of any prejudice about sexual orientation, but the Dean interrupted. 'I'll leave you to your networking. I'll organise a police clearance for Don. I can't imagine any problems.'

*

The Lesbian Mothers Project was vastly more interesting than the genetic factors influencing vulnerability to cirrhosis of the liver in mice, which had been the focus of my research for the past six years. The stimulus for it was an Israeli study that had observed different responses to male and female parents. Babies' oxytocin levels rose during cuddling by the mother but not by the father, and during active play with the father but not with the mother. Very interesting. But it appeared that the motivation for the project was a newspaper article titled *Research Proves Kids Need a Mom* and *a Dad*. Someone had written the word *crap* in red beside the article. It was an excellent start. Scientists need to cultivate a suspicious attitude to research.

My reading of the original paper provided no indication that the research was crap. The newspaper article offered a typically inexact interpretation, but its broad argument that fathers and mothers had different impacts on babies was supported by the published results.

The original study had involved only heterosexual couples. The B Team would examine lesbian couples. Their hypothesis was that the secondary carer playing with the child would cause the same oxytocin response as the father.

It all seemed straightforward, and I wondered why the Dean had bothered to involve me. But observing the actual research would provide the perfect background for fatherhood, provided I considered myself equivalent to a lesbian secondary carer. The research itself would clarify whether that identification was valid.

The only problem was the police check, which the Dean was arranging. To the risk of prosecution and deportation, I could now add a third consequence of professional disgrace if Lydia gave me an adverse report.

I assumed Rosie would be interested in the Lesbian Mothers Project and impressed that I was acquiring knowledge of babies and parenting. After a week of intense familiarisation, time-shared with ongoing reading on obstetrics, I was ready to discuss it with some authority.

I planned to introduce the topic at dinner. Rosie was now spending so much time on her medical study and thesis that meals and morning subway rides were becoming our only time together, with the exception of bed.

Gene and I had drunk half the bottle of wine before Rosie joined us at the table. She had a glass in her hand.

'Sorry guys, had to finish what I was doing or I'd have lost the thread.' She poured a half-glass of wine for herself. 'I need an hour of being human.'

'I've just started a new research project,' I said. 'The basis is a paper by –'

'Don, can we not talk genetics right now? I just need to chill for a bit.'

'It's not genetics. It's psychology.'

'What are you talking about?'

'I've been added to a psychology research team to provide scientific rigour.'

'Because the psychologists aren't up to it?' said Rosie.

Gene had screwed his face up and was making small but rapid shaking movements of his head.

'Correct,' I said.

'Great,' said Rosie. 'I should be getting some rigour into my thesis instead of wasting time drinking wine with my husband and my supervisor.'

She took her glass into her study.

'You're invading her territory, Don. Not for the first time,' said Gene after Rosie closed the door.

'How can we have interesting discussions if we don't identify common domains?'

'I don't know, Don. But Rosie is not fond of geneticists telling psychologists what to do. Case in point, me. Second case in point, you.'

I explained how the Lesbian Mothers Project would provide me with valuable knowledge relevant to parenthood.

'Good work,' said Gene. 'You can tell her how to do motherhood as well as psychology.' He put his hands up in dual stop signs. 'I'm being sarcastic. You do *not* want to tell her how to be a mother. If you learn something from the project, wonderful, but surprise her with your skills rather than beating her over the head with your knowledge.'

Gene recommended that I not raise the topic of the Lesbian Mothers Project again.

21

The Good Fathers Program was scheduled for Wednesday, 9 October on the Upper West Side. As with the Paedophile Assessment, I was astonished at how long it had taken to deliver support to a potentially dangerous person.

I told Rosie that I had organised a boys' night out and, in the interests of minimising deception, called Dave and invited him to participate. Gene was having dinner with Inge.

'I ought to catch up on some work,' Dave said. 'I've got a pile of paperwork this high.'

Obviously, I was unable to see whatever signals Dave was making to indicate the height of the pile, but I had a strong argument.

'I recommend you do something baby-related,' I said. 'Sonia is unimpressed by your lack of interest. She considers it a result of your focus on work. Which you are currently demonstrating.'

'She told you that? When?'

'I don't remember.'

'Don. There's a lot of things you do, but forgetting isn't one of them.'

'We had coffee.'

'She never told me.'

'You probably failed to ask. Or were too busy with work. I'll meet you at 42nd Street A-Train uptown platform at 6.47 p.m. and we can attend together. I've estimated thirteen minutes for travel to the venue.'

'I figured.'

The class was held in a room attached to a church. Dave and I were joined by fourteen other men, including the convenor, age approximately fifty-five, estimated BMI twenty-eight, appearance notable for the combination of frontal baldness and very long hair, plus a beard. The evening was warm, and he was wearing a t-shirt that made it apparent he had invested heavily in tattoos.

He introduced himself to the class as Jack, and explained that he had been a member of a motorcycle club, had spent time in jail and at one time had a bad attitude to women. It was quite a long speech but omitted some important information. I assumed he was being modest. When he asked if anyone had questions, I raised my hand.

'What are your professional qualifications?'

He laughed. 'The university of life. The school of hard knocks.'

I would have liked more information as to the disciplines, but did not want to dominate question time. As it turned out, nobody else asked anything, and it was our turn to introduce ourselves. Everyone provided only their names. Due to mumbling, Jack had to ask several times for a name to be repeated before he could match it on his list. When Dave's turn came, Jack shook his head.

'You're not on the list. Don't worry, they screw this up all the time. Spell your name for me, slowly.'

Dave provided the information.

'Bechler. Yugoslavian?'

'Serbo-Croatian, I think. Way back.'

'We get quite a few Serbs. Something in the genes. Not that I want to encourage stereotypes. Any other Serbs here?'

No hands went up.

'Your wife's pregnant?'

'Yes.'

'Who told you to come here?'

Dave indicated me.

Jack looked at me for a few moments. 'You're his buddy?'

'Correct.'

'You brought him along because you thought it'd be good for him?'

'Correct.'

'Smart move, Don. If we all looked after our buddies like Don here, there'd be a lot less mothers showing up at the emergency room, a lot less babies shaken to death by men who won't ever be able to look at themselves in the mirror again.'

Dave appeared more shaken than the hypothetical baby.

'Now,' said Jack. 'Everybody's here for a reason, including Dave. You've all done something to someone that you probably regret. I want to hear about it, and I want to know how you feel about it now. Who's first?'

There was silence. Jack turned to Dave. 'Dave, you look like –'

I interrupted. I needed to save Dave from being revealed as a non-violent imposter.

'I'm willing to commence.'

'All right, Don. Tell us what you've done.'

'Which incident?'

'Sounds like there's been a few.'

Few was accurate. There had been three in my adult life, but the frequency had increased recently.

'Correct. Two in the past month. Prompted by the pregnancy.'

'That's not good, Don. Maybe they're a bit raw to think about now. Maybe go back a little, to an incident you've had time to do some thinking about. Do you understand what I'm saying?'

'Of course. You're suggesting that analysis of recent events may lack a broader context and be clouded by emotions.'

'Yeah. That. So go back a bit.'

'I was at a restaurant. My costume was criticised. There was an altercation which escalated, and two security personnel attempted to restrain me. I responded with the minimum force needed to disable them.'

One of the other men interrupted. 'You took out two bouncers?'

'You're an Aussie, right?' This was another student. 'You took out two Aussie bouncers?'

'Correct and correct. I disabled them in self-defence.'

'Two guys diss his threads and *bam. Bam, bam, bam.*' The student performed a punching action in time with his bams.

'No bamming was required. I used a low-impact throw and a simple hold.'

'Judo?'

'Aikido. I am also proficient in karate, but the aikido is safer in these situations. I used aikido on the neighbour who damaged my clothing –'

'Do *not* mess with this man's threads.' The student was laughing.

'– and on the police officer –'

'You threw a cop? Not here? In New York? Where was his partner?'

Jack interrupted. 'I guess there were consequences for Don. Whoever won the fight, you got arrested, right?'

'Correct.'

'And then?'

'Total disaster. Threat of criminal prosecution, deportation, lack of access to my child, restrictions on working with children, forced attendance . . . And the necessity of deceiving my wife, which is incredibly stressful and has unpredictable consequences.'

'You were too ashamed to tell your wife what you'd done, right? That you'd got yourself into trouble again.'

I nodded. Although my justification for not telling Rosie had been to protect her from stress, there was some truth in Jack's observation.

Jack addressed the group. 'Doesn't sound so clever now, does it? We all get angry and we fuck up. Why? What makes us angry?'

Again, nobody raised his hand. I could empathise with Jack. It was like the first class of the semester with new students. As a fellow teacher, it was my responsibility to help Jack out.

'To understand anger,' I began, 'it is necessary first to understand aggression, and its evolutionary value.' I continued for approximately a minute. I had not even begun to explain the consequent evolution and internalisation of anger as an emotion when Jack stopped me.

'That'll do for now, Professor.' The use of the formal title was encouraging. I was surely the top student at this point, and I could not see any challengers. 'We're going to take a break, and afterwards I'm going to be looking for some contributions from the rest of you. Don, you've earned your gold star and you can shut the fuck up.'

Everyone laughed. I was class clown again.

Most of the students walked outside and the requirement for the break became obvious. Several, including Jack, were nicotine addicts. I stood in the courtyard drinking my instant coffee with Dave.

One of the students, a man of about twenty-three, BMI approximately twenty-seven as a result of muscle rather than fat, approached us, dropped his cigarette, and stamped it out with his boot.

'Wanna show us some moves?' he said.

'We will be returning inside shortly,' I said. 'Exercise

will make us hot and uncomfortable and unpleasant to others.'

He performed some shadow-boxing moves. 'C'mon. I wanna see what you can do. Beside talk.'

This was not the first time someone had challenged me to demonstrate my martial-arts skills. I did not need Jack's advice to know that it was unwise to spar with an unknown opponent in poor light with no protection. Fortunately I had a standard solution. I stepped a few paces away to create some space, removed my shoes and also my shirt to minimise the perspiration problem, then performed a *kata* I had prepared for my 3rd Dan karate grading. It requires four minutes and nineteen seconds. The students gathered in a circle to watch and at the end clapped and made noises of appreciation.

Jack walked up beside me and addressed the group. 'This stuff's pretty, but nobody's invincible.' Without any warning, he grabbed me in a chokehold. It was competently executed, and I suspected he had used it many times with success. I predicted that this was the first time he had applied it to a 4th Dan aikido practitioner.

The safest defence is prevention and I automatically moved to block him from applying the hold. Part way through the manoeuvre, which would have ended with him immobilised on the ground, I made a decision to allow Jack to complete the hold. He was attempting to illustrate a point, and my action would undermine his lesson. I expected that Jack would hold me for a few moments to demonstrate the technique's effectiveness and then release me.

Before he could do so, a strange voice said, 'That's enough. Let him go. Now.' The voice was strange because it was Dave doing his Marlon Brando–Woody Allen combination. Jack let me go, looked at Dave, and nodded.

Dave was shaking.

We returned to class, and I followed Jack's instruction to shut the fuck up. Nobody else spoke much at all. Jack's advice on self-control consisted of two principles, repeated numerous times:

1. Don't get drunk (or consume methamphetamines).
2. Walk away.

They had zero relevance to my interaction with the police, but there was a clear connection to my meltdown problem, though on the most recent occasion I had run rather than walked. What if it was infeasible to walk away? What if I was in a lifeboat after a shipwreck? Or in a space station? I needed Jack's advice, but was under instructions to remain silent.

I whispered to Dave, 'Ask what to do if you can't walk away.'

'No.'

'It's further practice for self-confidence,' I said. Dave had stopped shaking.

He put his hand up. 'What should someone do if they can't walk away?'

'Why wouldn't you be able to walk away?' said Jack.

Dave was silent. I was about to offer assistance when

229

he said, 'Maybe I'm minding the baby, and I have an anger attack. I can't leave because I need to look after it.'

'Dave, if you can walk away, walk away. Better to leave the baby for a while. But you need to calm down fast, that's what I'm hearing. So, deep breathing, try to visualise a relaxing scene, talk to yourself, say a calming word or sentence over and over.'

Jack made us all choose a calming phrase, and practise saying it multiple times. Dave began saying *calm, calm*. It struck me that the word might have a paradoxical effect: it reminded me of someone trying to shut me down. The man on the other side of me began chanting in a language I could not identify, but one of the words triggered an association, due to its similarity to Ramanujan, the name of the eminent Indian mathematician. The Hardy–Ramanujan number is the lowest natural number that can be expressed as the sum of two cubes in two different ways. Mathematics. The unassailable world of rationality. As Jack passed, I was repeating the name of the number in the same tone as my chanting neighbour. The technique seemed to have the required effect; I felt distinctly relaxed. I mentally filed it for future use.

At the end of the class, Jack asked me to stay. 'I want to know something. Could you have got out of that chokehold?'

'Yes.'

'Show me.'

He applied the chokehold and I demonstrated, without actual impact, three techniques for breaking it. I also showed him how to prevent it being applied, and a refinement which made it more secure.

'Thanks. Good to know,' he said. 'I shouldn't have done that, out there, you know. Bad example. Solving a problem with violence.'

'What problem?'

'Forget it. No problem. You ever hit a woman or a kid?'

'No.'

'I figured. You embarrassed a cop and they threw the book at you. Wasting my fucking time again. Ever thrown the first punch in a fight?'

'Only in class. There have been three external confrontations, none of which required striking, excluding one with my father-in-law which took place in a gymnasium with appropriate equipment.'

'Your father-in-law. Jesus. Who won?'

'There was no judge or referee, but he suffered a broken nose.'

'Look me in the eye and tell me you're never going to hit a woman or kid. Ever.'

Dave had been listening. 'Better he doesn't look you in the eye.'

'Go on,' said Jack.

I looked directly into Jack's eyes, while I repeated the promise.

'Jesus,' said Jack. 'I see what you mean.' But he was laughing. 'I'm in deep shit if I give anyone an early pass out of this class and they reoffend, but I think I'm safe with you. Better for both of us.'

'I don't need to come back?'

'You're not *allowed* to come back. I'll tell your social worker you've graduated.'

He turned to Dave. 'I can't make you come back, but you ought to think about it. You're dealing with some dangerous thoughts.'

Dave and I detoured via a bar before going to our respective homes, as I would have aroused suspicion if I returned from a boys' night out without smelling of alcohol. Dave had similarly not told Sonia about the Good Fathers Program.

'There's no reason not to tell Sonia,' I said.

'Best she doesn't know. Men's business.'

Sonia of course knew about the Good Fathers Program, but she couldn't tell Dave without revealing the Rosie impersonation.

Rosie was in bed but not asleep when I arrived home. 'How was your night?' she asked.

I had solved one part of the problem arising from the Playground Incident and gained new knowledge. Dave had increased his self-confidence in dealing with conflict, although he had needed two burgers to recover from the trauma.

I wanted to tell Rosie all about it, but everything led back to the Playground Incident and Lydia. The potential of the revelation to cause stress had diminished, but I was now worried that a full explanation would reveal Lydia's assessment of my competence in the father role, and increase Rosie's own doubts.

'Excellent,' I said. 'Nothing to report.'

'Likewise,' she said.

The martial-arts demonstration had reminded me of Carl and his attempts to surprise me with a punch. The routine had been mandatory on visits to Gene and Claudia's, and inevitably ended with Carl immobilised and minor damage to decorative objects. Now, there was a risk that Carl's punching ability would be applied to his father.

'Have you spoken to Carl yet?' I asked Gene the following evening.

Gene had purchased some port, which had three advantages over cocktail ingredients:

1. Existence. We had largely exhausted the supplies of anything alcoholic, except George's beer.
2. Improved taste. Some cocktail ingredients are not palatable by themselves.
3. Lower alcohol than spirits. I had identified alcohol as the likely cause of recurrent morning headaches.

'Carl won't speak to me. Believe me, I've tried. There's no way past the fact that I was unfaithful to his mother.'

'There's always a way.'

'Maybe with time. But it's my problem, not yours.'

'Incorrect. Rosie wants you to leave, hence I am required to ask you to leave. The best solution is that you return to Claudia, but you can't until we solve the Carl problem.'

'Apologise to Rosie on my behalf. I'm working on somewhere to live. I'd give anything to sort out the situation with Carl, but I can't change the past.'

'We're scientists,' I reminded him. 'We shouldn't be defeated by problems. If we think hard enough, a solution will present itself.'

22

The Lesbian Mothers Project protocols were straight-forward to review. The obvious limitation was the absence of a control group of heterosexual couples or unrelated adults.

'There were no same-sex couples in the original study,' B2 said.

I had been instructed by B1 to conduct all liaisons with the team via B2 who had recently completed her PhD. 'That was an exploratory study,' I said.

'This is an exploratory study, too. We're entitled to equal consideration.'

My police clearance had come through, presumably because Margarita Cop was still holding my report, pending advice from Lydia, and I was now permitted to observe the experiments.

The B Team had constructed a small living room with sofa and armchairs. The protocol was trivially simple: B3, the nurse, took a sample of oxytocin from the baby; then one of the baby's carers cuddled the baby. B3 then took another sample. At a later time, the carer would return and repeat the exercise, except that this time she would play with the baby rather than cuddling it. Then the experiment would be repeated with the second mother.

'What are the early results?' I asked B1.

'You of all people should know that it's inappropriate to draw conclusions based on early raw data. Don't you have mice to dissect? Seriously, we've got a women's group visiting this afternoon and it'd be nice if you weren't hanging around.'

B3 had been watching. 'Can I buy you a coffee?' she said.

'It's 3.13 p.m. Caffeine has a half-life –'

She turned, but intercepted me again outside the front door. 'You want to know what the early data is saying? I'll meet you at the café.'

Secrets, secrets, secrets. Rosie didn't know why I was working on the project. She didn't know about the Playground Incident, Lydia, and the Good Fathers Evaluation. Gene had deceived Claudia for years. Now B3 was sharing data that B1 would not. Once, there had been no secrets in my life. And my relationships, albeit few, had not been in danger. I suspected a correlation.

'I'm taking the samples and I have to key in all the results,' said B3. 'The first job's because I'm a nurse. So's the second. So's getting the coffee, for that matter. But you don't need a PhD to see what's happening. The oxytocin goes up with cuddling, doesn't move with play. For either mother. Looks like only fathers can make the play thing happen. They're changing the way they do the play so it's more like cuddling. Not when you're around, of course. They'll find a reason to dump the early results.'

I walked back with B3.

236

'Maybe come back tomorrow,' she said. 'Briony's a bit edgy.' B1.

In a social situation, I would have taken the subtle hint that I was not wanted. But this was science. Sometimes it is convenient to be immune to subtlety.

When I returned, a group of thirteen women was being greeted. B1 and B2 ignored me, but one of the women (age approximately sixty-five, BMI twenty-six) approached me directly.

'Are you the token male?' She laughed.

I used David Borenstein's words. 'I've been assigned by the Dean to ensure that the research is not influenced by lesbian politics.'

She laughed again. I detected friendliness. 'What did you do to earn that job? Sleep with the Dean's daughter?'

B1 interrupted and pointed to a woman with a baby beside her in a mid-quality pram. 'When the baby wakes up, this woman is going to play with her baby, and we're going to measure the baby's oxytocin. She's the non-gestational mother, and we're finding that the baby's oxytocin rises when she plays with the baby. Just as it did for fathers in the Israeli study.'

I added, 'In the Israeli study there was no control group of unrelated males or females, so there is no evidence that the men and women had to be parents or carers in order to raise the oxytocin levels.'

B1 looked at me in a way that Rosie would look at someone if she meant 'Shut the fuck up'. I suspected the meaning was the same. But the situation was not. Science is about honesty and transparency.

Friendly Woman asked, 'What would happen to the baby's oxytocin if an unrelated man or woman played with it?'

'Exactly!' I said.

B1 interrupted. 'It's not part of the study. And we can't have strange men coming in here and touching the babies.'

The baby in the pram began crying. I had to act quickly before any cuddling or play process commenced. I ran over to the pram.

'Is it all right if I play with your baby?' I asked the mother. 'I'm a member of the research team and I am approved by the police for baby handling.'

'I guess.' She smiled. 'I thought it was going to be me, but sure. If you don't upset him.'

I had no idea about how a baby might react to a large adult male. I had never handled one, except possibly my brother. I had a vague recollection of my mother giving Trevor to me to hold, and of handing him back to her as quickly as possible.

I realised it was critical not to drop or threaten the baby. I solved both problems by lying on my back before the mother gave it to me. I steadied it with my hands and let it crawl over me. My human body repulsion reflex did not activate. It was great fun, and the baby was making hilarious noises. Women in the visitor group were taking photos. We continued for approximately two minutes, then I looked around for B3. I waved to her and she put down the video camera.

'Test please.' I suspected my own oxytocin levels had risen, but only the baby's were relevant.

'No,' said B1. 'It's not part of the protocol.'

'Incorrect,' I said. 'The protocol is modified so as not to exclude serendipitous data, this being an exploratory study. Or the protocol will not be approved by the medical school.'

Friendly Woman smiled and nodded.

B3 opened the baby's mouth and took the swab. The mother let me play with the baby for another minute.

The pram I had ordered arrived in my absence. Rosie had unpacked it and now insisted we return it.

'Don, you know I'm not girly and I'm not into frilly baby stuff, but this is like some sort of industrial-military . . . tank. The Hummer of prams.'

'World's safest pram.' I meant this literally. The base model had been the safest available, and I had augmented it with numerous custom enhancements. I was confident Bud would be unhurt in a rollover, and would survive a low-speed automobile encounter, particularly if he or she was wearing the helmet I had purchased as an accessory. The only negatives were an increase in size and some complexity in access to the baby. And, of course, cost.

'Is appearance more important than safety?' I asked.

Rosie ignored the question. 'Don, I appreciate you're trying, I appreciate it a lot, but this just isn't you, is it?

Babies aren't really your thing. Prams, big metal prams with rubber bumpers, are more your thing.'

'I don't know. I have limited experience with both.'

My chances of increasing my experience through the Lesbian Mothers Project were looking poor. The protocol change I had suggested, involving each baby having a 'crawl over Don' experience, was subject to approval from the mothers. After my initial success, all had refused. I gave B2 and B3 my phone number in case any changed their minds.

'Don't stay up waiting for a call,' said B2.

But B3 sent me a text message: *Oxytocin through the roof on your intervention. Highest result from play activity. And you're not even a carer!*

The implication was that my gender had affected the result, but a single instance was of value only to prompt further investigation.

B1 wrote to David Borenstein, and did not copy the email to me.

'Just skim it,' said the Dean, indicating his computer screen.

I am not accustomed to skimming. Skimming involves ignoring some words. What if I ignored a *not?* It was a long message, but I noted the words *unprofessional, disruptive* and *insensitive*.

'Basically, she wants you off the study, and she says they're discarding the one-off result because it didn't fit the protocol, was not serendipitous but was the outcome of a deliberate intervention, blah blah.'

'Did she say what the result was?'

'She implied they hadn't tested it. Fat chance. If it had tested low, she'd have been falling over herself to include it.'

'Terrible science.'

'Agreed. I made a good call putting you on the job, didn't I?'

'It's possible that a person who cared about appropriate social behaviour would have given it priority over the research objective.'

The Dean laughed.

'I have to say, Professor Tillman, you're a fine scientist, but I sometimes wonder how Rosie copes.'

Rosie was not coping well with me.

One of the curious things about animals, including humans, is that we spend approximately one-third of our lives sleeping. There is no practical way around this inefficiency. In my twenties, I had conducted a series of trials to establish my minimum sleep requirement, and had settled on scheduling seven hours and eighteen minutes per night, excluding all light from the bedroom, and never using amphetamines again.

As we age, we sleep less soundly: one evolutionary explanation is that in the ancestral environment the young hunters and warriors required undisturbed sleep, while the older members of the tribe acted as watchdogs and needed to be woken by the slightest noise.

In sleep terms, Rosie was already a watchdog. She woke frequently, and exacerbated the problem by visiting the toilet and making herself a cup of hot chocolate, which of course began a vicious circle. Before she was pregnant Rosie would sometimes go to bed early, exhausted or intoxicated; on other occasions she would study until after 1.00 a.m. and come to bed animated and even wanting to initiate a conversation. At 1.00 a.m.! Sometimes she would also be interested in sex, in which case I accommodated the change to my routine and scheduled additional sleep for the following night.

I had become accustomed to being woken, and generally managed to fall asleep again within a few minutes. But the aggregate effect could not be ignored and I was forced to reschedule my bedtime to thirteen minutes earlier.

The pregnancy aggravated the problem. As predicted by The Book, the expanding baby and its associated support system had reduced Rosie's bladder capacity. And Rosie had begun snoring, not loudly but enough to be disruptive. I had to reschedule bedtime again.

We had a discussion about the problem at 3.14 a.m.

'You shouldn't have had the hot chocolate. It's going to recreate the toilet problem. And then you'll have another hot chocolate –'

'The hot chocolate helps me sleep.'

'Ridiculous. Chocolate contains caffeine. Caffeine is a stimulant with a four-hour half-life. It's inadvisable to drink coffee or eat chocolate after 3.00 p.m. I never –'

'*You* never. I know you never. But I do. It's my body, remember?'

'Caffeine is a restricted substance.'

'I'm allowed two coffees. I'm off coffee, so this makes up.'

'Have you calculated the caffeine in the chocolate?'

'No. I'm not going to, either. How about I solve your problem? And my problem too.'

Rosie pulled the duvet from the bed and walked out.

Now my own body rebelled and refused to sleep. I used the time to reflect on Rosie's departure. Was it for one night or permanently? Rationally, it was a good solution to the problem, which was at least in part temporary. After the pregnancy was over, Rosie could begin sleeping normally again. For now, we would need to purchase another bed. Then I realised that Rosie had nowhere to sleep: there was no other bed in the house. *Unless she was sleeping with Gene.*

I jumped from the bed and tiptoed towards Gene's room. Rosie's study door was open and she was curled up in an armchair, covered by the duvet. She did not move. I returned to the bedroom, dragged the mattress off the bed, and manoeuvred it into Rosie's study, which was considerably bigger than our bedroom. Rosie woke.

'Don? What are you doing?'

'Creating a temporary bed.'

'Oh. I thought –'

She did not complete her thought, but half staggered from the chair to the mattress and lay down. I covered her with the duvet and returned to the bedroom, where I succeeded in sleeping on the padded bed base. It was perfectly satisfactory, and my karate teacher would doubtless regard it as good discipline. In fact, the bed had been a compromise between Rosie's personal desire for softness and the optimum firmness as recommended by scientific studies. I had now created an arrangement more satisfactory to both of us.

Rosie obviously agreed, as she continued to sleep in her study every night, and I reinstated my original sleeping hours.

23

I had the spaceship nightmare again. It was, as far as I could remember, exactly the same, with the same fatal result. Except this time, when I woke up, Rosie was not there.

Gene was also concerned by the change in sleeping arrangements, which he noticed two days later. In his analysis, Rosie sleeping in the other room equated to a rejection of me.

'Be practical, Don. Why do people sleep together?'

'Sex.' It was always likely to be the correct answer to a question from Gene about motivation. 'Which is not required by evolution now that she is pregnant.'

'Too glib, my friend. Humans conceal their fertility to encourage ongoing closeness. For all sorts of reasons. We may not be monogamous, but we're all about pair-bonding and Rosie is sending you a big message.'

'What have I done wrong?'

'Let me tell you, Don, you're not the first man to ask that question. Usually after he's come home to find the television gone.'

'We don't own a television.'

'So I've noticed. Whose idea was that?'

'There's no requirement for a television. Higher-quality news is available from other media without advertisements; movies are available on bigger screens in theatres, and for all other requirements we have individual computer monitors.'

'That's not what I asked. Whose *idea* was it?'

'The decision was obvious.'

'Did Rosie ever mention buying a television?'

'Possibly. But her arguments were flawed. You're suggesting that our marriage is in trouble because of the lack of a television? If so, I can –'

'I suspect it goes a bit deeper than that. But if you want a specific answer to the question "What did I do wrong?", then it's the ultrasound. You should have gone. That's the point where Rosie started to wonder if you really wanted to be a father. Not whether you were capable, which is another matter, but whether you were even *interested*.'

'How can you be so certain?'

'I'm the head of a psychology department, you've already confided in me about your own doubts, which Rosie will surely have picked up on, and I'm aware that Rosie's own background includes a problematic father situation.'

'That problem was solved.'

'Don, problems that originate in childhood are never *solved*. Psychotherapists make a living out of that.'

'What if you're wrong and there is no problem? I may create a problem by responding to an imaginary one. Like falling over because you think there's a step and there isn't one.'

Gene stood up, walked to his office door, looked out,

then returned. 'There's a saying among wine experts: a glance at the label is worth twenty years' experience.'

'You're being obscure.'

'Rosie told me. She said the two of you were going through a rough patch and she wasn't sure you wanted to be a father.'

'She volunteered the information about the state of our marriage? Unprompted?'

'I asked her. Actually, Stefan gave me a bit of a heads-up.'

Stefan! Now Rosie was sharing critical data with him rather than the person who could make best use of it.

Although the method of transmission was frustratingly indirect, the identification of the Ultrasound Error was excellent input into improving my competence as a prospective father and demonstrating my interest to Rosie.

Gene's advice was that I should have attended the examination with a knowledge of the procedure and its possible outcomes. Fortunately, I had a second chance. Rosie had agreed to an exact date for the second sonogram: Twenty-two weeks, zero days and zero hours from the nominal beginning of gestation, which had been established at the first appointment as Monday, 20 May. I calculated the date – 21 October – and reserved the entire day in my schedule. This time I would be prepared.

I studied The Book for further events that might offer similar potential for error, or for compensatory high performance. There was one obvious example – the birth. The parallels with the sonogram appointment were striking:

1. Attendance at a specialist facility.
2. A critical point at which problems might be identified.
3. A low probability of problems, but high anxiety.
4. Expected presence of the partner despite him or her having no role in the procedure.

From The Book and further research, the best description that I could formulate of my role was 'reduce partner's anxiety'. This could be achieved through familiarity with the birth process so that the partner could be informed at all times as to what was happening while she concentrated on execution of the procedure. Knowledge is something I am good at. As a medical student, Rosie would have a basic understanding, but I planned to become an expert on birth, including the full range of possible complications and outcomes. I reopened *Dewhurst's Textbook of Obstetrics and Gynaecology* and renewed my efforts to supplement theory with practice.

After multiple requests to assist with or even merely observe an actual birth, David Borenstein finally gave me contact details for Dr Lauren McTighe, who was based in Connecticut.

She called on a Saturday evening as the boys' group finished take-out pizza at George's. I explained the situation to my companions and, to my surprise, not only Dave but also George and Gene decided to join us.

'You don't need the knowledge,' I said.

'Male bonding,' said George. 'Isn't that what we're supposed to be about?'

I called Lauren back to ensure that their presence would not be a problem.

'If you want. But you better warn them about the complications. It may not have a happy ending.'

We hailed a taxi and I gave the driver Dave's address so we could collect his vehicle.

'Bugger that,' said George. 'This is an emergency, right?'

'A breech birth,' I said. 'Apparently there are additional problems. I'm expecting to learn a great deal.'

'We're going straight to Lakeville, Connecticut,' said George to the taxi driver. 'I want you to wait and drive us back.'

'I don't take this cab anywhere past –'

George, who was in the front seat, gave the driver some money held together by a rubber band, and the driver was silent as he counted it. He did not object further.

It was hard to believe that George had acquired such wealth during the brief period that the Dead Kings had been popular almost fifty years ago. I assumed that, being a rock musician, he would have wasted the majority on illicit drugs. His payment of the taxi driver provided a good opportunity to ask.

'Where do you get all your money from?'

'That's what I like about you, Don. Straight to the point.'

Being straight to the point is what people generally *don't* like about me.

'Straight question, straight answer,' said George. 'Alimony.'

Gene laughed. 'Let me guess. You had to work so hard to pay off four wives that you accidently ended up making some for yourself. Or one of them died and the quarter you got back was enough to live like a king.'

'Close enough,' said George. 'My first wife died three years ago. Cancer. I left her when the band started to get noticed. Thought I could do better. Rock star and all. I never really did. I could say they were all the same, but the problem was *I* was all the same. When you have the same problem with four women, you start to think it might have something to do with you.'

'Not sure how that helped financially,' said Gene. 'You're not saying she left you all her money?'

'I *am* saying that. Not all of it, but enough. I had to pay two-thirds of my income to her back in the day, and when we had a few hits that turned out to be quite a bit. I was pissing my third up against the wall and she was buying property. When she died she left half of it for me.'

'Very generous of her,' said Gene.

'It was me or our son. He's already blown his share. She must've seen that coming; left some to me so I could bail him out. She was no Jerry Hall, but I never did any better. Take note, young Donald.'

I had taken note. George's advice, generalised and

then particularised for my situation, seemed clear. If I couldn't make it with Rosie, I couldn't make it with anyone. If my marriage failed, I would not try again. My choice was Rosie or the remainder of my life without a partner. Or a child.

The journey took two hours and sixteen minutes, eight minutes longer than predicted by my navigation application.

'You're just in time,' said Lauren (age approximately forty-five, BMI twenty-three). 'I've been holding off till you arrived, but she's in quite a bit of distress and I couldn't leave it much longer. This is Ben.'

She indicated a man in a checked shirt (age approximately forty, BMI thirty) standing a few metres away. He came over and we shook hands according to convention. His hand was extremely sweaty; I diagnosed anxiety. It was a good opportunity to practise my reassurance techniques.

'The mother's survival prospects are close to 100 per cent, although the difficult birth may result in a temporary reduction in fertility. The baby's survival probability is approximately eighty-five per cent.'

Ben looked relieved. 'Not bad odds,' he said. 'Fingers crossed.'

George looked at the mother. 'Poor cow,' he said.

Lauren was brilliant! It is always fascinating to watch a competent professional at work. She explained exactly what she was doing, and provided additional commentary on alternative possibilities and procedures. George held a halogen light powered from the battery in Lauren's vehicle while I assisted her to alter the position of the calf. The cow was held in a corral, hence unable to move far.

It was aesthetically unpleasant work, but I was familiar with the necessary mindset from dissecting mice and the intellectual stimulation exceeded the unpleasantness. It was so interesting!

Gene talked with Ben. Dave, who was not feeling well, sat in the taxi.

'All right,' said Lauren. 'We're going to need the tractor.'

Lauren reached inside the cow and explained that she was attaching a chain to the unborn calf's feet. George gave the light to Gene and began talking to the mother, who was making noises indicating distress.

Ben attached the other end of the chain to the tractor, and the pulling process began. In a human birth, forceps would have taken the place of the tractor. Or – more likely – a caesarean would have been performed. Nevertheless there were numerous anatomical similarities, and the three-dimensional experience was invaluable.

'All right, Don. You're going to have to help me catch it.' Fortunately 'catching' did not require the coordination of catching a ball – Lauren and I merely had to take the weight of the calf as it emerged. It did, along with vast quantities of fluid, drenching both of us. It was extremely slippery but we managed to avoid dropping it. One leg was at an odd angle, but the calf began breathing. The mother was still standing.

'Broken leg,' said Lauren. 'What do you want to do?'

'What do you think?' said Ben.

'I'm afraid it's probably best to put it down, unless you want to hand feed it.'

Dave staggered from the taxi. 'Don't shoot it. I'll take it home if I have to.'

My immediate thought was that this was a brilliant idea. Dave and Sonia's baby would have its immune system strengthened by cohabiting with a farm animal. But a moment's reflection revealed multiple problems with raising a lame calf in a New York apartment.

Ben smiled. 'I owe you guys. What's your name, again?'

'Dave.'

'Okay, Dave, meet Dave the calf. He owes you his life. And Lauren – all you guys. My wife'll feed him. She'll curse you every day.'

24

After making a phone call for advice, George commanded the taxi to detour via a bar in White Plains. It was 10.35 p.m. and we had not eaten. I was wearing clothes lent to me by Ben the Farmer to replace those soaked during the delivery of Dave the Calf.

'Beer tonight,' said George. He ordered four. We drank them rapidly and George ordered more.

'I'll let you in on a secret,' he said. 'Looking after that poor cow was good karma. Made up a wee bit for not being at the birth of my first kid.'

'The one with the thrifty mother?' said Gene.

'That's the one. I was on the road.' He paused. 'They rang the hotel and I was with a groupie. That's the way it was back then.'

I was amazed. 'You were having sex with another woman while your wife gave birth to your son?'

'How did you know it was a boy?'

'You mentioned it earlier. And it's on the internet.'

'I've got no bloody secrets. Except what I just told you.'

'We should all share a secret,' said Gene. 'One each. Tell us one of yours, Don.'

'A secret?' In the sixteen weeks since the Playground Incident, I had accumulated multiple secrets, but it seemed unwise to disclose any after drinking beer. Conversely, George's decision to share an example of morally repugnant behaviour seemed to be a gesture of friendship, allowing each of us to disclose something immoral or illegal and receive advice from the others, knowing that our behaviour was unlikely to be as shameful as George's. It was a subtle social manoeuvre, but my analysis had taken some time.

'I'll go first, then,' said Gene. 'But this goes no further, all right?'

George made us perform a ludicrous four-handed handshake.

'Guess how many women I've slept with.'

'Less than me,' said George. 'If you can count them, it's less than me.'

'More than me,' I said.

Gene laughed. 'Go on.'

I remembered Gene's map, with a pin for each nationality. I allowed for a further fifty per cent to accommodate multiple women of the same origin and more recent conquests.

'Thirty-six.'

'Way off.' Gene drank some more beer, then held up an open hand. 'Five.'

I was astonished. Was Gene lying? It was a reasonable hypothesis, given that, if he was not lying now, he must have lied repeatedly in the past. Perhaps, being unable to compete with George for the highest total, he was aiming to be the least promiscuous.

Dave also appeared astonished. Astonishment was the appropriate reaction. 'Five?' he said. 'I mean, that's –'

'– less than you, right?' Gene was smiling.

'I don't cheat on my wife, but –'

It was only four more than me! 'What about the open marriage? What about the map?'

'The open marriage never got off the ground. The first woman had issues. Bunny-boiling types of issues. I had enough of that with my first wife.'

'Game isn't worth the candle,' said George.

'Not at this age, anyway,' said Gene.

'What about the map?' I asked – again. There were twenty-four pins in Gene's map before he had temporarily reformed and pulled it down. 'What about Icelandic Woman?'

'I buy dinner. If they're up for having dinner one-on-one, I reckon that's a date. You don't go out to dinner by yourself with a married man unless you're up for it. The rest would follow if I wanted it to.'

This was incredible. The consequences of Gene lying to make his behaviour appear *worse* than it was had been disastrous. I pointed out the obvious.

'Claudia threw you out because you admitted to having sex with Icelandic Woman. But you only purchased dinner. Correct?'

'Actually, I had to fight her off. She was – what is it you say, George?'

'No Jerry Hall?'

Gene laughed.

I brought the discussion back on track. 'So tell

256

Claudia the truth and she'll accept you back. All problems solved.'

'It's not as easy as that.'

'Why not?'

We all looked at Gene. Nobody spoke. We were acting like therapists. I was wishing that I could fix the Rosie problem simply by telling the truth.

'I doubt Claudia would have any interest in me if I wasn't who she thinks I am. It's part of why she's attracted to me.'

'She's attracted to you because you cheat?' I said. 'All theories . . . *your* theories –'

'Women like men who can attract other women. They need to be reminded that they've got someone other women want. Look at George. All that form didn't stop you finding three more wives.'

'If I hadn't had the form, maybe I could have got by with one. But Don's got a fair point – there's nothing to lose by coming clean.'

'It's deeper than that. We let it go too long, till it was past saving. If I look back, it was after Eugenie was born. I started playing the game, even if I didn't take it all the way. You can't neglect a marriage for nine years and expect to go back. Anyway, I've found someone else.'

'Who?'

'You know who. I've shared my secret.' He turned to Dave. 'What about you?'

Dave looked back at Gene. 'You'll understand what this means. The baby's not mine.'

257

We were stunned into being therapists again and waited for Dave to speak.

'We did the IVF thing, and I've got some problems. Some to do with the weight, some not. So in the end it was her egg and some other guy's wriggler.'

I presumed *wriggler* was a synonym for sperm and not penis.

'Now I'm wondering if me not being around, working late – all the stuff Sonia complains about – is because I don't want to put time into some kid who doesn't have my genes. I mean, subconsciously.' He looked at Gene. 'Like you said.'

'Shit,' said Gene. 'There's nothing wrong with working hard to earn a dollar. '

'Funny,' said Dave. 'Until you told me about how the gene thing worked, I was afraid that Sonia would leave me. Now I realise I've got no more investment in our baby than I have in Dave the Calf. And if she figures that out, then why would she want me around?'

Gene laughed. 'Sorry, I'm not laughing at you. I'm laughing at the complexity of the whole business. Trust me, Sonia won't leave you because of that. The great thing about homo sapiens is that we've got a brain that can override our instincts. If we want it to.'

I had been so interested in the revelations from George, Gene and Dave – astonishing revelations – that I had not had time to think of one of my own. George saved me.

'Don told us his bit the other night, when he said he

was doing it hard with his marriage. Want to give us an update?'

'I'm acquiring knowledge of the birth process. I have professional-level expertise on the subject of attachment of babies to same-sex and mixed-sex couples, and the consequent impact on oxytocin levels. And I'm seeing a therapist to review progress.'

'How's the relationship?' said George.

'With Rosie?'

'That'd be the one.'

'No change. I haven't had a chance to apply the knowledge yet.'

We were all silent in the taxi on the way home. Two thoughts were occupying my mind: Gene's lies had cost him his marriage. And telling the truth could no longer save it.

When the elevator stopped at my floor, George asked if I had a few minutes to check something upstairs.

'It's extremely late,' I said, although I suspected I would have trouble sleeping. I had not drunk sufficient alcohol to counteract the effects of adrenaline from the excitement of Dave the Calf and, despite reinstating my original bedtime schedule, I had slept erratically since the removal of the mattress.

'It'll only take a few minutes,' he said.

'The alcohol will affect my judgement. Better to check in the morning.'

'All right,' said George. 'Guess I'll just do some drum practice to wind down.'

Gene was holding the elevator door open. 'George wants to talk to you "one on one",' he said. 'That's fine. Have a drink for me.'

I had no choice but to follow George to his apartment. He poured two large glasses of Balvenie twenty-one-year-old Scotch.

'Here's to you,' he said. 'I said I didn't want to be part of a men's group, but you've kept it going. None of us would bother if it wasn't for you calling up and making us put it in our *schedules* every week.'

'You're suggesting we abandon the group? That I'm the only one benefiting?'

'On the contrary. I'm just saying that these things need a champion or they drift apart. If it wasn't for Mr Jimmy, the Dead Kings would've been finished thirty years ago. And we'd all be the worse for it.'

I drank my Scotch. I assumed George had delivered his message, but he refilled our glasses. I suspected the second glass would solve the sleeping problem – possibly the standing problem.

'You know I said I didn't have any secrets?' he said.

I nodded.

'I lied. My son, the one whose birth I didn't get to. He's a drug addict. That's no secret. This is the secret. It was my fault. I caused it. He never even drank, didn't smoke. He was a jazz drummer. A bloody good drummer.'

'You consider that some failure in your parenting caused him to take addictive drugs?'

'It wasn't his genes, I can tell you that.' George took a long time to finish his glass of Scotch. I followed the therapist rule and stayed silent. George filled his glass again. 'I put him onto it. I goaded him into doing it. Told him he was afraid to try things, afraid to grab hold of life. Gene'll tell you why I did it.'

'I thought this was a secret. Do you want me to tell Gene?'

'No. But if you did, Gene would tell you I wanted to bring him down to my level. Unconsciously, I suppose. But not that unconsciously.'

George was now unambiguously distressed. I hoped I would not be required to put my arm – or arms – around him.

'So there you go,' he said. 'You're the only one who knows, besides me and him. He's never said a word against me.'

'Do you require help to solve the problem?'

'If I did, you'd be the first person I'd ask. Too late for that. I just wanted to tell someone who would see it straight, see it for what it is. If I'm going to be judged, I want to be judged by someone I respect.' He raised his glass as if in a toast, then consumed its contents. I followed his example.

'Ta for that,' he said. 'I owe you one. If you find a solution for drug addiction, let me know on the way to collecting your Nobel Prize. If I had to put my money on anyone to do it, you'd be my man.'

Our apartment was dark when I returned from George's. I had unpacked my wet clothes from the garbage bag, brushed my teeth and checked my schedule for the following day when a thought formed. I was compelled to act on it.

Gene was asleep and not happy to be woken.

'We need to call Carl,' I said.

'What? What's happened? Has something happened to Carl?'

'Something might. He may begin taking illicit drugs. Due to his mental state.'

Gene had provided an argument, albeit an unconvincing one, for not telling Claudia the truth. But it was obvious that the lie was causing Carl to hate Gene. Hate causes distress, potentially leading to mental and physical health problems. Adolescents are highly vulnerable. It was too late to save George's son, but we were in a position to save Carl.

'His mental state is based on an incorrect assumption about your behaviour. You need to correct it.'

'Save it for the morning.'

'It's 2.14 a.m. 5.14 p.m. in Melbourne. Perfect time to call.'

'I'm not dressed.'

This was true. Gene had been sleeping in his underwear, an unhealthy choice. I began to explain about the risk of *tinea cruris* but he interrupted.

'Let's get it done, then. Don't turn the video on.'

Calculon was online. I connected and she summoned Carl. I remained in text mode.

Greetings Carl. Gene (your father) wants to speak to you.

No thanks. Sorry Don, I know you're only trying to help.

He has a confession.

I don't want to hear any more about the stuff he's done. Goodnight.

Wait. He didn't have sex with multiple women. It was a lie.

What?

I judged this as the perfect moment to switch to video. Carl's face filled the screen. He had neglected his shaving, in the manner of Stefan, and looked capable of patricide.

'What are you saying?'

I punched Gene in the arm in what I considered a traditional signal to speak.

'Shit, that hurt, Don.'

'Give Carl the information.'

'Um, Carl, you should know I didn't sleep with all those women. I was just big-noting myself. Don't tell Claudia.'

There was silence. Then Carl said, 'You're such a loser,' and terminated the connection.

Gene began to stand up from the edge of the bath but, doubtless due to intoxication, fell back in on top of my clothes, which had been soaked in bovine amniotic fluid. They did not smell pleasant. Gene did not appear to be hurt, and from my position on the toilet it was easier to let him get out by himself.

Gene's yell as he fell into the bath must have woken Rosie. She opened the bathroom-office door and looked at us strangely, presumably because of Gene's attempts to exit the bath and my unfamiliar costume – Ben the

Farmer's trousers were too large for me and were held up by rope. Gene was, of course, in his underwear.

Rosie quickly turned away from Gene and looked at me. 'Have a good night?' she said.

'Excellent,' I replied. The large mammal delivery represented an important milestone in restoring our relationship.

Rosie did not seem interested in further conversation. Gene fell back in the bath.

'Sorry,' I said to Gene. 'I should not have classified the night as excellent. We appeared to make no impression on Carl.'

'I think you're wrong,' said Gene. 'He just needs time to think about it.'

I stood up, but Gene had not finished.

'Don, one day soon you're going to have a child of your own. You'll understand how far you'd go to protect your relationship with him or her.'

'Of course. I encouraged you to make maximum efforts to solve the Carl problem.'

'Then if you ever work out what I did, I hope you'll at least understand. Even if you don't forgive me.'

'What do you mean?'

'Carl wouldn't have believed that story coming from anyone but you.'

'Why aren't you at work?' asked Rosie on the Monday morning. It was 9.12 a.m. and she was preparing breakfast for herself. It appeared healthy, which was probably inevitable as the fridge contained only pregnancy-compatible foodstuffs. Her shape was, as expected, changing; it was currently consistent with the diagrams in The Book for the fifth month of pregnancy. I was seeing variations of the world's most beautiful woman. It was like listening to a new version of a favourite song. 'Satisfaction', sung by Cat Power.

'I've scheduled the full day off. To attend the second sonogram examination,' I said. I had not mentioned it previously in order to maximise the impact of my improved level of participation. A surprise.

'I didn't say anything to you about a sonogram,' said Rosie.

'You're not having one?'

'I had it last week.'

'Ahead of schedule?'

'Twenty-two weeks. Like you insisted a couple of months ago.'

'Correct. Last week was twenty-one weeks and some variable number of days.' We had agreed: twenty-two weeks and zero days.

'Fuck,' said Rosie. 'I ask you to come and you don't show up, and now I don't ask and you take the day off.' She turned away and filled the kettle. 'You didn't really want to come with me, did you, Don? You didn't come to the last one.'

'That was an error. Which I wanted to rectify.'

'Why?'

'It's generally accepted that men should attend sonogram examinations. I was unaware of that convention. I'm sorry about the mistake.'

'I don't want you to come because it's generally accepted.'

'You didn't want me to come?'

Rosie poured hot water onto a 'herbal' tea bag (in fact not herbal but fruit-based and caffeine-free).

'Don, we're at cross-purposes. It's not your fault, but you're not really interested, are you?'

'Incorrect. Human reproduction is incredibly interesting. The pregnancy has prompted me to acquire knowledge –'

'You know, it's kicking. It moves around. I watched it on the screen. I can feel it when I'm lying in bed.'

'Excellent. Movement is normally experienced from approximately eighteen weeks.'

'I know,' she said. 'I'm living it.'

I made a mental note to record the information on the Week 18 tile. Gene's fall into the bath had smudged some of my earlier diagrams, but the recent tiles had escaped. Rosie was looking at me as if she expected something further.

'A good sign that things are progressing normally. Which the sonogram would have confirmed.' I was making an assumption. '*Is* everything proceeding normally?'

'Thanks for asking. All components are in place according to schedule.' She sipped her fruit tea. 'You know, they can tell whether it's a boy or a girl,' she said.

'Not always. It depends on the position.'

'Well, it was in the right position.'

I had an idea. 'Do you want to go to the Natural History Museum? It will be less busy on a weekday.'

'No thanks. I'll do some reading. You go. Do you want to know if we're having a boy or a girl?'

I could not see how the information would be useful at this point, except to encourage purchasing of gender-specific products, which I was sure Rosie would regard as sexist. My mother had already asked what colour socks to purchase.

'No,' I said. I am more competent at interpreting Rosie's expressions than those of other people, due to practice. I detected sadness or disappointment – definitely a negative response. 'I've changed my mind. Yes. What gender?'

'I don't know. They could tell but I didn't want to know.'

Rosie had engineered a surprise for herself. It solved the socks problem.

I collected my backpack from my bathroom-office. On the way out, Rosie stopped me, took my hand, and put it on her belly, which was now noticeably distended. 'Feel, it's kicking.'

I felt and confirmed the fact. It had been some time since I had touched Rosie, and my brain formed the thought of purchasing a triple-espresso coffee and a blueberry muffin. But they were both on the banned substances list.

25

Rosie had completed her PhD thesis. In keeping with the conventional practice of celebrating milestones, I booked dinner for two at a prestigious restaurant, and confirmed that they could produce a pregnancy-compatible meal. At Rosie's request, I delayed the celebration to enable her to focus on study for a dermatology exam, which she completed that afternoon.

There had been no significant change to our relationship since the Second Ultrasound Misunderstanding. The previous Saturday, I had completed Tile 26 – in fact two adjacent tiles. Bud no longer fitted on a single tile.

I had stopped travelling with Rosie on the subway. With the arrival of cooler weather, I established a routine of jogging through the Hudson River Park to and from Columbia. There had been no sex. In my early twenties, I had shared a house with other students. Our current situation felt similar.

Rosie was already home in her study-bedroom when Gene and I arrived. She called out, 'Hi guys. How were your days?'

'Interesting.' I called back from the living room as I removed the access panel to the beer storage to check the system and draw off two samples for taste-testing.

'Inge discovered a statistically significant anomaly in group 17B.' After Rosie's initial reaction to the Lesbian Mothers Project, and Gene's advice that it was in Rosie's 'territory', I considered it best to limit my report to the safe ground of the mouse-liver research. 'She used a Wilcoxon signed-rank test – temporary interrupt – I'm checking the beer.'

Gene took the opportunity to hijack the conversation. 'How did your exam go?'

'My memory's like a fucking sieve. Stuff I know I studied, I couldn't remember.'

I returned with the two filled pint glasses and gave one to Gene. The cooling system was functioning perfectly and I wondered at what point George would realise that he could dispense with my services.

I was in clear speaking range again. 'The analysis indicated an unexpected –'

'We were talking about Rosie's exam,' said Gene. Rather than point out that we had been talking about the mouse results prior to that and had not completed the discussion, I made a rapid mental adjustment and joined the exam conversation.

'Impairment of cognitive function is a common side-effect of pregnancy. You should ask for special consideration.'

'For being pregnant?'

'Correct. The science is quite clear.'

'No.'

'That seems an irrational response. Which is also an established side-effect of pregnancy.'

'I just had a bad day, okay? I probably passed. Forget it.'

People cannot forget things on command. Being instructed to forget something is analogous to being instructed not to think of a pink elephant, or not to buy certain foodstuffs.

Did the lowering of cognitive power in pregnancy have some evolutionary value, or did it reflect the diversion of some resource to the reproductive process? The latter seemed more likely. I reflected on it as Gene offered the formulaic statements of reassurance that lecturers use to fend off students in the period between examination and results, then I presented a summary of my conclusion.

'Chances are your exam failure will lead to a higher-quality baby.'

'What? Don, go and get dressed for dinner.'

Rosie walked back into her study-bedroom, presumably also to dress for dinner. Gene was still in interruption mode. I suspected too much coffee or Inge-related stimulation.

He called out to Rosie. 'Think about the thesis. The exam's one small blip. The thesis is six years' work. If it helps the celebration tonight, I can tell you it'll get through, with minor amendments at worst. Whether or not I agree with you philosophically, it's a real contribution and you should be proud of yourself. I've been giving you a hard time to keep you honest. So go out and have a good time.'

'Aren't you coming with us?' Rosie called back.

'I'll grab a pizza.'

I said, 'I assumed you would be dining with Inge.'

'Not every night. Not yet.'

'I thought you'd be joining us. You're a big part of this,' said Rosie.

'No, I'll leave you to it.'

'Seriously, I want you to come. I'd really like you there tonight. Please.'

Rosie was creating a problem – a totally unexpected problem. She had complained constantly about Gene as a supervisor, house guest and in general as a human being, so I had assumed she would not want him present as she celebrated what she had frequently referred to as 'finally being free of that jerk'. I had booked for two and the restaurant was extremely popular. I explained the situation, leaving out the negative statements about Gene, but Rosie was insistent.

'Bullshit. They can put another chair at the table. They won't turn us away.'

Based on my conversations with the restaurant staff earlier in the day, I suspected Rosie's second statement was likely to be true.

The restaurant in the Upper East Side was within walking distance, though Gene and Rosie seemed to struggle for the final twenty blocks. Both needed to work on their fitness. I mentioned this to Rosie as a possible use of the time freed up by the completion of the thesis and exam.

There was a greetings person at a lectern just inside the door. I addressed her in the conventional manner.

'Good evening. I have a reservation in the name of Tillman.'

It was as if I had said, 'We have detected bubonic plague in the restaurant.' She walked off rapidly.

'What's up her nose?' said Rosie. 'You're wearing a jacket.' This was true, although the restaurant did not have a formal dress code. I realised it was a reference to the night Rosie and I first had dinner together. The series of events that began with me being refused entry to a restaurant due to some confusion about the definition of 'jacket' ultimately led to our relationship. So much had changed since then.

Bubonic Plague Woman returned with a formally dressed person whom I assumed was the maître d'.

'Professor Tillman. Welcome. We've been expecting you.'

'Of course. I made a reservation. For this time. Exactly.'

'Yes. Now it was for two people, am I right?'

'Correct. *Was*. Now three.'

'Well, we're very full. And the chef has gone to some trouble, I understand, to accommodate your specific requirements.'

Very full was a modified absolute. I was pleased my father was not with us. But it was obviously unacceptably rude to exclude Gene, now that he had walked to the restaurant. I turned to leave. 'We can find somewhere else,' I said to the maitre d'.

'No, for God's sake, no, we'll sort something out. Just wait a moment.'

A couple arrived and he turned his attention to them. 'Reservation for two at eight,' said the man. It was now 8.34 p.m.

They did not identify themselves but the maître d' apparently recognised them, as he made a mark on his list. I looked again. It was Loud Woman from the night I was fired from my cocktail job!

She was definitely pregnant. As far as I could tell, she was not drunk. At least the sacrifice of my job to protect her baby from foetal alcohol syndrome had not been based on a misjudgement.

Her companion spoke to her. 'You're going to die for the truffled brie.'

Die. His choice of word was potentially accurate. I had no choice but to intervene. 'Unpasteurised cheeses may carry listeria and are hence inadvisable in pregnancy. You'll be putting the foetus at risk. Again.'

She looked at me. '*You!* The cocktail nazi! What the fuck are you doing here?'

The answer was obvious and I was not required to give it, as the maître d' interrupted.

'Actually, we're doing a very special degustation menu tonight. We had a customer with some unusual require-ments, and in the end the chef decided to prepare the meal for the whole restaurant.' He looked at me in an odd way and spoke slowly. 'In order to preserve his sanity.'

'Is the truffled brie on? What about the lobster sash-imi?' Loud Woman asked.

'Tonight, the brie will be replaced by an artisanal local

273

ewe's milk cheese and the Maine lobster will be cooked in a broth enhanced by –'

'Forget it.'

'*Madame*, if I might be so bold, you might find tonight's menu particularly appropriate for your . . . situation,' said the maître d'.

'My *situation*? Holy fuck.' She pulled her partner towards the door. 'We'll go to Daniel.'

Twice I had saved this woman's baby, or at least given it another chance. I deserved to be its godfather. I could only hope that Daniel would be cognisant of the risks of food poisoning in pregnancy.

Rosie was laughing. Gene was shaking his head. But a problem had been solved.

'You now have two seats available,' I said to the maître d'. 'And a reduction in the crowding problem.'

We were guided to a window table.

'They've guaranteed all food will be compatible with a baby under development according to the strictest guidelines and that the aggregate nutrition will be perfectly balanced. And incredibly delicious.'

'How can they do that?' asked Rosie. 'Chefs don't know about that sort of stuff. Not at your level of . . . detail.'

'This one does. Now.' I had spent two hours and eight minutes on the phone explaining, supplemented by several follow-up calls. Gene and Rosie thought it was hilarious. Then Gene raised a glass of champagne to toast Rosie's success, and, in accordance with convention, Rosie and I raised our mineral water and champagne glasses respectively.

'The future Doctor Jarman,' said Gene.

'Doctor *Doctor* Jarman,' I pointed out. 'When you've finished the MD, you'll have two doctorates.'

'Well,' said Rosie, 'that's one of the things I wanted to tell you. I'm deferring.'

At last! She had listened to reason. 'Correct decision,' I said.

Food arrived.

'Vitamin A,' I said, 'packaged in calf's liver.'

'You're really taking my renunciation of pescatarian-ism literally, aren't you?' said Rosie.

'If you want to minimise environmental impact, you eat the entire animal,' I said. 'And it's delicious.'

Rosie took a bite. 'It's not bad. Okay, it's good. Great. Whatever happens, I'll never say you were insensitive about food.'

After the carob-based low-sugar petits fours and decaffeinated coffee arrived, I asked for the bill – *the check, please* – and Gene returned the conversation to Rosie's plans.

'Full-time at home with the baby? Won't you go nuts?'

'I'll get a part-time job so that we're self-sufficient. I'm thinking about different options. I might go home for a while. To Australia.'

There was a contradiction in the sentence. So that *we're* self-sufficient. *I* might go home. My hope that Rosie might simply have made a grammatical error was extinguished when I realised that *we* must be referring to her and Bud. If *we* referred to Rosie and me, or to Rosie, me and Bud, our aggregate self-sufficiency did not require her to have a job. Nor had she consulted with me about moving back. I was stunned. The waiter brought the bill and I automatically put my credit card on it.

Rosie took a deep breath and looked at Gene, and then at both of us. 'I guess that sort of brings me to the other thing I wanted to talk about. I mean, I don't think it's any secret – you don't have many secrets living in the same house . . .'

She stopped as Gene stood up and waved at the waiter who approached our table with my credit card on a silver tray. I calculated the tip and filled it out, but Gene took the tray from me before I could sign.

'What sort of tip is that?' he said.

'Eighteen per cent. The recommended amount.'

'Exactly, judging by the odd cents.'

'Correct.'

Gene crossed out my writing and wrote something else.

Rosie started to speak. 'I really need to say –'

Gene interrupted. 'I think we owe them a little more, tonight. They've given us a pretty special, and slightly crazy evening.' He raised his coffee cup. I had never seen a coffee cup used in a toast, but I copied his action. Rosie did not raise her cup.

'To Don, who put so much into this evening and who makes life just a little bit crazier for all of us.' There was a pause. Rosie slowly lifted her cup and clinked it with Gene's and mine. No one spoke.

As we left the restaurant, we were assaulted by the flashing of cameras. A group – a *pack* – of photographers was photographing Rosie!

Then one called out, 'Wrong one. Sorry guys.' We caught a cab home and went to our separate bedrooms.

26

Gene confirmed my analysis the following evening. Rosie had been planning to end our marriage.

'It was only because last night at the restaurant reminded her why you two got together in the first place that she stopped short. But that's not the problem.'

'Agreed. The problem is not my suitability as a partner. It's my suitability as a father.'

'I'm afraid you're right. Claudia would say they're inseparable, but Rosie seems to have made the separation.'

Rosie was in bed. Rosie, who had encouraged me to look beyond my limitations, who was the reason for my life being more than I had ever envisioned. I was sitting with my best friend on a balcony in Manhattan, looking over the Hudson River to the lights of New Jersey, with the world's most beautiful woman and my potential child asleep inside. And I had almost lost it. I was still at risk of losing it.

'The trouble,' said Gene, 'is that the things that Rosie loves you for are exactly the things that make her think you're too . . . different . . . to be a father. She may be a risk-taker with relationships, but no woman's a risk-taker with her kids. In the end it'll come down to persuading her you're . . . average enough to be a father.'

It seemed like a sound analysis. But the solution remained the same. Work hard on fatherhood skills.

Although I had made enormous progress, thanks to my obstetric studies, supplemented by delivering Dave the Calf and the work with the Lesbian Mothers Project, my new skills had not been visible to Rosie due to the absence of a baby to apply them to. Other initiatives, such as the pram, had had an unexpectedly negative impact.

I anticipated that things would improve after the birth, but was now faced with a challenge to survive the final fourteen weeks of the pregnancy without Rosie rejecting me. One inadvertent error could make the difference: given my propensity to make such errors, it was vital that I create a buffer zone.

I needed expert input to create the optimum survival plan.

Dave was shocked.

'You and Rosie? You're kidding me. I mean, I knew you were having some problems, but no worse than Sonia and me.'

'She's prioritised the baby over our relationship. Which is leading to marriage failure.'

George laughed.

'Sorry, not laughing at you. But welcome to the real world. I wouldn't say your marriage is over just because she's behaving like every other woman. It's in their genes, isn't it, Gene Genie?'

'I'm not going to win a Nobel Prize for telling you

that women are programmed to focus on the baby. But I think Don does have a problem.' Gene looked at me. 'It started when he didn't go to the sonogram.'

'Shit,' said Dave. 'I took time off for that and I *never* take time off. You missed something, Don.'

'I saw the hardcopy of the image.' I was feeling defensive. I *had* screwed up.

'It's different. We could see the baby moving around and – I mean – after all the effort, there it was.' Dave was showing signs of emotion.

George pulled a bottle from under the table, and I applied my corkscrew. The baseball season was long over and we were at Arturo's Pizza in Greenwich Village. George's extreme tipping allowed us to violate the rules and bring his ludicrously expensive Tuscan wines, which he now claimed to prefer to English ale. The break in conversation allowed some time for thinking.

Gene tasted the wine.

'What do you think?' asked George.

'About the wine? Only one of the ten best bottles I've ever tasted. And I'm with three blokes in a pizza parlour. I shouldn't have ordered the *diavolo*. But about Don and Rosie . . .'

Gene swirled his wine around in the glass, which was too small for fine-wine appreciation.

'There's no point sugar-coating the pill with Don. Rosie doesn't think he can cut it as a father. Think about repeating patterns. Rosie was brought up by a single parent, so maybe she sees that as her destiny as well.'

Gene's insight was of no practical use to me. I could not change the past.

Dave had been silent, finishing the first shared pizza.

'I'm trying to make this refrigeration business work. It's like playing baseball,' he said. 'All I can do is try to execute right every day and hope the results come. And that Sonia doesn't give up on me in the meantime. All Don can do is try to be the best he can and hope that Rosie comes around.'

Dave was right. I needed to do everything I could to be the best father I was capable of being. I had made a start. Unknown to Rosie, I had interacted so successfully with a baby that I had raised its oxytocin levels. But I needed to do more.

I had obtained input on the crisis from 42.8 per cent of my friends, including my new friend George. I had distilled their messages into: *There is a problem* and *Don't give up*.

I decided not to call the Eslers. I did not want them to join Rosie, Gene, George, Dave, Sonia and Stefan– Stefan! – in knowing there was a problem.

That left Claudia. World's best psychologist.

This time she decided to use voice rather than text when I connected with her on Skype. I had not yet worked out what determined her preference, but the speed of voice communication allowed me to explain the problem in less than an hour.

Claudia delivered her analysis almost as soon as I had

finished. 'She's looking for perfect love. She's idealised something that she lost before she could understand that love is never perfect.'

'Too abstract.'

'Her mother died when she was ten. Even if her mother – her mother's love – wasn't perfect, Rosie had no chance to find out. So she went off looking for a perfect father, who didn't exist, of course, and then she found a perfect husband.'

'I'm not perfect,' I said.

'In your own way, you are. You believe in love more than any of us. There's no grey with you.'

'You're suggesting I'm incapable of dealing with continuous concepts; that my mind is somehow Boolean?'

'You're never going to cheat on Rosie, are you?'

'Of course not.'

'Why?'

'It's not right.' I realised what I was saying. 'Unless you have an open marriage, of course.'

'Let's not go there, Don. This is about you and Rosie. But at some point Rosie will have discovered that you're human. You forget an anniversary, you don't read her mind.'

'It's unlikely I would forget a date. But mind-reading is not my strongest attribute.'

'So now she's on another quest for perfect love.'

'Repeating patterns,' I said.

'Where did you get that from? Don't bother answering. But it's valid in this case. And from what you're saying, she's not seeing you as part of that perfect love.

Being yourself probably works beautifully with just the two of you, but not so well with a baby. In her mind.'

'Because I'm not an average father.'

'Perhaps. But average may not be enough. Her picture of a father is problematic. She had a lot of issues with her own father, didn't she?'

'The problems with Phil have been resolved. They're friends.' Even as I said it, I remembered Gene's observation about childhood problems.

'It doesn't change the past. It doesn't change her subconscious.'

'So what do I do?'

'That's always the hard part.' I was reaching the conclusion that psychology researchers needed to give more attention to problem-solving. 'Keep working on being a father. Maybe try to discuss the issue with Rosie. But not in the terms I've used.'

'How can I discuss it without using the terms you've used to explain it?' It would be like trying to explain genetics without mentioning DNA.

'You've got a point. Maybe just keep trying and let her know you're committed.'

There's a problem. Don't give up.

'And, Don.'

I waited for Claudia to finish the sentence.

'I'd rather you didn't say anything to Gene, but I'm seeing someone. I'm in a relationship with a new man. So I think the time has passed for you to worry about getting Gene and me back together.'

The conversation appeared over, so I terminated the

call. Claudia obviously had not finished. She sent me
two text messages.

Good luck, Don. You've surprised us all so far.
Then: I think you know the new man in my life. Simon
Lefebvre – Head of the Medical Research Institute.

The data-gathering stage of the Lesbian Mothers Project was complete, and I had reviewed the initial draft
paper. At my request, B3, the helpful nurse, had sent me
the raw data, and I had undertaken my own analysis. The
results were fascinating and definitely a useful contribution to the field. There were numerous ways to improve
the paper, and I sent my notes to B2. She did not respond,
but B1 demanded a meeting with the Dean who invited
me to join them.

'Don's demanding that we include data that was gathered before the protocols were properly in place. It's
misleading.'

'It's the most interesting data,' I said. 'It establishes
that neither mother raises the baby's oxytocin levels
through play rituals.'

'That's because the original play rituals were male-
biased. The female carers weren't comfortable with
them. The babies sensed this. We had to make them
more appropriate to women.'

'They would be classified as cuddling,' I said.

'You didn't see them. You weren't there.'

The second part was true. Emails advising me of the
schedule had failed to arrive, and the technicians I had
contacted had not located the problem despite multiple

follow-ups and escalation. Fortunately B3 had found a more efficient solution.

'I was provided with video.'

'Who –'

'Does it matter?' asked David. 'Don's surely entitled to see the video.'

'He's not qualified to determine the difference between play and cuddling.'

'Agreed,' I said. 'I sent the videos to experts for analysis.'

'Who? Who did you send the videos to?'

'The original researchers in Israel, obviously. They confirmed that the second protocol should be classified as cuddling. Hence your research establishes that the secondary carer, if female, stimulates the production of oxytocin in the child by cuddling rather than play. Which is a clear difference from the results with male secondary carers. Hence interesting.'

It seemed that B1 had not understood my point, as she stood up with an expression that I provisionally diagnosed as angry. I clarified. 'Hence highly publishable. The researcher I spoke to on Skype was extremely interested.'

'What Don's done is totally unethical,' said B1. 'Showing our results to other researchers.'

'Naive, perhaps. Not unethical. This is the Columbia medical school, open and cooperative with researchers around the world. Don has our support.'

After B1 had left, the Dean congratulated me on my persistence. 'They tried to cut you out, Don. I think most researchers would have walked away. Refusing to take no for an answer has given us a good result.'

The weather had turned cold, as was usual for early December. Bud's diagram was now taking up four tiles. At twenty-nine weeks, with the medical services available in New York, he could possibly survive in the external world.

Our marriage was surviving in shared-house mode.

Rosie had invited her study group to our apartment to celebrate the end of classes prior to exams and also her deferral from the course.

'It'll probably be the last time I see these guys,' she said. 'We've got nothing much in common – most of them are younger than me.'

'Only by a few years. They're adults.'

'Just. And they're not into babies and stuff. Anyway, if you and Gene want to go out with Dave –'

'We had a boys' night out last night. Dave is being criticised for insufficient attention to Sonia and also has to perform paperwork. Gene has a date with Inge.'

'A date.'

'Correct.' It was pointless to use a less accurate term. Gene had confessed that he was in love with Inge. George had argued that the age difference was irrelevant, and Dave had no opinion. Gene's visa allowed him to remain in the US for a month's vacation on completion of his sabbatical, and he planned to spend the time looking for a permanent position in New York.

'How about George?' Rosie had not met George.

286

The persistent suggestion of alternatives led to an inevitable conclusion. I had learned something from the Lesbian Mothers Project.

'You don't want me here?'

'It's my study group.'

'This is also my apartment. The study-group meeting is a social occasion. I'm your partner. Are other people bringing partners?'

'Maybe.'

'Excellent. I am RSVPing in the affirmative.'

The Dean would have been impressed.

27

Gene provided me with some guidelines for hosting a party.

'Loud music, low lights, salty food, plenty of booze. Fresh shirt and jeans. The shoes you wore for Dave the Calf, if you've cleaned them. Don't tuck your shirt in. The unshaven look is fine. Shake hands, serve food, serve drinks, don't do anything to embarrass Rosie.'

'What makes you think I'll embarrass her?'

'Experience. And she told me. Not in so many words, but she tried to get me to break my date with Inge so I could take you off her hands. Fat chance. This is the big one.'

'The big one? You plan to have sex with Inge?'

'Believe it or not, it's been remarkably chaste so far. But my professional instincts tell me that tonight's the night.'

I made the party arrangements, and Rosie confirmed that all was going according to plan when I arrived home.

'What's all this booze?' she asked. 'I had to sign for five cases of liquor. We can't afford to be spending like this.'

'Delivery was free. And there was a discount for the quantity. Based on past behaviour, you'll be drinking to excess again once Bud is born.'

'I told people to bring their own. We're just students.'

'I'm not,' I said.

'And Don, I'm thinking of moving back to Australia, remember. Before the baby is born. I won't be around to drink it.'

I had moved my weekly discussion with my mother forward by thirty minutes to accommodate the party and made a decision to lie in order to avoid inflicting emotional pain.

'Has it arrived yet?' my mother asked.

I told the truth. 'It arrived on Thursday.'

'You should have called. Your father was in a state about it. It cost a fortune to send. God knows what he's spent on it already. He was talking to people in Korea – *Korea* – half the night and then the boxes arrived and he had to sign all these documents about patents and secrecy and of course he had to read every word – you know what your father's like, he's worked on it day and night, Trevor's had no help in the shop for weeks . . . I think you should speak to him.' She turned away and called out, 'Jim, it's Donald.'

My father's face replaced my mother's. 'Is it what you wanted?' he said.

'Excellent. Perfect. Incredible. I've tested it. Meets all requirements.' This was true too.

'What does Rosie think?' asked my mother in the background.

'Totally satisfied. She considers Dad the world's greatest inventor.'

This was a deception. I had not shown Rosie the crib. It was in Gene's closet. After the pram problem, I considered there was a high probability that she would reject my father's most amazing project.

The first to arrive for the study-group celebration was a couple, vindicating my decision to be present. Rosie introduced them.

'Josh, Rebecca, Don.'

I extended my hand which they shook in turn. 'I'm Rosie's partner,' I said. 'What would you like to drink?'

'We've brought some beer,' said Josh.

'There's cold beer in the fridge. We can drink it while yours returns to optimum temperature.'

'Thanks, but this is English beer. I worked in London in a pub for six months. Got a taste for it.'

'We have six real ales on tap.'

He laughed. 'You're kidding me.'

I showed him to the coolroom and drew off a pint of Crouch Vale Brewers Gold. Rebecca followed and I asked if she wanted beer or would prefer a cocktail. The social protocols were familiar and I was feeling very comfortable as I mixed her a Ward 8 and performed a few tricks with the cocktail shaker.

Other guests arrived. I mixed cocktails to their specification and handed around the salted Padrón peppers and edamame. Rosie turned off the music I had selected and replaced it with a more current recording. The noise level remained high, lights low, alcohol consumption steady. People appeared to be having fun. Gene's formula was working. So far, there were no indications that I had embarrassed anyone.

At 11.07 p.m. there was a knock. It was George. In one hand he had a bottle of red wine and in the other a guitar case.

'Revenge, eh? Keeping an old man awake. Mind if I join you?'

George was our de facto landlord. It seemed inadvisable to refuse him entry. I introduced him, took his wine and offered him a cocktail. By the time I returned with his martini, all of the guests were seated and George had started playing and singing. Disaster! It was 1960s style music similar to that which Rosie had turned off earlier. I assumed George's performance would be similarly unacceptable to young people.

I was wrong. Before I could think of a way of silencing George, Rosie's guests were clapping and singing along. I focused on refilling drinks.

While George was playing, Gene arrived home. We had an apartment full of young people, a significant percentage of whom were unaccompanied women, disinhibited by alcohol. I was worried that he might behave inappropriately, but he went directly to his bedroom. I presumed his libido had been exhausted.

The party finished at 2.35 a.m. One of the last to leave was a woman who had introduced herself as Mai, age approximately twenty-four, BMI approximately twenty. We spoke together in the beer fridge while I selected liquor for her final cocktail.

'You're so not like what we were expecting,' she said. 'To be honest, we all thought you'd be some kind of geek.'

It was a notable milestone. Tonight, at least in this limited domain of social interaction, I had managed to convince a cool young person, and apparently her fellow students, even in the face of a preconception, that I was within the normal range of social competence. But I was concerned with how the preconception had arisen.

'How did you deduce that I was a geek?'

'We just thought – well, you're with Rosie, the only person on the planet doing an MD and a PhD at the same time. And the way she just says what she thinks, how we've got to drag her into doing anything social . . . and then it's like, oh yeah, I'm having a baby but let me get these stats done first. We thought she'd have gone for someone the same and here you are with the apartment and the cocktails and the muso buddy and the retro shirt.'

She sipped her cocktail.

'This is awesome. Is it okay to ask, is she getting any help with the clinical thing?'

'What clinical thing?'

'Sorry. I'm sticking my nose in. But we've talked about it because we want to help. She's so obviously using the pregnancy as a way out.'

'Of what?'

'Her clinical year. I mean she wants to do psych, and she'll never have to touch a patient after next year if she can get some help to get through it. I gather there was some sort of trauma in her childhood – a car accident or something that's freaked her out about emergency medicine.'

Rosie had been in the car when her mother was killed and Phil badly injured. It would seem reasonable that confronting the injuries of others might stimulate traumatic memories. But she had never said anything to me.

Inge asked to see me urgently on the Monday morning after the party, then offered to buy me coffee. 'It's more of a personal matter,' she said.

I can see no logical reason why personal and social topics need to be discussed in a café and accompanied by beverages, whereas research topics can be discussed in both the work environment and in cafés. But we changed location and purchased coffee to enable the conversation to begin.

'You were right about Gene. I should have listened to you.'

'He attempted to seduce you?'

'Worse. He says he's in love with me.'

'And that emotion is not reciprocated?'

'Of course not. He's older than my father. I thought of him as a mentor, and he treated me like an equal. But I never did anything to suggest . . . I can't believe he got it so wrong. I can't believe *I* got it so wrong.'

In the evening, I knocked on Rosie's door and entered. I had expected she would be performing some task at her computer, but she was lying on the mattress. There was no book visible. The lack of distractions created an ideal opportunity to raise an important topic.

'Mai told me there was some problem with clinical activities. A phobia about patient contact. Is this correct?'

'Fuck. I told you, I'm dropping the medical program. The reasons don't matter.'

'You said you were deferring. David Borenstein –'

'Fuck David Borenstein. I *am* deferring. Who knows, I may go back, I may not. Right now I'm a bit busy with exams and having a baby.'

'Obviously if there is some obstacle preventing you from achieving a goal, you should investigate methods for overcoming it.'

I could empathise with Rosie, and was in a position to help. I had faced an almost identical situation when I switched my studies from computers to genetics. My revulsion at handling animals increased in proportion to the size of the animal. It was irrational but felt instinctual, hence difficult to overcome.

I undertook hypnotherapy, but attributed my cure to the Cat Rescue Incident, in which it had been necessary to save a housemate's kitten which had jumped into the toilet – a doubly unpleasant task. I learned that I could create an intellectual separation from the physical sensation in an emergency. Once I knew the brain configuration, I was able to reproduce it well enough to dissect mice and assist in the delivery of a calf. I was confident that I could function in a medical emergency, and that I could coach Rosie to do so too.

I began to explain, but she stopped me. 'Forget it, please. If I wanted to do it enough, I'd sort it out. I'm just not that interested.'

'Do you want to see a play? Tonight?'

'What play?'

'It's a surprise.'

'So you haven't bought tickets or anything. Haven't you got stuff . . . scheduled?'

'I've scheduled a play. For both of us. As a couple.'

'Sorry, Don.'

I saw Gene next. He was also in his room lying on the bed. Our household was aggregately depressed.

'Don't say anything,' he said. 'Inge spoke to you, right?'

Gene had asked me not to speak, then asked a question that required me to answer. I decided that the latter overrode the former.

'Correct.'

'Christ, how do I face her? I've been a complete idiot.'

'Correct. Fortunately she has been similarly imperceptive in failing to note that your interactions with her were aimed at seduction. I recommend –'

'It's okay, Don, I don't need your advice on etiquette.'

'Incorrect. I'm extremely experienced at dealing with embarrassment resulting from insensitivity to others. I'm an expert. I recommend an apology and admission that you are a klutz. I have recommended to her that she apologise for not making her position clear. She is similarly embarrassed. Nobody else knows except me.'

'Thanks. Appreciate it.'

'Do you want to go to a play? I have tickets,' I said.

'No, I'll stay in, I think.'

'Bad decision. You should come to the play with me. Otherwise you'll reflect on your error but make zero progress.'

'All right. What time?'

Don Tillman. Counsellor.

Before leaving, I prepared a meal for Rosie and put the other two serves in the fridge for Gene and me to eat later. I had a minor problem with managing the cling wrap, as a result of poor dispenser design. Rosie got up from the table and pulled out a new sheet.

'I can't believe you can't manage cling wrap. How would you ever fold a nappy? Can't you just be normal about some things?' She turned around. Gene had joined us from his bedroom. 'I'm sorry. I didn't mean that. Forget I said it. I just get frustrated sometimes because you have to do everything differently.'

'No, he doesn't,' said Gene. 'Don's not the only man who has trouble with cling wrap. Or can't find things in the fridge. I remember your friend Stefan back in Melbourne throwing a wobbly over someone stealing the sugar from the tearoom. He went on for about five minutes, and by the time he'd finished half the department was standing there, all looking at the sugar bowl, right in front of him.'

'What's Stefan got to do with anything?' said Rosie.

*

'Do you or Rosie want to do a shift?' It was Jamie-Paul, the following night, texting from the wine bar that used to be a cocktail bar.

I texted back: 'Has Wineman forgiven me?'

'Who's Wineman? Hector's gone.'

Rosie offered to join me, but Jamie-Paul had said 'you *or* Rosie', which I interpreted as per common English usage as an exclusive *or*.

It was not quite the same as before, in part due to the absence of Rosie, but Jamie-Paul informed me that former clients were returning and asking for cocktails. Wineman had been dismissed following an incident in which nobody could produce a satisfactory whiskey sour for the owner's brother. Christmas was only fifteen days in the future and the bar was busy – hence the need for my services. I left Rosie and Gene to eat the dinner I had prepared.

It was a good feeling making cocktails, an incredibly good feeling. I was competent and people appreciated my competence. Nobody cared about my opinions on gay couples raising children or whether I could guess what they were feeling or if I could manipulate cling wrap. I stayed past the end of my shift, working unpaid until the bar closed and I could walk home in the snow to an apartment made empty in a virtual sense by its occupants being asleep.

It did not work out exactly as planned. As I was writing a note to advise Gene and Rosie not to disturb me before 9.17 a.m., Rosie's door opened. Her shape had definitely changed. I had a feeling that I was unable to name: some combination of love and distress.

'You're very late,' she said. 'We missed you. But Gene was nice. It's difficult for all of us at the moment.'

She kissed me on the cheek, to complete the set of contradictory messages.

28

I had an opportunity to compensate for failing to attend the two ultrasound examinations.

The antenatal briefing was to be conducted at the hospital where Rosie had arranged for the birth to take place. I was determined to attend and perform well. The Good Fathers class, where I had graduated after only one session, was the benchmark.

Dave had already attended an antenatal class. 'It's mainly for the fathers,' he said. 'About what to expect, how to support your partner, that sort of stuff. The women know it all already. The guys embarrass themselves and their wives by how little they know.'

I would not be an embarrassment to Rosie.

'I'm only doing this because it's part of the deal,' said Rosie as we rode the subway to the hospital. 'I was tempted not to show up, just to call their bluff. What are they going to do? Not let me have my baby? Anyway, I'm probably not even going to have it here.'

'It would be unwise to take any risk on such a crucial matter.'

'Yeah, yeah. But like I said before, you didn't have to come. They'd be discriminating against single mothers if they made the fathers come.'

'Fathers are expected to attend,' I said. 'Fathers are provided with an understanding of what to expect in a supportive, non-threatening and fun environment.'

'Thanks for that,' said Rosie. 'Non-threatening is good. Wouldn't want a karate exhibition.'

Rosie's statement was completely unjustified, as she was unaware of the two occasions on which I had used martial arts in *reasonable self-defence* in New York. She was presumably referring to the Jacket Incident on our first date, and confirming her recent selective memory for events that cast me in a bad light, *even though she had been amused at the time and come home with me.*

In the foyer there was an urn, a selection of low-quality instant beverages, including several that were caffeinated, and sweet biscuits which were definitely not on the list of pregnancy power foods. We were three minutes early, but there were approximately eighteen people already present. All the women were at various stages of pregnancy. I did not see anyone who appeared to be a lesbian secondary carer.

A group of three introduced themselves to us: two pregnant women and a man. The women were named Madison (estimated age thirty-eight, BMI not estimated due to pregnancy but probably low under normal conditions) and Delancey (approximately twenty-three, BMI probably above twenty-eight under normal conditions). I pointed out that Madison and Delancey were both New York street names. My mind was working at maximum efficiency, hence noticing interesting patterns. The man, who was the husband of Madison and aged approximately fifty, BMI approximately twenty-eight, was named Bill.

'There's also a William Street,' I said.

'No big surprise there,' said Bill, reasonably. 'Got a name picked out for your boy or girl yet?'

'Not yet,' said Rosie. 'We haven't even talked about it.'

'Lucky you,' said Bill. 'It's all we talk about.'

'What about you?' Rosie asked Delancey.

'Madison and I talk about it a lot, but it's a girl and it's going to be Rosa after my mom. She was a single mom too.' Repeating patterns.

Rosa was a similar name to Rosie. If her surname was Jarmine her name would be an anagram of 'Rosie Jarman'. Or if it was Mentilli, it would be an anagram of 'Rosie Tillman' which would only be interesting if Rosie had adopted my surname when we were married.

'I recommend avoiding a name associated with your ethnicity. To reduce prejudice,' I said.

'I think you might be the one bringing your prejudices with you,' said Madison. 'This is New York, not Alabama.'

'Bertrand and Mullainathan's study of discrimination in job applications was based on research in Boston and Chicago. It would seem unwise to take the risk.'

Another idea popped into my head unbidden. 'You could call your child Wilma. A combination of William and Madison.'

'There's a name that's due to come back,' said Bill. 'Since prehistoric times. What do you think, Mad?' He was laughing. I was performing well – *hyper-well* – socially.

'And how do you and Madison know each other?' Rosie asked Delancey.

Madison answered. 'Delancey's my best friend. And our housekeeper.'

The relationship sounded very efficient. Interestingly, the first two letters of *Delancey* appended to the first two letters of *Madison* made (*made!*) *made* which was a homophone for Delancey's role. Which was an anagram of *Dame*, which seemed to relate to Madison's role. Also *Edam*, which is a cheese and *mead*, which is a honey-based alcoholic drink. It would be interesting to create a meal in which all foods were paired with anagram drinks.

My racing mind was interrupted by the late arrival of the convenor. Before she could be distracted by educational tasks, I informed her of the catering problem, in some detail.

Rosie interrupted. 'I think she's got the message, Don.'

'Oh, I'm glad we have a dad who knows about nutrition in pregnancy. Most don't have a clue.' Her name was Heidi (age approximately fifty, BMI twenty-six) and she seemed very friendly.

The education component commenced with introductions, followed by a video of actual births. I moved to the front row when one male student vacated his seat and left the room hurriedly. I had already watched numerous online videos covering the most common situations and complications, but the bigger screen was a definite benefit.

At the end, Heidi asked, 'Any questions?' She moved to the whiteboard in the front corner.

Remembering Jack the Biker's recommendation, I shut the fuck up initially to give others an opportunity.

The first question was from a woman who identified herself as Maya. 'In the breech presentation, wouldn't they normally do a caesarean?'

'That's right. In this case, I guess they didn't pick it up until labour was well along, and it was too late. And, as we all saw, it still worked out fine.'

'I've been told I have to have a caesarean unless the baby turns. I really wanted a natural birth.'

'Well, there are risk factors with a natural birth in breech position.'

'How risky is it?'

'I can't give you all the facts and numbers –'

Fortunately, I could. I walked to the whiteboard and, using the red and black markers, showed how the umbilical cord could be crushed in a breech birth, and provided a breakdown of factors contributing to the decision to perform a caesarean section. Heidi stood beside me with her mouth open.

Maya was expecting her third child, so the risk was reduced. 'Your pelvic bones and vagina will already be well stretched.'

'Thanks for sharing that, buddy,' said her husband.

When I had finished, everyone clapped.

'I gather you're an OBGYN,' said Heidi.

'No, just a father, recognising that I have a valuable and fulfilling role to play in the pregnancy.'

She laughed. 'You're an example to us all.'

I hoped Rosie, sitting at the back, had taken notice.

We covered a number of topics, most of which I was able to expand upon. I was conscious of Jack's advice, but I seemed to be the only knowledgeable person in the room other than Heidi. Everything seemed to be going very well. The topic moved to breastfeeding, where I had extended my research beyond The Book.

'It won't always be easy, and you fathers have to support your partners' choice to breastfeed,' said Heidi.

'Or not,' I added, since the word *choice* implies an alternative.

'I'm sure you'd agree, Don, that breastfeeding is always the preferred option.'

'Not always. There are numerous factors which may affect the decision. I recommend a spreadsheet.'

'But one huge factor is the immunity that breastfeeding gives to the child. We need a very strong reason to deny our child the best immune system.'

'Agreed,' I said.

'Let's move on then,' said Heidi. But she had left out a critical fact!

'Maximum immunity is achieved by sharing babies among mothers. In the ancestral environment, mothers fed one another's children.' I pointed to the Street Women. 'Madison and Delancey are best friends, living in the same house with babies due concurrently. Obviously they should co-feed each other's babies. In the interests of creating the best possible immune systems.'

I continued the argument with Rosie on the train home. In retrospect it was probably more of what Rosie

would call a rant than an actual argument, due to all contributions being made by me.

'Chapped nipples are reported to cause agony, but
mothers are expected to continue feeding to improve
the immune system. Yet a social convention, a *constructed*
social convention with minimal underlying rationale, is
enough to prevent a simple extension that –'

'Please, Don, just shut up,' said Rosie.

Rosie apologised a few minutes later, walking home
from the subway. 'Sorry I told you to shut up. I know it's
who you are and there's nothing you can do about it. But
you were just so embarrassing.'

'Dave predicted embarrassment. It's normal.'

But I was conscious that it was unlikely that anyone at
Dave's class had been the catalyst for the public breakup
of two best friends and their employment relationship
and an unstructured discussion involving most of the
participants that violated the promise that the classes
would be 'non-threatening'.

'Keep executing,' Dave had said. To extend his baseball
analogy, I was in imminent danger of being dropped from
the roster. I needed help from the coach: my therapist.

'I'm not your therapist, Don.'

I intercepted Lydia as she left the clinic at the end of
the day. I'd had no success securing an appointment and
detected obstruction. She refused my offer of coffee and
insisted on returning upstairs to her office. I had come
alone.

I told her everything, excluding the Rosie–Sonia sub-stitution. More correctly, I *planned* to tell her everything, but the description of the Antenatal Uproar, which I commenced with in response to her question 'What prompted you to come to see me?', occupied thirty-nine minutes and was not finished when she interrupted. She was *laughing*. I could not have imagined Lydia laughing, but now she was laughing *inappropriately* at a situation that had driven my marriage to the brink of disaster.

'Oh God, breastfeeding Nazis. Women whose maids are their best friends. You know what David Sedaris says? None of these women have someone *else's* maid as their best friend.'

It was an interesting observation, but not useful in solving my problem.

'All right,' said Lydia. 'We didn't get off to a very good start, you and I, and that's partly my issue. We do need people like you. You should know that I cleared you with the police after the first session. The only child you're a danger to is your own.'

I was shocked. 'I'm a danger to my own child?'

'I thought there was a risk. That's why I used the lever of the police report to see you again. I wanted to make sure you were safe. Report me if you like, but I was doing it for a good reason, and now you've come back voluntarily.' She looked at the clock. 'Do you want a coffee?'

I almost missed the social signal because it was so unexpected. She wanted to continue the conversation. 'Yes, please.'

She left me and returned with two coffees.

'I'm officially finished for the day. I'm an hour past officially finished. But I want to tell you something. It might help to explain a few things.'

Lydia sipped her coffee and I did likewise. It was of the quality I would expect from a university tea-room. I continued drinking it anyway, and Lydia proceeded with her explanation.

'About a year ago, I lost a patient. She had postpartum psychosis. You know what that is?'

'Of course. One birth in 600. Frequently no prior history. More common in *primagravidae*. First births,' I explained.

'Thank you for the clarification, Doctor,' she said. 'Anyhow, I lost her and the baby. She killed the baby and committed suicide.'

'You failed to diagnose the psychosis?'

'I never saw it. The husband didn't report anything wrong. He was . . . insensitive, so insensitive he didn't notice his wife was psychotic.'

'And you considered me capable of similar insensitivity?'

'I know you're trying to do the right thing. But I thought Rosie might be at risk of depression and you wouldn't pick it up.'

'Postnatal depression occurs in between ten and fourteen per cent of births. But I'm adept at administering the Edinburgh Postnatal Depression Scale.'

'She completed the questionnaire?'

'I asked her the questions.'

'Trust me, Don, you're not adept. But I've met Rosie. She's remarkably robust, probably a result of her early life in Italy. She's got your number. She obviously loves you, she's got purpose and structure through her medical studies, she's worked through her family issues, she's got a good network of friends.'

It took me a moment to remember she was talking about Sonia.

'What if she wasn't studying? And didn't have friends? And didn't love me? Surely even the support of an insensitive husband would be better than zero.'

Lydia finished her wine and stood up. 'Luckily that's not the position you're in. But, paradoxically, having a husband like that is worse than having no supports. He may well keep the woman from taking some positive action by herself. In my opinion – and there's research to support it – she'd be better off without him.'

29

I spent the next day at work, alone, attempting to deal with the problem generated by Lydia's observations. I undertook some supplementary research on the desirable attributes of a father.

Non-violence was at the top of the list. My actions had led to arrest and referral to an anti-violence class. My meltdown was virtually indistinguishable from the outbreaks of anger that Jack the Biker had discussed. I did not consider myself a threat to others, but I presumed many violent people would make the same self-assessment.

Drug Use – Lack of. My alcohol consumption, already at the highest daily limit I had been able to find, had risen significantly during the pregnancy. This was doubtless a response to stress. Jack the Biker was right: it probably made me more vulnerable to meltdowns.

Emotional stability. One word. Meltdown.

Sensitivity to Child's Needs. One word. Empathy. My most serious weakness as a human being.

Sensitivity to Partner's Emotional Needs. See previous.

Reflective Functioning. As a scientist probably good, but the fact that I had been unable to find a solution to my relationship problem suggested I could not apply it to the domestic environment.

Social Supports. This was the only redeeming item in an otherwise disastrous list of shortcomings. My family was in Australia, but I was fortunate to have incredible support from Gene, Dave, George, Sonia, Claudia and the Dean. And, of course, I had professional help from Lydia.

Honesty was not included in the list, but was obviously a desirable attribute. I had hoped that when the Playground Incident was resolved, I could share it with Rosie. But it was an instance of weird behaviour, and weird behaviour was no longer acceptable.

I created a spreadsheet and it rapidly became obvious that the negatives outweighed the positives. As a potential father, I was manifestly unsuitable, and it was increasingly clear that I was no longer required in my role as a partner.

Further research confirmed that it was not unusual for relationships to fail during pregnancy or shortly after the birth. The woman's attention naturally shifted to the baby, at the expense of the partner. Alternatively, the male partner wanted to avoid the responsibility of fatherhood. The first had definitely occurred in our case. And while I was willing to take on the responsibilities of fatherhood, I had been rated as incapable by both a professional therapist and my wife. And now by my own self-assessment.

My research provided some guidance on separation: better results were achieved by swift and definite action rather than prolonged discussion. This was consistent with the portrayal of relationship termination in two films I had watched during the Rosie Project: *Casablanca* and *The Bridges of Madison County*. In keeping with these films, I prepared a short speech of nine pages outlining the situation and the inevitability of my conclusion. It was emotionally painful work, but the process of articulating the argument helped to clarify it in my mind.

Jogging home, with the speech prepared, I allowed my thoughts to wander. I had spent sixteen months and three days married to Rosie. Falling in love with Rosie had been the single best event of my life. I had worked as hard as I could to maintain the situation, but – like Dave with Sonia – I had always suspected that there had been some sort of cosmic mistake that would be discovered and that I would be alone again. Now it had happened.

It was, of course, not the fault of the cosmos but of my own limitations. I had simply got too many things wrong, and the damage had accumulated.

I left work early to arrive home before Gene. Once again, Rosie was on the mattress. This time she was reading, but it was a formulaic romance novel of the kind my aunt read. I had made Rosie so unhappy that she was seeking relief in fantasy.

I began my speech. 'Rosie, it seems obvious that things are not going well with us. There is some fault –'

She interrupted. 'Don't say any more. Don't talk about faults. I was the one who got pregnant without talking to you. I think I know what you're going to say. I've been thinking the same thing. I know how hard you've tried, but this relationship has always been about two independent people who had fun together, not about a conventional family.'

'Why did you get pregnant then?'

'I guess because having a baby is so important to me, and I had a fantasy that we could be parents together. I didn't think it through.'

Rosie said more, but my ability to process speech, especially speech about emotions, had been impaired by my own emotions. I realised I had hoped that Rosie would disagree with me – possibly even laugh at some error in my thinking – and things would return to normal.

Finally she said, 'What are we going to do?'

'You indicated you would return to Australia,' I said. 'Obviously I will provide financial support for Bud as per convention.'

'I mean, now. Can I stay here?'

'Of course.' I was not going to make Rosie homeless. She had no close friends in New York besides Judy Esler. And I did not want the Eslers to know about the separation yet. I still had an irrational hope that the problem would be resolved. 'I'll stay with Dave and Sonia. Temporarily.'

'It won't need to be long. I'll book a flight home. Before they won't let me fly.'

Rosie insisted it was too late to go to Dave's that evening, so I slept at the apartment. In the middle of the night, I woke to hear her performing her hot-chocolate and bathroom ritual, then the door opened. In the light from the living room, which was never completely dark, she looked interesting, in an extremely positive way. Her shape had changed even further and I was disappointed not to have been able to monitor it through closer contact.

She was going to fly home. I would stay for a few days with Dave and Sonia and move back into the apartment alone. Perhaps I would also fly back to Australia at some stage. It made little difference. I am not particularly interested in my physical surroundings. I liked the job at Columbia, with David Borenstein, Inge, the B Team and, at least currently, Gene.

Somewhere in the world I would have a child, but my role would be little different from that of a sperm donor. I would send money to assist Rosie with the costs, and perhaps resume my cocktail-making job to supplement my income and social contact. Even in New York, I lived efficiently. My life would revert to the way it was prior to Rosie. It would be better for the changes Rosie had stimulated me to make and for the new ways I had of perceiving reality. It would be worse for knowing that it had once been even better.

Without speaking, Rosie climbed into bed with me. She was moving differently with the additional weight of Bud and his or her support system, leaning back to take advantage of the third wedge-shaped vertebra that human females have for that purpose. It seemed that she should ask permission, as it had never occurred to me to join her after she had relocated to her study. But I was not going to object.

She put one arm around me, and I wished I had thought to freeze an emergency supply of blueberry muffins. To my surprise, the preliminary ritual was not necessary.

In the morning, I slept past my automatic wake-up time. Rosie was still there. She would be late for her Saturday morning tutorial.

'You don't have to go,' she said.

I parsed the sentence. She was giving me an option. But she was not suggesting she would change her plans to return to Australia. And she was not saying, 'I want you to stay.'

I packed a bag and, after taking over an hour to create an accurate picture of Bud on Tile 31, I took the subway to Dave's.

When Sonia arrived home from visiting her parents, she wanted Dave to drive me back to my apartment. Immediately. Dave had already helped me to move into his office, which was also the bedroom for their baby under construction, due to arrive in ten days.

'She's pregnant,' said Sonia. 'We all have ups and downs. Don't we, Dave?' She turned to me. 'You can't walk out on her just because you've had a fight. It's your job to make the relationship work.'

I checked Dave's expression. He looked surprised. Any psychologist, including Rosie, would surely agree that relationship success was a joint responsibility.

'We haven't had a fight. I've seen a therapist. It's clear I'm a negative influence on Rosie. She's going back to Australia. She'll have proper support.'

'You're the proper support.'

'I'm unsuited to fatherhood.'

'Dave. Drive Don home. Help him sort this out.'

It was 7.08 p.m. when we arrived at the apartment. Gene was home, as his social life with Inge was over.

'Where have you been?' he said. 'You're not answering your phone.'

'It's in my bag. At Dave's. I'm now living with Dave.'

'Where's Rosie?'

'I assumed she was here. She's usually home before 1.00 p.m. on a Saturday.'

I explained the situation. Gene was in agreement with Sonia that we should attempt some sort of reconciliation.

'I've been trying to make the relationship work,' I said. 'I think Rosie has too. The fault is intrinsic to my personality.'

'She's got your kid on board, Don. You can't walk away from that.'

'According to your theory, women seek the best genes from the biological father but make a separate decision as to who they want to care for the child.'

'One thing at a time, Don. Like I said to Dave, it's theory. Priority one is to find Rosie. She's probably off in some bar drowning her sorrows.'

'You think she'd drink alcohol?'

'Wouldn't you?'

'I'm not pregnant.'

If Gene was right, we had an emergency. Perhaps Rosie had left some clue in her study.

I entered, and her computer was on. A Skype message was on the screen. From a person with the Skype name of *34*, time zone Melbourne, Australia.

I told you I'd be here for you. Stay strong. I love you.

I love you! I opened the application and looked at the preceding conversation:

Everything's turned to shit. It's over with me and Don.

Are you sure?

Are you sure you'll still have me? With a baby and everything?

Rosie walked in. She did not appear drunk.

'Hello, Dave. What are you doing in my room, Don?'

It was obvious what I was doing.

'Is there some other man?' I asked.

'Since you ask, yes.' She turned away from Dave and me and looked out the window. 'And he tells me he loves me. I think I feel the same way about him. Sorry, but you asked.'

Repeating patterns. Rosie's mother had slept with one man and married another who remained loyal to her despite them both believing Rosie was the original man's child. Rosie had deceived me, just as I had deceived Rosie. And for the same reason, no doubt: in order not to cause distress.

Dave drove me home to his apartment. He had heard the conversation. Neither of us could think of anything useful to say. Despite the plausibility – possibly the inevitability – of what I had just learned, I was stunned. I had no doubt who the other man was: Stefan, Rosie's conventionally attractive study partner, whom she acknowledged had been pursuing her in Melbourne before we became a couple. He had been thirty-two when I met him, and could be thirty-four now. She had chosen him ahead of me to help with her statistics. Now she had chosen him to help her raise Bud. I considered him stupid enough to use an unstable string of characters as his identifier.

30

Dave's office, which was now my bedroom, was a disaster! His desk was covered in paperwork, the stack of seven filing trays was overflowing and the cardboard boxes with dividers that he was using instead of a filing cabinet were in danger of tearing from internal pressure. It was obvious to me why his business was failing.

Lectures were over for the year. My mouse-data analysis was being performed competently by Inge and I was not required by the Lesbian Mothers Project. It would have been a perfect opportunity for joint activities with Rosie. Instead I had vast unscheduled time. I volunteered as a filing clerk.

Dave was desperate enough to entrust his business to a geneticist with an aversion to administration. And I was looking for anything to divert my brain from constructing mental images of Rosie and Number 34.

'Invoice copies go in this file,' said Dave.

'But you have them on the computer already. There's no need to print.'

'What if the computer blows up?'

'You revert to backup, obviously.'

'Backup?' said Dave.

It took only two days of focused work, omitting lunches, to fix the system.

'Where are the files?' said Dave.

'On the computer.'

'What about the paper files?'

'Destroyed.'

Dave looked surprised, in fact shocked. Correction, devastated.

'Some of that stuff came from customers: orders, authorities, sketches. It's all paper.'

I indicated the scanner function of the device I had acquired for $89.99 and identified the remaining problem.

'You're creating your invoices individually. Don't you have an application for that?'

'It's too hard to use.'

I seldom find computer programs difficult to use, but I struck some problems with accounting rules, due to not being an accountant. While Dave was at work, I enlisted professional help from Sonia, who had now ceased working in anticipation of the birth. She was unfamiliar with the software, but was able to answer all of my accounting questions.

'I can't understand why Dave didn't ask me for help with this. He's always saying it's under control, but it obviously isn't.'

'I suspect that once he deceived you – in order to spare you stress – he found it increasingly difficult to admit to his deception over a long period.'

'Married couples shouldn't need to have secrets. I've told Dave that,' said the woman who had posed as an Italian medical student and told me not to tell Dave because he was a worrier.

'Can you print an aged debtors' ledger for me?' Sonia asked when the system was configured and all data had been entered. 'I want to know how much we're owed.'

The report was available from the menu.

'$418.12, current.'

'What about overdue?'

'$9245, from four invoices. All issued more than 120 days ago.'

'Oh, God,' she said. 'Oh my *God*. No wonder he didn't want to buy a pram. If it's been four months, there's probably some problem with the work. Can you show me the invoices? The overdue ones?'

'Of course.'

Sonia looked at the screen for a few moments, then pointed to the phone on the newly acquired four-in-one utility.

'Does this work?'

'Of course.'

Sonia spent fifty-eight minutes on the phone, employing a variety of tactics apparently tailored to create guilt, pity, fear or, in one case, merely awareness. She was incredible. When she had finished, I told her so.

'I spend half my life doing it to ordinary people who've overspent on trying to have a baby. Something I can relate to. After that, this is a breeze.'

'Are they going to pay?'

'The wine bar on West 19th is going to need a call to the owners. There's been a change of management since Dave did the work and it sounds like the last guy left a mess. But the other three are okay. They just needed a little push.'

Sonia raised the topic subtly at dinner.

'I need some money to pay my credit card. Do you have anything?'

'Not right now,' said Dave. 'I'm just waiting for money to come through. Everyone's slow, but the work's all good.'

'How much did you say we were owed?'

'Plenty,' said Dave. 'Don't worry about it.'

'I *am* worried. If we need the money, maybe I can go back to work after the baby. Part-time.'

'You don't need to do that. I just need to get the money in.'

'Tell me how much we're owed, and I'll decide.'

Dave shrugged. 'You know me, I don't keep track exactly. Twenty, thirty thousand. We're good.'

The next morning, Sonia was angry with Dave – not *at* Dave as he had gone to work early. She was directing her anger towards me.

'He's out all day and half the night and he's not earning any money. Is he actually working? Maybe he's going to the library, like these guys who lose their jobs and can't tell their wives. Is that what's going on, Don?'

It was unlikely. Dave discussed his work with me, in detail. He seemed to have plenty of it, but perhaps he was not charging enough, or was lying about the clients' satisfaction level. I had been wrong about my friends before. I was still unsure if a central component of Gene's identity was a manufactured fiction. Claudia was in a relationship with Simon Lefebvre. And Rosie was in love with another man.

'If I have to go back to work, he can stay home and look after the baby. Maybe it'll force him to take an interest.'

I retreated to Dave's office and worked on the problem. One possibility was that Dave had not entered all of the invoices into the computer. This had been the case, but I had rectified the problem. There had only been two small ones. When I thought more about it, it seemed odd that Dave was almost up-to-date in recording his invoices.

A metaphorical light bulb went on. The obvious explanation was not that Dave had been unusually conscientious in one aspect of his administration. No! Dave had been consistently lax. He had failed to create the invoices at all.

I opened the file of scanned worksheets and began to match them with invoices. I was right. Most of his work had not been entered into the computer, hence not billed to the clients. There was a limit to what I could do to rectify the situation. Creating invoices required accounting knowledge that I did not have. If I made errors in billing, Dave might be perceived as incompetent or a cheat.

Fortunately I had access to a qualified accountant. It took Sonia and me until 3.18 p.m. to create the invoices: state taxes varied, invoices for labour and materials were filed separately, Dave had offered a variety of inconsistent mark-ups and discounts.

Sonia contributed comments that alternated between sympathetic and critical: 'God, this is so complex. No wonder he put it aside.'

'Eight thousand dollars. From three months ago!'

'We've been living on cash from George. Dave's an idiot.'

When we were finished we had a pile of envelopes ready for posting and had emailed numerous other bills.

'Show me the creditors' total first. I want to know what we owe before I get too excited.'

I checked: $0.00.

'That's Dave for you,' said Sonia. 'We can't afford to eat, but no fridge manufacturer is going to have a cash flow problem because of Dave Bechler. Now you can show me the debtors' total. I've been too scared to keep track.'

'$53,216.65,' I said. 'Dave's estimate of twenty to thirty thousand was incorrect. And it's reduced because payment has arrived online for two of the invoices you phoned about.'

Sonia began crying.

'You were hoping for more?' I asked.

Sonia was now laughing and crying simultaneously. How can it be possible to make sense of such displays of emotion?

'I'm going to make a coffee to celebrate,' she said. 'A real coffee.'

'You're pregnant.'

'You noticed.' It would have been impossible not to notice. Sonia was huge. The reminder to moderate caffeine could not have been more obvious.

'How many have you had today?'

'I'm Italian. I'm having da coffee alla da time.' She laughed.

'I'll have an alcoholic drink with Dave when he gets home.' I was being empathetic to Dave at a distance.

'Dave caused this.' The crying appeared to have stopped. 'Don, you've saved my life.'

'Incorrect. I –'

'I know, I know. Don, when you said a therapist told you that you weren't right for Rosie, I couldn't ask in front of Dave, but you weren't talking about Lydia, were you?'

English is annoying in not having unambiguous responses for answering a question framed in the negative. The simple addition of the equivalent of the French word *si* ('*Yes*, I *am* talking about Lydia') would solve the problem. Sonia, however, must have read my expression, as no verbal reply was required.

'Don. Lydia doesn't even know Rosie. She knows *me*.'

'That's the problem. I was approved for parenthood with you, but not with someone like Rosie. Lydia described Rosie perfectly.'

'Oh God, Don, you're making a terrible mistake.'

'I'm following the best advice available. Objective, research-based, professional advice.'

Sonia would not accept the clear evidence that Rosie

did not want me, evidence that was additional to Lydia's assessment.

'Do you want this marriage to work or not?' she said.

'My spreadsheet identified —'

I interpreted Sonia's expression as *I don't want to hear about your fucking spreadsheet. Do you, emotionally, as a whole mature person, want to live the rest of your life with Rosie and the Baby Under Development or are you going to let a computer make that decision for you, you pathetic geek?*

'Work. But I don't think —'

'You think too much. Take her out to dinner and talk it over.'

31

Gene, Inge and I had a total of seven connections to the Momofuku Ko website: a notebook computer and a mobile phone each, plus the desktop computer in my office at Columbia. I was issuing instructions, calculated to maximise our chances of securing a table when reservations opened.

Gene had supported Sonia's idea of taking Rosie to dinner. 'Regardless of whether you can repair this, you're going to be parents of a child. She doesn't seem to have many other friends, besides her Jewish mama who's been around every day.' I assumed he was referring to Judy Esler.

On our first visit to New York together, a year and eight months earlier, Rosie had organised dinner at Momofuku Ko, and it had been the best meal of my life. Rosie had been similarly impressed.

At exactly 10.00 a.m. we clicked the reservation button. Available slots on the newly opened day popped up and we selected different times as planned.

'Gone,' said Gene. Someone had taken his slot already. 'Trying the second option.'

'Mine are also gone,' said Inge.

'Missed that one too,' said Gene.

'Gone,' said Inge.

My messages came back. We had failed, mere humans attempting a task better handled by software.

I refreshed the screen. It was possible that someone employing a similar strategy had secured multiple bookings and would now release one. I refreshed again. No success.

'What's wrong with that one?' said Inge, who had been looking over my shoulder. She pointed to the screen.

I had been focused on the newly opened bookings ten days ahead and had not observed a single unreserved spot at 8.00 p.m. under today's date. It had probably been there all the time. I clicked on it, and the booking program responded with a request for credit card details. I had a reservation for two for this evening!

'Believe me,' said Gene. 'She won't have made plans. I'll lock her in for dinner with me to make sure, and you can roll up and surprise her.'

'What happened to your shirt?' said Sonia.

'A laundry accident.'

'It looks like you tie-dyed it. You can't go out looking like that.'

'The restaurant is highly unlikely to refuse me entry. If my shirt was unhygienic or I had failed to wash or –'

'It's not about the restaurant. It's about Rosie.'

'Rosie knows me.'

'Then it's about time you were a bit less predictable. In the right direction.'

'I'll borrow –'

'You will not borrow one of Dave's. Have you looked at Dave lately?' Dave's weight reduction project was going as badly as my marriage.

I detoured to Bloomingdale's on the way to the apartment. There were other menswear shops closer to the route, but it would be inefficient to navigate an unfamiliar layout. Expert salesmanship resulted in a new pair of jeans to accommodate a change in my waist measurement. I estimated my current BMI at twenty-four, an increase of two points. This was totally unexpected. My return to a version of the Standardised Meal System meant my carbohydrate intake was again tightly managed. My exercise effort of running, cycling and martial-arts classes had been stable, and I should have been burning additional kilojoules in the cold weather. A few seconds of reflection sufficed to identify the variable factor: alcohol. I now had another reason to reduce my drinking.

As I walked towards the apartment building, a man of about my own age approached from the opposite direction carrying a coffee in each hand. He smiled and waited for me to enter the security code for the front door. University laboratories and computer rooms are similarly secured, and our compulsory training had covered exactly this scenario.

'Let me take one of your coffees,' I said. 'So you can enter the code and I am not complicit in a security violation.'

'Don't trouble yourself,' he said. 'Game's not worth the candle.' He began to walk away.

It seemed that I had foiled an attempted break-in. Unless I alerted the police, the man would be back to take advantage of a less conscientious tenant. He could be a murderer, rapist or a person who might violate one of the many building bylaws with impunity. And Rosie was in the building!

As I unclipped my phone from my belt to dial 911, another possibility occurred to me. The man's accent was familiar, as was the metaphor comparing the cost of illumination with the enjoyment of recreation. I called out to him.

'Are you visiting George?'

He walked back.

'That was the idea.'

'You can press the buzzer. He's on the top floor.'

'I know. I wanted to knock on his door.'

'Better to use the buzzer. That way if he doesn't want to see you he doesn't have to open the door.'

'You worked it out.'

I had made the right decision. It was easy to forget that George was a rock star, or at least a former rock star, and therefore likely to be pursued by autograph hunters and other stalkers.

'Are you a fan of the Dead Kings?' I said.

'Not really. I got enough of them growing up. George is my father.'

My facial-recognition ability is poor, and humans tend to over-recognise patterns, due to the greater risk of failing to recognise them. But there was a distinct resemblance in the thin face and the long, curved nose.

'You're the drug addict?'

'I think the term they use here is *recovering addict*. I'm George.'

'George too?' I said.

'Actually, George Four. Started with my great-grandfather George. So my old man's George the Third. You've met him?'

'Correct.'

'So it fits, doesn't it? The madness of George the Third. And I'm George the Fourth, the Prince Regent. That's what my family used to call me. The Prince.'

It was possible that the Prince was an imposter, an inventive autograph hunter, but I was confident I could protect George from him if necessary. Assuming he wasn't armed.

'I'm going to check you for weapons then take you up,' I said. The formulation seemed natural, though it was possibly derived from visual entertainment rather than direct experience.

The Prince laughed. 'You're having me on.'

'This is America,' I said, in what I hoped was an authoritative voice, and patted him down. He was clean.

George was not home or not answering. It was now 7.26 p.m. and I needed to allow thirty-five minutes to travel to the restaurant.

I could not leave the Prince in the building unsupervised.

'I propose telephoning your father.'

'Don't bother. I'm not planning to be around after tomorrow. It was just on the off-chance.'

'If he says no, it's the same result as if you leave. You don't see him.'

'It's not the same. Not by a long shot. But go ahead.'

George's phone was not responding.

'I'll be off, then,' said the Prince.

'Shall I give George a message?'

'Tell him it wasn't his fault. We make our own lives.'

I did not want to let the Prince leave. George had seemed upset about the damage he had caused to his son, and it would be good for him to hear directly that it was not his fault. But there was no obvious way I could keep the Prince in the building without remaining there myself or violating security.

'I recommend you return later.'

'Thanks. I might do that.'

I knew with absolute certainty that the Prince was lying and would not return. It was an odd feeling to be so sure of something for which I was unable to cite concrete evidence. There must have been some information that I had subconsciously processed. I was still trying to work out what it was when I knocked on the door of my own apartment.

Rosie opened it, looking incredibly beautiful. She was wearing makeup and freshly applied perfume, and a tight dress that adhered to her new shape. Gene was standing behind her.

She smiled. 'Hi, Don, what are you doing here? I thought Gene was taking me to dinner.' She smiled again.

'He is,' I said. 'I just needed to check the beer. But there's no sign of flooding. Inspection complete.'

I ran back to the elevator, pushing my foot into the crack before the door closed. Gene followed me.

'What the hell, Don? Where are you going?'

'It's an emergency. I'm unavailable. Rosie was expecting you to take her out. The change is transparent to her.'

'I'm not taking Rosie to Momofuku Ko.'

There was no time to argue.

At the ground level I looked up and down the street and saw him, standing on the street waving for a taxi. I started running as one pulled over and arrived just in time to drag him away from the opened door. The driver was not happy with my intervention, and I ended up with my arms around the Prince as he drove away.

'What the hell?' said the Prince, expressing his surprise in the same words as Gene.

'I'm going to buy you dinner,' I said. 'At Momofuku Ko. World's Best Restaurant. While we wait for your father to return.'

I had made the connection just as Rosie opened the door and startled me with her beauty. A wave of pain had run over me, a realisation that I was going to lose her, and a consequent feeling that life would not be worth living. It was an extreme emotion and an irrational conclusion, and both would have passed, as they had passed in my twenties, when I had looked into the pit of depression and managed to step back. That was what I had recognised in the Prince. He was at the edge of the pit. He had said he would not be around after tomorrow.

I was trusting my least reliable skills when I decided

to follow him. It was possible I was losing the last chance to save my marriage. I was sure that Rosie or Gene would have told me I had got it wrong. But the risk associated with an error was too great.

I released the Prince.

'You're going to have to explain before you take me anywhere,' he said. 'Who are you?'

'I'll explain as we walk. Our first priority is to catch the subway. Reservations are forfeited fifteen minutes after the scheduled arrival time.'

I was trying to think of a way of discovering if my depression hypothesis was correct without asking the question directly. I tried to recover the mindset I had in the bad times to work out what sort of question might have elicited an honest response. It was not pleasant.

'Are you okay?' said the Prince.

'Revisiting some bad memories,' I said. 'I was once so depressed I considered suicide.'

'Tell me about it,' he said.

I texted Gene to say I would be using the booking, in case he changed his mind about going with Rosie. The Prince and I arrived twelve minutes late, three minutes inside the tolerance limit. I would have preferred to be dining with Rosie, but there would have been the problem of what to say. Despite Sonia's encouragement, I still had no solution to the Marriage Problem.

But dinner with the Prince was fascinating.

'George told me he convinced you to take drugs which ultimately resulted in you becoming an addict.'

'He told you that?'

'Correct.'

'Fair play to him. I suppose I can tell you the whole story then.'

The waiter came to take our drinks orders. The Prince ordered a beer. Apparently his recovery program allowed alcohol, so I recommended sake as more compatible with the food. I ordered a club soda for myself.

'Basically, Dad was doing the whole rock'n'roll thing, and I was the opposite. Except for the drumming. No artificial stimulants for me.' The Prince used a non-standard intonation for the last sentence, as though he was impersonating a cartoon superhero. 'But I meant it. And he said, "You can't go through life without ever getting just a little bit high. Without knowing what it's like." And I was such a geek – you know what I'm saying – that I decided if I was going to have one experience, it'd be the best one I could have.'

'You researched drugs?'

'I know, it seems crazy.'

It seemed completely sensible. I wondered why I had fallen into drinking alcohol and caffeine without proper research into alternatives – or indeed into the impacts of these two. They were legal, but so were cigarettes. Legality was surely less important than the risk of death. The exception had been amphetamines, which I saw as having a precise, focused purpose. I explained my own experiment as a student, and the exam disaster that resulted.

'The professor showed me the paper that I had

334

demanded to have re-marked and it was incomprehensible. A rant!'

The Prince laughed. 'Anyway, I decided that acid was the pick of them – for quality of experience. And safety, everything.'

'You chose lysergic acid diethylamide? As the optimum drug?'

'I took one tab of LSD. And you know how everyone says one dose can't make you an addict? Well I'm the guy they should put in the education videos. Because it was just the best, the most fantastic experience of my life. All I wanted to do was keep repeating it. And you know what?'

'No.'

'I couldn't. Not reliably, anyway. I had bad trips, so-so trips, I had all sorts of shit, and then I started trying other stuff. I tried everything. For a long time. I never got what I wanted again. So I started backing off. Which is where I am now. Just this.'

He waved his sake glass. I was not drinking alcohol, as a result of my recent resolution. It was interesting to watch the Prince's mood change as the drink took effect. It struck me that Rosie probably had the same experience watching Gene and me descend into intoxication, now that she was temporarily a non-drinker.

'So you've solved the problem,' I said.

'Except for wasting the best years of my life. No partner, no kids, no job.'

'No job?' Disaster. 'You require a job. The other things are optional, but you need a job.'

'I'm a drummer. An all-right drummer. You know how many all-right drummers there are in the world? I thought I might have got something going here, but it didn't work out.'

My phone vibrated. It was Gene.

With Rosie at Café Wha? WTF are you?

I texted Gene back and he invited me to join them. *Commanded* me to join them.

'Do you want to hear some music?' I asked the Prince. He remained my first priority and, although his emotional state seemed much improved, my own experience told me the problem was not solved.

'Why not? Maybe the band won't turn up and I can play a couple of hours of drum solos.'

I told the Prince not to speak. I needed to think. Walking is good for thinking, as are other repetitive activities. Unfortunately, the walk to Greenwich Village was insufficiently long to generate a solution to the Prince's problem.

The venue was downstairs. As we opened the door, I realised why Gene had uncharacteristically chosen to spend his evening listening to live music. On the front of the band's drum kit were the words *Dead Kings*. Behind the drums was George.

I looked at the Prince.

'You knew he was playing here?' he said.

'No. It's a result of human interconnectedness.'

Although I had heard George practising multiple times, I had never seen him undertake his most characteristic repetitive activity. We stood inside the door and observed for a while. The Prince was watching his father and I was looking for Rosie and Gene. Due to the large number of patrons, I did not succeed in locating them.

I asked the Prince's opinion of his father's competence.

'Better than he used to be.'

'Better than you?'

'He's good for the Dead Kings. It's not all about technical expertise. It's about how you work together. People used to criticise Ringo, but he was a great drummer for the Beatles.'

We waited by the entrance for another three songs. While we listened, my mind completed the problem-solving process. I made a mental note to be less critical of my students' use of earphones while studying.

The singer announced a short break and I tracked George as he walked to a table in front of the stage. Rosie's red hair was unmistakable. I instructed the Prince to wait and walked over. George and Gene were pleased to see me, Rosie possibly less so.

'Nice of you to join us,' she said. 'I gather you've eaten.'

'Correct. I need to speak to Gene.'

'Of course you do.'

I pulled Gene away and explained what I wanted to achieve. I had a theoretical solution, but the social protocols were too complex for me to execute. Gene, of course, was totally confident.

'I'll speak to George. You speak to whatever-his-name-is.'

'The Prince.'

'The Prince. Right. I'm doing this on two conditions, Don. Number One is you've got to, *got to*, make an effort to fix things up with Rosie.'

'I've made all possible efforts.'

'Didn't look like it tonight. Number Two is you have to break a rule.'

A chill ran through my body. Gene was asking a high price. He pointed to a sign: *Absolutely no recording or photography*.

'Get your phone out. This is going to be a moment for the ages.'

Gene returned to his table. I could see him speaking to George, who responded by looking around frantically. But the timing was perfect. The band was reassembling and George was required on stage.

They played one song, then George, who had his own microphone, made an announcement.

'My son is here tonight. I haven't seen him for a very long time. His name is also George and last time I heard him play he was a sight better than I am.' There was applause, and the Prince waved. George beckoned him up, and he refused, but I pushed him, and informed him that I would persist if necessary.

The Prince stepped onto the stage and George indi-cated that he should take his place behind the drums. The band started playing, and George and I sat with Rosie and Gene. George was focused on the stage. The Prince seemed competent. When the song was over, George started to get up. I put down my phone, which had been running the video application that had led to my arrest, and stood in front of him.

'The change of roles is permanent,' I said. 'The Prince requires a job and you need to escape the repeating pattern of Atlantic cruises.' I detected resistance. 'It also compensates for the error you made, which temporarily destroyed his life.'

George sat down again and poured himself a glass of red wine.

'And since he is a superior drummer, the cruise ship patrons will receive better entertainment.'

32

'Rosie. I need to discuss something with you.'

I was visiting the apartment to check the beer. The system was functioning well; prior to leaving I had checked it only once per week. But the weather was unusually warm for December, and it seemed reasonable to visit more frequently. I had also taken the opportunity to draw the Week 32 diagram of Bud on the tiles. His or her development remained interesting, despite the reduced connection to my own life. Having gone this far, it seemed reasonable to complete the forty weeks.

'I closed the door for a reason, Don. It doesn't make it easy for me, you coming in twice a day.'

Gene had indicated that Rosie was not currently receptive to a surprise dinner – or even a scheduled dinner – or to relationship discussions.

'I'm afraid you're going to have to give it time,' he said.

But I was not discussing the relationship.

'This is a research question. Since you're considering returning to psychology, you'll find it interesting.'

'I'll reserve judgement.'

I explained the Lesbian Mothers Project. Any justification for refraining from mentioning it was no longer relevant. It was time to begin disclosing the information I had withheld. This was the first, and least risky, step. My participation in the project was not illegal, unethical or weird.

'This is the project you started to tell me about, right,' said Rosie. 'You never mentioned it again.'

'I didn't want to invade your territory.'

'You mean you didn't want to tell me you were invading my territory.'

'Correct. The problem is that they don't want to publish the results.'

'Why do you think that is?' asked Rosie.

'If I knew the answer, I wouldn't have woken you up to ask.'

'What do you think of people who take scientific findings out of context to push their own barrows?'

'You're referring to Gene?' I said.

'Him too. These women are trying to make a point that two women can bring up a child as well as a heterosexual couple.' She sat up in bed. 'They don't want to publish something that suggests otherwise.'

'Surely that's pushing their own barrow.'

'Not to the extent of some dinosaur who's going to pick it up and say kids who don't have a father are deprived. Which is an issue that's a little close to my heart right now. So don't expect me to be rational about it.'

'But the results don't indicate any requirement for a father,' I said. 'Both carers can raise the baby's oxytocin. It's just that an unconventional parent uses an unconventional method. I predict zero problem for the child.'

'Don't expect the *Wall Street Journal* to see it that way.'

I had turned to leave when Rosie spoke again.

'And, Don. I've got a flight home tomorrow. Judy's taking me to JFK. I got the cheapest fare. It's non-refundable.'

I was leaving to check the beer again before dinner when Sonia stopped me.

'Wait an hour and I'll come with you.'

'Why?'

'We're going to see Lydia.'

'She indicated she was unavailable for further consultation. And it's a Sunday. A Sunday evening.'

'I know. I called her. I told her that you and Rosie – you and I – had split up as a result of what she said to you. She was a bit blown away: she thought she'd reassured you to stay with me – with Rosie.'

'She merely provided objective advice.'

'Well, she's feeling responsible now. She overstepped the line and she knows it. We're meeting at your apartment. I couldn't do it here because of Dave. I've told him I'm taking you to see Rosie before she flies home. I haven't mentioned Lydia. Obviously.'

'What about Rosie?'

'Gene's taking her out.'

'Gene's involved in this?'

'Everyone's involved, Don. We think you're both making a mistake, and if you won't listen to anyone except Lydia, then she can tell you. I'm going to channel Rosie – I'll *be* Rosie – and Lydia is going to tell us to stay

342

together. And when she does, you're going to solve the Marriage Disaster Problem. Am I speaking your language?'

Sonia and I arrived at the apartment two minutes before Lydia was due. I realised Sonia had never visited; it had not occurred to me to invite her and Dave to dinner. It was probably a social error.

'My God, what's that smell?' she said. 'I think I'm going to throw up. I've been feeling terrible all day.'

'Beer. There's a small leak that's impossible to access. Dave blames the workman who replaced the ceiling.'

Sonia smiled. 'That's so Dave. How does Rosie cope with it?'

'Humans adapt to smells quite quickly,' I said. 'It's only recently that regular washing has been conventional. Prior to that humans did not wash for months, and there was no problem. Except disease, obviously.'

Lydia arrived on time.

'My God, what's that smell?' she said.

'Beer,' said Sonia. 'Humans adapt to smells quite quickly. It's only recently that regular washing has been conventional.'

'I guess hygiene was not quite at New York standards in a small Italian village.'

'That's right. Lucky Don's a hygiene freak or the baby –'

I gave Sonia a look intended to remind her that she was supposed to be Rosie, who would not be defending weirdness and had not been raised in a small Italian village with poor hygiene. Of course, neither had Sonia. I suspected things were going to become confusing.

Then one of the Georges began drumming.

'What's that?' asked Lydia.

It was a reasonable question, as the initial beats could have been confused with the discharge of a firearm. But the drumming became more rhythmic, and a bass and two electric guitars joined in. Now the answer would be obvious to Lydia, which was fortunate as she could not have heard mine.

We attempted to communicate in rudimentary sign language for approximately three minutes. I deduced that Lydia was asking, 'How will the baby sleep?' and Sonia was responding, 'Skull, bye-bye, bird, kangaroo, no, no, no, eating spaghetti.'

The music stopped. Sonia said, 'I am thinking about flying home to Italy.'

'And if you stay? If you and Don are able to get through this misunderstanding?'

I led them to Gene's room, where I had stowed the gift from my father.

'Oh God, it's a coffin,' said Lydia. 'A transparent coffin.'

'Don't be ludicrous,' said Sonia. 'I feel like you're trying to find reasons to criticise Don.'

'What is it then? A spaceship?'

In fact the soundproof crib was incompatible with space travel as it was permeable to air. I set the alarm on my phone, and as soon as it started ringing put it in the crib and secured the lid. The noise disappeared.

'But if the phone needed to breathe, it could do so,' I said.

'What if it cries?' asked Lydia.

'The phone?' I realised my error and pointed out the microphone and transmitter in the crib. 'Rosie will sleep with earphones. I will have earplugs, hence not be disturbed by the baby myself.'

'Nice for you,' said Lydia. She looked around. 'Is someone else sleeping here?'

'My friend. His wife evicted him for immoral behaviour and now he's living with Rosie.'

'In the baby's room.'

'Correct.'

'Rosie,' Lydia said, and Sonia glanced at the door before realising that Lydia was speaking to her. 'You're comfortable with this?'

Sonia's response suggested extreme *dis*comfort. She returned to the living room and looked around frantically. I diagnosed panic.

'I need to use the bathroom. Where's the bathroom?' she asked in what was supposed to be her own apartment.

We were standing just outside my bathroom-office. I opened the door for Sonia.

'There's a desk in the bathroom,' said Lydia as Sonia closed the door behind her. I was aware of this. I had not taken it with me to Dave and Sonia's, as it would have been impractical to carry it on the subway.

We were interrupted by Sonia calling from the bathroom-office. 'I've got a problem.'

'With the plumbing?' I asked. The toilet sometimes jammed in flush mode.

'With *my* plumbing. Something's wrong.'

It is socially *extremely* inappropriate to enter a bathroom containing an unrelated individual of the opposite gender. I was aware of this, but my behaviour was justified by the probability that the problem was related to Sonia's advanced state of pregnancy. I guessed the onset of labour.

I entered the forbidden zone, and Sonia explained the problem. Her description of the symptoms was unambiguous.

'What are you doing?' asked Lydia. 'Is everything okay?'

'Making a phone call,' I said. 'No.'

'What's wrong?'

'Prolapsed umbilical cord. I've called an ambulance. The problem should not require immediate intervention if labour hasn't commenced.'

'Oh God,' said Sonia. 'I think it has.'

Following my instructions, Lydia assisted Sonia to Rosie's study, and I once again dragged the mattress from the main bedroom which Rosie had resumed using. I needed space to manoeuvre. Sonia lay on the mattress. I had already specified maximum urgency when I phoned 911, so there was no point in phoning again and adding a load to the system that might delay assistance to other emergencies.

Sonia was extremely agitated, almost hysterical. 'Oh

God, I read about this. The baby's head crushes the cord and there's no oxygen, oh shit, shit, shit –'

'Potentially,' I said. I attempted to adopt a bedside manner, the exact thing that had dissuaded me from considering medicine as a career. 'The chances of maternal death are virtually zero. Without intervention, the baby will probably die. However, intervention has been summoned.'

'What if it doesn't come? *What if it doesn't come?*'

'I consider myself capable of the necessary intervention. I've had significant practice.' I thought it unnecessary to mention that there had been no prolapsed cord in the birth of Dave the Calf.

'What practice? *What practice?*' Sonia's hysteria seemed to be causing her to say everything twice.

I reassured her. 'The procedure is straightforward. I'm going to have to perform an examination.' I was not looking forward to this: the thought of intimate contact with a human female who was a close friend was causing a wave of revulsion, but I could not be responsible for failing to do everything possible to ensure the survival of the baby. It would be extremely disappointing if Dave and Sonia's five-year project failed at the final stage. I did my best to imagine Sonia as the mother of Dave the Calf. I would probably have some sort of post-traumatic stress to deal with later.

Lydia was pacing aimlessly. I diagnosed anxiety. 'Do you know what you're doing, Don?' Very poor bedside manner.

347

'Of course, of course.' I was feeling much less sure, but was adhering to the principle of inspiring calm: profess total confidence even at the expense of honesty. I was about to commence the examination when I heard the external door open.

'Hello? Is that you, Don?' It was Rosie's voice. Gene was with her. They stood in the doorway of Rosie's study. 'What's happening?'

I explained the problem. 'I need to do an examination.'

'*You* need to do an examination?' said Rosie. '*You're* going to examine her? I don't think so, Professor. Everybody out. Including you.' She indicated me.

'Thank God you got here in time,' said Lydia to Gene and Rosie.

Rosie evicted us and closed the door. Less than a minute later, she opened it again, exited, and closed it behind her.

'You're right,' she said, speaking in a loud whisper. 'Oh my God, what are we going to do? I haven't done obstetrics.'

I attempted to match the volume of her whisper. 'You've done anatomy.'

'What the fuck use is that? We need someone who knows what to do, right now.'

'I know what to do.'

'I'm the medical student, I should know what to do.'

Rosie's tone indicated a descent into irrationality.

'They're sending medical students now?' said Lydia to Gene. She also sounded panicked.

Sonia was calling out incoherently. Gene had been right about Italian women.

'I know what to do,' I said to Rosie again.

'Bullshit, you've got no experience.'

'Theory will be sufficient. You will need to execute my instructions.'

'Don, you're a geneticist: you don't know anything about obstetrics.'

I did not want to remind Rosie of an incident that had been instrumental in our relationship breakdown, but it was more important that she had confidence in my obstetric knowledge than in my social skills.

'Heidi the antenatal class convenor was convinced I was an OBGYN.'

I was feeling calm now that I had been relieved of the human-contact aspect. Then I remembered Rosie's problem with physical medicine.

'Do you have a problem touching Sonia?' I said.

'Not as big a problem as having you do it, Professor. Just tell me what to do.'

Lydia turned to Gene. 'Can't you do something? You're qualified, aren't you?'

'Full professor,' said Gene. 'New to this city. My wife and I parted company and Columbia made me an offer I couldn't refuse.' He extended his hand. 'Gene Barrow.'

I left Gene speaking to Lydia, while I instructed Rosie on the procedure. Essentially, the objective is to keep the baby's head from putting pressure on the cord, by pushing it back if necessary. It was apparently difficult. Rosie kept saying 'Fuck,' which made Sonia hysterical, which in turn caused Rosie to say 'Fuck'. Meanwhile, I was repeating the information that we were totally competent, which seemed to have a short-term positive effect on Sonia. It would have been easier if we could each have said, in turn, 'Oh God, it's going to die,' 'Fuck, keep her still,' and 'Don't panic, we're in control,' with an instruction to iterate as necessary.

Unfortunately humans are not computers. The intensity of our conversation increased, with Sonia actually screaming and not keeping still, Rosie shouting 'Oh fuck,' and me attempting to create calm by lowering the pitch and raising the volume of my voice. Our verbal efforts were rendered irrelevant when the band started up again.

After no more than ninety seconds, the band stopped. Approximately thirty seconds later, the study door opened. Gene entered, followed by George the Third, the Prince and the remaining Dead Kings, whom I had met in Greenwich Village on the night of the Passing of the Batons. There was also a woman of about twenty (BMI in normal range, no more accurate estimate possible due to overall confusion) and a male of about forty-five, with a camera around his neck. A few seconds later, three uniformed paramedics pushed through the crowd with a stretcher.

'Are you a doctor?' one (female, approximately forty, BMI normal range) asked Rosie.

'Are you?' said Rosie. I was impressed. Rosie's emotional state had transformed during the musical performance from panicked to professional.

'The medical situation is under control,' I said. I gave the officer a quick briefing.

'Outstanding work,' she said. 'We can take it from here.' I watched her take over from Rosie. In keeping with the bedside-manner protocol, I advised Sonia of the status.

'The paramedic appears competent. The chances of your baby's survival have increased significantly.'

Sonia wanted Rosie and me to ride in the ambulance with her, but one of the other paramedics (male, approximately forty-five, BMI approximately thirty-three) provided further reassurance in a highly professional manner, and Sonia allowed them to carry her to the ambulance. The photographer took photos. The overweight paramedic gave me a card with the hospital location.

Lydia pushed through the crowd to me. 'You're not going with her?'

'I see no reason. The paramedics seem highly competent. My contribution is complete. I plan to drink a glass of beer.'

'Jeeesus,' she said. 'You don't have any feelings at all.'

I was suddenly angry. I wanted to shake not just Lydia but the whole world of people who do not understand the difference between control of emotion and lack of it, and who make a totally illogical connection between inability to read others' emotions and inability to experience their own. It was ridiculous to think that the pilot who landed the plane safely on the Hudson River loved his wife any less than the passenger who panicked. I brought the anger under control quickly, but my confidence in Lydia's qualifications to advise me had been reduced.

Rosie interrupted my thoughts. 'I'm going to take a shower. Can you clear everybody out?'

I realised I had failed to perform the basic social ritual of introductions, due partly to not knowing some of the people who had arrived. I began by filling in what gaps I could.

'Lydia, this is George the Third and the Prince, Eddie, Billy, Mr Jimmy. Guys, Lydia is my social worker.'

George introduced the journalist (Sally) and photographer (Enzo) who had been interviewing the Dead Kings about the change in line-up.

'Who was the lady?' said George.

'Dave's wife.'

'You're in shock. You're dissociating,' said Lydia to me. 'Try to take some deep breaths.'

'Has someone rung Dave?' said George.

I had forgotten about Dave. He would definitely be interested.

I waited for the Dead Kings and the journalists to leave, then phoned Dave. Lydia walked to the kitchen and filled the kettle. I diagnosed confusion.

Dave seemed panicked. 'Is Sonia all right?' he asked.

'The risk to Sonia was minimal. The danger –'

'I'm asking you, is Sonia all right?'

I needed to reply to Dave's question several times. He seemed to have caught the sentence-repetition problem. Obviously my answer did not change, so our dialogue was like a looping error. Finally I managed to force an interrupt and was able to convey details of the hospital. As he did not ask, I did not inform him of the risk to the baby. I drew myself a glass of beer from the beer room. Lydia followed me.

'Would you like a beer?' I asked. 'We have unlimited beer.'

'Nothing surprises me anymore,' she said. 'Actually, I will have one.'

33

When Rosie returned from the shower, changed into clean clothes, Lydia and I were sitting on the sofa.

'Who are you?' Rosie asked Lydia. I detected a minor level of aggression.

'I'm a social worker. Lydia Mercer. I came to see Don and Rosie, and then all this happened.'

'Don didn't say anything about it. Is there some issue?'

'I don't think it's something I can discuss with . . . Did you just take a shower? I thought you were with the ambulance team. The *first* ambulance team. With the tall professor.'

It was an odd description of Gene, who is five centimetres shorter than I am and hence approximately the same height as Lydia. And Lydia seemed to have confused herself. Why would a professor be included in a paramedical team?

'Gene left with the band,' I explained. 'But he'll be back. He lives here.'

'I'm Rosie,' said Rosie. 'I live here too. So I hope you don't have a problem with me using the shower.'

'Your name's Rosie?'

'Is there a problem with that? You just said you came –'

'No . . . just a coincidence with Don's – Don-Dave's – wife being . . . Rosie too.'

'There is no Rosie II,' I explained. 'Only the Georges are numbered.'

'I'm Don's wife,' said Rosie. 'Is that okay with you?'

'You're his wife?' Lydia turned to me. 'I need to speak to you privately, Don-Dave.'

I assumed Lydia had concluded I had two wives, both named Rosie, both pregnant and living in the same house, and referred to as Rosie I and Rosie II to avoid confusion. This was improbable, but so were the chances of the real situation occurring randomly. Of course it had not. I took a few moments to contemplate its cause. I, Don Tillman, had woven a web of deceit. Incredible. Fortunately there was no longer any purpose in deception. And Lydia could now provide advice based on her assessment of the real Rosie.

'No privacy is required,' I said.

I began to tell them both the story. In detail. I refilled Lydia's glass and then mine and also drew a glass for Rosie, which I justified on the basis of three facts:

1. Her pregnancy was in the third trimester, where the risk of damage to the foetus from small quantities of alcohol was minimal as shown by research previously cited by Rosie.
2. English ale has a lower alcohol content than American or Australian lager.
3. Rosie said, 'I need a drink,' with an expression that indicated something bad would happen if this need was not met.

Approximately twenty minutes into the story, when

Rosie was interspersing her usual requests for 'overview' and 'cutting to the chase' with profane expressions of astonishment, Gene returned.

'You might as well join us,' said Lydia. 'What sort of professor are you?'

'I'm the head of the Department of Psychology at Australia's highest-ranked university, currently undertaking research at Columbia.' Gene's statement was correct, but did not actually answer the question, which could have been responded to precisely and accurately with a single word: *Genetics*. And I was the one being accused of unnecessary detail.

'Well,' said Lydia, 'it's nice to have some professional support. Let me summarise what Don's told us, which so far is not news to me. But apparently it is to this Rosie.'

'Not necessary,' I said. 'Gene is familiar with the Playground Incident and the requirement for psychological assessment.'

Rosie looked at Gene. She did not appear happy.

'Sworn to secrecy,' he said. 'Don didn't want to upset you.'

I continued the story. 'So then I asked Sonia to impersonate Rosie.'

I had not told Gene this part. I had allowed him to think that the pending charges had been dropped after the first meeting with Lydia. Another component of the web of deceit.

The reactions of Rosie, Gene and Lydia varied in intensity and detail, but were all variants of 'You did *what*?'

'Wait, wait, wait,' said Lydia. 'You're saying she' – she pointed at Rosie – 'is your wife? Rosie is Rosie?'

This question could be answered with zero contextual knowledge. It was the simplest of tautologies and the fact that it was asked at all was an indicator of Lydia's confusion. Rosie had also stated explicitly that she was my wife.

Gene took the opportunity to make some sort of witticism.

'A Rosie is a Rosie is a Rosie,' he said.

I tried to help. 'There is only one Rosie relevant to this story. She has red hair. She is my wife. I have exactly one wife. This is her.'

'Who's Sonia, then?' asked Lydia.

This was easy. 'You've met Sonia. She's currently delivering a baby.'

'No. *Who* is she? You recruited some Italian village girl . . .'

'She's Dave's wife.'

'Dave?'

'Oh my God,' said Rosie. 'We need to call Dave. I was so caught up in not screwing up, I forgot about Dave.'

'Dave?' said Lydia to me. 'There's another Dave? Your father? I thought he was another Don.'

'I've called Dave,' I said.

'This is getting surreal,' said Gene. 'Now we're relying on Don to look after the people issues.'

We were becoming distracted. Distractions were everywhere. Text messages, Lydia consulting her watch, Gene responding to Lydia consulting her watch.

'Do you have to be somewhere?' he said to Lydia.

'Not really, but I have to eat. I feel like this is going to take a while.'

'I'll order pizza,' said Gene.

While Gene was on the phone, there was a knock. It was the young journalist and the photographer who had been interviewing the Dead Kings: Sally and Enzo.

'Sorry to interrupt,' said Sally. 'We just wanted to check that everything was okay with the lady who went to hospital. And . . . it seems there's a story here, if you'd like to share it.'

'Not if it means Don going through it again,' said Gene, who had rejoined us. He paused. 'I suppose I'm here all night anyway. I'll get some pizza for you guys too.'

'We won't be that long,' said Sally.

'That's what you think,' said Gene. 'Family-size margheritas and pepperonis to share?'

Sally the journalist was *obsessed* with the details of the Sonia Emergency, whereas I remembered Rosie's and B1's concern about misreporting of the Lesbian Mothers Project. I considered it vastly more important for their readers to have information about important research than an isolated instance of a pregnancy complication. Although I did my best to relate both stories accurately, while accommodating Sally's frequent requests to omit detail, I suspected she did not achieve a full understanding of events. Rosie spent most of the time on the phone.

After Sally and Enzo left, I resumed the conversation

with Lydia, Rosie and Gene. I had classified it as very important, but not so urgent as to require refusing the press interview. I was having to perform some real-time schedule adjustment to maintain sanity.

'I've been trying to reach Dave,' Rosie said.

'Why?'

'To find out what's happened with Sonia and the baby, that's why.'

'Emergency caesarean, as predicted. No permanent damage to either party.'

'What? How do you know?'

'Text message from Dave 138 minutes ago.'

'Why didn't you tell us?'

I explained about priorities. Now I could resume the explanation of the therapy deception.

'Boy or girl?' said Rosie.

'Male, I think.' I checked my message. 'No, female.' It was a detail that could have waited. It would be years before the difference was important.

'Wait,' said Lydia. 'Why did Sonia do all this for you? She could have gotten herself in a lot of trouble. She still could.' The last statement was obviously a threat, but even I could see that Lydia lacked conviction.

'She said it was in compensation for assistance that I gave to Dave. I did some work that was necessary to prevent his business failing. In fact, it was necessary but not sufficient. Dave's filing and computer systems were also inadequate. His invoice generation procedure –'

Rosie interrupted. 'Dave's business is in trouble?'

'*Was.* I've now rectified all problems. Except the lack

of time for administration. I sourced a Hewlett Packard four-in-one and reconfigured –'

It was Gene's turn to interrupt. 'Dave's filing system is all very interesting but can we focus on the Number One priority: Don's got it into his head that he's not going to make it as a father. That Rosie's better off without him. And Rosie's picked up on that and thinks he doesn't *want* to be a father. That's crap. Don can do whatever he puts his mind to. Am I right, Lydia?'

'Technically, I'm sure he can,' said Lydia. 'My concern was about him understanding others' needs and being supportive.'

'Like understanding that his friend's business is failing and that if it happens everything is going to come tumbling down, marriage and all? And then fixing it?'

'I'm talking about emotional –'

'I only provide practical advice,' I said. 'I avoid emotional issues.'

'I try not to provide advice at all,' said Lydia. 'This is something you have to work out for yourselves.'

'Not so fast, Lydia,' said Gene. 'Don left Rosie because you told him he was bad for her. He made a life-changing decision based on your advice.'

'In response to a fictitious scenario. An accountant pretending to be an Italian peasant girl pretending to be an Australian medical student.'

I corrected Lydia's oversimplified scenario. 'You assessed me as unsuitable prior to meeting Sonia.'

She spoke to Gene. 'I was concerned. I'd met Don before. Over lunch.'

Rosie stood up. I recognised anger. 'You had lunch with Don? And then saw him as a patient? When did you have lunch with him?'

'With my friend, Judy Esler.'

'*My* friend Judy Esler. At the Japanese fusion place in Tribeca? So you're the bitch from hell who diagnoses autism at twenty paces? Fuck.'

'Judy called me that?'

Lydia stood up, then Gene stood up and put one hand on Rosie's shoulder and the other on Lydia's. 'Let's hear Lydia out first. She's not the only one who overstepped the mark.'

Lydia sat down. 'Look,' she said, 'I was out of line at lunch. Don got under my skin. I stayed involved because I felt for Rosie . . . Sonia . . . because I felt sorry for any woman having a baby with a man who wasn't connected.'

Rosie sat down too.

'After all this,' Lydia continued, 'I'm not concerned with Rosie becoming psychotic or depressed and nobody noticing. If you'd told me you had an eminent professor of psychology, a trained observer, living in the house' – she smiled at Gene and Gene smiled back – 'I would have let it go.'

It seemed that the problem was solved. But Lydia had not finished.

'I'm not Don's therapist. But you two are going to have some challenges. I don't think Don's dangerous, and I'm sure he's done many good things for his friends, but he's –'

I saved Lydia the problem of finding tactful words. 'Not exactly average.'

She laughed. 'Good luck working it out. You're both smart people but parenting isn't easy for anyone. And forget any of that evolutionary-psychology crap that idiot friend of yours told you.'

The evolutionary-psychology crap was presumably the information I had shared about sexual compatibility on the day of the Bluefin Tuna Incident.

'How are you getting home?' said the person Lydia had just called my idiot friend.

'I'll get the subway.'

'I'll come for the walk,' said Gene. 'Sounds like we have a common issue with these geneticists who think they've got human behaviour sewn up.'

Rosie and I were left alone in the apartment. There was some pizza left over. I pulled out the cling wrap and Rosie moved to take it from me. I held on to it and in a practised motion – a *very* practised motion – I tore off a perfectly sized sheet and wrapped the pizza.

Rosie watched. She had not spoken since identifying Lydia as someone that Judy Esler had criticised.

'You don't have to go back to Dave's tonight,' she said. 'But you know I've got a ticket home tomorrow, don't you?'

'Lydia's assessment didn't change your mind?' I asked.

'Did it change yours?'

'My reason for leaving was that I was a net negative in

your life. Based primarily on Lydia's evaluation of me as an unsuitable father.'

'Don, she's wrong. It's the opposite. You're probably the world's greatest father. For the right partner. You know everything. You know about diet and exercise and what pram to buy. You know stuff about prolapsed cords that I don't even know as a medical student. We'd be arguing all the time and you'd be right all the time. As you always are.'

'Incorrect. I –'

'Don't give me your counter-example. I'm sure you've been wrong once. I'm speaking broadly. I want to care for and love and bring up my baby without you telling me what to do. I don't want to be just a pair of hands. Like I was tonight.' Rosie stood up and walked around. 'Or a part of your Baby Project. I just want to have a relationship with my baby that's my own.'

'You think my input would be in opposition to yours?' Claudia had been right. Rosie wanted a perfect new relationship without interference.

Rosie walked to the kitchen and activated the kettle. The hot-chocolate cycle was commencing for the night. I spent the time trying to construct an argument that would keep Rosie in New York. Approximately six minutes passed before she returned to the living-room zone.

'Maybe we wouldn't disagree on anything. That'd be a problem too. I have no other role now except to be a mother. And you'd just keep walking in and doing it better. Part-time. Trying not to be a fuck-up as a mother is hard enough without having a partner who reminds me every time I get it wrong.'

'Maybe I can transfer my knowledge to you rather than apply it directly.'

'No! Maybe I'm being too nice. I'm making you sound like Superdad, but there's more to being a parent than theory. Babies need more than the nappy being folded the right way.'

'You're definitely going home? Without me?'

'Don, I didn't want to bring it up, but I told you: there's someone else. It's the hardest decision I've ever made. I did a spreadsheet.'

34

We slept in the same bed again, for what I expected would be the last time. Sex did not seem appropriate, especially considering the existence of 'someone else', and we were both extremely tired. I had vast amounts of confusing information to process, and I knew that there was no point beginning until my head was clear again. There was no longer any urgency. I would conduct a post-project review in due course.

'I can't face Dave and Sonia,' Rosie said in the morning. 'I'll stay here. Judy's picking me up at ten.'

This was the second goodbye to Rosie, after my original departure for Dave's. The research I had read earlier indicated that complicated separations generated more pain. My experience supported it.

Rosie was packing up her study when I returned from my scheduled run. She looked extremely beautiful, as always, but her new shape contributed an additional dimension.

'Is it still moving around?' I asked.

'I'd be worried if it wasn't.'

'I mean right now.'

'Not right now. A few minutes ago.'

I was conflicted. I knew, from talking to Dave, that someone who was exactly average would have wanted strongly to feel the baby under development 'kicking'. I didn't. There were three possible reasons:

1. If it turned out to be a powerful emotional experience, I would be increasing the pain I would feel at Rosie leaving. If Dave or another average person was in the same circumstance, he might well have reached the same conclusion.
2. I was still in some form of denial that an actual baby existed, relating back to the lack of planning. Feeling it move would act in opposition to that comfortable denial.
3. My natural aversion to body contact with strangers. Rosie had slept with me the previous night, but there had been a definite change in our relationship.

I knew that I might influence Rosie's opinion of me if I acted differently, but the behaviour would be deceptive. Instead, I behaved with integrity – as myself.

'Can I have a copy of your spreadsheet?' I asked. My best chance was that she had made an error.

Gene and I went to see Sonia in the hospital. He had not met Sonia prior to the previous evening, but his motivation made sense.

'We're there for Dave. Men hand out cigars because they need something to do. There's stuff-all to do for the first six months. And don't talk to me about bonding. If

Dave's expecting the baby to throw its arms around him and say "dada," he'll be waiting a while.'

Gene's advice was in line with what I had read. Males were advised to assist with domestic chores, work that could easily be subcontracted, particularly in a country which had a low minimum wage. Dave's focus on working at his profession, earning a higher hourly income, was rational.

'Where's Rosie?' asked Sonia as soon as we arrived. The baby was sleeping in a crib in a dormitory, while Sonia had a private room. Dave was due to arrive once he finished a job, but he had already viewed the baby. It had no apparent faults and its appearance would not change substantially on a day-to-day basis.

'Unfortunately, no change in status. In fact, separation has been confirmed. Rosie is on her way home to Australia.'

'No! Why? What you did for me – you guys were such a great team.'

Sonia's logic was faulty. According to it, professionals working on a common project would transition into permanent relationships. Obviously this happened sometimes, but it was insufficient in our case.

The discussion was interrupted by the arrival of a nurse carrying a baby, which I assumed was Sonia and Dave's. I was well aware from the Antenatal Uproar that social convention took precedence over maximising immunity through the sharing of breast milk.

Sonia commenced the nutrition and immunity-improving process.

'So what happened?' she said, once the baby was attached. 'With you and Rosie? If it's Lydia, I'm going to report her. Seriously.'

Sonia was an accountant. She would understand the logic of decision-making. I took Rosie's spreadsheet from my pocket and gave it to her. She held it with one hand while steadying the baby with the other. I was impressed with her proficiency after such a short period.

'My God, you guys are both nuts,' she said. 'Which is why you should be together.' She looked at the spreadsheet for a few more seconds. 'What's this about *already purchased the air ticket*?'

'Rosie's ticket was non-refundable. She felt obliged not to waste the investment. It was obviously a factor in her decision to go home.'

'You'd break up over the price of an air ticket? Anyway, she's wrong. It's the sunk-cost fallacy. You don't take non-recoupable costs into account in making investment decisions. What's gone is gone.'

Gene took the spreadsheet from her. 'Strike the air ticket. Nice work, Sonia. Sometimes you need to speak to these guys in their own language.'

He looked at the spreadsheet. 'Rosie's been lying to you.'

'How do you deduce that?'

'Where's her other man? Your Number 34? Who, if you want my opinion, is not Stefan. I know Stefan. He'd run a mile from a woman with a baby. Even Rosie. If he was a factor, he'd be the biggest factor and she wouldn't need a spreadsheet.'

It was true that there were no emotional factors on the spreadsheet. The focus was on practicalities such as child care (father and extended family in Australia), job opportunities (approximately equal) and whether or not to continue the MD (multiple factors, no clear result).

'Maybe she made the spreadsheet to make me feel better,' I said.

'You know,' said Gene, 'a statement like that is only possible in your and Rosie's relationship. You need to be together to protect the rest of us. Don, there is no Number 34. He's an excuse.'

'There was a Skype message.'

'I don't know about any Skype message. What I know practically is that Rosie is a handful. And theory tells me that men don't generally volunteer to take over a baby who doesn't have their genes.'

Sonia gave Gene an incomprehensible look. 'If you worked in IVF –'

But my mind was working in another direction. Rapidly. I have always been better with numbers than names. Now I remembered where I had seen the number thirty-four.

Before I had time to process the information, Sonia said, 'Do you want to hold Rosie?'

It seemed an inappropriately personal question, until I realised what she was saying. Given names are not unique identifiers.

'The baby is called Rosie?'

'Rosina. But we'll call her Rosie. If the sonogram had been wrong and it had been a boy, he would have been Donato. She's only here because of you. You and Rosie.'

'It's going to be confusing.'

'I hope so. It'll mean you've got Rosie back into your life. Which you have to do. Here.' She passed me the baby. I held it for a few moments, but my mind was still analysing the consequences of the Number 34 insight. I gave Rosie II back to Sonia.

'What's the total?' I asked Gene. 'With the sunk cost deleted.'

'It takes nine points off. Hence minus two.'

'Are you sure?' I recalled the ticket counting for only four points. I reached for the spreadsheet to check, but Gene gave it to Sonia.

'You want to check my arithmetic?' he said.

'Minus two,' said Sonia.

I was stunned. 'She's made an error? The spreadsheet recommends remaining together?'

'In the world you live in, yes. I don't know about Rosie. She may want to add three points for the pain of changing the decision. How would I know?'

Dave walked in as I was planning my response.

'Is everything okay?' he asked.

'Zero change in the baby situation,' I said. 'Do you have your vehicle?'

'Yeah, it's —'

'JFK,' I said. 'Immediately.'

Dave was waving his keys but Sonia would not let me go without further advice.

'Don't try to argue her to death. And don't forget to tell her you love her.'

'She knows that.'

'When did you last tell her?'

'You're suggesting I need to tell her multiple times?'

Love was a continuous state. There had been no significant change since we were married – perhaps a diminution in limerence, but it seemed unhelpful to provide Rosie with progress reports on that.

'Yes. Every day.'

'Every day?'

'Dave tells me he loves me every day, don't you, Dave?'

'Uh huh.' Dave waved his keys again.

35

I booked my ticket online on the way back to the apartment. Only full-price tickets were available, but they had the advantage of being refundable. Rosie was notoriously disorganised, but in important matters such as international travel she over-compensated by arriving early. I hoped she might not have passed through security by the time we arrived. Rosie did not have the 'special' status that I had been awarded by the airline as a result of past contributions, so could not access the airline lounge. I would text her if necessary to find her, but did not plan to warn her.

We stopped at my apartment to get my passport.

'You don't need it,' said Gene. 'It's a domestic flight as far as Los Angeles. You can use your driver's licence.'

'I don't have one. It expired.'

'Aren't you taking anything else? I'd pack a bag, just in case.'

'I'm only going as far as the airport.'

'Just throw a few things into a bag.'

'I can't pack without a list.'

'I'll tell you what to pack.'

'No.' I was reaching a stress limit and Gene must have sensed it.

I retrieved my passport from my bathroom-office

cabinet. I would use the travel time between the apartment and the airport to solicit advice from Dave and Gene. It was critical to optimise my argument before I saw Rosie. I realised that there was an opportunity to improve the advisory panel. On the way out, I visited George and he agreed to join us.

I sat in front with Dave. Gene and George sat in the back seat.

'What are you going to say to her?' said Dave.

'I'm going to tell her she made an error on her spreadsheet.'

'If I didn't know you so well, I'd think you were kidding. All right, I'm going to play Rosie. Ready?'

I supposed that if Sonia could imitate Rosie, there was no reason why Dave could not. I looked out the window to avoid being distracted by his anomalous physical appearance.

'Don, I've thought of something I missed on the spreadsheet. You snore. Five points off. Goodbye.'

'You can use your normal voice. I don't snore. I've checked with a recorder.'

'Don, whatever you say, I'll find something else to put on the spreadsheet because it's only there to convince you I've made the right decision.'

'So you won't come back no matter what I do?'

'Maybe. Do you understand what you did that made me leave?'

'Explain it again.'

'I can't. I'm Dave. *You* explain it to *me* to make sure you understood it.'

'I was doing things that you could do already, only in an annoying way.'

'Right. You were in my face all the time. The toughest thing for fathers is to find a role. For me, it's being the breadwinner.'

'You want to be the breadwinner? I thought you wanted to look after the baby, then get a research job.'

'I'm being Dave now. You've got to work out where you fit. What position you play. She thinks she doesn't need you. There's only one relationship in her mind now: her and the baby. That's biology.'

'You've been paying attention,' said Gene.

One relationship. Our relationship had been usurped, superseded, rendered obsolete by the baby. Rosie had what she wanted. Now she didn't need me.

'This must happen with all relationships,' I said. 'Why don't all relationships split up?'

'Groupies,' said George. 'Seriously, you've got to find your own way. None of my relationships was ever the same after the first kid.'

'Give it six months,' said Gene. 'It gets better.' Gene seemed to have chosen a timescale that supported his argument, like a populist denier of global warming. Obviously his marriage was now in a worse state than six months after the birth of Eugenie. But he had recently resumed contact with Carl. It seemed reasonable to conclude that happiness in marriage was not a simple function of time, and that instability was part of the price of an improvement in overall wellbeing. My experience was consistent with this.

Dave added: 'What you're supposed to do is take the load off your wife so she has time for you. Do the washing, vacuum the house. That's what everybody says. Everybody who's never tried to run a business.'

'Sonia can take responsibility for all paperwork,' I said. 'Hence freeing you up for relationship-enhancing activities.'

'I can run my business,' said Dave. 'I don't need help from my wife.'

'I reckon if your wife offers to do the books for you,' said George, 'you say, "Thank you very much," and do the bloody vacuuming, and when you're done you use the spare time for a well-earned bonk.'

Dave did not speak again until he pulled into the drop-off zone. 'Do you want me to wait?'

'No,' I said. 'It's more efficient to catch the Airtrain.'

'No carry-on, sir?'

The security officer (estimated age twenty-eight, estimated BMI twenty-three) stopped me after I had passed through the scanner without incident.

'Just my phone and passport.'

'Can I see your boarding pass? You checked a bag?'

'No.'

'You're going to LA with no bags?'

'Correct.'

'Can I see some ID?'

I gave him my Australian passport.

'Step over here, sir. Someone will be here to talk to you momentarily.'

I knew what *momentarily* meant in American.

In the interview room, I was conscious of Rosie's flight time approaching. Fortunately my interviewer, a male (approximately forty, BMI twenty-seven, bald), dispensed with formalities.

'Let's cut to the chase. You just decided to go to LA, right?'

I nodded.

'You didn't have time to pack underwear, but you remembered your passport. What do you plan to do there?'

'I haven't made plans yet. I'll probably fly home.'

After that, they performed a thorough inspection of my clothes and body. I did not object because I did not want to waste time. It was only marginally more unpleasant than my routine check for prostate cancer.

I was returned to the interview room. I decided it might be helpful to share further information.

'I need to join my wife on the flight.'

'Your wife's on the flight? With the bags? Why didn't you say so before?'

'It would have added complexity. I'm frequently accused of providing unnecessary detail. I just want to board the plane.'

'What's your wife's name?'

I provided Rosie's details and the officer made a confirmatory phone call.

'She's checked through to Melbourne, Australia. You're not.'

'I wanted to accompany her on the flight. To maximise time with her.'

'You must enjoy talking to your wife more than I do.'

'That seems probable, since she and I chose to be married and you haven't met her.'

He looked at me oddly. It was not the first time. 'Your flight's on final call. Better move your ass. There's a new boarding pass for you at the gate. They've done a seat switch so you're beside your wife.'

The gate lounge was empty: Rosie was already on the plane. My only option was to board also.

She was surprised when I sat beside her. Extremely surprised.

'How did you get here? What are you doing here? How did you get on the plane?'

'Dave drove me. I've come to persuade you to return. I purchased a ticket.'

I took advantage of her silence to begin my argument, which, thanks to Dave's advice, did not begin by identifying the sunk-cost error on the spreadsheet.

'I love you, Rosie.' It was true but probably sounded out of character.

'Did Sonia tell you to say that?'

'Correct. I should have stated it more often, but I was unaware of the requirement. However, I can confirm that the feeling has at no time disappeared.'

'I love you too, Don, but that's not what it's about.'

'I want you to get off the plane and come home with me.'

'I thought you said you had a ticket.'

'I purchased it only to enable me to access the airport.'

'It's too late, Don. My ticket's non-refundable.'

I began to explain the sunk-cost fallacy. But Dave was right about the spreadsheet.

'Stop, stop,' Rosie said. 'The spreadsheet was just to show you I'd thought about it rationally. There's a whole bunch of other things – things I can't quantify. I told you, there's someone else.'

'Phil.' The 34 had been visible on his football shirt in photographs on the wall of Jarman's Gym.

Rosie looked embarrassed, or at least I assumed that her expression was one of embarrassment for deceiving me. 'Why didn't you tell me it was your father?'

Rosie was provided with additional thinking time by a loud cabin announcement that was not compatible with conversation.

'We're just waiting on three passengers from a connecting flight –'

'I wanted to make it easier, simpler.'

'By inventing an imaginary boyfriend?'

'You invented an imaginary me.'

It was possible that Rosie was offering a deep psychological insight, or she could have been referring to Sonia. It was irrelevant.

'You're replacing me with Phil, world's worst father.' This was not, of course, my current view of Phil, but it reflected Rosie's comments prior to their reconciliation. Accuracy was not my priority right now.

'I guess he must have been,' said Rosie. 'Look how I've turned out. A mess who can't make a marriage work and is going to be a single parent like he was.'

Repeating patterns. One rainy morning, after Rosie had rejected my first offer of marriage, I had ridden to the university club to try again, as I was trying again now. But on that occasion I had a plan – a better plan than the sunk-cost fallacy.

Three passengers walked down the aisle.

'The plane is about to depart,' I said.

'So you have to get off,' said Rosie.

'There are numerous reasons for remaining in New York.' I was improvising, not giving up, though I knew that the probability that Rosie would be convinced by anything I could think of now was minimal. 'Number One is the prestige of the Columbia medical program, which . . .'

'All electronic devices must now be switched off.'

It was probably better for my sanity that Rosie stopped me.

'Don, I so appreciate what you're trying to do, but think about it. You're not really engaged with this baby. Not emotionally. You're engaged with me. I believe that, I believe that you love me, but it's not what I need right now. Please, just go home. I'll Skype you as soon as I arrive.'

Rosie, unfortunately, was essentially correct. Claudia was right about her motivation and no rational argument would change her decision. Bud was still a theoretical construction in my mind. I could not fool Rosie that I was emotionally configured as a father. I pushed the call button. A flight attendant (male, estimated BMI twenty-one) appeared almost instantly.

'Can I help?'

'I need to get off the plane. I've changed my mind about flying.'

'I'm sorry, we've closed the doors. We're about to taxi.'

The man sitting in the aisle seat next to me offered his support. 'Let him off. Please.'

'I'm sorry, we'd have to unload bags. You'd delay the flight for everyone. You're not ill, are you?'

'I don't have bags. Not even carry-on.'

'I'm truly sorry, sir.'

'Passengers and crew please take their seats.'

In retrospect, it was the realisation that if I *had* claimed to be ill I would have been let off the flight that pushed me to the line between sanity and meltdown. It came on top of the stress of the previous day's life-threatening emergency, my failure to save my marriage, administrative incompetence and gross invasion of personal space. One more deception, a small deception, and I could have walked off. But I had reached my limits in all dimensions.

I couldn't walk away. I was being *prevented* from walking away.

I closed my eyes and breathed deeply. I visualised numbers, alternate sums of cubes behaving with predictable rationality, as they had before humans and emotions, and as they would for all time.

I was aware of someone leaning over me. The flight attendant.

'Excuse me, sir, would you mind bringing your seat fully forward for take-off?'

Yes, I would fucking mind! I had already tried and it was broken, and the almost *zero* probability that it would make any difference to anyone's survival . . .

I breathed. In. Out. I did not trust myself to speak. I felt the steward reaching across my neighbour, jiggling my seat as the meltdown began, and the seatbelt prevented me from moving. *I could not let this happen in front of Rosie.*

I started my mantra, steadying my breathing again and keeping my voice toneless. *Hardy-Ramanujan, Hardy-Ramanujan, Hardy-Ramanujan.*

I don't know how many times I said it, but when my mind cleared, I could feel Rosie's hand on my arm.

'Are you okay, Don?'

I was not, but the reason had reverted to the original problem. And I had a further five hours to find a solution.

36

'Don, I have to sleep. I'm not going to change my mind between here and Los Angeles. I really, really appreciate you trying. I'll call when I get home. Promise.'

Shortly after Rosie put her seat back and closed her eyes, the steward returned and offered our neighbour an upgrade. I assumed the seat would remain vacant: I was accustomed to having empty seats beside me, except on full flights, as a result of my special status with the airline. A win-win outcome for my neighbour and me. But he was replaced by another male, estimated age forty, BMI twenty-three.

'I guess you've figured out who I am,' he said.

Perhaps he was a celebrity who expected to be recognised – but I doubted that celebrities travelled in economy class. I provisionally diagnosed schizophrenia.

'No,' I said.

'I'm a federal air marshal. I'm here to look after you – and the rest of the passengers and crew.'

'Excellent. Is there some specific danger?'

'Maybe you can tell me that.'

Schizophrenia. I was going to have to share my flight with a mentally ill person. 'Do you have ID?' I asked. I was trying to distract him from his delusion that I possessed special knowledge.

To my amazement, he did. His name was Aaron Lineham. As far as I could tell from approximately thirty seconds of close examination, the ID card was genuine.

'You got on the plane with no intention of travelling, am I right?' he said.

'Correct.'

'What was your purpose in boarding the flight then?'

'My wife is returning to Australia. I wanted to persuade her to stay.'

'That's her, in the window seat, right?'

It was definitely Rosie, making the low-level sleeping noises that had begun during the baby-development project.

'She's pregnant?'

'Correct.'

'Your kid?'

'I presume so.'

'And you couldn't persuade her to stay with you. She's leaving you for good and taking your kid?'

'Correct.'

'You're pretty unhappy about that?'

'Extremely.'

'And you decided to do something about it. Something a little crazy.'

'Correct.'

He pulled a communications device from his pocket. 'Situation confirmed,' he said.

I guessed that my explanation had been satisfactory. He was silent for a while, and I looked beyond Rosie into a clear sky. I watched as the wing dipped and centrifugal force held me in my seat. Without the horizon as a reference point I would not have known the plane was turning. Science and technology were incredible. As long as there were scientific problems to solve, I still had a life worth living.

Aaron the Marshal interrupted my reflections.

'Are you afraid to die?' he asked.

It was an interesting question. As an animal, I was programmed to resist death to ensure the survival of my genes, and to be afraid in circumstances that threatened pain and death, such as a confrontation with a lion. But I was not afraid of death in the abstract.

'No.'

'How long do we have?' asked Aaron.

'You and me? How old are you?'

'I'm forty-three.'

'Approximately the same age as me,' I said. 'Statistically, we both have approximately forty years, but you appear to be in good health. I am also in excellent health, so I would add five to ten years each.'

We were interrupted by an announcement. 'Good afternoon. This is the first officer. You may have noticed the aircraft turning. We've had a minor problem, and air-traffic control have asked us to return to New York. We'll be commencing our descent into JFK in approximately fifteen minutes. We're sorry for any inconvenience, but your safety is our first priority.'

Almost immediately, conversations commenced around us.

'Is there some mechanical problem?' I asked Aaron.

'It's going to take us about forty minutes to get back to New York and deplane. I've got a wife and kids. Just tell me, am I going to see them again?'

If it was not for the evidence of the plane turning back, I would have insisted on a more thorough examination of Aaron's ID. Instead I asked, 'What's happening?'

'Pregnant woman buys a ticket home, checks three big bags. Man known to the airline for unusual behaviour follows her without any bags, acts suspiciously, then tries to get off the plane before it leaves. Gets agitated when he's refused. Then he prays out loud in a foreign language. That was plenty – but now you tell me she's leaving you. What would you make of that?'

'I'm not skilled at analysing human motivations.'

'I wish I was. I don't know if they've got it wrong or if we've turned around in time. Or if you're the coolest guy I've ever met, sitting here chatting while your life ticks away.'

'I don't understand. What is the nature of the danger?'

'Mr Tillman, have you packed a bomb in your wife's bags?'

Incredible. They had profiled me as a terrorist. On reflection, it was not incredible. Terrorists are not exactly average. My non-standard behaviour was reasonably interpreted as increasing the probability I would do something else non-standard, such as commit mass murder because my wife was leaving me.

It was flattering to be judged as cool, even if on a false premise. But now a planeload of passengers was returning to New York. I suspected the relevant authorities would want to blame me in some way.

'There is no bomb. But I would advise you to assume I am lying.' I would not want a marshal to rely on the word of a suspected terrorist in deciding whether there was a bomb on board. 'Assuming I am telling the truth, and there is no bomb, have I done anything illegal?'

'Not as far as I can see. But I'd be willing to bet on TSA finding something.' He leaned back. 'Tell me the story. I'm not going anywhere. And I'll try to work out if we're all going to die.'

I tried to think of some way of reassuring him.

'Surely if there were a bomb, the scanners would have detected it.'

'We like to think so, but you can draw your own conclusions.'

'If I wanted to kill my wife, I could have done it without killing a planeload of people. In our home. With my bare hands. Or a variety of domestic items. I could have made it look like an accident.' I looked into his eyes to demonstrate my sincerity.

As Aaron the Marshal requested, I told my story. It was difficult to know where to start. Numerous events required context for full understanding, but I estimated that there was insufficient time to include the complete

story of my life prior to becoming a terrorism suspect. I
began with my initial meeting with Rosie, since the
events of interest to Aaron were Rosie-related. Predictably, this meant leaving out important background
information.

'You're saying basically that before you met your wife,
there was no one else.'

'If "basically" means "excluding dates that did not
lead to relationships", the answer is yes.'

'First time lucky,' he said. 'I mean, she's a good-looking
lady.'

'Correct. She vastly exceeded any expectations I had
for a partner.'

'You thought she was out of your league?'

'Correct. Perfect metaphor.'

'So you didn't think you deserved her. Now you've
got the chance for a family. Mr Don Tillman, husband
and father, that's another league again. You think you're
up to playing in it?'

'I've done considerable research on parenthood.'

'There you go. Overcompensating. If I was a motiva-
tional speaker, I'd have some advice for you.'

'Presumably. It would be your job to motivate me.'

'What I would say is you haven't *visualised* it. If you
want something you've got to visualise it. You've got to
see yourself where you want to be, and then you can go
get it. I was a security guard, going nowhere, when I
heard about the air marshals' jobs after 9/11. So I visualised it and here I am. But without the vision, nix.'

One thing I had learned about pregnancy was that there was no shortage of advice.

Rosie slept through my conversation with Aaron and the agitated conversation of other passengers, but was woken by the announcement to prepare for landing.

'Wow. I slept all the way to LA,' she said.

'Incorrect. We're returning to New York. There's a suspected terrorist on board.'

Rosie looked frightened and grabbed my hand.

'No cause for fear,' I said. 'It's me.' It struck me that Rosie and I were probably the only people on the plane who were not terrified.

When we landed in New York, Rosie and I were taken to separate interrogation rooms while her bags were checked. It took a long time and I was left alone. I decided to use the opportunity to visualise being a parent.

I am not good at visualisation. I do not have a graphic representation of the streets of New York in my brain, or an instinctive sense of direction. But I can list the streets, the intersections, the landmarks and the subway stations, and can read the orientation information – *14 St & 8 Av SE Corner* – when I exit the subway. It seems equally effective.

I did not have a picture of Rosie and me with an actual baby. At some level I did not believe in it, perhaps because of my original Lydia-induced fear of being a parent, or perhaps – as Aaron the Marshal had suggested – I did not consider myself worthy. There had been some amelioration of both of these concerns: Lydia had given me provisional endorsement, and Gene, Dave, Sonia and even George had recently provided positive feedback about my worth as a human being beyond the domain of genetics research.

Now I had to imagine the outcome.

It took a deliberate effort of will. I attempted to integrate four images of a baby and my emotional responses to them.

I imagined the pictures of the developing baby on the wall of my bathroom-office. No response. The process of drawing them had definitely had a calming effect, but the recollection of an image of a picture of a generic foetus or even the ultrasound photos did not have any power.

The mental picture of Rosie II, Dave and Sonia's baby, was not particularly helpful – she was also still a generic baby.

The memory of the older baby that had crawled over me during the Lesbian Mothers Project was more satisfactory. I remembered the experience being fun. I suspected the level of fun might increase with the baby's age, obviously with some limit. I recalled the fun generated by the LMP baby as being of the same order as that induced by a margarita. Perhaps two margaritas, but not sufficient to motivate me to life-changing actions.

The final image was of the actual Bud. I envisaged Rosie and the bump. I even envisaged it moving, evidence of human life. Minimal emotional impact.

I faced the same problem as I had during the Rosie

Project. I was crippled – *challenged* – incapable of the feelings needed to drive normal behaviour. My emotional response was to Rosie. It was of a very high level, and if I could have redirected some of it towards the baby, as Rosie had apparently done with her feelings for me, the problem would have been solved.

Finally, an official (male, approximately fifty, BMI approximately thirty-two) opened the door.

'Mr Tillman. We've checked your wife's baggage and everything seems to be in order.'

'No bomb?' The question was automatic and, on reflection, stupid. I had not packed a bomb and it was extremely unlikely that Rosie had.

'No bomb, smart guy. Nevertheless, we have broad laws against inciting an incident and –'

At this point the door opened again – no knock – and another official (female, age approximately thirty-five, estimated BMI twenty-two) entered. Given that I was dealing with officialdom, and probably at risk of some sort of penalty, this was annoying. I was definitely better at one-on-one interactions than situations involving multiple people. With Margarita Cop I had been fine; with Good Cop and Bad Cop less so. With Lydia alone I had made progress; the involvement of Sonia had required subterfuge that inevitably led to confusion. Even in our informal men's group, the move from one relationship to six had created dynamics that I had overlooked. Dave apparently did not approve of Gene. I only knew this because Dave had told me so directly.

I barely noticed what the new official was saying, because my train of thought had led me to a massive insight. I needed to share it with Rosie as soon as possible.

'We understand you've been subjected to some inconvenience, Professor Tillman,' said the female officer.

'Correct. Reasonable precautions to prevent terrorism.'

'That's very understanding of you. The flight will be leaving again in approximately an hour, and you and Ms Jarman are both welcome to board. They're going to hold the Melbourne flight in LA for delayed passengers. But if you'd rather have some recovery time, we can arrange a limousine to your home and fly her business class on tomorrow's flights through to Melbourne. We'll upgrade you too if you choose to fly with her.'

'I will need to consult with Rosie.'

'You can do that momentarily. But we'd like you to do something for us, in exchange for my colleagues not taking this further. Which they might be under pressure to do, even though we do realise it was all a misunderstanding.'

She put a three-page document in front of me, paced around the room for several minutes, left, and then re-entered, while I read the legal wording. I considered asking for a lawyer, but I could see no serious negative implications in signing. I had no intention of discussing the incident with the media. I just wanted to talk to Rosie. I signed and was released.

*

'Will you accept the offer of staying overnight in New York?' I asked Rosie.

'I'll stay. Anything's better than twenty hours pregnant in economy. I'm going to miss life being this crazy.'

'You need to call Phil,' I said. 'To tell him you'll be a day late.'

'He doesn't expect me till January,' said Rosie. 'It's going to be a surprise.'

37

I had been given a final chance to find a solution. My plan was straightforward, but made difficult by the limited amount of time available. We arrived back at the apartment at 4.07 p.m. Gene was there, and assumed Rosie had returned permanently. The result was an awkward conversation.

At the end Gene said, 'To be honest, I was expecting Don to come home alone and had an exciting evening planned for him.'

I had my own exciting evening planned.

'We'll have to reschedule it. Rosie and I are going out and won't be home until late.'

'It's not reschedulable,' said Gene. 'Medical faculty break-up party. Starts at five-thirty, be over by seven. You can have dinner later.'

'It's not just dinner. It's a series of activities.'

'I'm really tired,' said Rosie. 'I'm not up for activities. Why don't you go with Gene and pick up something on the way home?'

'The activities are critical. You can drink some coffee if necessary.'

'If the plane hadn't turned around we wouldn't be doing anything. You'd be on a flight back from LA. So it can't be critical. Why don't you just tell me what you had planned?'

'It's intended to be a surprise.'

'Don, I'm going home. I'm guessing that you're trying to do something that will make me change my mind. Or something nostalgic that'll make me sad, like going to the cocktail bar and making cocktails together or eating at Arturo's or . . . the Museum of Natural History's closed.'

Her expression was 'smiling but sad'. Gene had gone to his room.

'Sorry,' she said. 'Tell me what you'd planned.'

'What you said. You only missed one item. You guessed seventy-five per cent, including the museum which I rejected for the same reason.'

'I guess that says something about what we managed to do together. I finally got into your head just a bit.'

'Incorrect. Not just a bit. You are the only person who has succeeded in understanding me. It commenced when you reset the clock so I could cook dinner on schedule.'

'The night we met.'

'The night of the Jacket Incident and the Balcony Dinner,' I said.

'What didn't I guess?' said Rosie. 'You said I got seventy-five per cent. I'm guessing ice-cream.'

'Wrong. Dancing.' The Science Faculty ball in Melbourne, where Rosie had solved a technical problem with my dancing skills, had been a turning point. Dancing with Rosie had been one of the most memorable experiences of my life, yet we had never repeated it.

'No way. With me like this.' She put her arms around me briefly, demonstrating how her modified shape would have interfered with dancing. 'You know what? If we had gone out tonight, something would have gone wrong. Something crazy. It would have been different from what you planned but better and that's what I love about you. But now, crazy isn't going to work. It's not what I need. It's not what Bud needs.'

It was odd, paradoxical – *crazy* – that what Rosie seemed to value most about me, a highly organised person who avoided uncertainty and liked to plan in detail, was that my behaviour generated unpredictable consequences. But if that was what she loved, I was not going to argue. What I was going to argue was that she should not abandon something she valued.

'Incorrect. You need less crazy, not zero crazy. You need a scheduled optimum amount of crazy.' It was time to explain my analysis and solution. 'Originally there was only one relationship. You and me.'

'That's a bit simplistic. What about Phil and –'

'The domain under consideration is our family unit. The addition of a third person, Bud, increases the number of relationships to three. One additional person, triple the number of binary relationships. You and me; you and Bud; me and Bud.'

'Thanks for that explanation. We wouldn't have wanted to have eight kids. How many relationships would that have been?'

'Forty-five, of which ours would have been one forty-fifth of the total.'

Rosie laughed. For approximately four seconds, it felt as though that our relationship had been rebooted. But Rosie had rebooted in safe mode.

'Go on.'

'The multiplying of relationships initially led to confusion.'

'What sort of confusion?'

'On my part. Regarding my role. Relationship Number Two was your relationship with Bud. Because it was new, I endeavoured to contribute to it, via dietary and personal maintenance recommendations that you reasonably considered to be interference. I was annoying.'

'You were trying to help. But I need to find my own way. And for once Gene is right – it's a biological thing. Mothers are more important than fathers, at first anyway.'

'Of course. But your focus on the baby has reduced your interest in our relationship, due to simple dilution of time and energy. Our marriage has deteriorated.'

'It happened gradually.'

'It was sound prior to the pregnancy.'

'I guess. But I realise now it wasn't enough by itself. I guess I knew that at some level even back then.'

'Correct. You require the additional relationship for emotional reasons. But you should not discard another high-quality relationship without investigating all reasonable means of retaining it.'

'Don, looking after a baby isn't compatible with the way we used to live. Sleeping in, going out drinking, turning planes around . . . it's a whole different life.'

'Of course. The schedule will have to be modified. But it should incorporate joint activities. I predict that, without the intellectual stimulation and craziness that you have become accustomed to, you will become insane. And possibly acquire some depressive illness as predicted by Lydia.'

'Depressed *and* insane? I'll find stuff to do. But I'm not going to have time to –'

'That's the point. Now that you're going to be occupied with Bud, I should take total responsibility for our relationship. For organising activities, obviously subject to baby requirements.'

'Relationships can't be one person's responsibility. It takes two –'

'Incorrect. There has to be a commitment from all participants, but one person can act as champion.'

'Where did you get this from?'

'Sonia. And George.'

'George upstairs?'

I nodded.

'So, the experts are onto it.'

'Experience rather than theory. The psychologists we know all have failed marriages. Or, in your case, marriages at risk.' This was a weak point in George's advice also, but I did not think it was helpful to inform Rosie of his marital history.

'I think most couples,' Rosie said, 'even the ones that stay together, just accept that the relationship has to take a hit for a while.'

'From which the participants never recover.' I was

drawing on George's experience again. And possibly Gene's. And potentially Dave's. 'My proposal is that we attempt to retain as much of our previous interpersonal relationship as possible, subject to baby demands. I offer to do all the required work: you merely need to accept the objective and offer reasonable cooperation.'

Rosie got up and began to make a fruit tea. I recognised this as code for *Just shut up for a few minutes, Don, I'm trying to think.*

I went to the cellar and drew off a beer to manage my own emotional state.

When Rosie sat down again, she had done some insightful thinking. Unfortunately.

'I think it matters more for you, Don, because you haven't connected with the baby. You haven't talked about the third relationship. You're still focused on you and me. Most men transfer some of their love to their children.'

'I suspect the transfer will take some time. But if I don't accompany you, then I'll have zero input. You consider me worse than zero as a father?'

'Don, I think you're wired differently. It worked with the two of us, but I don't think you're designed to be a father. I'm sorry to put it like that, but I sort of thought you'd come to the same conclusion.'

'You didn't think I was wired for love. You were wrong. You may be wrong again.'

Gene came out of the bedroom. 'Sorry to interrupt, guys, but I have to go to this medical school thing. You're not going out?'

'No,' said Rosie.

'Come with me, then. Both of you.'

'I'll stay,' said Rosie. 'I'm not invited.'

'Partners are. You should do this. It's your last night in New York. Don won't say this, but it's the right thing for him.'

'You really want me to come?' said Rosie to me.

'If not, I'll stay home,' I said. 'I want to make full use of the time remaining in our marriage.'

As we were leaving, my phone rang. I didn't recognise the number.

'Don, it's Briony.' It took me a moment to remember who Briony was. B1. B1 never contacted me directly. I prepared myself for conflict.

'I can't believe what you've done,' she said.

'What?'

'You haven't seen the *New York Post*?'

'I don't read it.'

'It's online. I don't know what to say. None of us would have guessed.'

I opened the door to my bathroom-office to check the *New York Post* website, and Rosie was sitting on the edge of the bath, facing the Bud tiles.

'What are you doing in here?' I asked. I was not being aggressive; the question was intended in its literal sense.

'I came in to steal one of your sleeping pills. For the flight tomorrow.'

'Sleeping pills –'

'Stilnox. Active ingredient Zolpidem. Third trimester,

399

one tablet. No adverse effects. Wang, Lin, Chen, Lin and Lin, 2010. It's more likely to make me take my clothes off and dance around the plane than harm the baby.'

She resumed looking at the Bud tiles. 'Don. These are just amazing.'

'You've seen them before.'

'When? I never come in here.'

'On the night of Dave the Calf. When Gene fell in the bath.'

'I saw my supervisor thrashing around naked. I didn't take time to check the pattern on the tiles.' She smiled. 'But this is our baby – Bud – every week, right?'

'Wrong. It's a generic embryo, foetus . . . Baby Under Development. Except Tiles 13 and 22 which were copied from the sonograms.'

'Why didn't you share this with me? I was looking at pictures in the book and here you were drawing the same pictures –'

'You told me you didn't want a technical commentary.'

'When did I say that?'

'Twenty-second of June. The day after the Orange Juice Incident.'

Rosie took my hand and squeezed it. She was still wearing her rings. She must have noticed me looking.

'My mother's ring is stuck on. It's a bit small and my fingers have probably puffed up a bit. If you want yours back you'll have to wait.'

She continued looking at the tiles as I located the *New York Post* article.

Father of the Year: A Celebratory Beer After Saving his Child for Lesbian Moms.

I was aware that journalists were frequently inaccurate, but the article, by Sally Goldsworthy, exceeded my imagination as to the possibilities of misreporting.

> *Don Tillman, an Australian visiting professor of medicine at Columbia and leading researcher on the link between autism and liver cancer, donated his sperm to two lesbians and then saved the life of one of his babies. In true down-under style, Professor Tillman drank a pint of beer to toast the emergency caesarean section he performed in his Chelsea apartment, and said he had total confidence in the ability of the two mothers to bring up his children without any involvement from him.*
>
> *And he showed that he's learned something about America, too.*
>
> *'Of course lesbian parents are not average,' he said. 'Hence we should not expect average outcomes. But it would seem un-American to seek averageness.'*

There was a photo of me, posing with my Santoku cook's knife as the photographer had requested.

I showed Rosie the newspaper article.

'You said this?'

'Of course not. The article is full of ludicrous errors. Typical of science reporting in the popular press.'

'I meant the quote about not-average outcomes. It sounds like you, but it's so . . .'

I waited for her to finish the sentence, but she seemed to be unable to find an adjective to describe my statement.

'The quote is correct,' I said. 'Do you disagree?'

'No, not at all. I don't want Bud to be average either.'

I emailed the link to my mother. She insisted on copies of all mentions of me in the press to show our relatives, regardless of accuracy. I included a note that I had not impregnated any lesbians.

'That'll explain why we're flying business class tomorrow and not sitting in Guantanamo Bay,' said Rosie. 'They didn't want a headline saying *Hero Surgeon Harassed by TSA for Being Exceptional*.'

'I'm not a surgeon.'

'No, but you're exceptional. You were right about the blood and mess phobia. I just had to do it once. We were a good team, right?'

Rosie was right. We had been an excellent team. A team of two.

38

The subway was full of people wearing Santa hats. Had I been acceptable as a father, I would one day have played that role. I would have been required to do all the things my own father had done. He had been an expert at producing non-average gifts and experiences for Michelle, Trevor and me.

I would have had to learn a whole new set of skills and master numerous activities. Based on observations of my parents and of Gene and Claudia, some of the activities would surely have been joint projects with Rosie.

The faculty party was held in a large meeting room. I estimated the number of guests as 120. Only one was unexpected. Lydia!

'I didn't realise you were employed by Columbia,' I said. If she was a colleague, there was surely some further ethical problem with our interactions.

She smiled. 'I'm with Gene.'

As is usual with these occasions, there was low-quality alcohol, uninteresting snacks and too much noise for productive interaction. Incredible to collect some of the world's most eminent medical researchers in one place and then dull their faculties with alcohol and drown out their voices with music that they would probably require their children to turn down at home.

It took me only eighteen minutes to consume enough food to eliminate any requirement for dinner. I hoped Rosie had done the same. I was about to find her and suggest we leave when David Borenstein made an amplified announcement from the stage. I could not see Rosie. She might not realise that the commencement of formalities was our signal to depart.

'It's been a big year for the College,' said the Dean. I might as well have been back in Melbourne; the Dean at home would have used the same words. It was always a big year. It had been a big year for me too. With a disastrous ending.

'There have been some significant achievements,' the Dean continued, 'and these will all doubtless be given due recognition in appropriate forums. But tonight I'd like to celebrate a few that may not . . .'

As the Dean called researchers to the stage to receive applause for achievements in support and teaching, showing poor-quality videos of them at work, I began to feel better. It was not my destiny to raise children directly, but there was every possibility that one day a good father – someone who was making a valuable contribution to his child's upbringing – would choose not to drink alcohol to excess as a result of a genetic test that indicated he was susceptible to cirrhosis, and would survive to raise his child. That test would be a result of my six years of work breeding mice, getting them drunk and dissecting their livers. Perhaps a lesbian couple would make better and more confident decisions about bringing up their child thanks to the Lesbian Mothers Project of which I was a part. I would have perhaps forty-five to fifty years more to make contributions, to live a worthwhile life.

I was going to miss Rosie. Like Gregory Peck in *Roman Holiday*, I had been granted an unexpected bonus that was destined to be temporary because of who I was. Paradoxically, happiness had tested me. But I had concluded that being myself, with all my intrinsic flaws, was more important than having the thing I wanted most.

I realised that Gene was standing beside me, jabbing me in the ribs with his elbow.

'Don,' he said, 'are you okay?'

'Of course.' My thoughts had blocked out the Dean's words, but now I focused on them again. *This was my world.*

'And, in the same spirit as the Australian Nobel Laureate who swallowed bacteria to demonstrate that it would give him an ulcer, one of our own Australians put himself on the line in the cause of science.'

Behind the Dean, a video recording had appeared on the screen. It was me, on the day I had lain on the floor and allowed a lesbian couple's baby to crawl over me to determine the effect on its oxytocin. Everyone started laughing.

'Professor Don Tillman as you've never seen him before.'

It was true. I was amazed to see myself. I was obviously happy, far more so than I remembered. I had probably not fully appreciated my emotional state at the time, due to my focus on conducting the experiment correctly. The video went for approximately ninety seconds. I became aware of someone on my other side. It was Rosie. She was gripping my arm hard and crying, profusely.

I had no opportunity to determine the cause of her emotional state, as David added, 'Or perhaps he was practising – Don and his partner Rosie are expecting their first child in the New Year. We have a small gift for you.'

I walked up to the stage with Rosie. It was possibly inappropriate to accept a gift that was given on the premise that Rosie and I were remaining together. I was considering what I should say, but Rosie solved the problem.

'Just say "thank you" and take it,' she said as we walked to the stage. She was holding my hand, which was bound to reinforce the incorrect impression.

The Dean gave us a parcel. It was obviously a book. After that he offered ritual season's greetings and people began departing.

'Can we wait a few minutes?' said Rosie, who seemed to have partially recovered.

'Of course,' I said.

Within five minutes, everyone had left, including Gene and Lydia. There was only David Borenstein, his assistant and us.

'Would you mind showing the video of Don again?' Rosie asked the Dean.

'I'm packing up,' said his assistant. 'You can have the DVD, if you want.'

'I thought it was the right touch to finish on at this time of year,' said the Dean. 'The soft side of the hard man of science. I suppose you know it well,' he said to Rosie.

We took the subway to what had been our home. Rosie did not speak. It was only 7.09 p.m. and I wondered whether I should try again to persuade her to participate in the memorable experiences I had planned. But I was enjoying holding her hand on our last night together and thought it advisable not to do anything that might change the situation. I was carrying the Dean's present in my other hand, so Rosie had to open the door to our apartment.

Gene was waiting with a magnum of champagne and multiple glasses – because we had multiple guests. More precisely, he had seven glasses. He filled them and distributed six of them to me, Rosie (in violation of pregnancy rules), Lydia, Dave, George and himself.

I had several questions, including the reason for the presence of Dave and George, but started with the most obvious.

'Who's the seventh glass for?'

The question was answered by a very tall, strongly built male, approximately sixty years old, walking in from the balcony, where I guessed he had been smoking a cigarette. It was *34* – Phil, Rosie's father, who was supposed to be in Australia.

Rosie squeezed my hand very tightly, as though to earn some hand-holding credits, then let go and ran over to Phil. As did I. My brain was taken over by a flood of sympathy for his distress on the night his wife had been killed. It was doubtless the result of the Phil Empathy Exercise and the resultant nightmares, and was so powerful that it overwhelmed my distaste for physical contact. I reached Phil approximately a second before Rosie did and threw my arms around him.

He was predictably surprised. I expect everyone was surprised. After a few seconds, with his encouragement, I let go. I remembered his promise to come over and beat the shit out of me if I screwed up. Obviously I had fulfilled that condition.

'What have you two done?' he said. He didn't wait for an answer, but took Rosie out to the balcony. I hoped the surprise had not motivated her to have a cigarette.

'He was waiting here when we got back,' said Gene. 'Camped outside the door with a carry-on bag.'

Not everyone was as vigilant as I was in preventing the entry of unauthorised visitors, though of course I would have recognised Phil and allowed him access.

'Did he explain why he came?' I asked.

'Did he need to?' said Gene.

I remembered that Phil did not drink alcohol, and quickly drank his glass to avoid embarrassment.

Gene explained that he had summoned Dave and George so they could collectively give me a present. From its size and shape I deduced that it was probably a DVD. It would be my only DVD, as I source my video material through downloads. I wondered if Lydia had been involved in making an environmentally irresponsible choice.

When Rosie and Phil returned, I opened the Dean's present. It was a humorous book on fatherhood. I put it down without saying anything.

Gene, Dave and George's present was a video recording of *It's a Wonderful Life*, which they advised me was a traditional Christmas movie. It seemed an unimaginative choice for three of my closest friends, but I was conscious that choosing gifts was extremely difficult. Sonia had suggested purchasing Rosie high-quality decorative underwear for Christmas, noting that gifts of this kind were traditional in the early years of marriage. It was a brilliant idea, and had allowed me to replace the items damaged in the Laundry Incident, but the process of matching the stock at Victoria's Secret with Rosie's purple-dyed originals had been awkward. The gift was still in my office.

'So,' said Gene, 'we're going to drink champagne and watch *It's a Wonderful Life*. Peace on earth and goodwill.'

'We don't own a television,' I said.

'At my place,' said George.

We all went upstairs.

'Metaphors are not Don's strength,' Gene said as George loaded the DVD. 'So, Don, we bought you this film because you bear some resemblance to George.'

I looked at George. It was an odd comparison. What did I have in common with a former rock star?

Gene laughed. 'There's a George in the movie. James

Stewart. He does a lot for his friends. Allow me to testify first. When my marriage was beyond saving, Don was the last to give up on it. He gave me somewhere to live even though Rosie had every reason to make that a hard decision for him. He was a mentor for my son and daughter and' – Gene took a breath and looked at Lydia – 'he set me straight when I screwed up. Not for the first time.'

Gene sat down and Dave stood up. 'Don saved my baby and my marriage and my business. Sonia's going to take over the administration. So I'll have some time with her and with Rosie. Our baby.'

Rosie looked at me and then back at Dave, and then at me again. She had not been informed of the choice of name.

George stood up. 'Don . . .' He was overcome by emotion and could not continue.

George attempted to hug me, and probably found me unresponsive. Gene took over. 'Rosie and I were there on the night that Don decided that the most important thing in his life could wait while he looked after someone else. For the rest of you, Don has the event on video.'

I was feeling embarrassed. I am adept at problem-solving, but only in the practical sense. Solutions such as suggesting that an accountant could contribute to her husband's business or recommending a change of personnel in a rock band were deserving of credit, but not such an emotional response.

Then Lydia – *Lydia* – stood up. 'Thank you for letting me be a part of this. Can I just say that Don's example has helped me overcome a ... prejudice. Thank you, Don.'

Lydia's testimony was a little less emotional, which was a relief. I was surprised that my arguments had persuaded her of the acceptability of eating unsustainable seafood.

Everyone looked at Phil for a few seconds, but he said nothing.

George started playing the movie, then all four of the Dead Kings, including the Prince, arrived. George the Third drew everyone beers and was about to start the movie again when the Eslers buzzed, followed shortly afterwards by Inge. Gene and Rosie had made phone calls. Lydia and Judy Esler went out on the balcony and were gone for some time.

It seemed appropriate that I should invite my remaining local friends. I called the Dean and Belinda – B3 – and within an hour we had the entire B Team as well as the Borensteins. George drew more beers and, for the first time, his apartment actually resembled a functioning English pub. He seemed extremely happy in his role as host. Rosie had resumed holding my hand.

The story of the James Stewart character's struggles and near suicide was interesting and highly effective at manipulating emotions. It was the first time I had cried at a movie, but I was aware that others were having the same response. I was also experiencing emotional overload due to Rosie's proximity, the endorsement of the most important people in my life and the pain of my marriage ending. Rosie was going to leave an awful hole.

She had to explain at the end of the movie that she had changed her mind.

39

Rosie and I had the *best Christmas ever*. We were on the plane from Los Angeles to Melbourne and crossed the International Date Line, thus virtually eliminating the day that had given me so much stress in the past. We were further upgraded to first class and the cabin was only half full. The stewards were incredibly friendly. Rosie and I talked about Christmases of the past, which had been painful to her also, due to the absence of her mother as a result of death. Phil's family and her mother's relatives were good people but annoyingly intrusive. I could relate to this.

We talked about our plans. Rosie had accepted my theory of three relationships and was willing to trial my approach to the division of responsibilities. My performance with the lesbian mothers' baby had given her reassurance that I would be able to relate emotionally to Bud. I warned her that it might take some time.

'That's fine,' she said. 'I guess I was worried that you would somehow mess up my relationship with him or her.'

'You should have just said so. I'm good at solving problems and following instructions. I would have done whatever was necessary to preserve our relationship.' The responsibility I had volunteered for aligned with my instincts in the same way that Rosie's giving priority to the baby aligned with hers.

Rosie would defer her decision about continuing at Columbia for a few months. This seemed sensible.

Phil decided to stay in New York for Christmas, sharing our apartment with Gene, as well as Carl and Eugenie, who were due to join their father for January. He was *extremely* happy about everything – seeing Rosie, the Bud situation, and Rosie and me being together – but recognised that we would enjoy some time in his house alone in Melbourne to recover from jet lag and acclimatise to summer.

Nobody else knew we were coming, so we had eight days together without interruption. It was incredible! The enjoyment of interacting with Rosie was amplified by the realisation that I had almost lost her.

Phil's house in suburban Melbourne had broadband-internet facilities, and that was all I needed to communicate with Inge and the B Team and continue writing up the two projects.

Phil returned on 10 January. All relatives wanted us to stay in Melbourne for the birth, and David Borenstein supported the decision. Rosie had already cancelled her US arrangements and booked at a Melbourne hospital after deciding to leave me, so it was less disruptive to plans overall.

We spent three days at my family home in Shepparton. The stress of interaction was alleviated by the debriefing of the Soundproof Crib Project with my father. We talked for *hours* beyond bedtime without the support of alcohol. My father had solved some practical problems with the use of the materials, and the Korean research team was negotiating the rights to the improvements and my father's ongoing participation. It was unlikely my father would become rich but, in a scenario reminiscent of the passing of the batons, he would need to hand the hardware store responsibilities to my brother Trevor. My brother was extremely pleased with this development. I wondered if one day I would hand over something of my life to Bud.

To my surprise, and in contradiction to predictions from Gene, my mother and Rosie got on well and seemed to have a great deal in common.

Our baby emerged without problems (other than the expected discomfort of birth, which my reading had prepared me for) at 2.04 a.m. on 14 February, the second anniversary of our first date, the Jacket Incident and the Balcony Dinner. *Everyone* noted that it was Valentine's Day, which explained why I had encountered difficulty in reserving a table at a prestigious restaurant two years earlier.

The birth process would have been fascinating to watch, but I followed Gene's advice to 'stay at the head end' and provide emotional support rather than observe as a scientist. Rosie was extremely happy with the outcome, and I was surprised to find that I had an immediate emotional reaction myself, though not as strong as when Rosie had decided to rejoin our relationship.

The baby's gender is male, and accordingly we have given it a conventional male name. There was some debate.

'We can't call him "Bud". It's a nickname. An American nickname.'

'American culture is pervasive. Bud Tingwell was Australian.'

'Who's Bud Tingwell?' said Rosie.

'Famous Australian actor. He was in *Malcolm* and *The Last Bottle.*'

'Name one scientist called Bud.'

'Our son may not be a scientist. Abbott from Abbott and Costello was Bud. Bud Powell was one of jazz's most important pianists. Bud Harrelson was an All-Star shortstop.'

'With the Yankees?'

'The Mets.'

'You want to name him after a Mets player?'

'Bud Cort was Harold in *Harold and Maude*. Bud Freeman. Another influential jazz player. A saxophonist. Plus numerous Buddys.'

'You've looked it up, haven't you? You don't know anything about jazz.'

'Of course. So I would have a convincing argument for retaining the name. It seems odd to change someone's name because of a single event in their lives. You didn't change your name when we got married.'

'We're talking about his birth. Anyway, it stands for Baby Under Development. First: he's not under development any more, he's an actual baby, and second: he won't always be a baby.'

'Unfortunately Hud isn't a name.'

'Hud?' said Rosie.

'Human Under Development.'

'It's the name of a prophet. An Islamic prophet. You're not the only one who knows stuff.'

'Unacceptable. Blatant connection to a religion is inappropriate.'

'Short for Hudson, maybe.'

I considered Rosie's suggestion for a few moments.

'Perfect solution. Concatenation of *Human Under Development* and *Son*. Connection to New York, the place of conception, via the river and the associated explorer. Australian usage with connection to the Terrorist Incident which saved our relationship.'

'What?'

'Hudson Fysh was the founder of Qantas. Common knowledge from the airline magazine.'

'And Peter Hudson, the footballer, was Phil's hero. One little problem. Remember what it stands for. *Under Development*. He's a full human now. Actually, it makes him sound like the *son* of a human under development.'

'Correct. Humans should be permanently under development.'

Rosie laughed. 'Hudson's father, in particular.'

'Since you nominated only one problem, and it has

been dismissed, I assume that he is now named Hudson.'

'Hard to argue with your logic. As always.'

Another joint task successfully completed. I gave Hudson back to Rosie to feed. I needed to schedule Phil to babysit so that Rosie and I could commence tango lessons.

Acknowledgments

The Rosie Project concluded with a long and probably incomplete list of acknowledgements, reflecting its five-year journey from concept to publication. I was learning to write at the same time, and many people helped me with general advice and encouragement as well as specific suggestions about the manuscript.

Thanks in good measure to the help I received from them, I approached *The Rosie Effect* with a clearer idea of what I was doing, and wrote the first draft with significant input from only two people. My wife, Anne Buist, to whom the book is dedicated, brought a writer's understanding of story as well as her expertise as a professor of psychiatry to the table (usually it was a table with a bottle of wine open). She takes no responsibility for Gene's views on attachment theory. My friend Rod, who, with his wife Lynette, was the inspiration for and dedicatee of *The Rosie Project*, was my other sounding board. Our conversations as we jogged beside Melbourne's Yarra River inspired the soundproof crib, the Bluefin Tuna Incident and the Antenatal Uproar.

I was unusually fortunate in the editing process: in addition to Michael Heyward and Rebecca Starford at Text Publishing, several of my international publishers provided me with detailed notes: Cordelia Borchardt at S. Fischer Verlag; Maxine Hitchcock at Michael

Joseph; Jennifer Lambert at HarperCollins Canada; Marysue Rucci at Simon & Schuster; and Giuseppe Strazzeri at Longanesi.

My first readers also provided valuable feedback: Jean and Greg Buist, Tania Chandler, Corine Jansonius, Peter McMillan, Rod Miller, Helen O'Connell, Dominique and Daniel Simsion, Sue Waddell, Geri Walsh and Heidi Winnen. Thanks also to Shari Lusskin, April Reeve and Meg Spinelli for their local knowledge of New York and American medical education, and to Chris Waddell for his advice on drumming. W. H. Chong designed the Australian cover.

The references to research in psychology and pregnancy incorporate the prejudices of fictional characters and should be taken with a grain of salt. In particular, Don's interpretation of *What to Expect When You're Expecting*, Rosie's use of various papers to support her dietary choices and the implicit reference to Feldman et al.'s work as a basis for the Lesbian Mothers Project do not necessarily represent their authors' intentions.

Many publishers, booksellers and readers around the world have contributed to making *The Rosie Project* a success and are already doing the same for *The Rosie Effect*. In Australia, thanks are particularly due to Anne Beilby, Jane Novak, Kirsty Wilson and their teams at Text Publishing who have supported my writing and been creative in bringing it to a wide audience.